DUGOUT
THE ZOMBIE STEALS HOME

BY SCOTT MORSE

graphix

An Imprint of

SCHOLASTIC

Library of Congress Control Number: 2018949530

ISBN 978-1-338-18810-3 (hardcover)
ISBN 978-1-338-18809-7 (paperback)

10 9 8 7 6 5 4 3 2 1   19 20 21 22 23

Printed in China   62
First edition, July 2019
Edited by Adam Rau
Book design by Shivana Sookdeo
Color by Guy Major
Creative Director: Phil Falco
Publisher: David Saylor

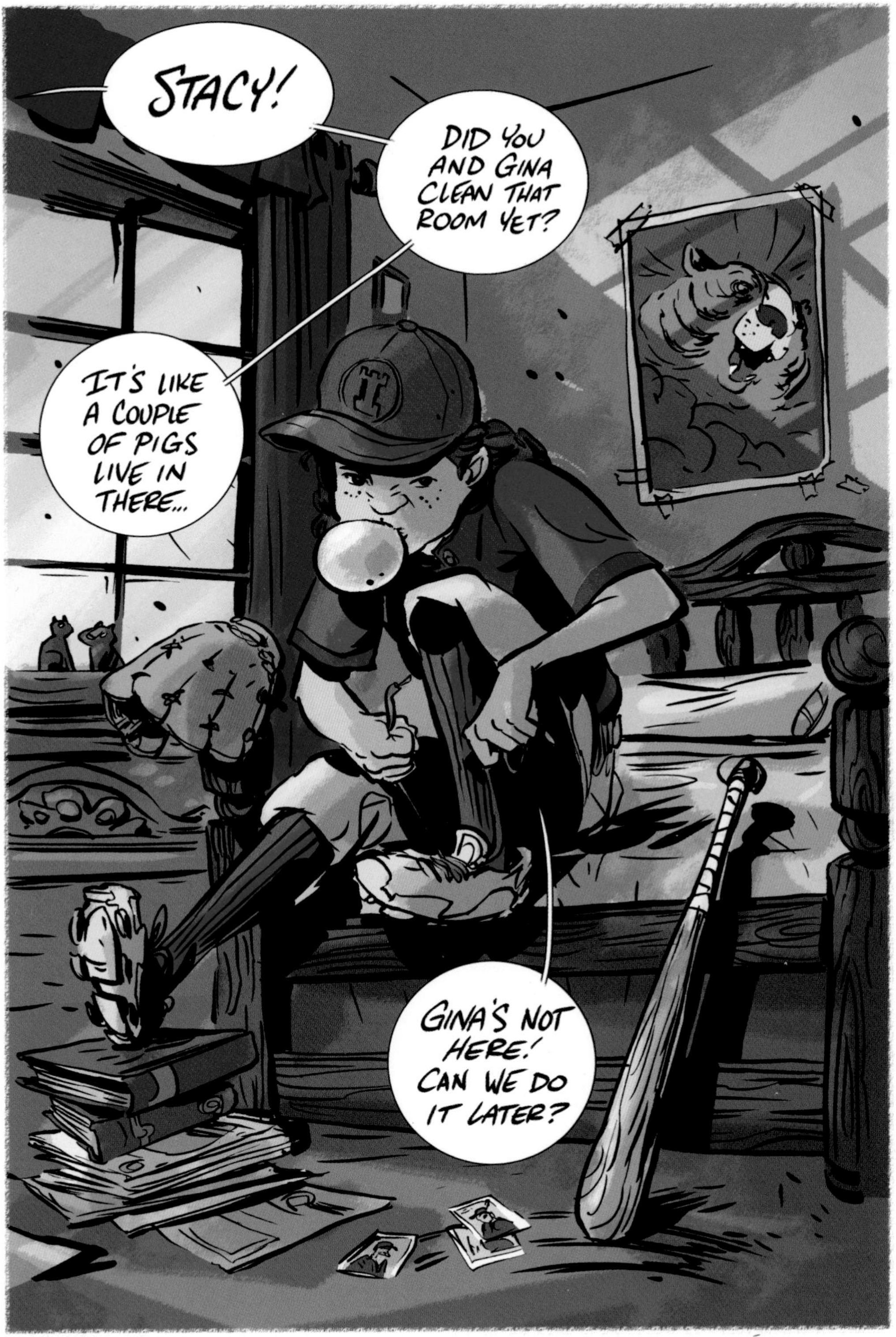
STACY!
DID YOU AND GINA CLEAN THAT ROOM YET?
IT'S LIKE A COUPLE OF PIGS LIVE IN THERE...
GINA'S NOT HERE! CAN WE DO IT LATER?

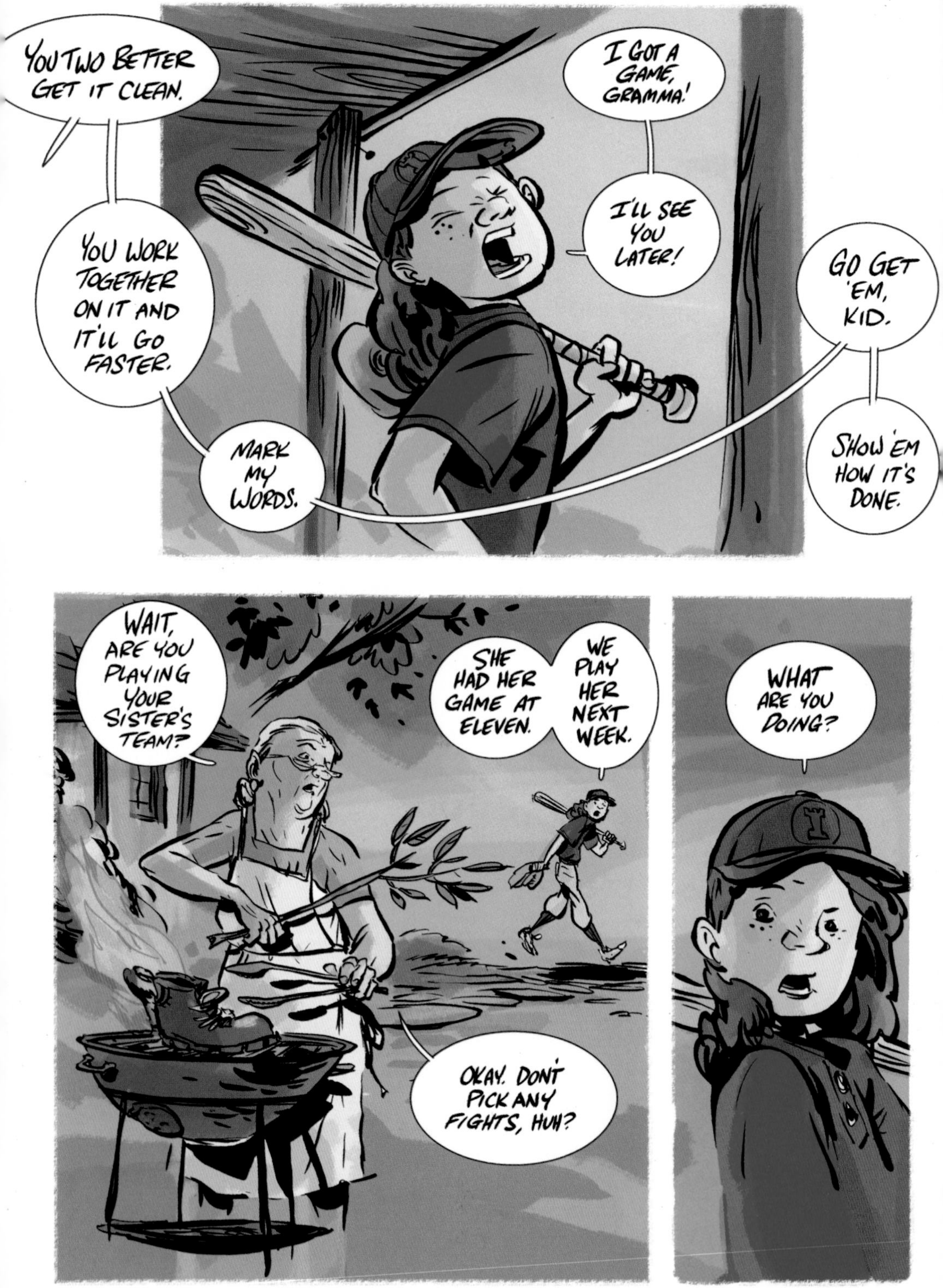
YOU TWO BETTER GET IT CLEAN.
YOU WORK TOGETHER ON IT AND IT'LL GO FASTER.
MARK MY WORDS.
I GOT A GAME, GRAMMA!
I'LL SEE YOU LATER!
GO GET 'EM, KID.
SHOW 'EM HOW IT'S DONE.
WAIT, ARE YOU PLAYING YOUR SISTER'S TEAM?
SHE HAD HER GAME AT ELEVEN.
WE PLAY HER NEXT WEEK.
OKAY. DON'T PICK ANY FIGHTS, HUH?
WHAT ARE YOU DOING?

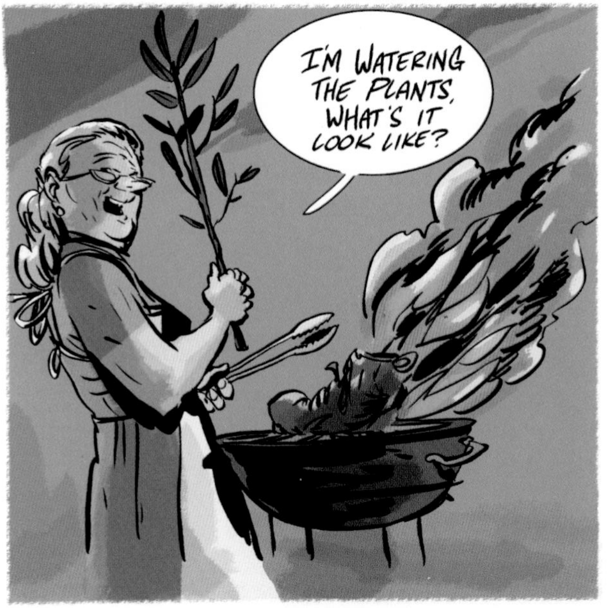
I'M WATERING THE PLANTS, WHAT'S IT LOOK LIKE?

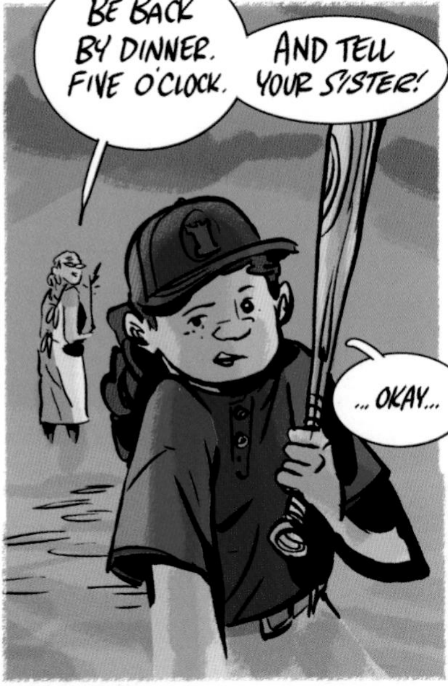
BE BACK BY DINNER. FIVE O'CLOCK.
AND TELL YOUR SISTER!
...OKAY...

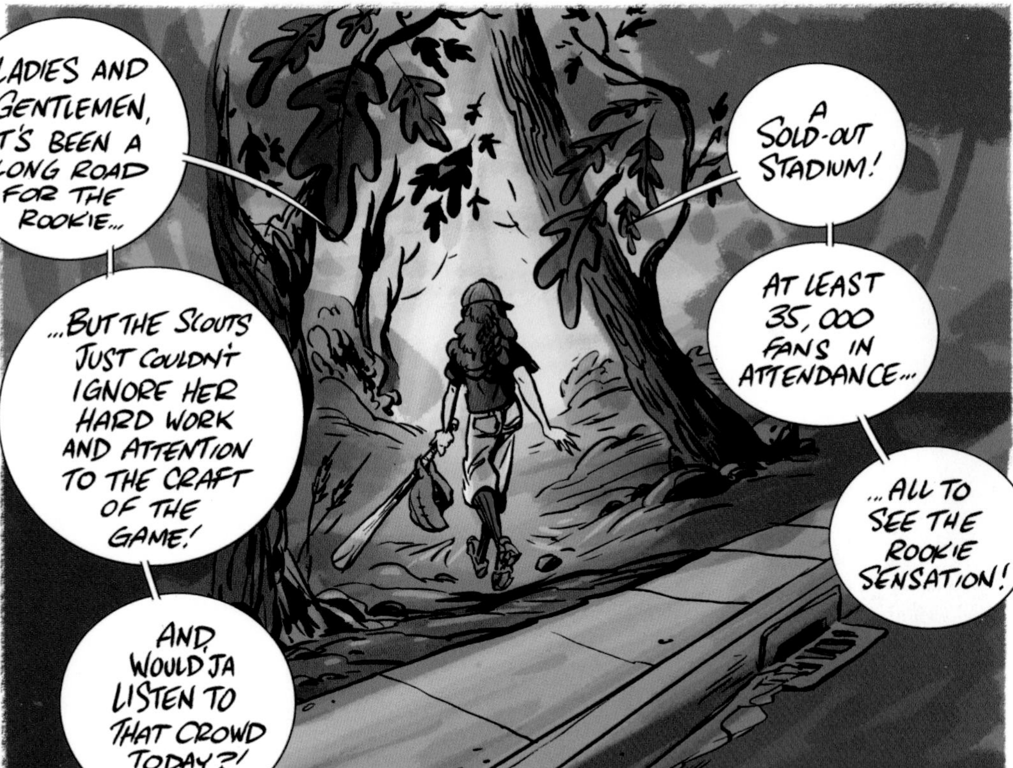
LADIES AND GENTLEMEN, IT'S BEEN A LONG ROAD FOR THE ROOKIE...
...BUT THE SCOUTS JUST COULDN'T IGNORE HER HARD WORK AND ATTENTION TO THE CRAFT OF THE GAME!
AND, WOULD'JA LISTEN TO THAT CROWD TODAY?!
A SOLD-OUT STADIUM!
AT LEAST 35,000 FANS IN ATTENDANCE...
...ALL TO SEE THE ROOKIE SENSATION!

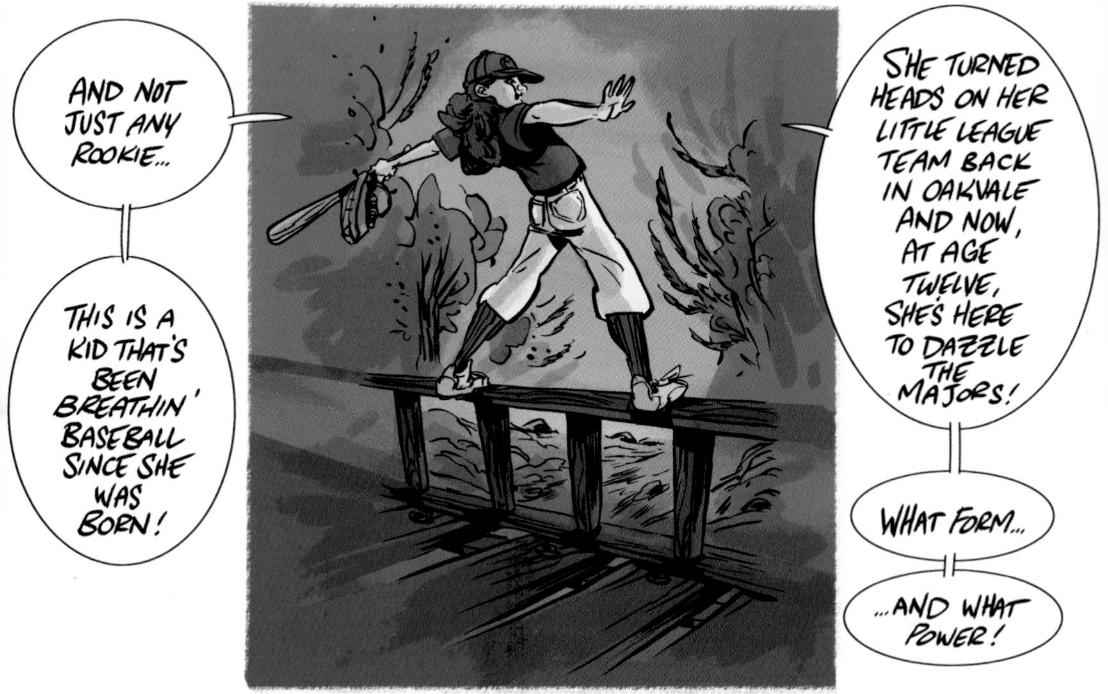
AND NOT JUST ANY ROOKIE...
THIS IS A KID THAT'S BEEN BREATHIN' BASEBALL SINCE SHE WAS BORN!
SHE TURNED HEADS ON HER LITTLE LEAGUE TEAM BACK IN OAKVALE AND NOW, AT AGE TWELVE, SHE'S HERE TO DAZZLE THE MAJORS!
WHAT FORM...
...AND WHAT POWER!

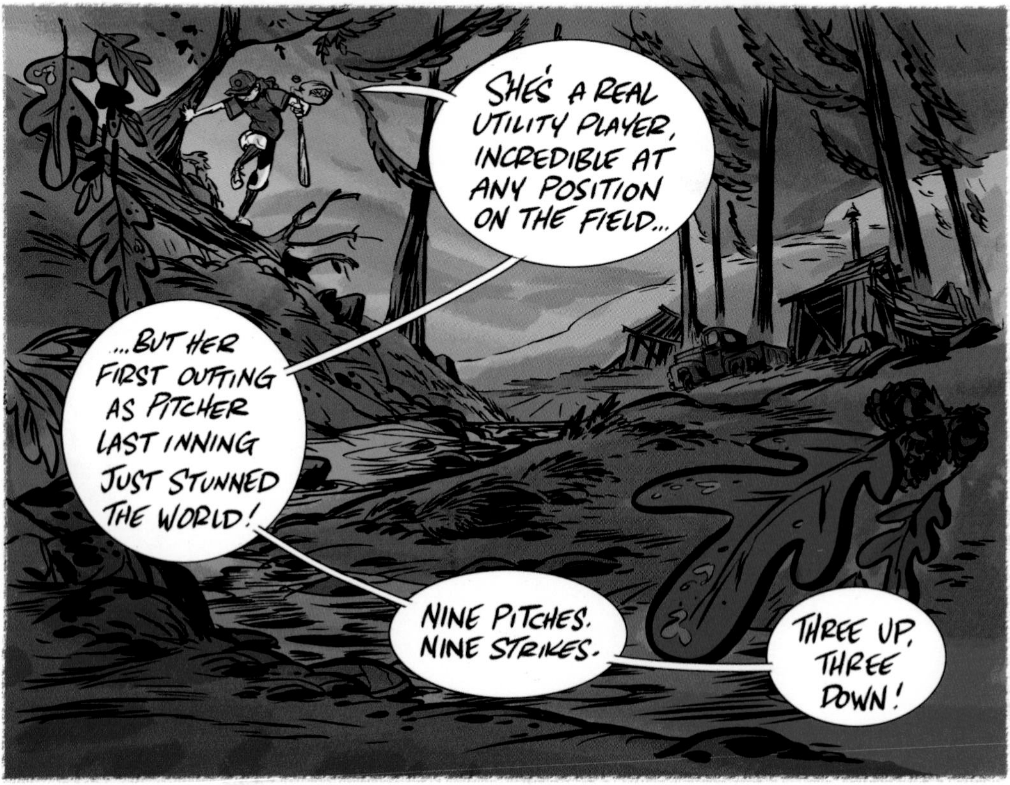
SHE'S A REAL UTILITY PLAYER, INCREDIBLE AT ANY POSITION ON THE FIELD...
...BUT HER FIRST OUTING AS PITCHER LAST INNING JUST STUNNED THE WORLD!
NINE PITCHES. NINE STRIKES.
THREE UP, THREE DOWN!

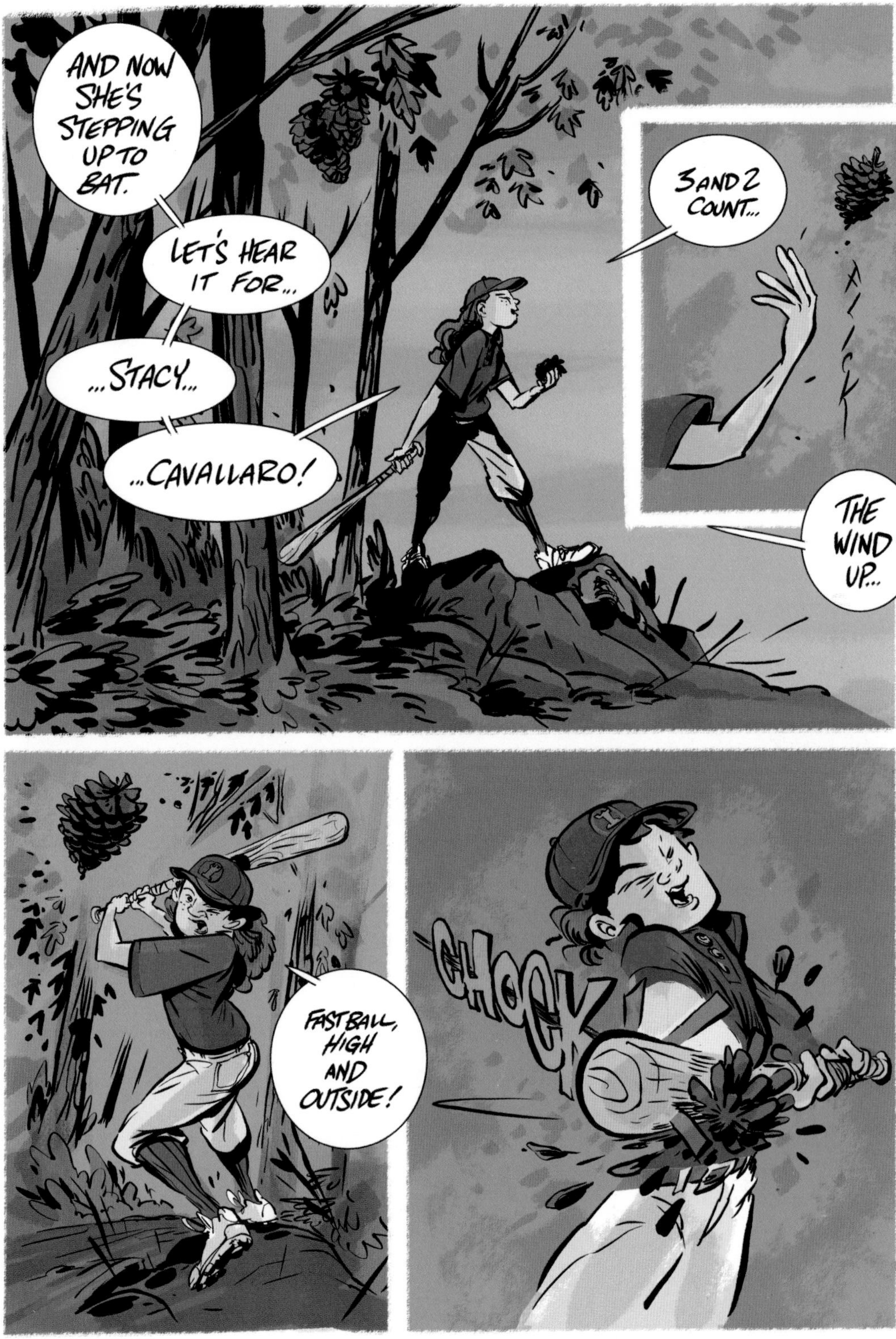
AND NOW SHE'S STEPPING UP TO BAT.
LET'S HEAR IT FOR...
...STACY...
...CAVALLARO!
3 AND 2 COUNT...
FLICK
THE WIND UP...
FASTBALL, HIGH AND OUTSIDE!
CHOCK

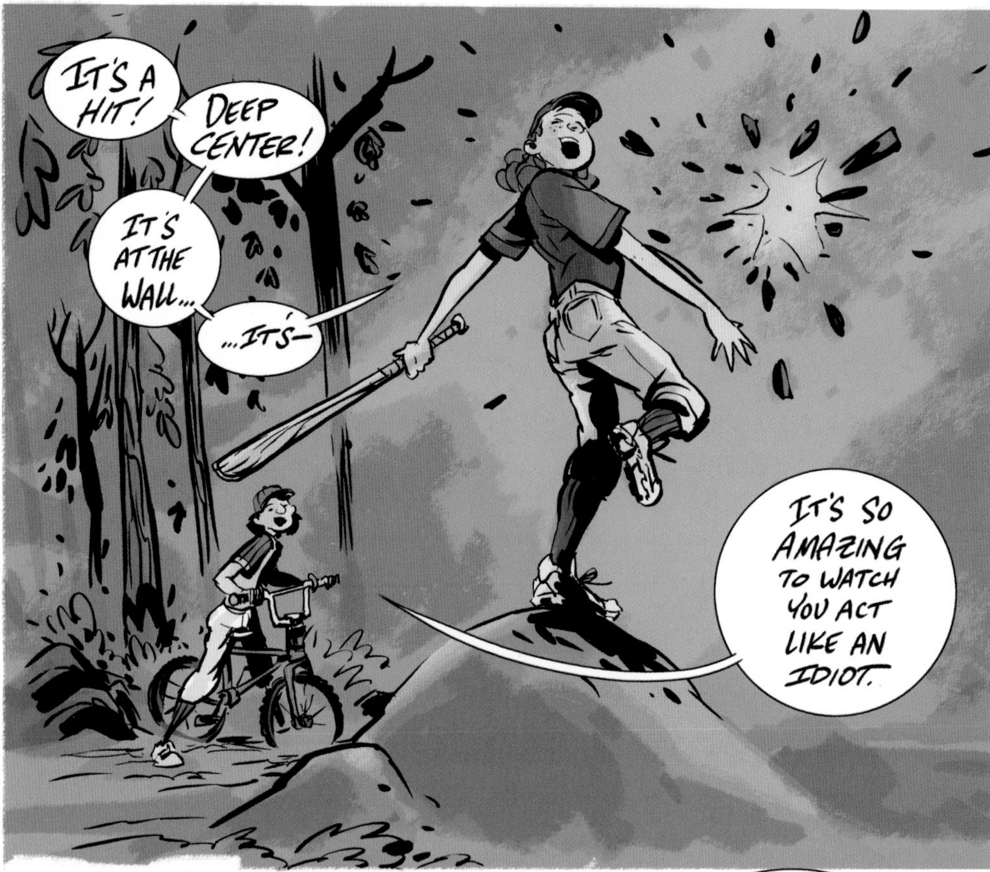
IT'S A HIT!
DEEP CENTER!
IT'S AT THE WALL...
...IT'S—
IT'S SO AMAZING TO WATCH YOU ACT LIKE AN IDIOT.

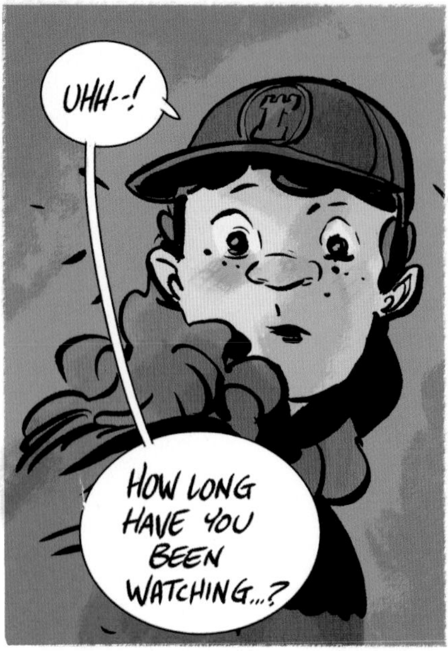
UHH--!
HOW LONG HAVE YOU BEEN WATCHING...?

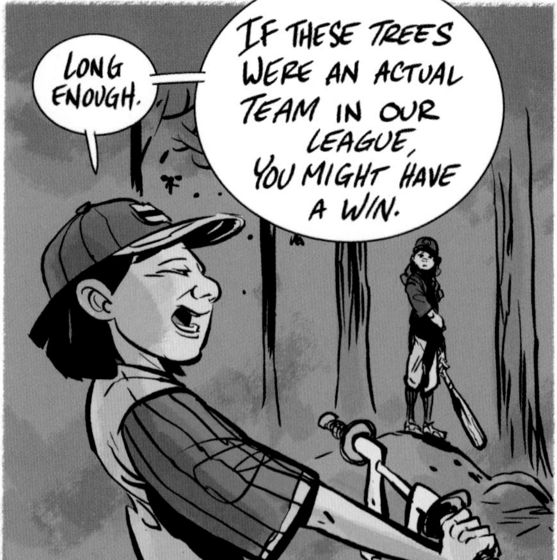
LONG ENOUGH.
IF THESE TREES WERE AN ACTUAL TEAM IN OUR LEAGUE, YOU MIGHT HAVE A WIN.

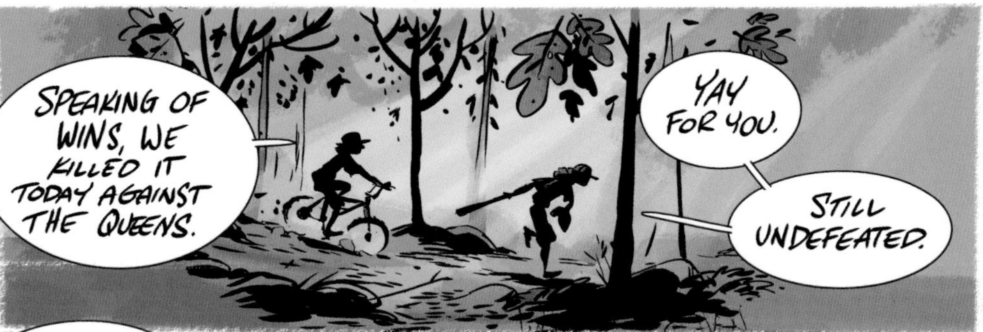
SPEAKING OF WINS, WE KILLED IT TODAY AGAINST THE QUEENS.
YAY FOR YOU.
STILL UNDEFEATED.

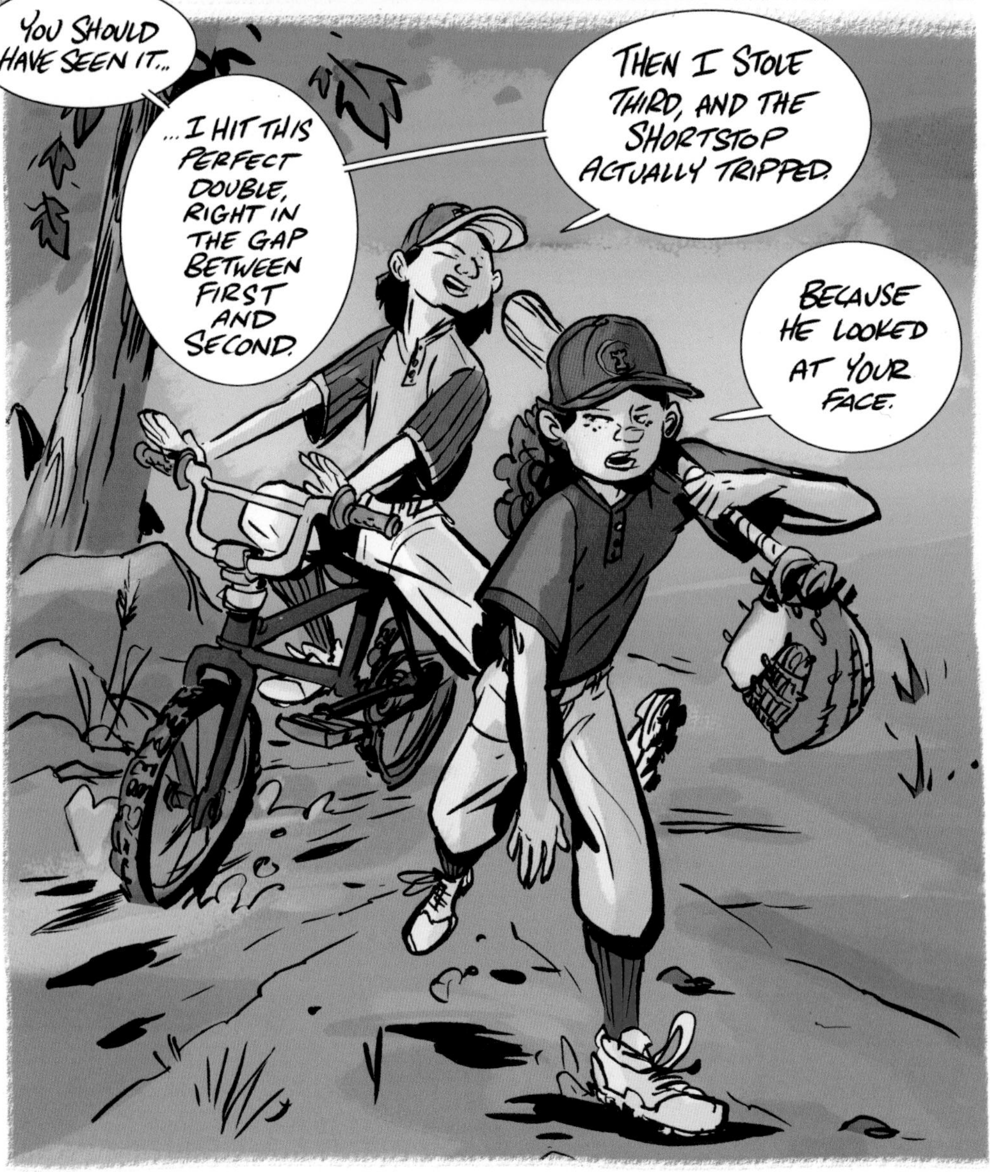
YOU SHOULD HAVE SEEN IT...
...I HIT THIS PERFECT DOUBLE, RIGHT IN THE GAP BETWEEN FIRST AND SECOND.
THEN I STOLE THIRD, AND THE SHORTSTOP ACTUALLY TRIPPED.
BECAUSE HE LOOKED AT YOUR FACE.

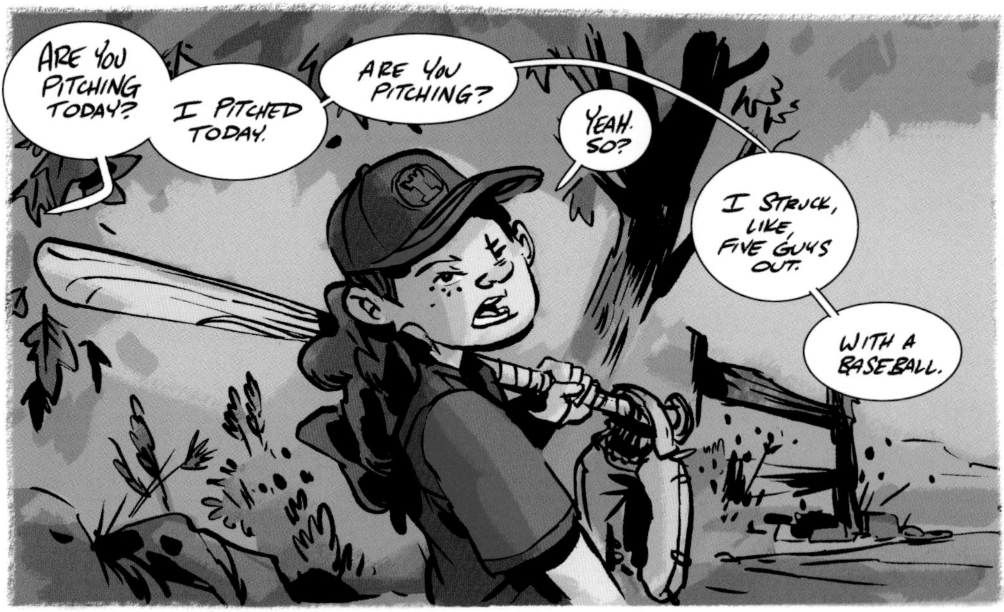
ARE YOU PITCHING TODAY?
I PITCHED TODAY.
ARE YOU PITCHING?
YEAH. SO?
I STRUCK, LIKE, FIVE GUYS OUT.
WITH A BASEBALL.

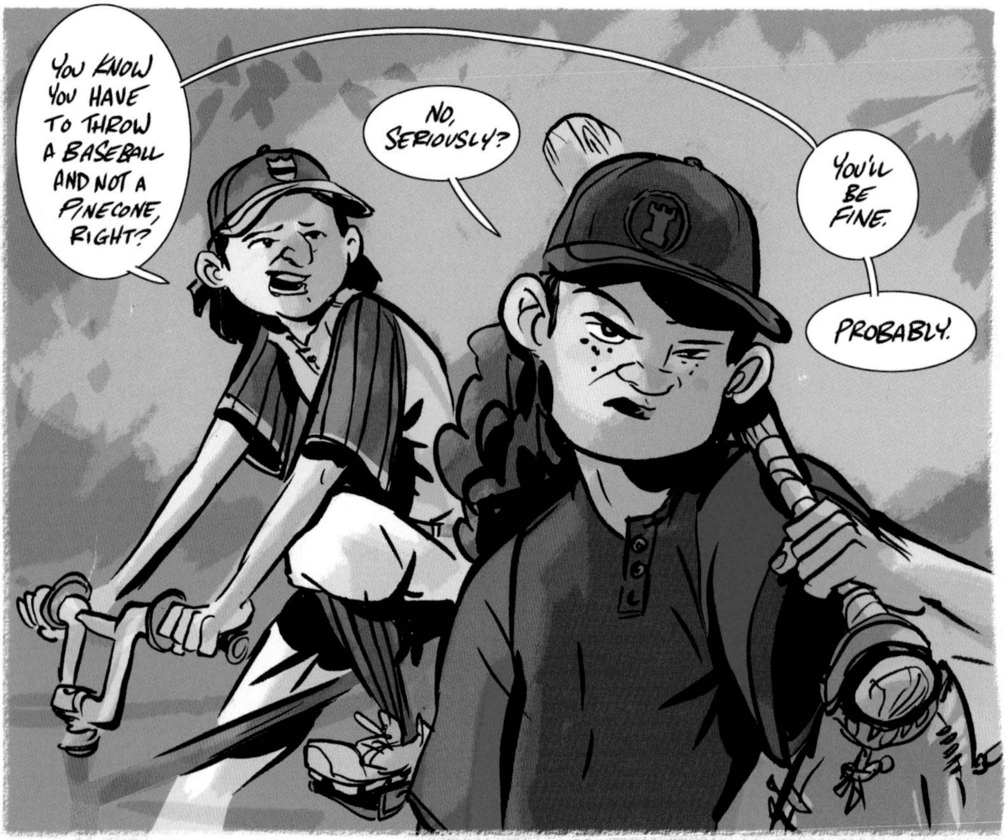
YOU KNOW YOU HAVE TO THROW A BASEBALL AND NOT A PINECONE, RIGHT?
NO, SERIOUSLY?
YOU'LL BE FINE.
PROBABLY.

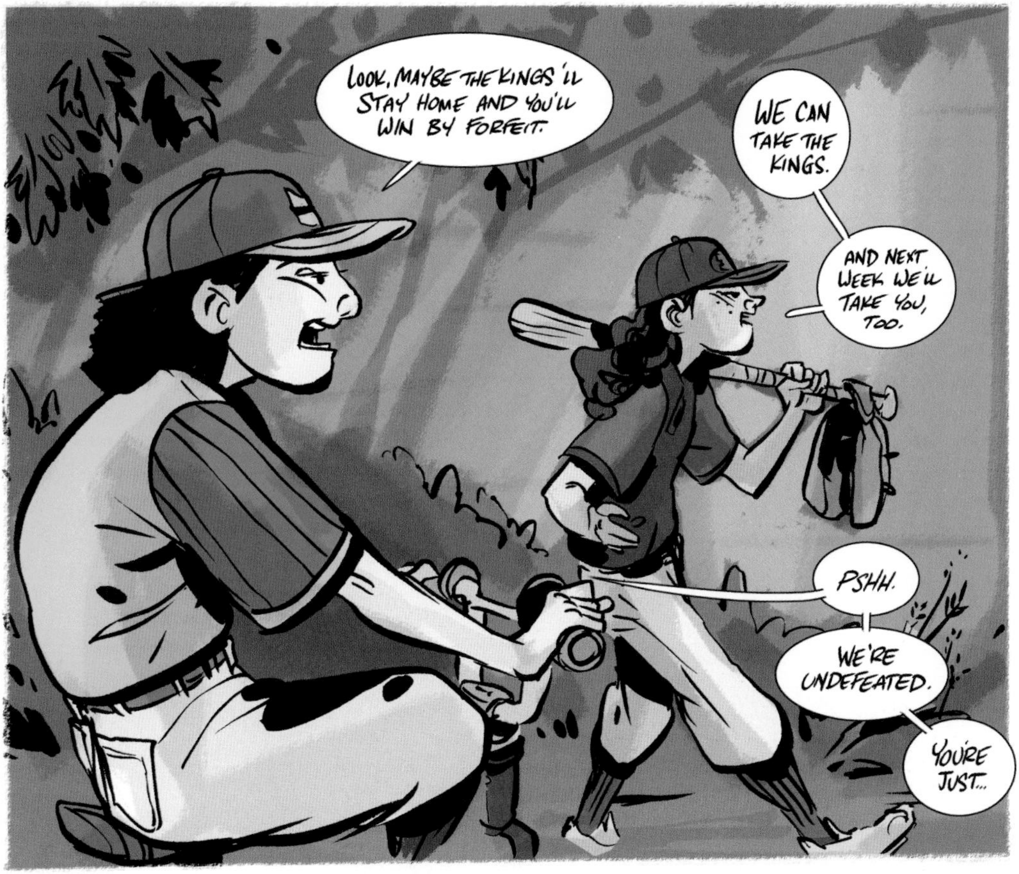
LOOK, MAYBE THE KINGS'LL STAY HOME AND YOU'LL WIN BY FORFEIT.
WE CAN TAKE THE KINGS.
AND NEXT WEEK WE'LL TAKE YOU, TOO.
PSHH.
WE'RE UNDEFEATED.
YOU'RE JUST...

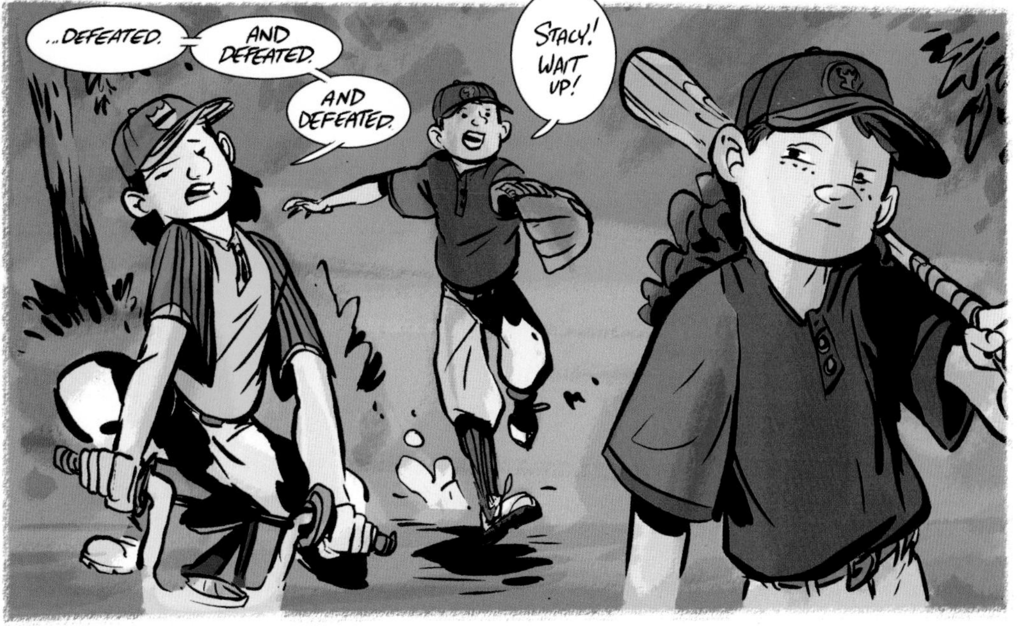
...DEFEATED.
AND DEFEATED.
AND DEFEATED.
STACY! WAIT UP!

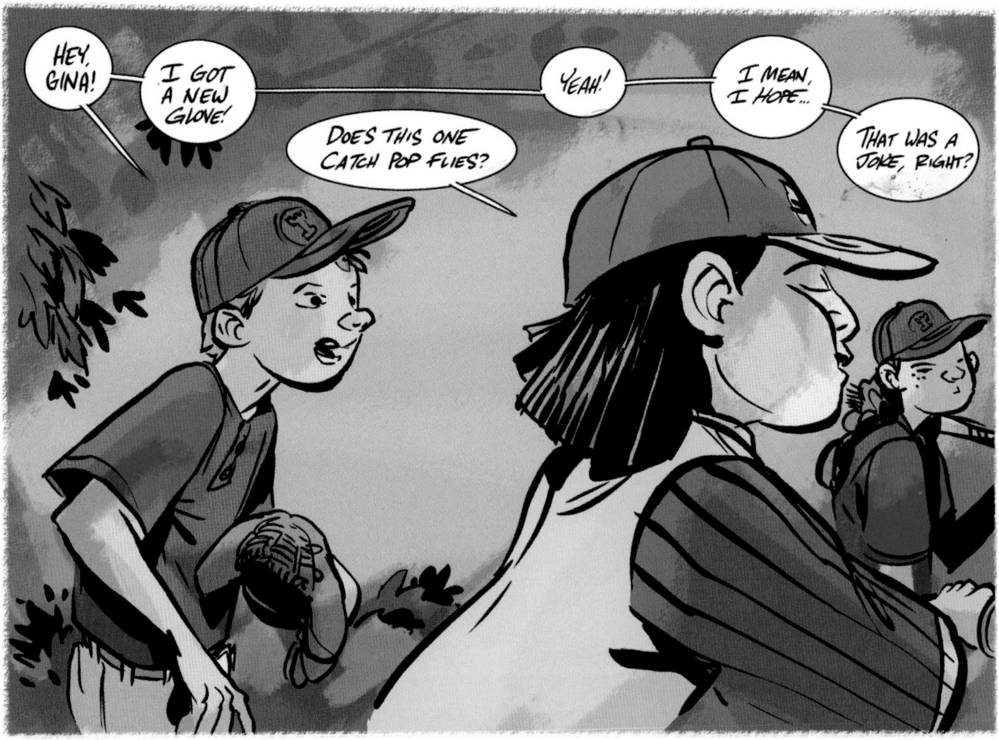
HEY, GINA!
I GOT A NEW GLOVE!
DOES THIS ONE CATCH POP FLIES?
YEAH!
I MEAN, I HOPE...
THAT WAS A JOKE, RIGHT?

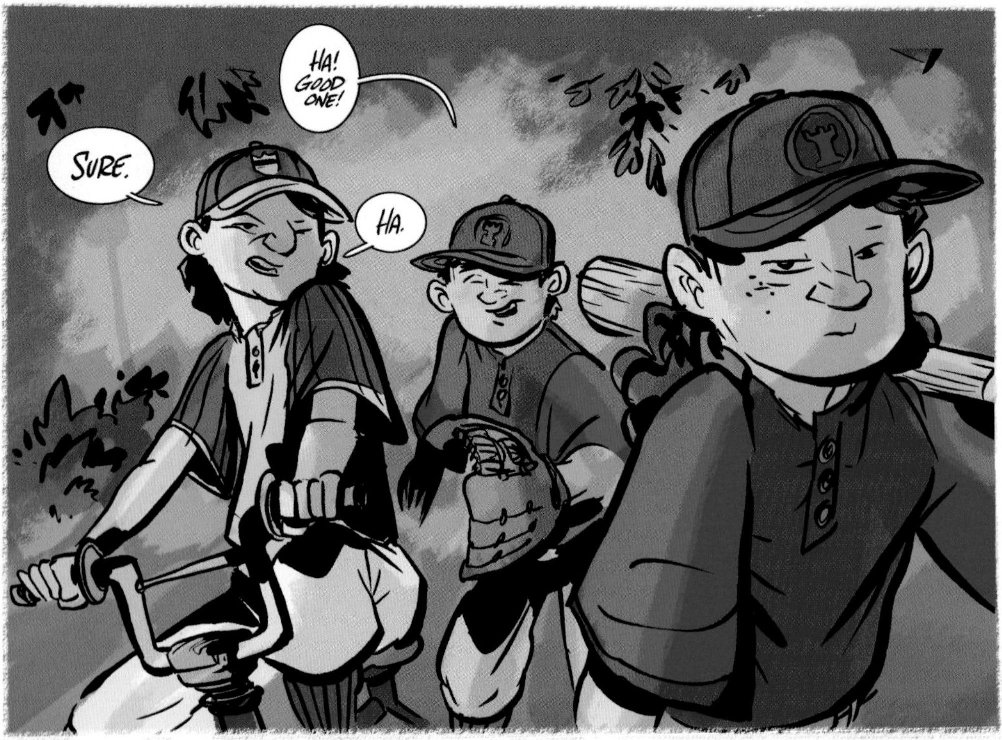
HA! GOOD ONE!
SURE.
HA.

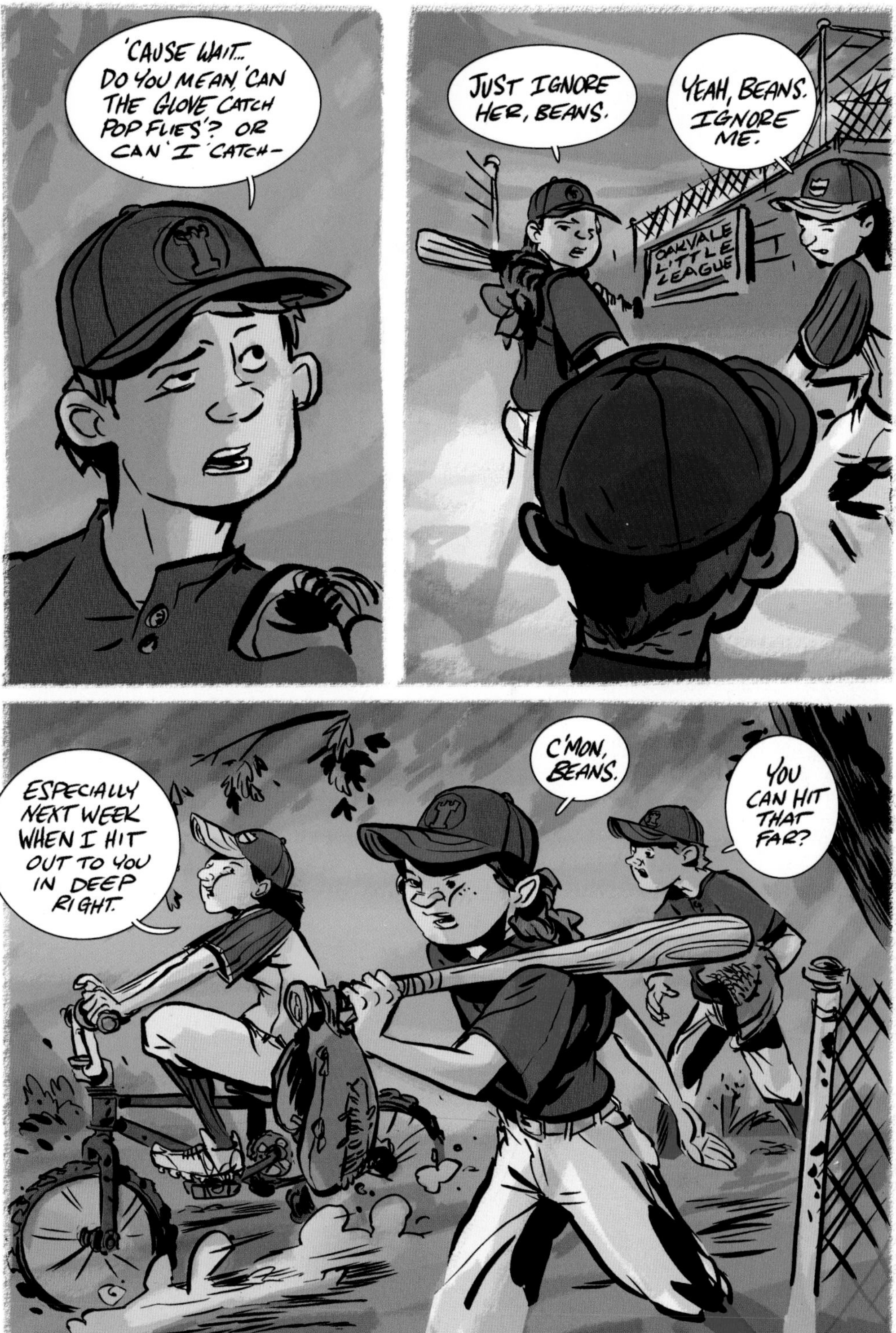
'CAUSE WAIT... DO YOU MEAN, 'CAN THE GLOVE CATCH POP FLIES'? OR CAN 'I' CATCH-
JUST IGNORE HER, BEANS.
YEAH, BEANS. IGNORE ME.
OAKVALE LITTLE LEAGUE
ESPECIALLY NEXT WEEK WHEN I HIT OUT TO YOU IN DEEP RIGHT.
C'MON, BEANS.
YOU CAN HIT THAT FAR?

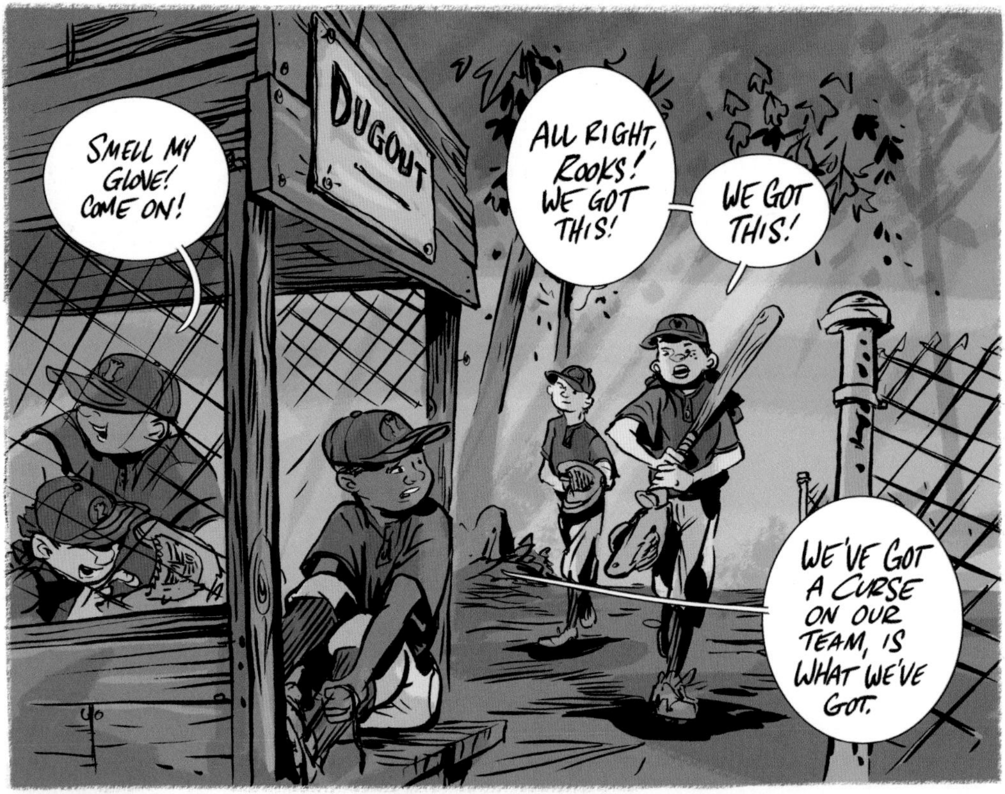
SMELL MY GLOVE! COME ON!
DUGOUT
ALL RIGHT, ROOKS! WE GOT THIS!
WE GOT THIS!
WE'VE GOT A CURSE ON OUR TEAM, IS WHAT WE'VE GOT.

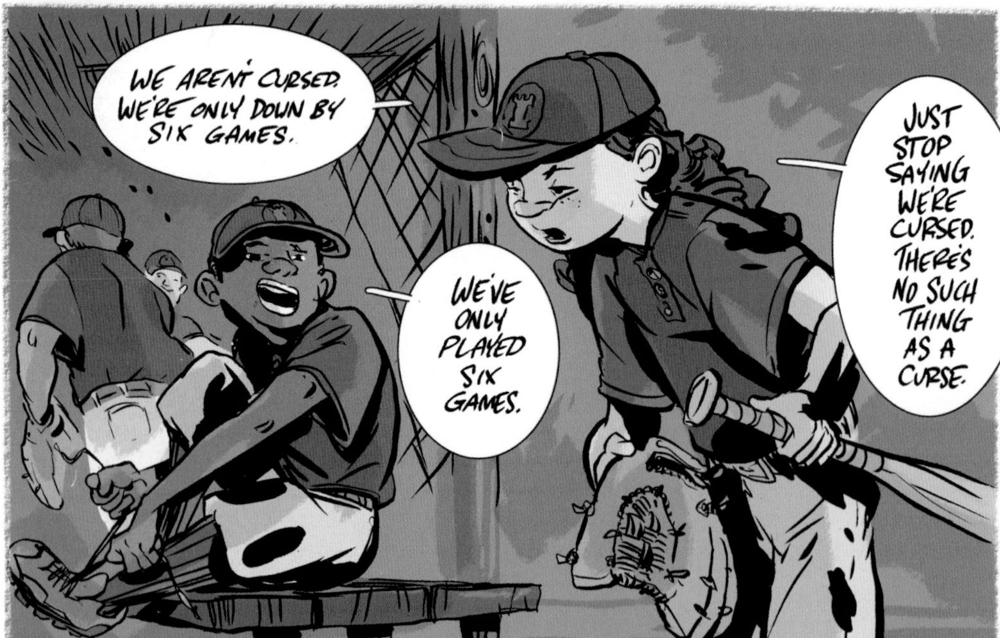
WE AREN'T CURSED. WE'RE ONLY DOWN BY SIX GAMES.
WE'VE ONLY PLAYED SIX GAMES.
JUST STOP SAYING WE'RE CURSED. THERE'S NO SUCH THING AS A CURSE.

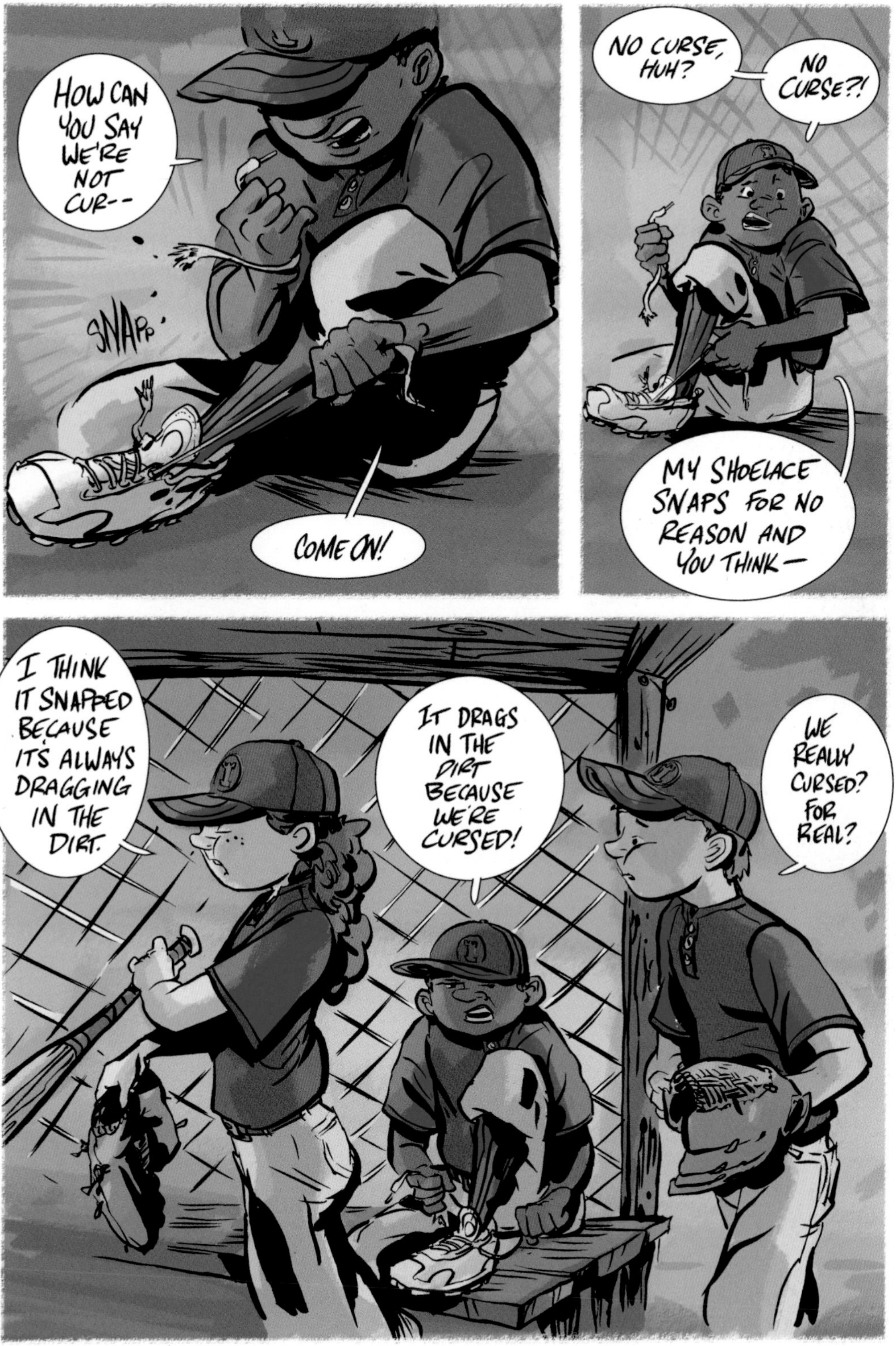
HOW CAN YOU SAY WE'RE NOT CUR--
SNAPP
COME ON!
NO CURSE, HUH?
NO CURSE?!
MY SHOELACE SNAPS FOR NO REASON AND YOU THINK—
I THINK IT SNAPPED BECAUSE ITS ALWAYS DRAGGING IN THE DIRT.
IT DRAGS IN THE DIRT BECAUSE WE'RE CURSED!
WE REALLY CURSED? FOR REAL?

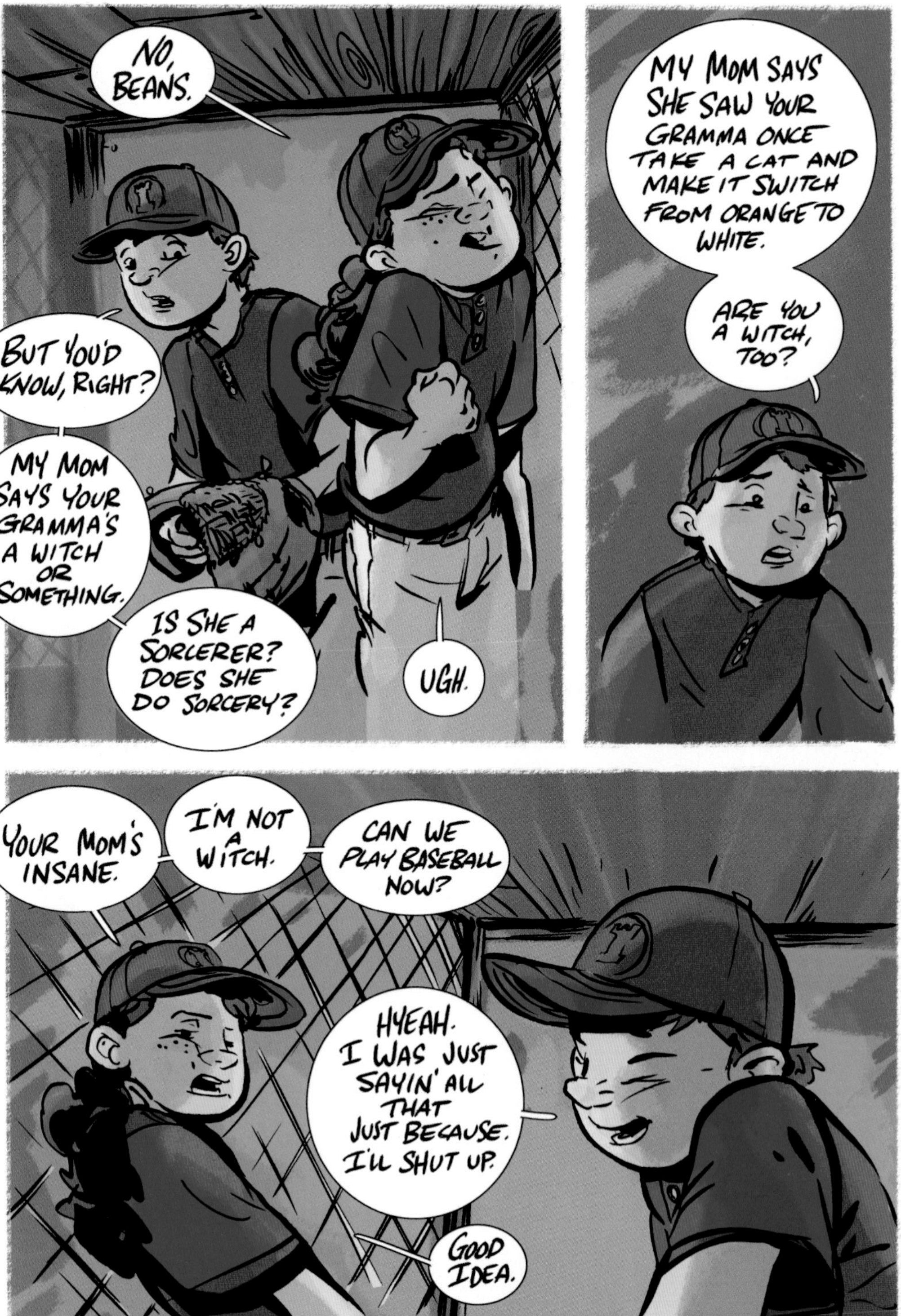
NO, BEANS.
BUT YOU'D KNOW, RIGHT?
MY MOM SAYS YOUR GRAMMA'S A WITCH OR SOMETHING.
IS SHE A SORCERER? DOES SHE DO SORCERY?
UGH.
MY MOM SAYS SHE SAW YOUR GRAMMA ONCE TAKE A CAT AND MAKE IT SWITCH FROM ORANGE TO WHITE.
ARE YOU A WITCH, TOO?
YOUR MOM'S INSANE.
I'M NOT A WITCH.
CAN WE PLAY BASEBALL NOW?
HYEAH. I WAS JUST SAYIN' ALL THAT JUST BECAUSE. I'LL SHUT UP.
GOOD IDEA.

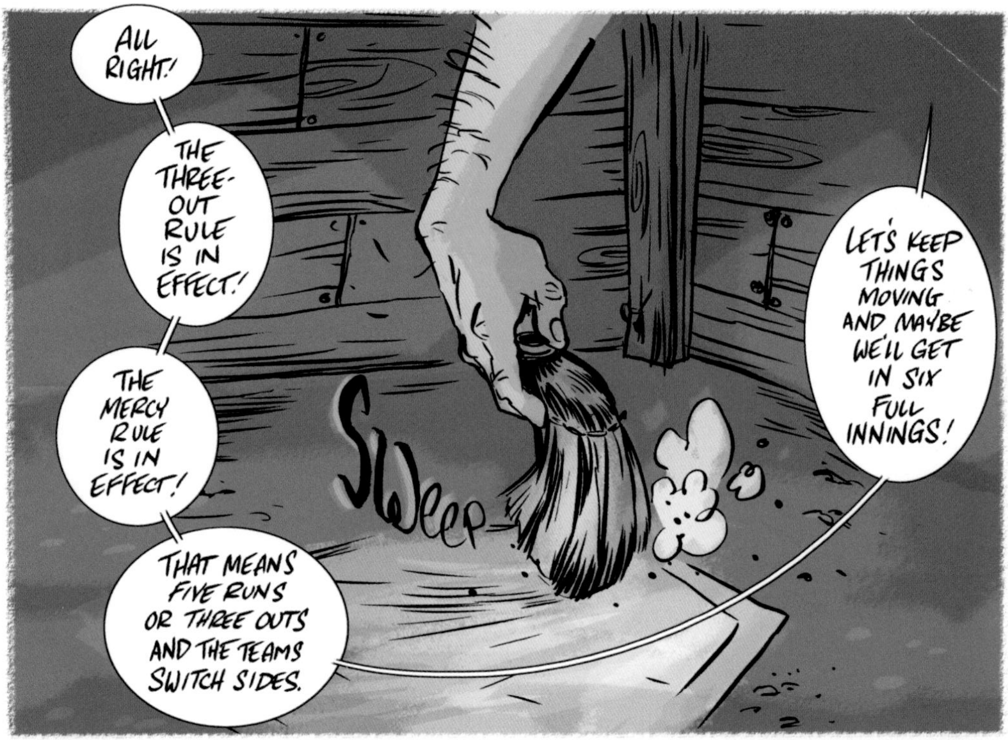
ALL RIGHT!
THE THREE-OUT RULE IS IN EFFECT!
THE MERCY RULE IS IN EFFECT!
THAT MEANS FIVE RUNS OR THREE OUTS AND THE TEAMS SWITCH SIDES.
LET'S KEEP THINGS MOVING AND MAYBE WE'LL GET IN SIX FULL INNINGS!
SWEEP

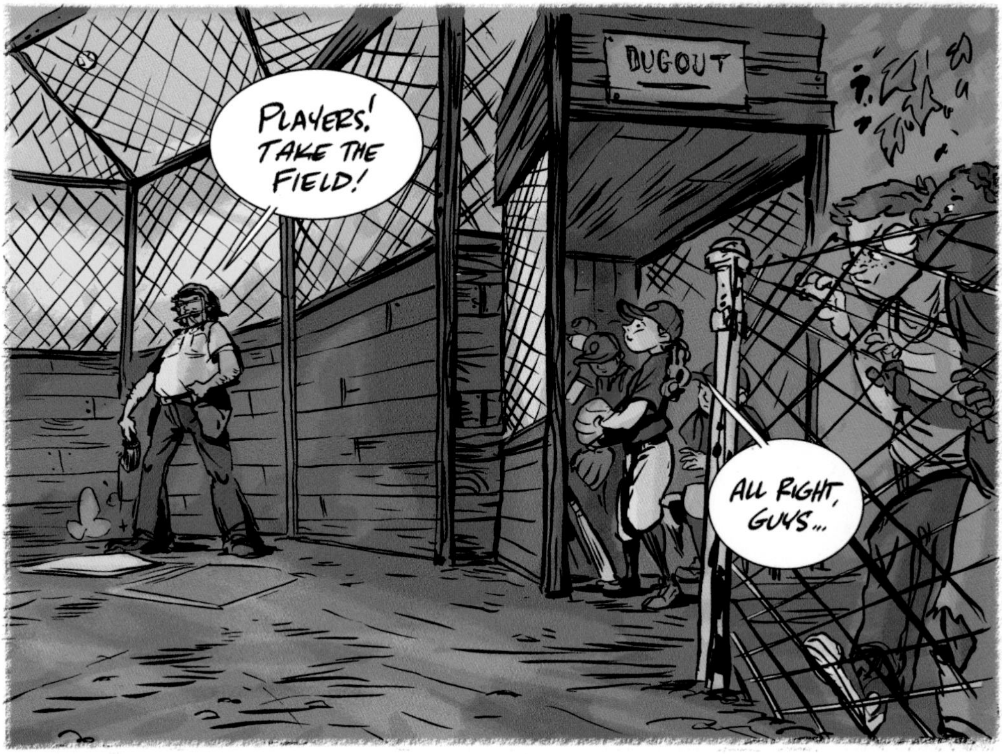
DUGOUT
PLAYERS! TAKE THE FIELD!
ALL RIGHT, GUYS...

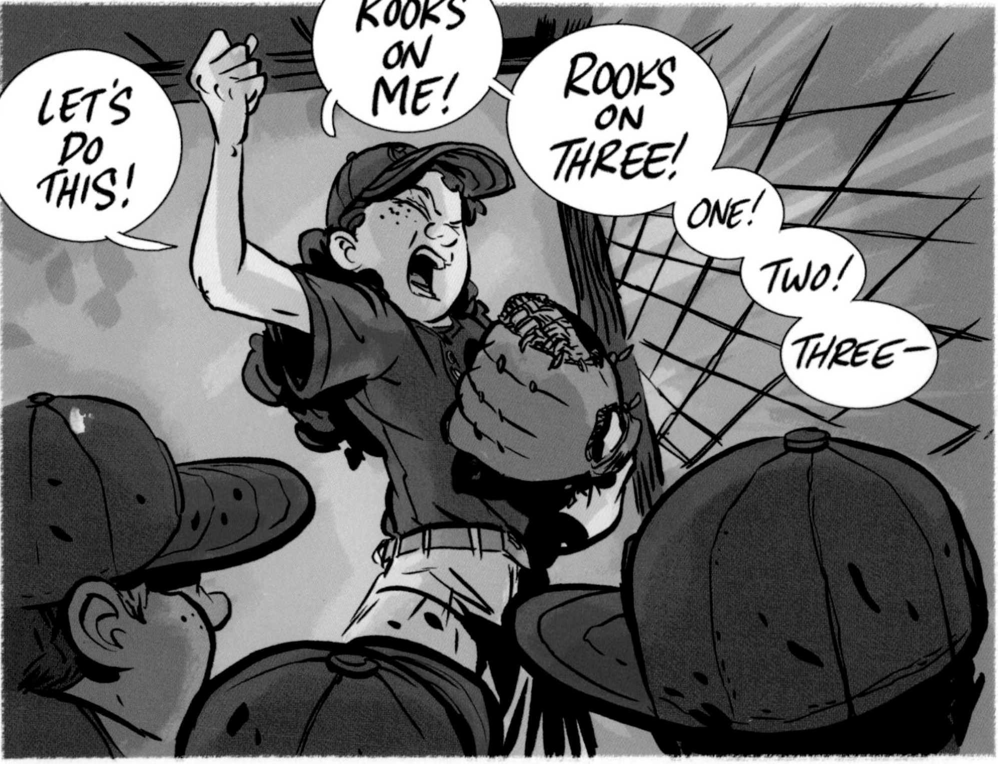
LET'S DO THIS!
ROOKS ON ME!
ROOKS ON THREE!
ONE!
TWO!
THREE-

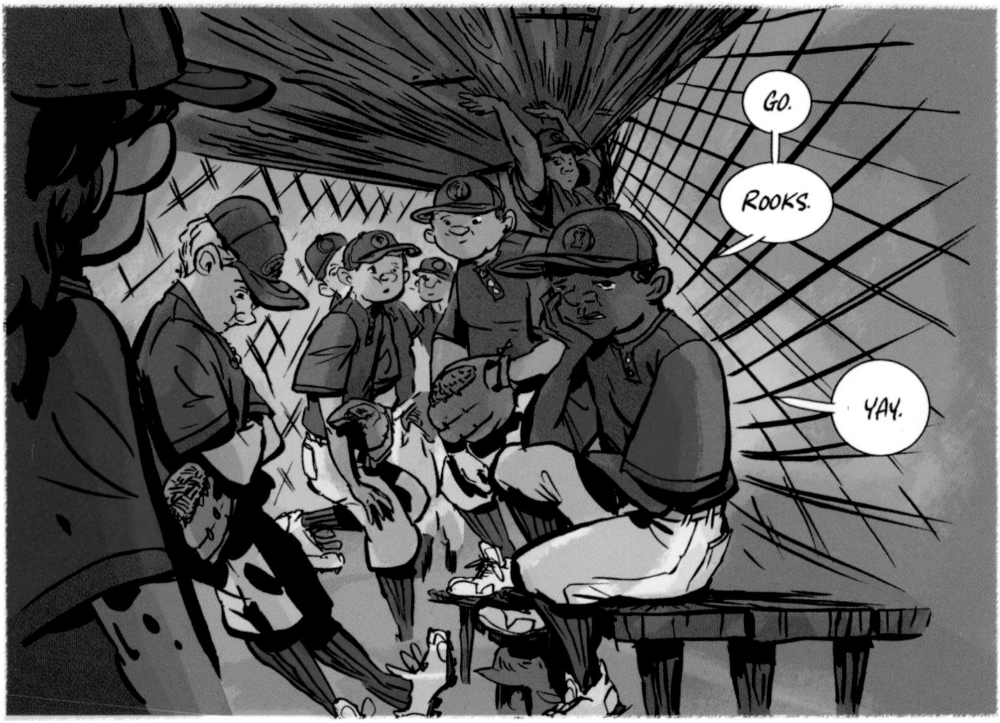
GO.
ROOKS.
YAY.

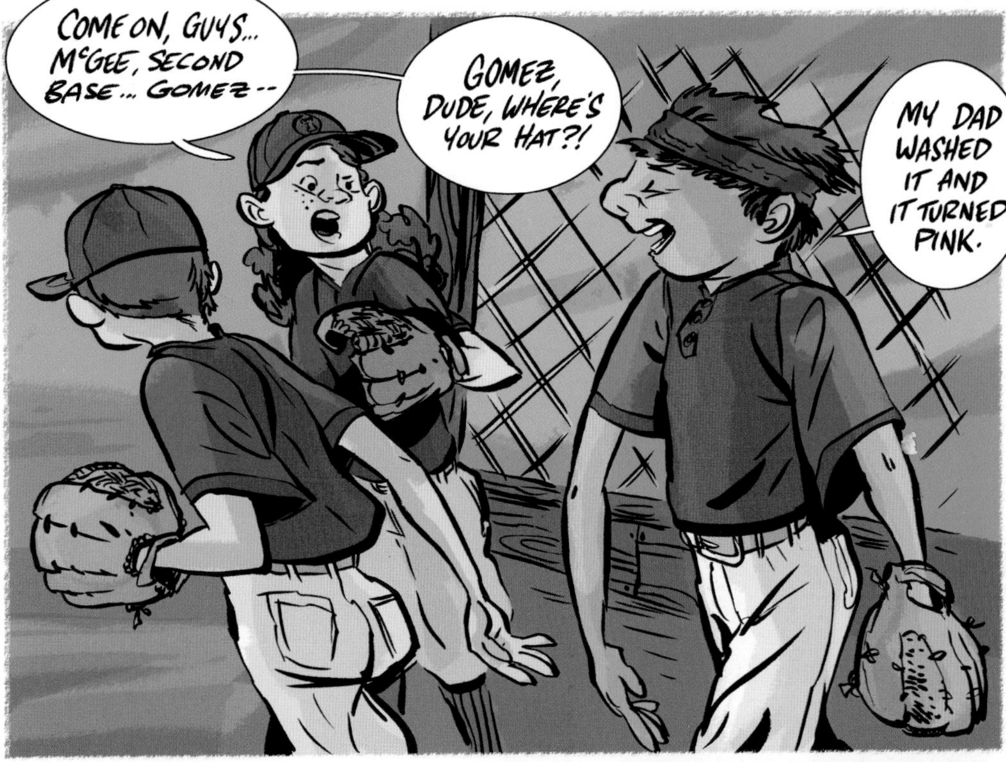
COME ON, GUYS... McGEE, SECOND BASE... GOMEZ--
GOMEZ, DUDE, WHERE'S YOUR HAT?!
MY DAD WASHED IT AND IT TURNED PINK.

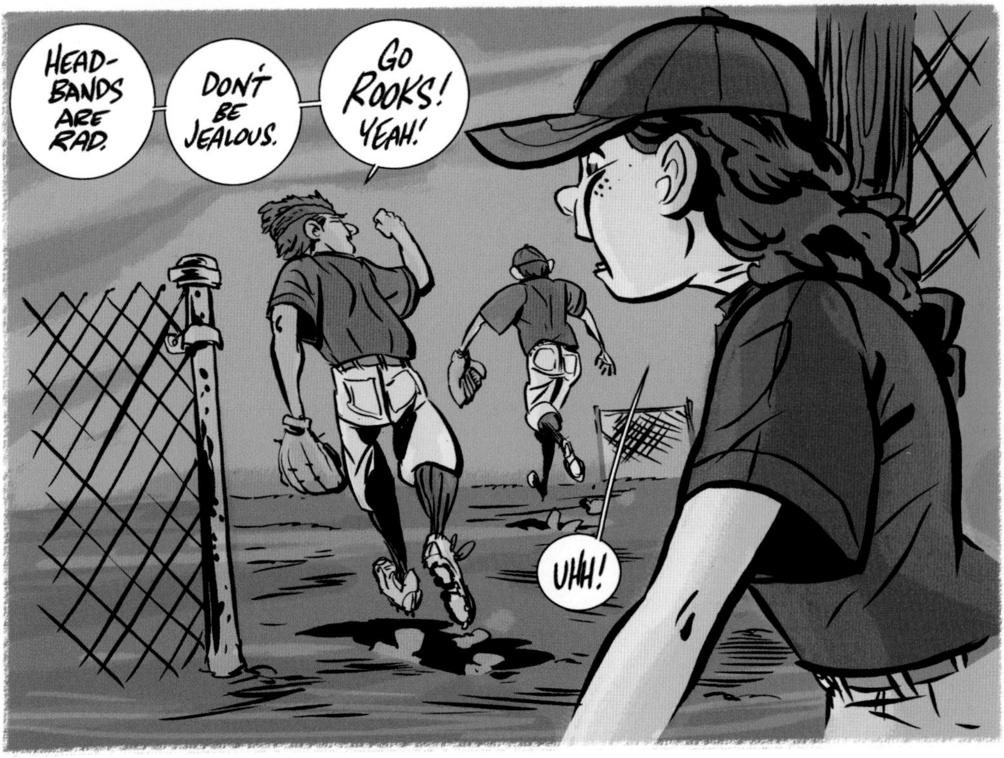
HEAD-BANDS ARE RAD.
DON'T BE JEALOUS.
GO ROOKS! YEAH!
UHH!

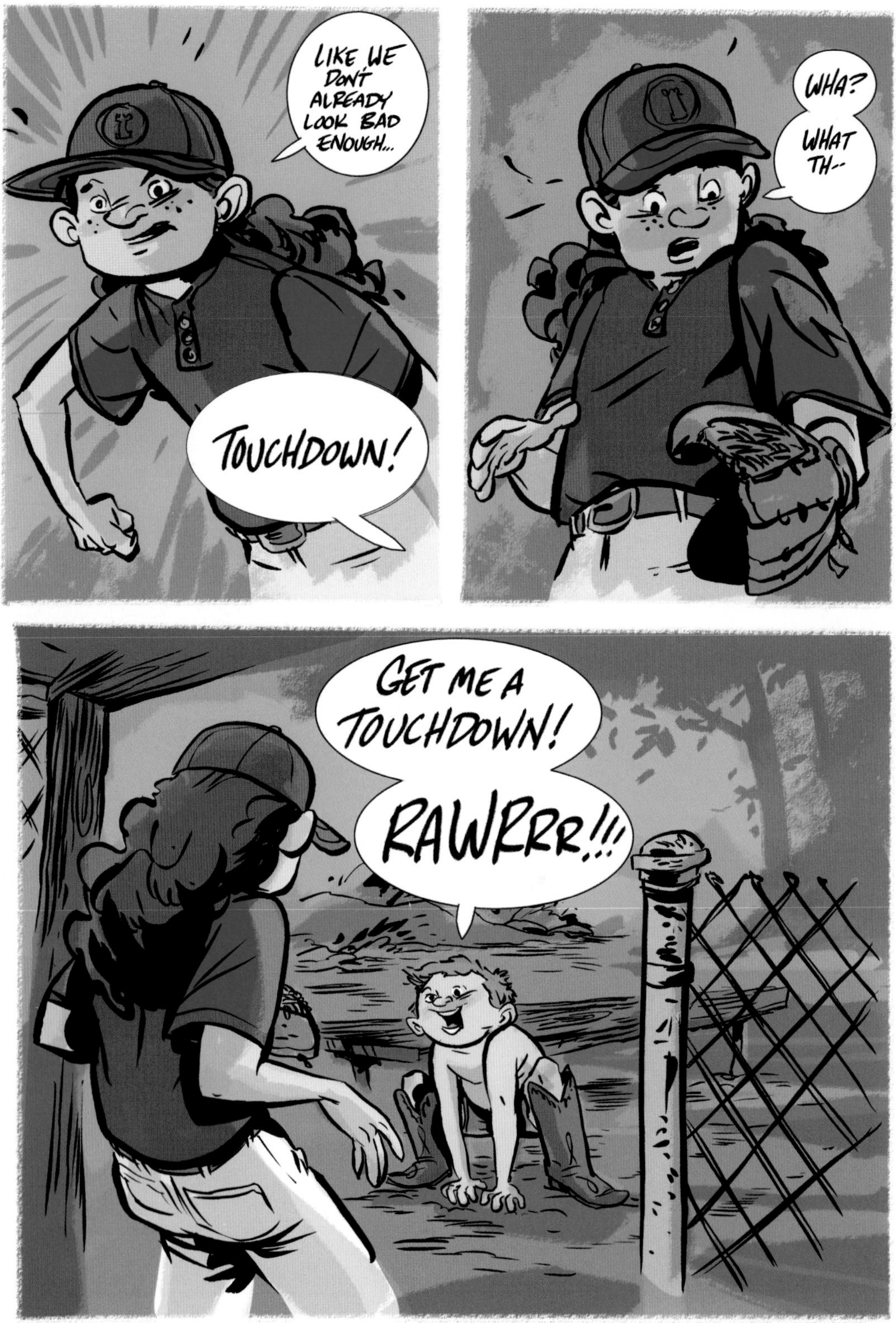
LIKE WE DON'T ALREADY LOOK BAD ENOUGH...
TOUCHDOWN!
WHA?
WHAT TH--
GET ME A TOUCHDOWN!
RAWRrr!!!

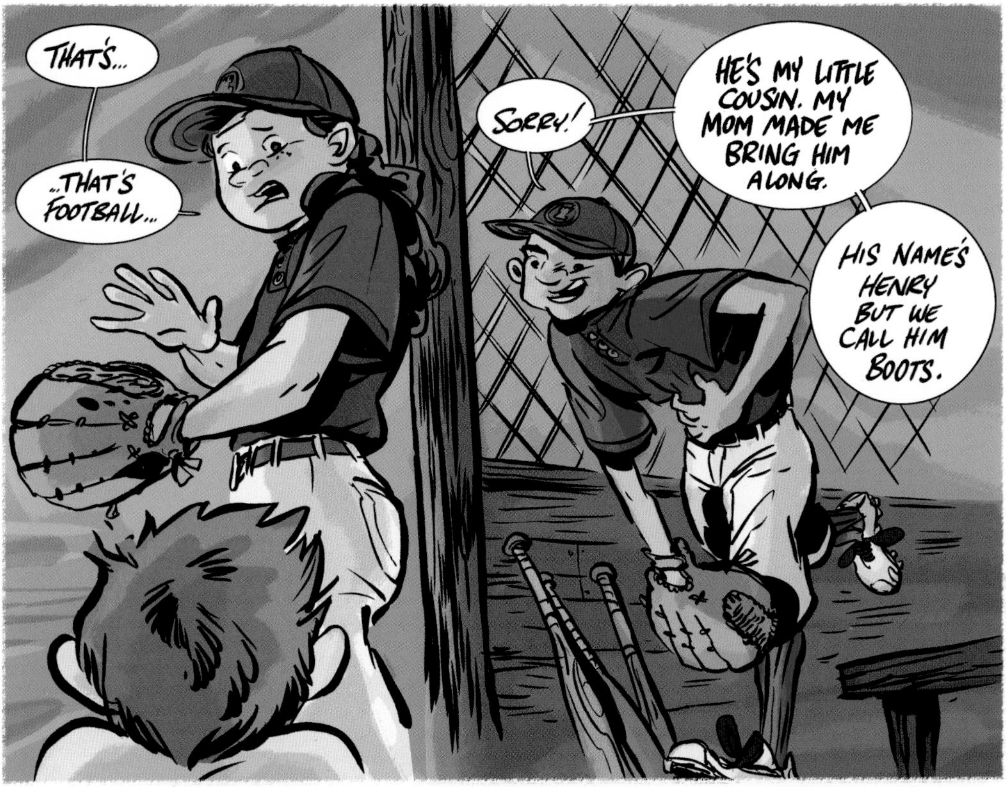
THAT'S...
..THAT'S FOOTBALL...
SORRY!
HE'S MY LITTLE COUSIN. MY MOM MADE ME BRING HIM ALONG.
HIS NAME'S HENRY BUT WE CALL HIM BOOTS.

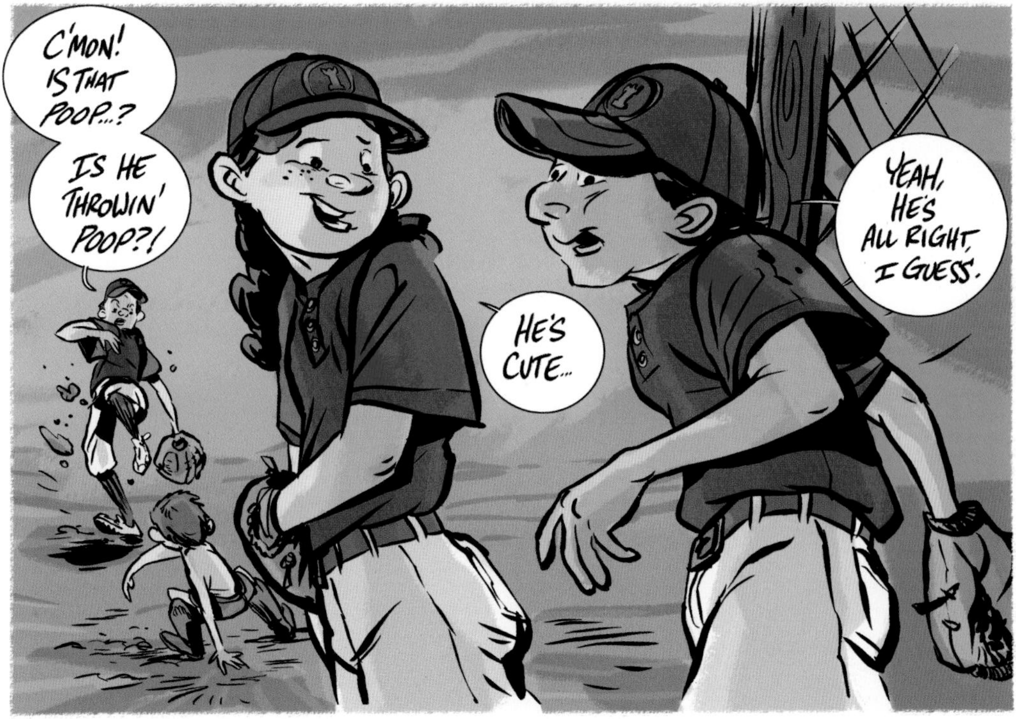
C'MON! IS THAT POOP...?
IS HE THROWIN' POOP?!
HE'S CUTE...
YEAH, HE'S ALL RIGHT, I GUESS.

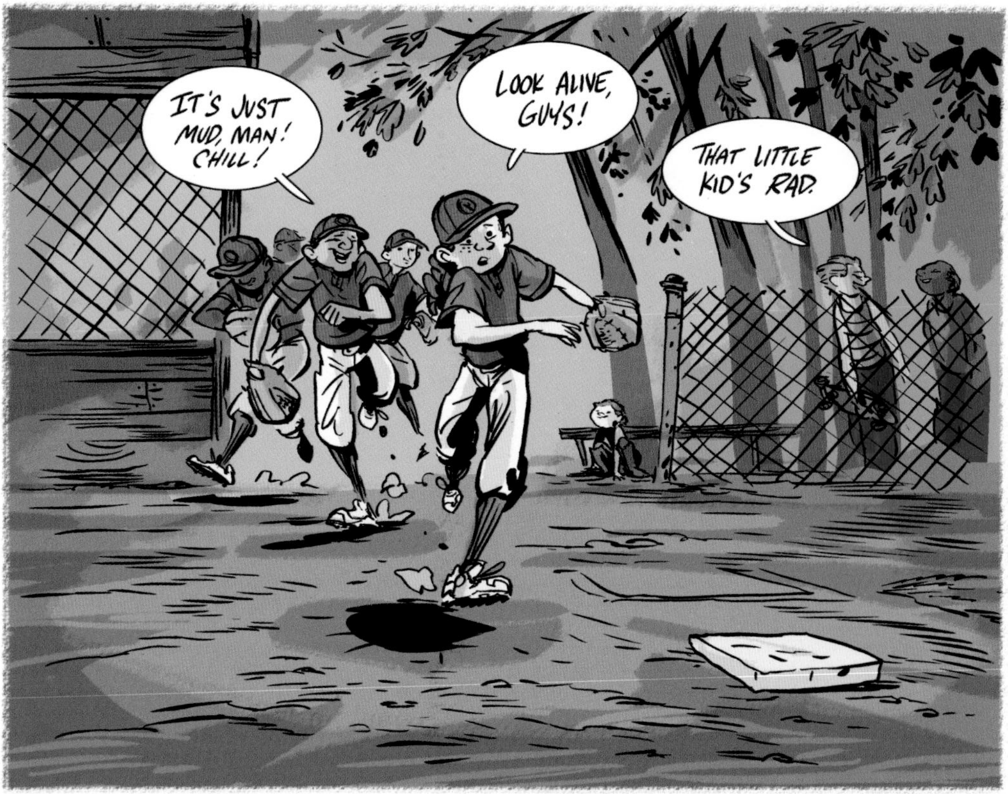
IT'S JUST MUD, MAN! CHILL!
LOOK ALIVE, GUYS!
THAT LITTLE KID'S RAD.

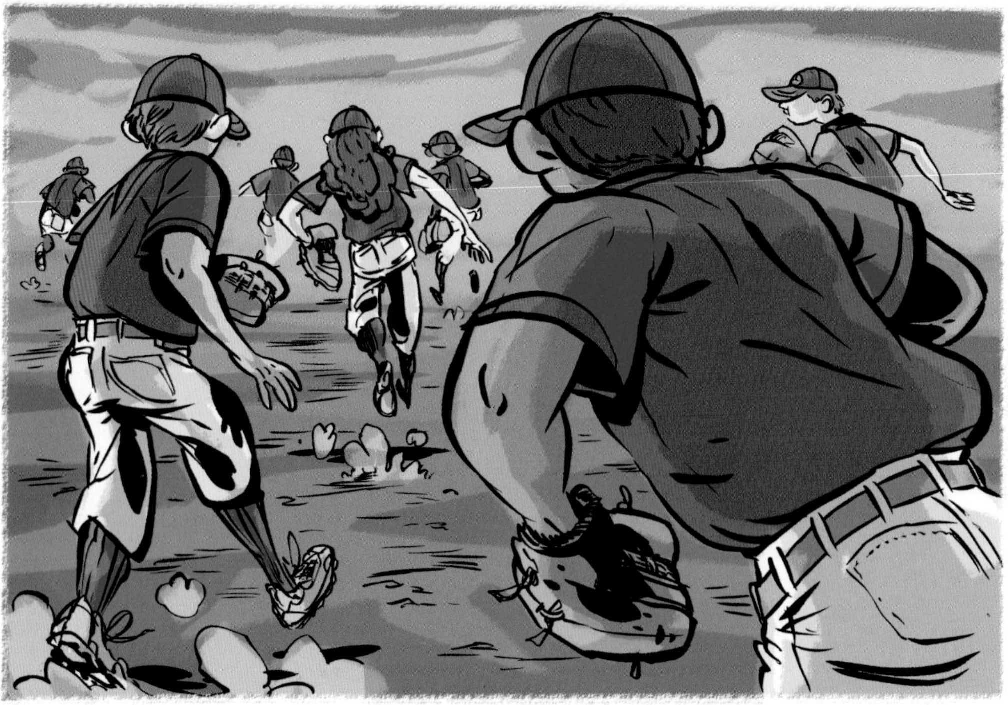

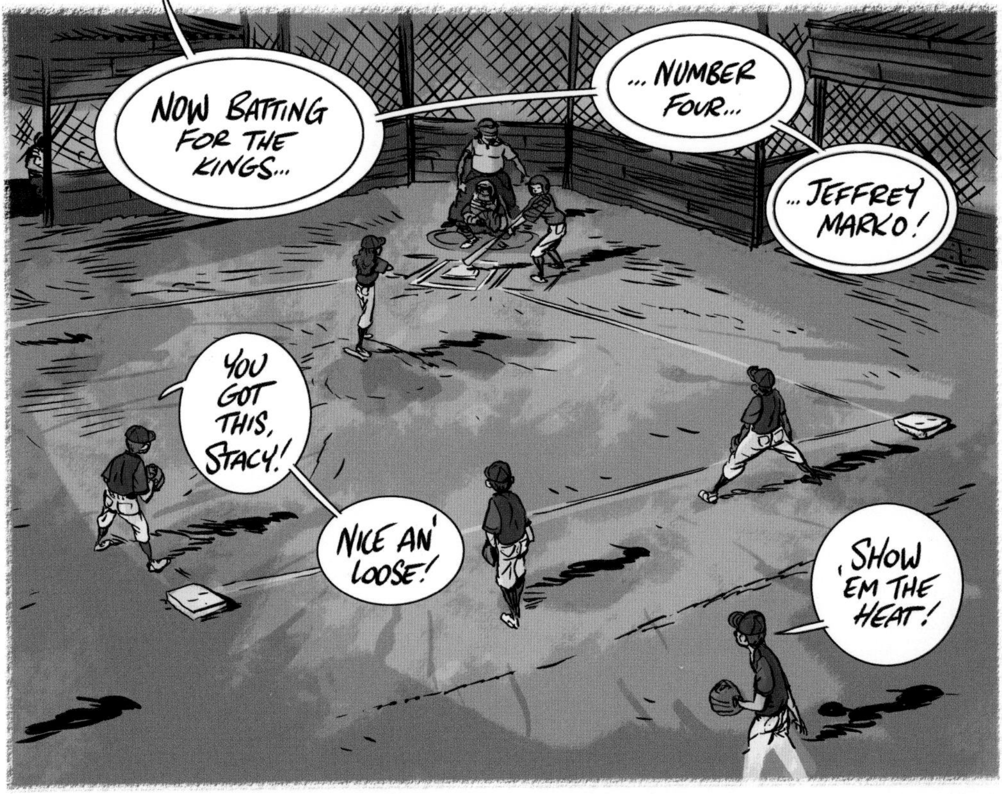
NOW BATTING FOR THE KINGS...
...NUMBER FOUR...
...JEFFREY MARKO!
YOU GOT THIS, STACY!
NICE AN' LOOSE!
SHOW 'EM THE HEAT!

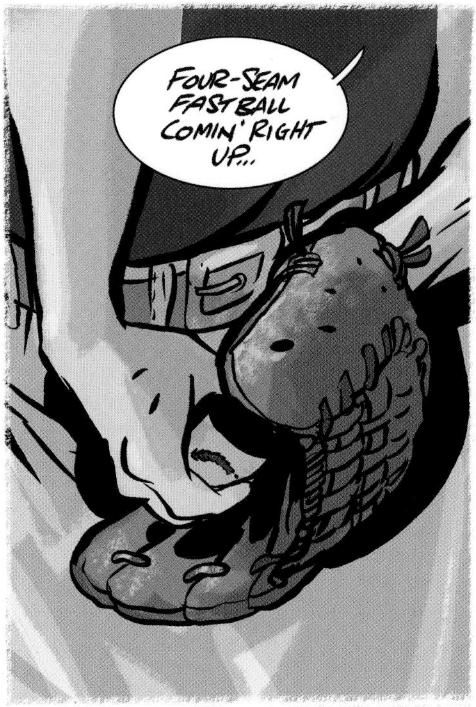
FOUR-SEAM FASTBALL COMIN' RIGHT UP...

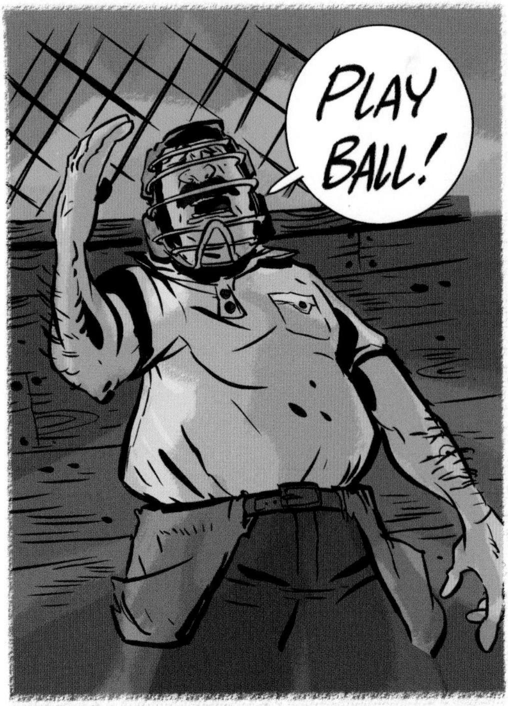
PLAY BALL!

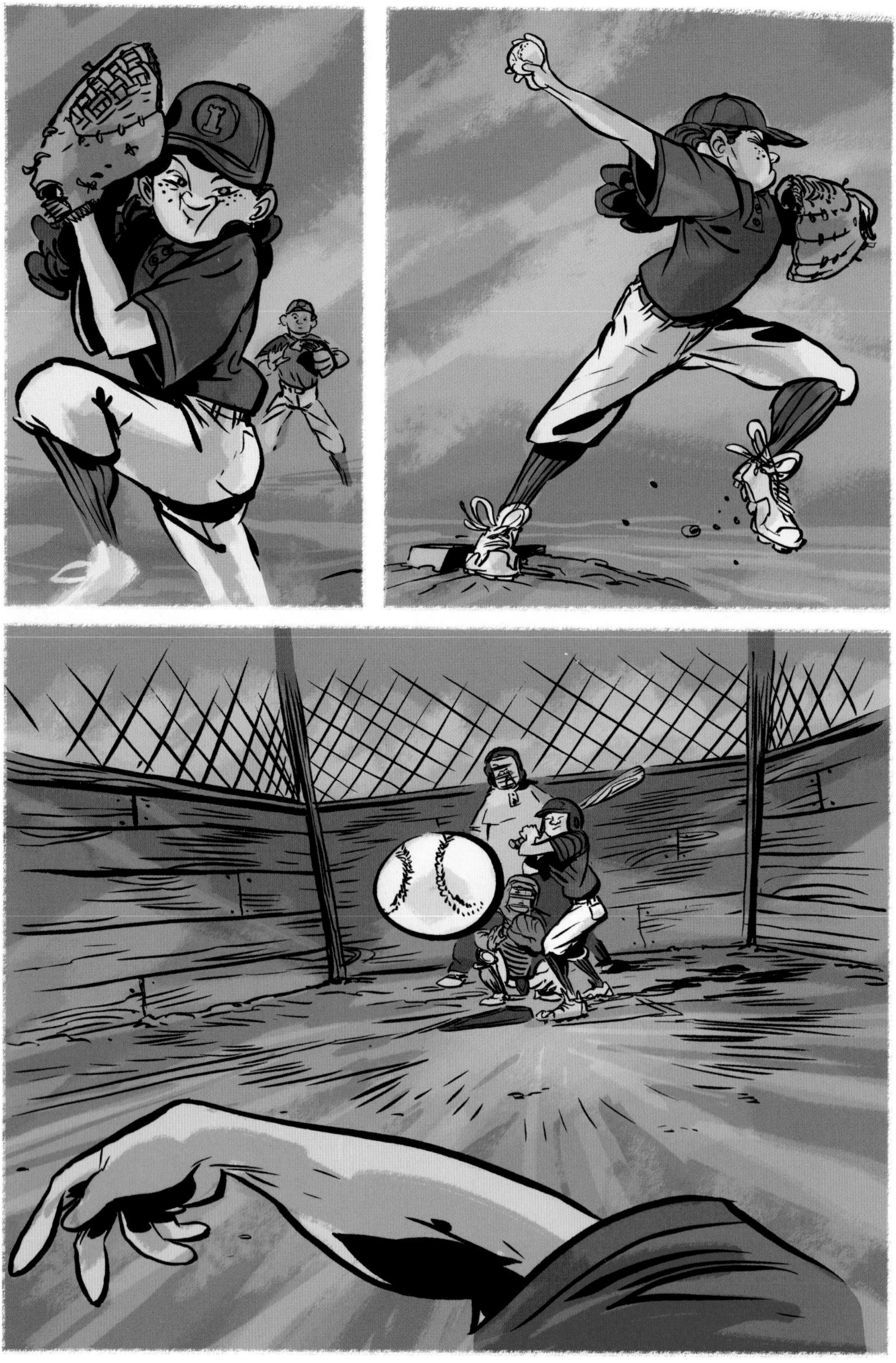

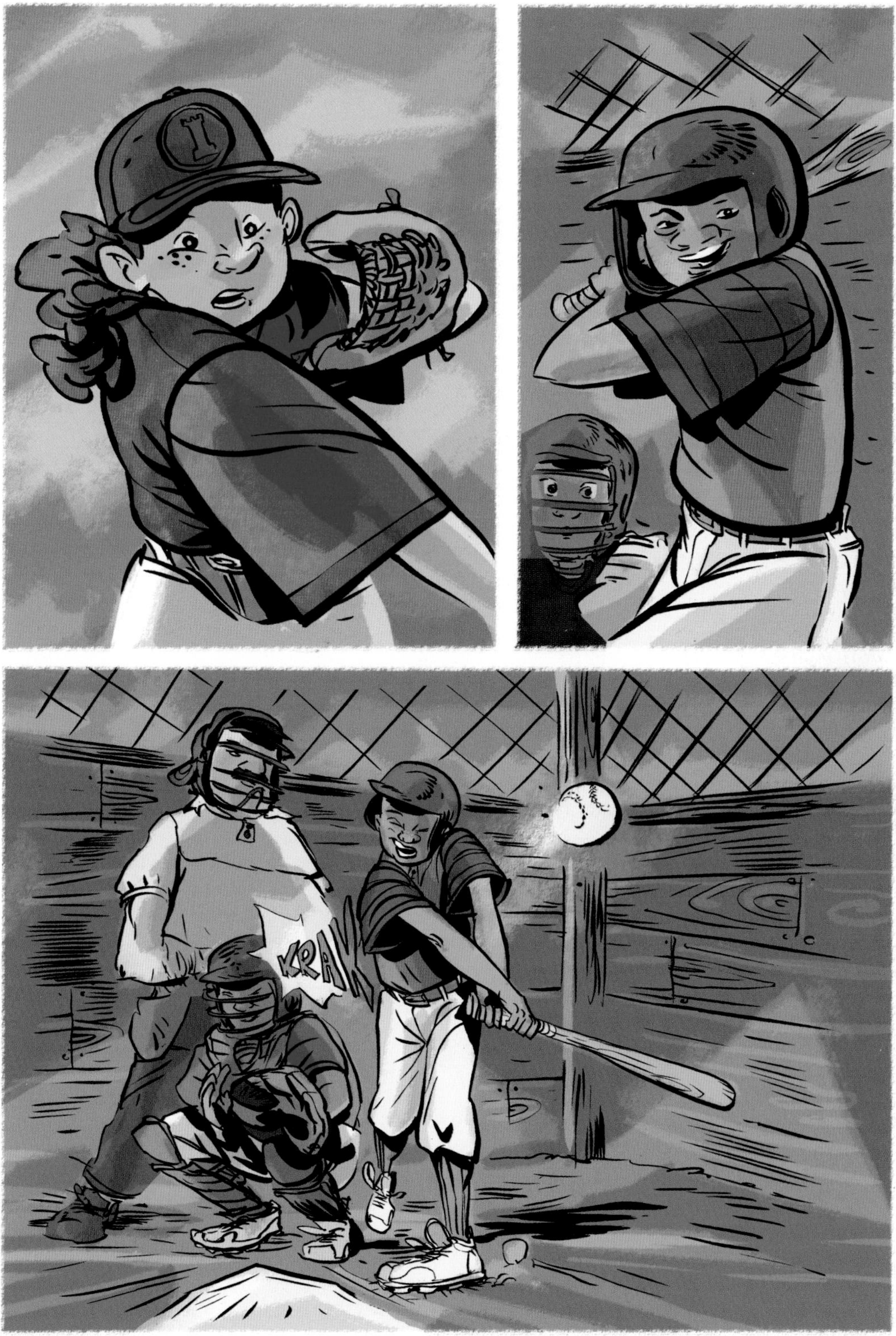
KRAK

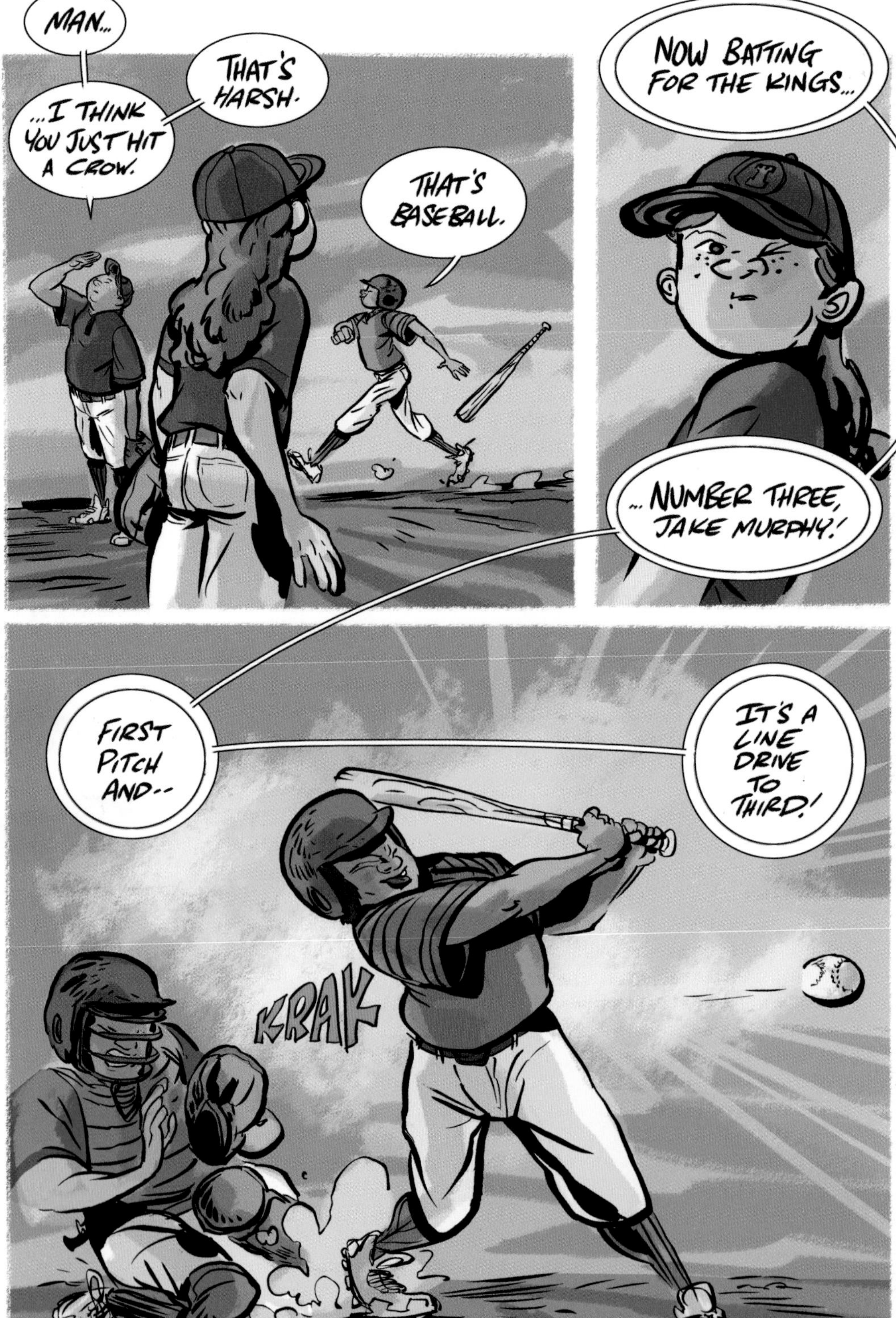
MAN...
...I THINK YOU JUST HIT A CROW.
THAT'S HARSH.
THAT'S BASEBALL.
NOW BATTING FOR THE KINGS...
...NUMBER THREE, JAKE MURPHY!
FIRST PITCH AND--
IT'S A LINE DRIVE TO THIRD!
KRAK

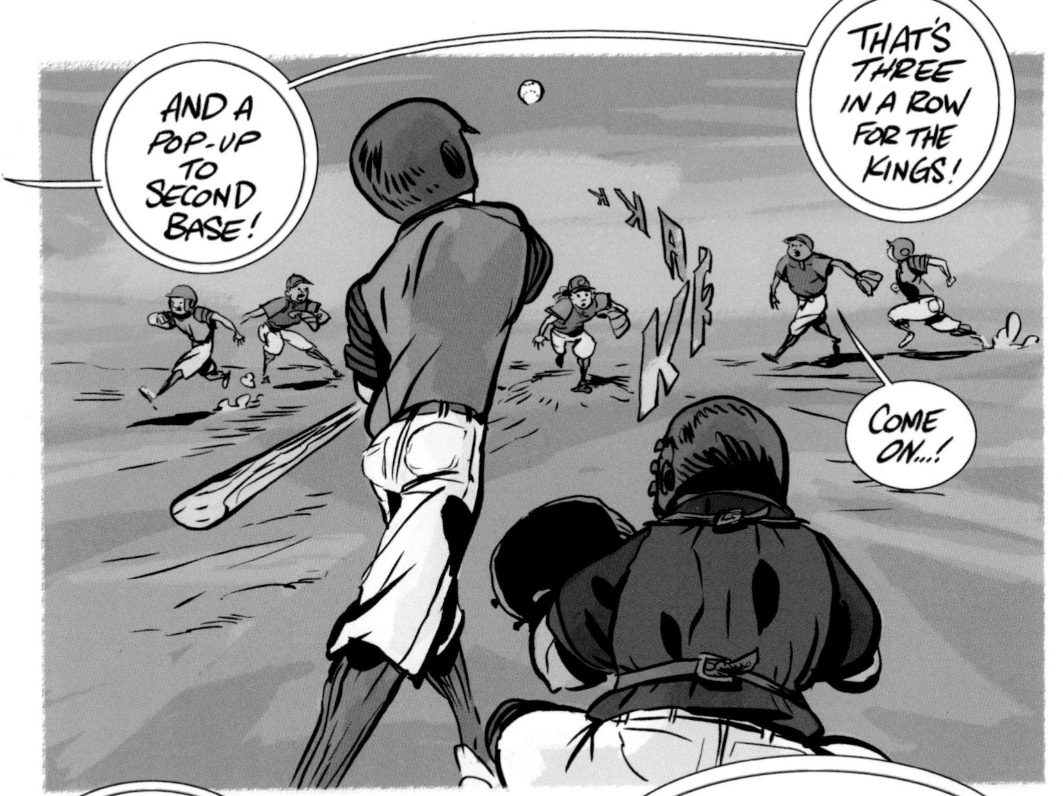

AND A POP-UP TO SECOND BASE!
THAT'S THREE IN A ROW FOR THE KINGS!
COME ON...!

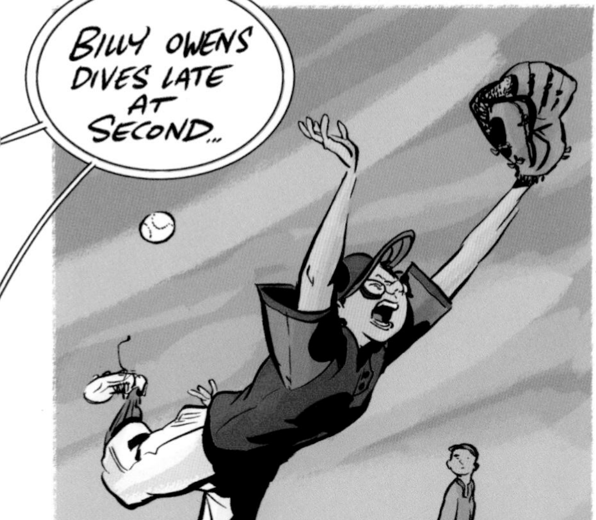

BILLY OWENS DIVES LATE AT SECOND...
...AS LEVI ISAACS WATCHES FROM CENTER!

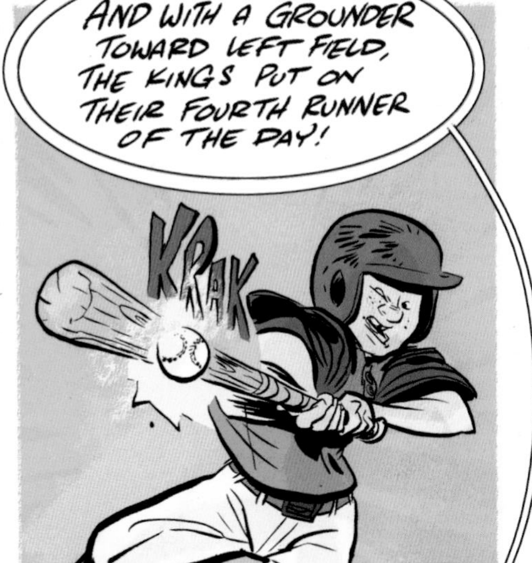

AND WITH A GROUNDER TOWARD LEFT FIELD, THE KINGS PUT ON THEIR FOURTH RUNNER OF THE DAY!
KRAK
THREE-NOTHING, KINGS!

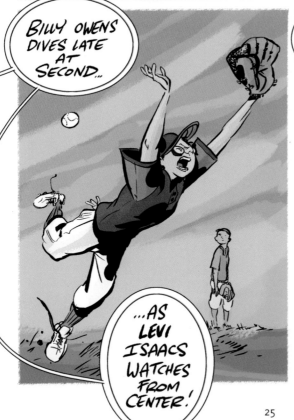

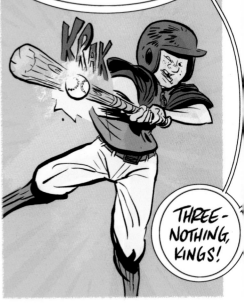

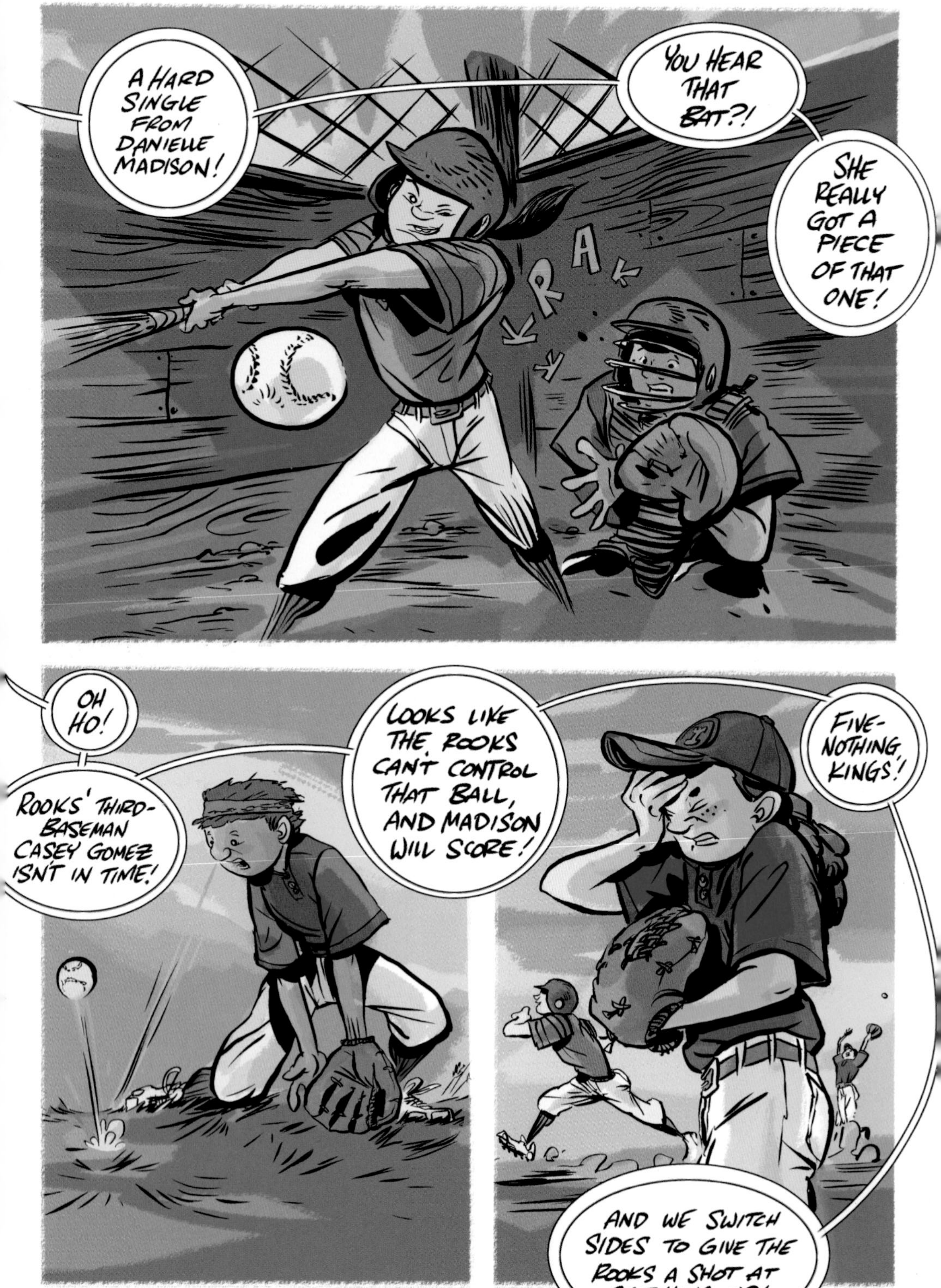
A HARD SINGLE FROM DANIELLE MADISON!
YOU HEAR THAT BAT?!
SHE REALLY GOT A PIECE OF THAT ONE!
KRAK
OH HO!
ROOKS' THIRD-BASEMAN CASEY GOMEZ ISN'T IN TIME!
LOOKS LIKE THE ROOKS CAN'T CONTROL THAT BALL, AND MADISON WILL SCORE!
FIVE-NOTHING, KINGS!
AND WE SWITCH SIDES TO GIVE THE ROOKS A SHOT AT CATCHING UP!

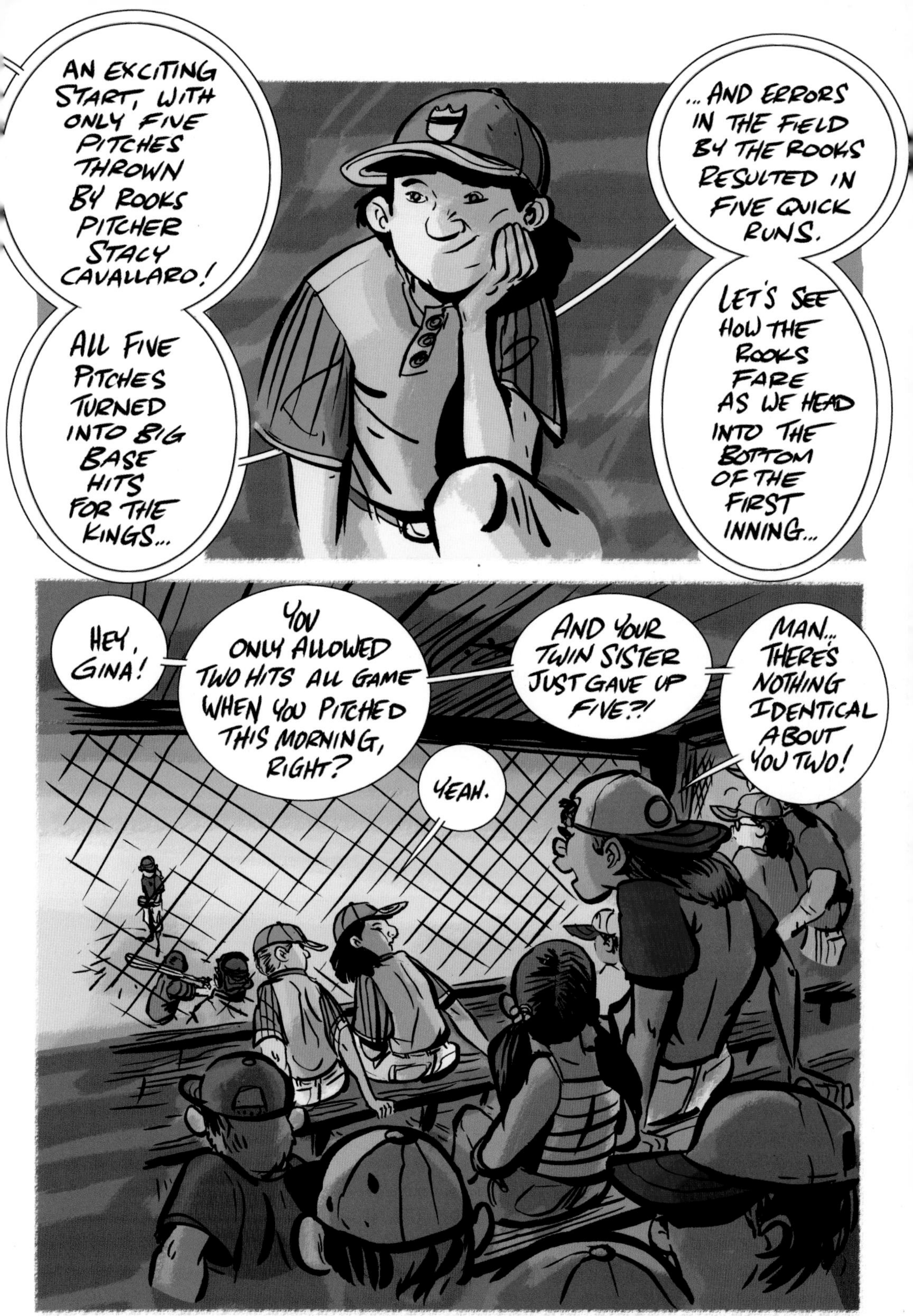
AN EXCITING START, WITH ONLY FIVE PITCHES THROWN BY ROOKS PITCHER STACY CAVALLARO!
ALL FIVE PITCHES TURNED INTO BIG BASE HITS FOR THE KINGS...
...AND ERRORS IN THE FIELD BY THE ROOKS RESULTED IN FIVE QUICK RUNS.
LET'S SEE HOW THE ROOKS FARE AS WE HEAD INTO THE BOTTOM OF THE FIRST INNING...
HEY, GINA!
YOU ONLY ALLOWED TWO HITS ALL GAME WHEN YOU PITCHED THIS MORNING, RIGHT?
AND YOUR TWIN SISTER JUST GAVE UP FIVE?!
MAN... THERE'S NOTHING IDENTICAL ABOUT YOU TWO!
YEAH.

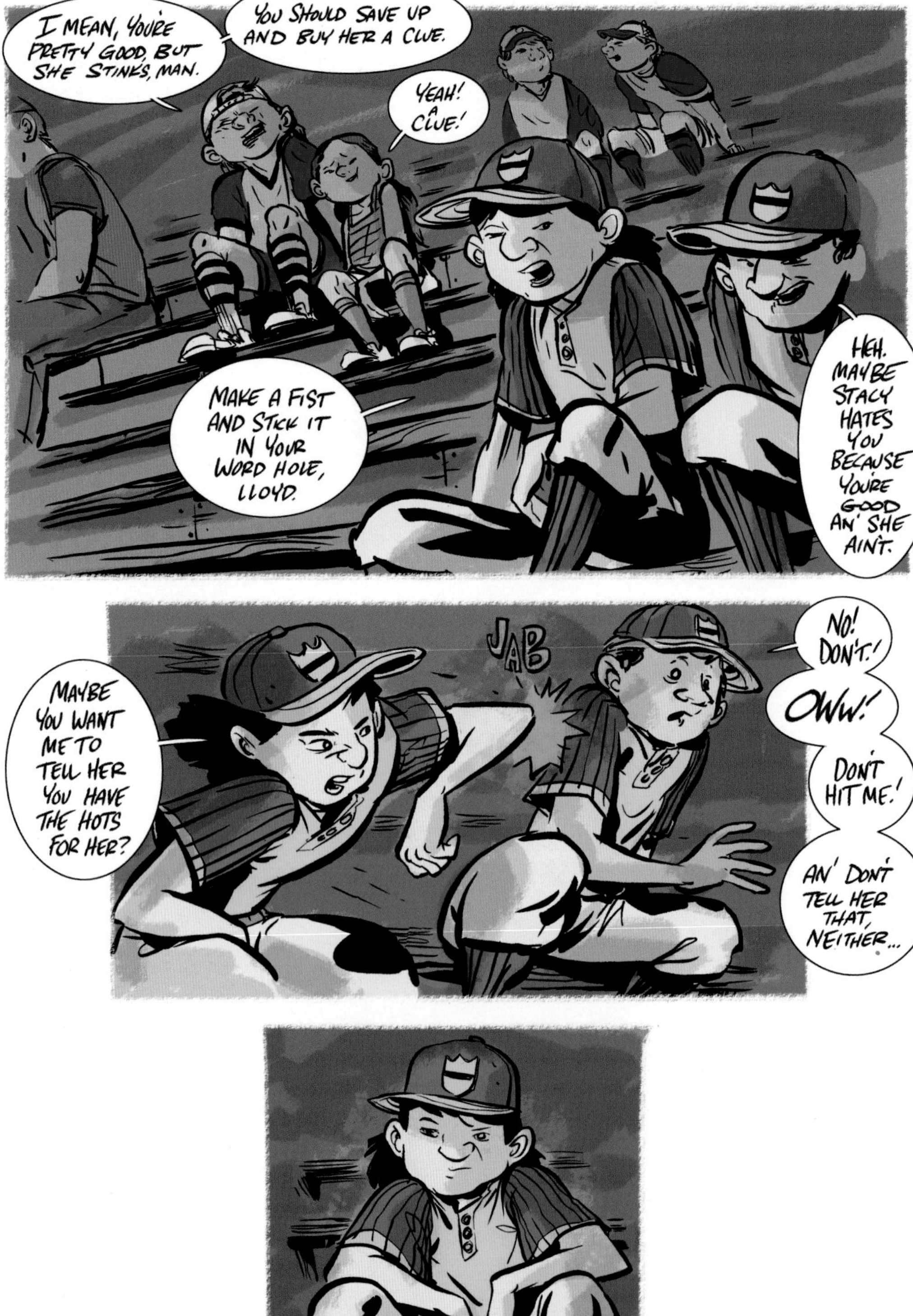
I MEAN, YOU'RE PRETTY GOOD, BUT SHE STINKS, MAN.
YOU SHOULD SAVE UP AND BUY HER A CLUE.
YEAH! A CLUE!
MAKE A FIST AND STICK IT IN YOUR WORD HOLE, LLOYD.
HEH. MAYBE STACY HATES YOU BECAUSE YOU'RE GOOD AN' SHE AIN'T.
MAYBE YOU WANT ME TO TELL HER YOU HAVE THE HOTS FOR HER?
JAB
NO! DON'T!
OWW!
DON'T HIT ME!
AN' DON'T TELL HER THAT, NEITHER...

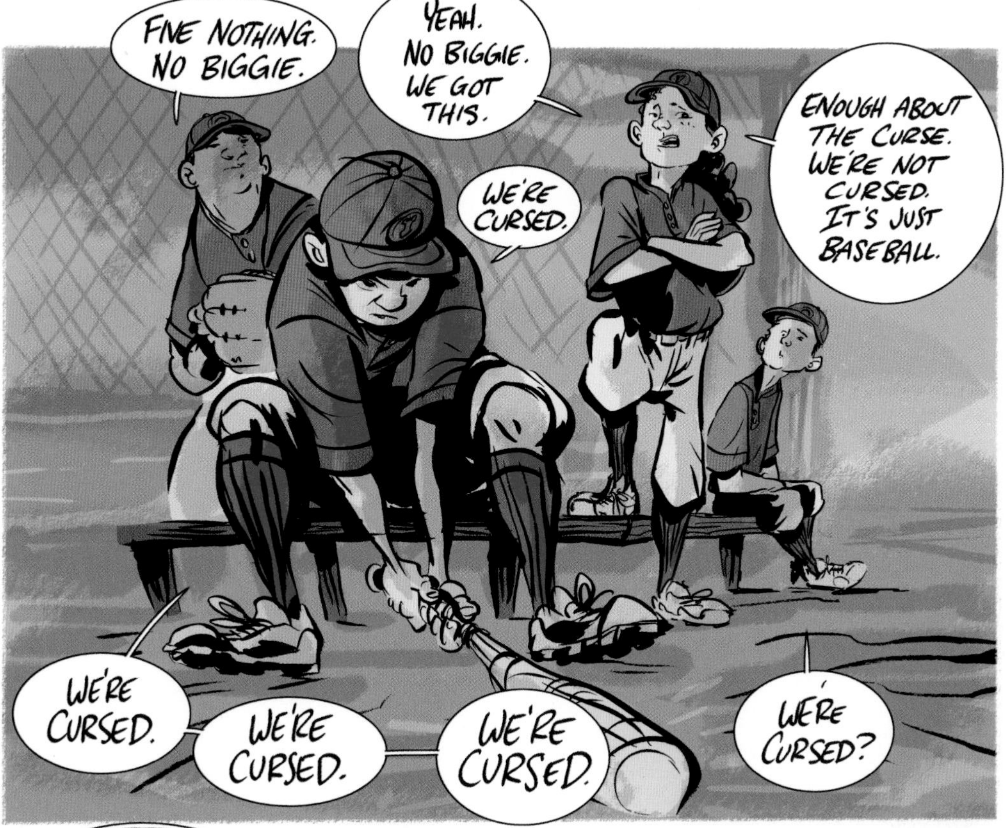
FIVE NOTHING. NO BIGGIE.
YEAH. NO BIGGIE. WE GOT THIS.
WE'RE CURSED.
ENOUGH ABOUT THE CURSE. WE'RE NOT CURSED. IT'S JUST BASEBALL.
WE'RE CURSED.
WE'RE CURSED.
WE'RE CURSED.
WE'RE CURSED?

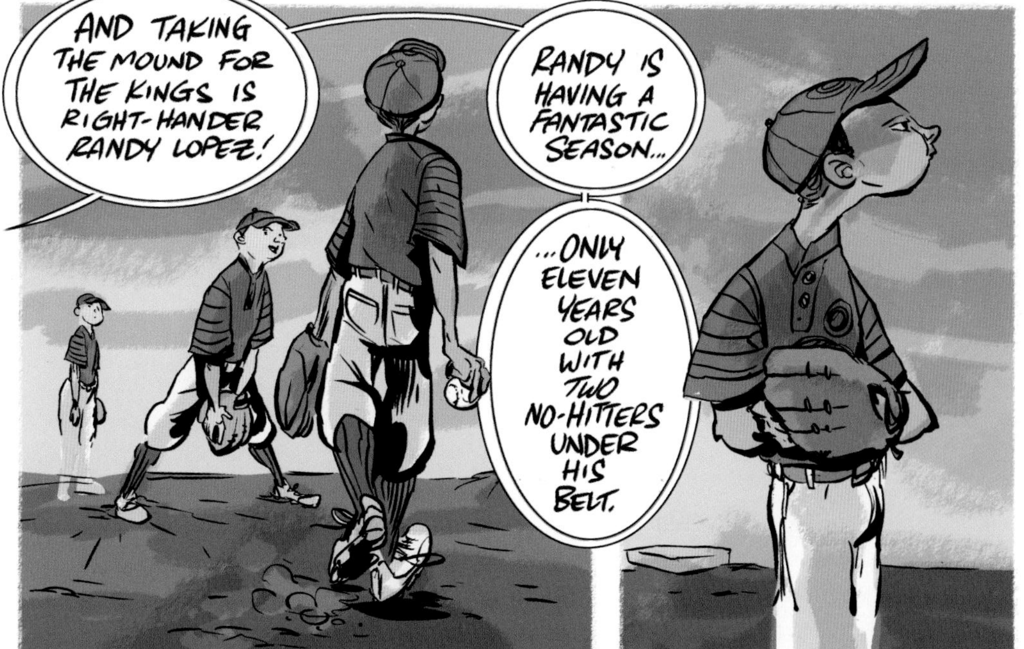
AND TAKING THE MOUND FOR THE KINGS IS RIGHT-HANDER RANDY LOPEZ!
RANDY IS HAVING A FANTASTIC SEASON...
...ONLY ELEVEN YEARS OLD WITH TWO NO-HITTERS UNDER HIS BELT.

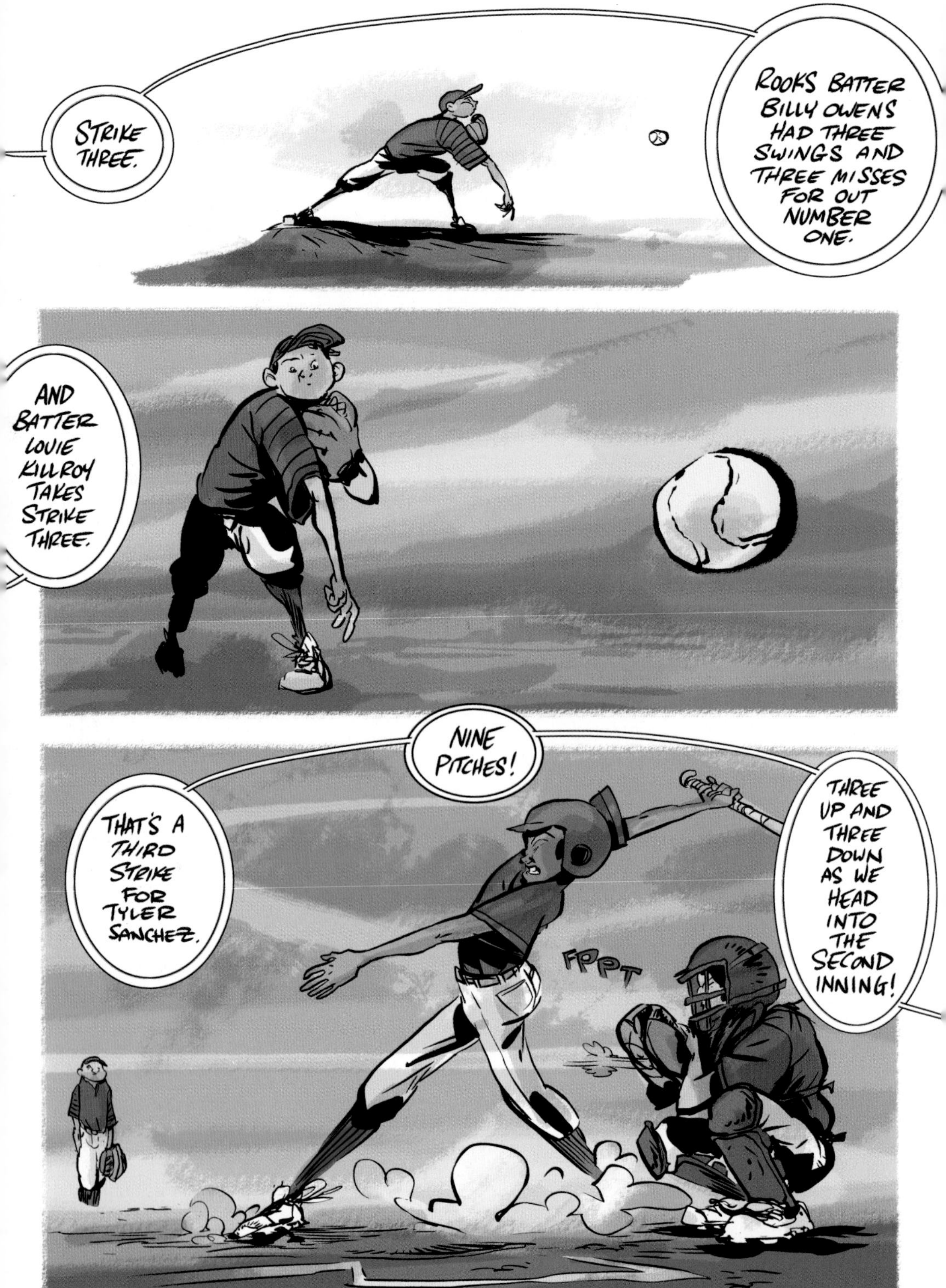
STRIKE THREE.
ROOKS BATTER BILLY OWENS HAD THREE SWINGS AND THREE MISSES FOR OUT NUMBER ONE.
AND BATTER LOUIE KILLROY TAKES STRIKE THREE.
THAT'S A THIRD STRIKE FOR TYLER SANCHEZ.
NINE PITCHES!
THREE UP AND THREE DOWN AS WE HEAD INTO THE SECOND INNING!
FPPT

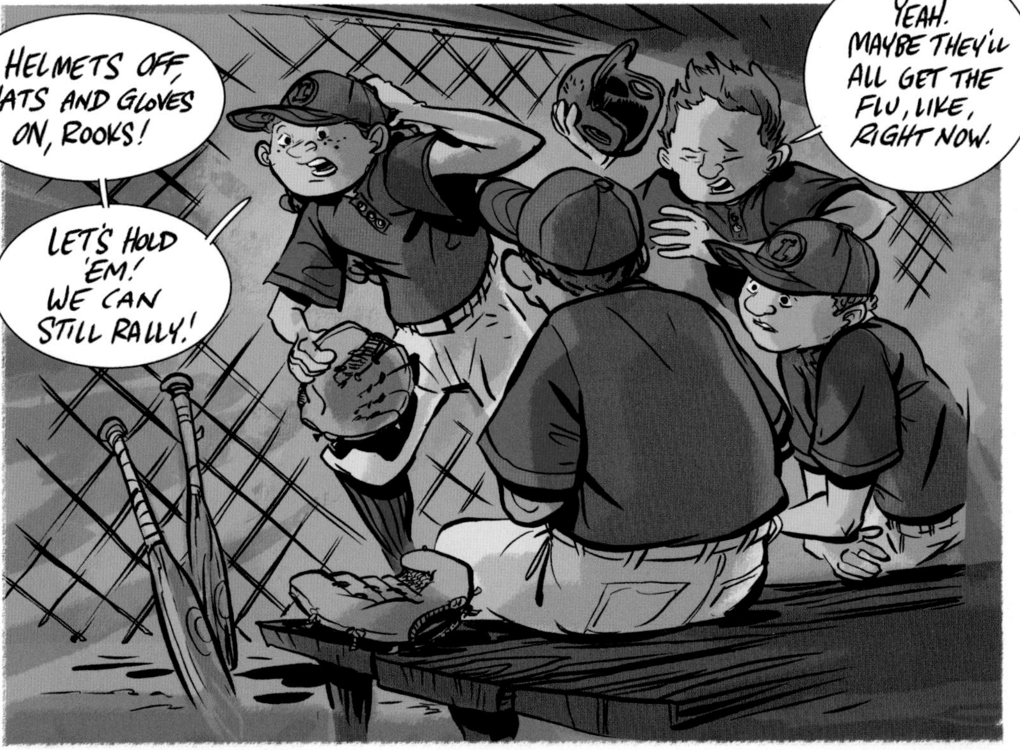
HELMETS OFF, HATS AND GLOVES ON, ROOKS!
LET'S HOLD 'EM! WE CAN STILL RALLY!
YEAH. MAYBE THEY'LL ALL GET THE FLU, LIKE, RIGHT NOW.

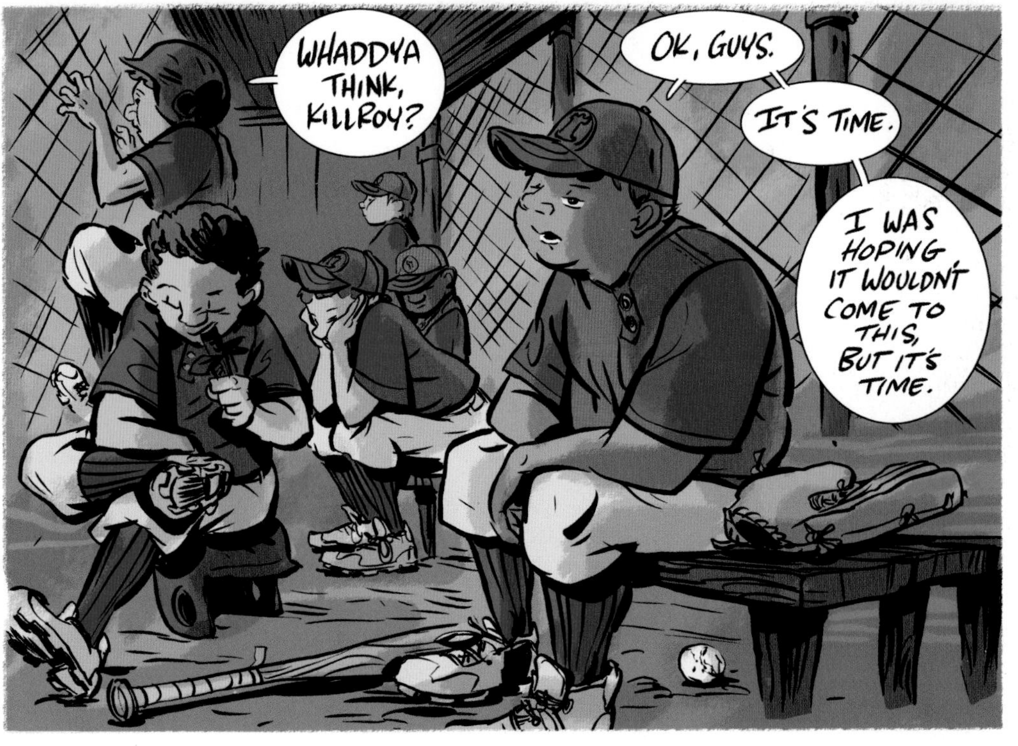
WHADDYA THINK, KILLROY?
OK, GUYS.
IT'S TIME.
I WAS HOPING IT WOULDN'T COME TO THIS, BUT IT'S TIME.

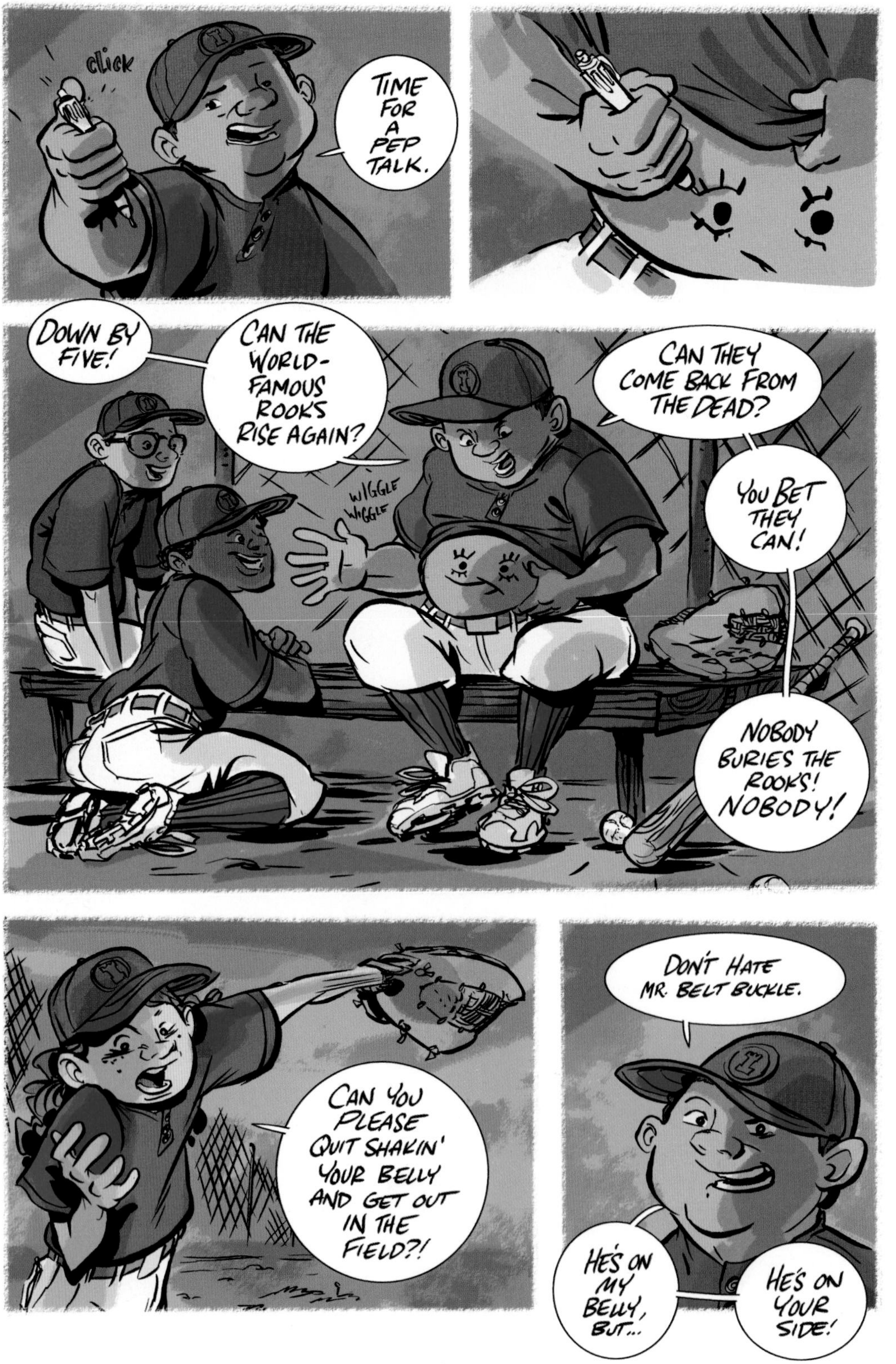
CLICK
TIME FOR A PEP TALK.
DOWN BY FIVE!
CAN THE WORLD-FAMOUS ROOKS RISE AGAIN?
WIGGLE WIGGLE
CAN THEY COME BACK FROM THE DEAD?
YOU BET THEY CAN!
NOBODY BURIES THE ROOKS! NOBODY!
CAN YOU PLEASE QUIT SHAKIN' YOUR BELLY AND GET OUT IN THE FIELD?!
DON'T HATE MR. BELT BUCKLE.
HE'S ON MY BELLY, BUT...
HE'S ON YOUR SIDE!

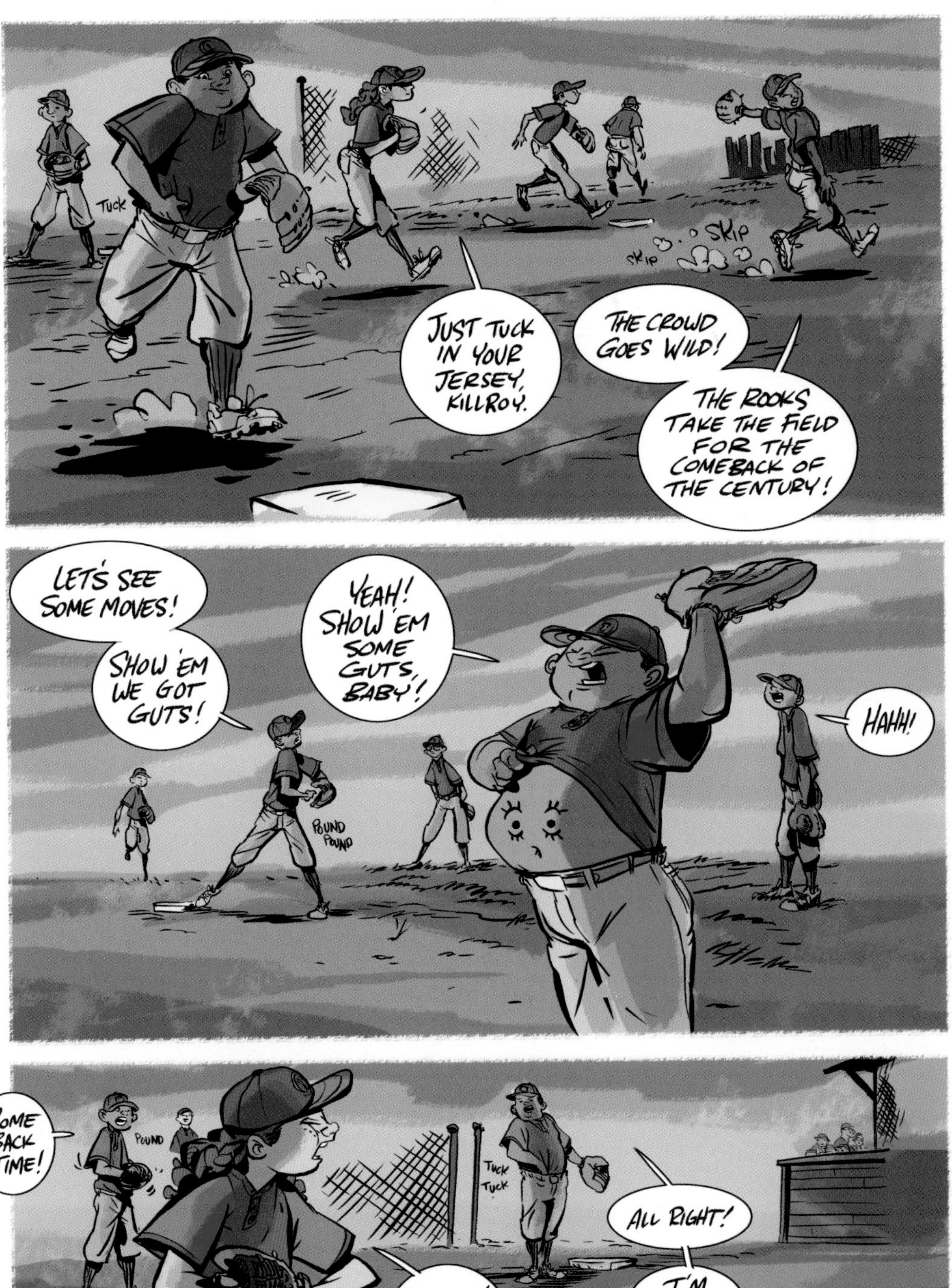
TUCK
SKIP
SKIP
JUST TUCK IN YOUR JERSEY, KILLROY.
THE CROWD GOES WILD!
THE ROOKS TAKE THE FIELD FOR THE COMEBACK OF THE CENTURY!
LET'S SEE SOME MOVES!
SHOW 'EM WE GOT GUTS!
YEAH! SHOW 'EM SOME GUTS, BABY!
HAHH!
POUND POUND
COME BACK TIME!
POUND
TUCK TUCK
KILLROY! JERSEY! TUCK IT!
ALL RIGHT!
I'M TUCKIN'!
I'M TUCKIN'!

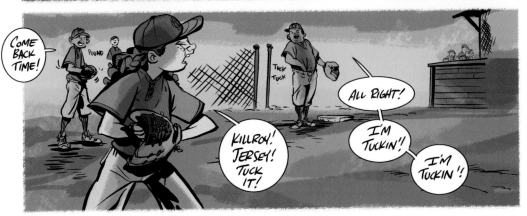

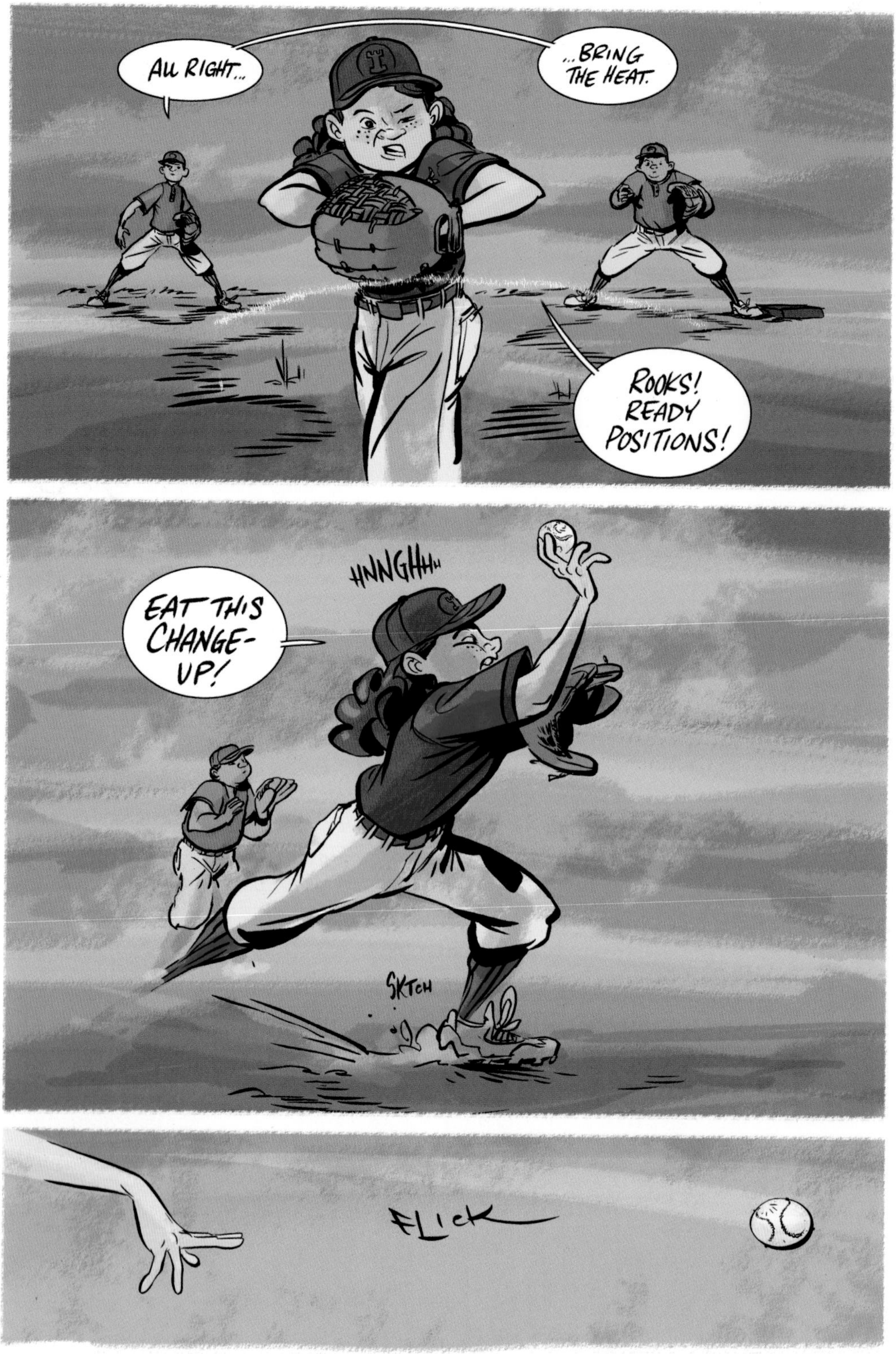
ALL RIGHT...
...BRING THE HEAT.
ROOKS! READY POSITIONS!
HNNGHH
EAT THIS CHANGE-UP!
SKTCH
FLICK

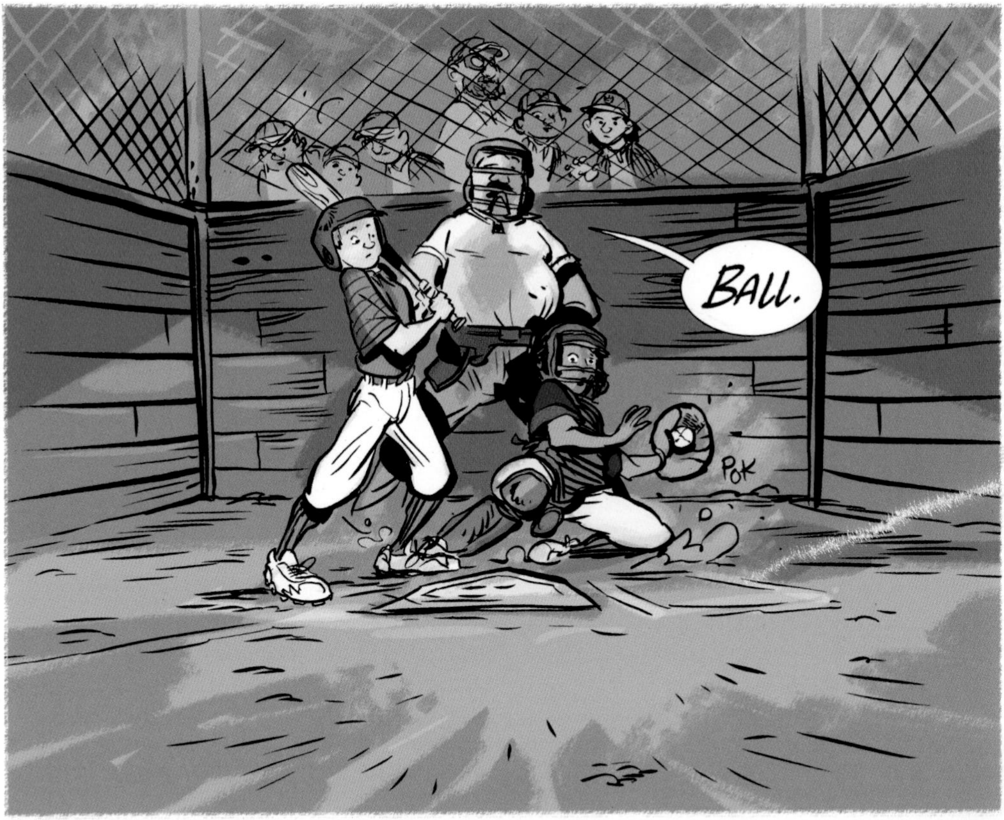
BALL.
POK

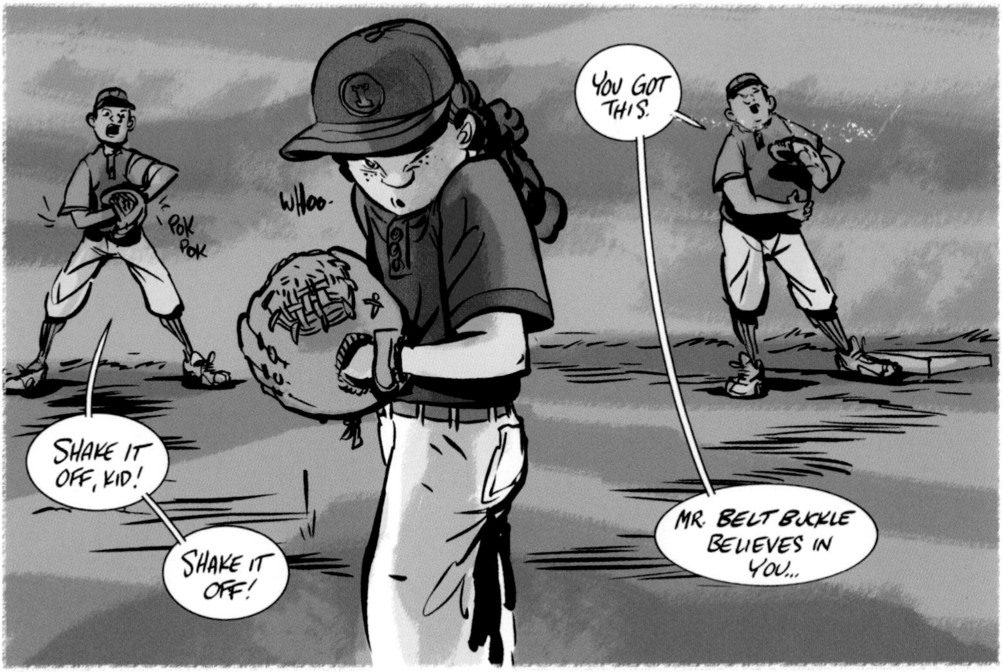
WHOO.
POK
POK
SHAKE IT OFF, KID!
SHAKE IT OFF!
YOU GOT THIS.
MR. BELT BUCKLE BELIEVES IN YOU...

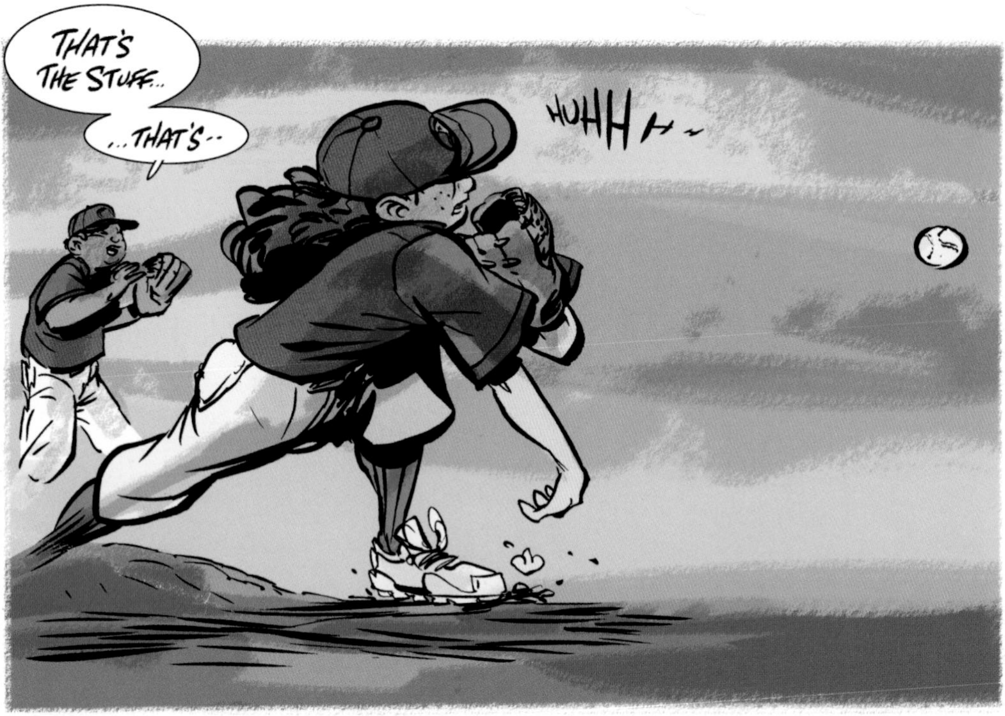
THAT'S THE STUFF...
...THAT'S--
HUHHH--

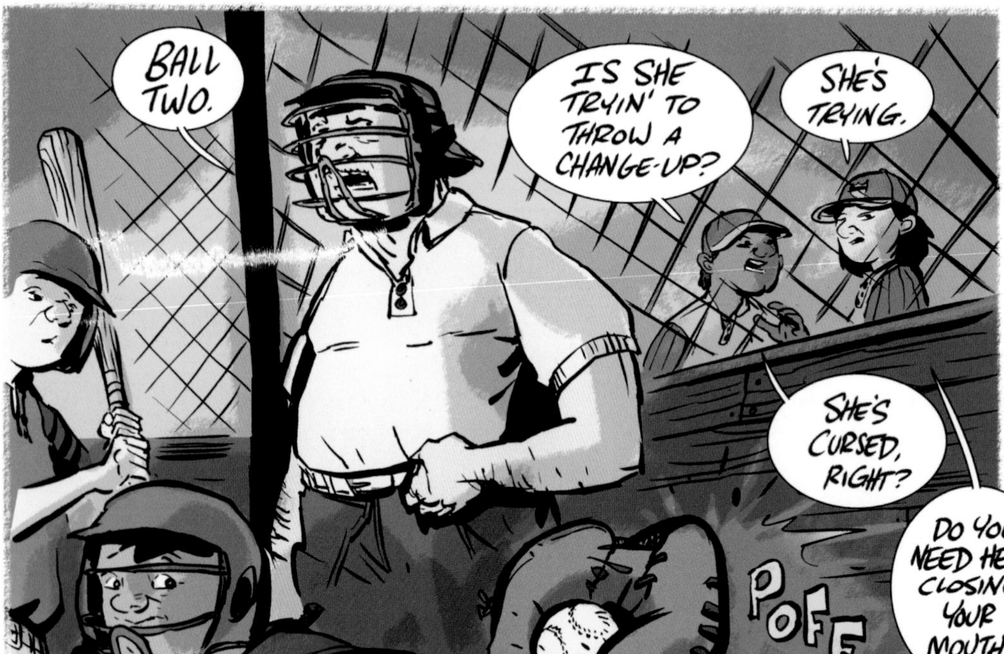
BALL TWO.
IS SHE TRYIN' TO THROW A CHANGE-UP?
SHE'S TRYING.
SHE'S CURSED, RIGHT?
DO YOU NEED HELP CLOSING YOUR MOUTH?
POFF

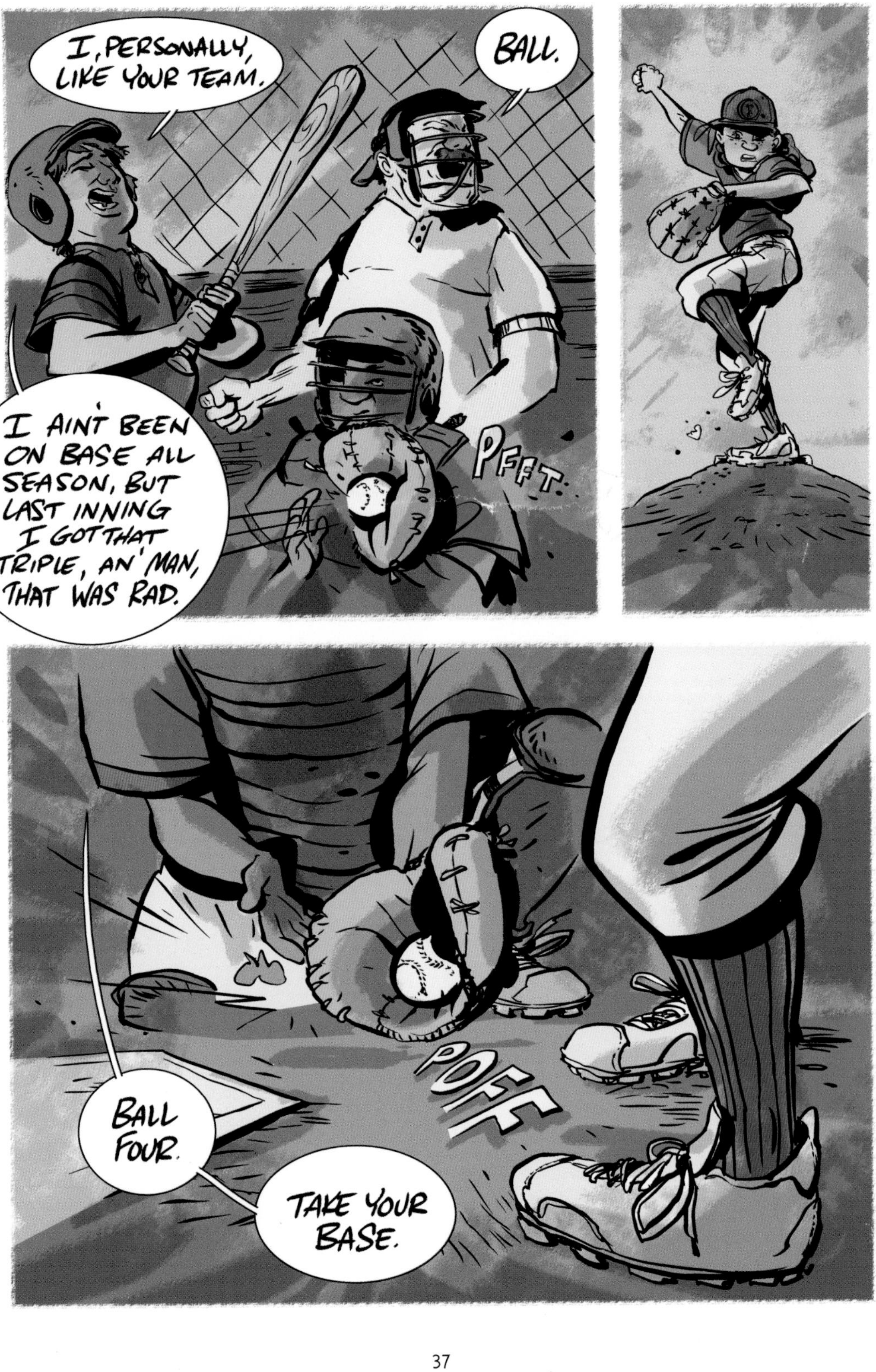
I, PERSONALLY, LIKE YOUR TEAM.
BALL.
I AIN'T BEEN ON BASE ALL SEASON, BUT LAST INNING I GOT THAT TRIPLE, AN' MAN, THAT WAS RAD.
PFFT...
POFF
BALL FOUR.
TAKE YOUR BASE.

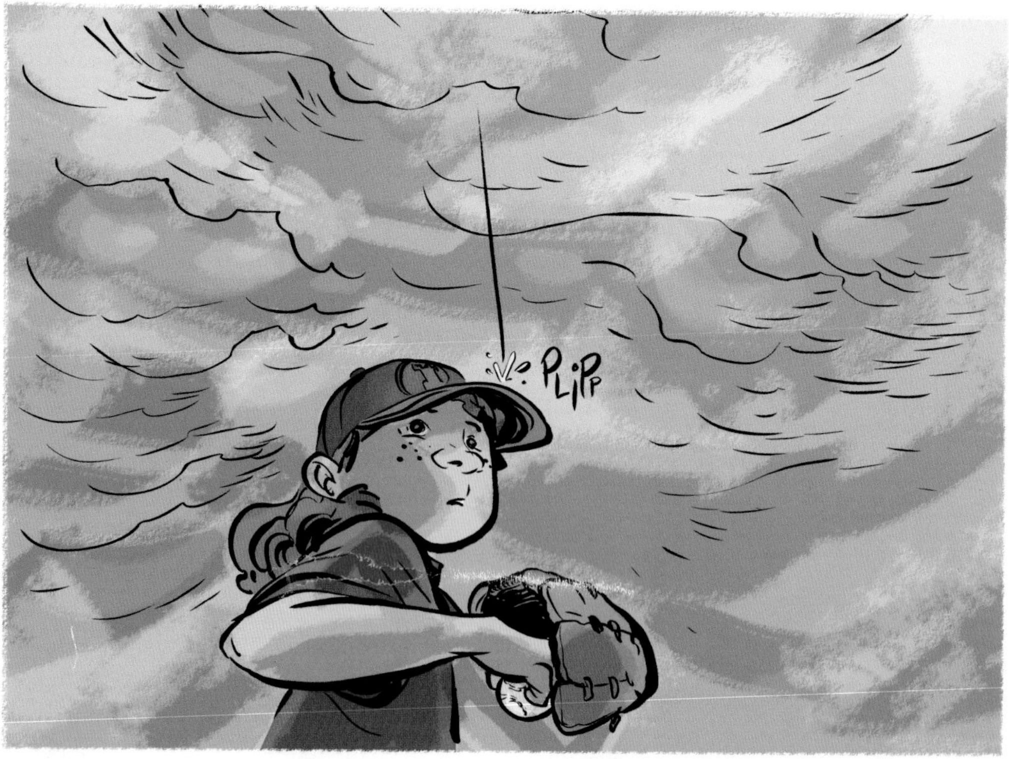
PLIPP

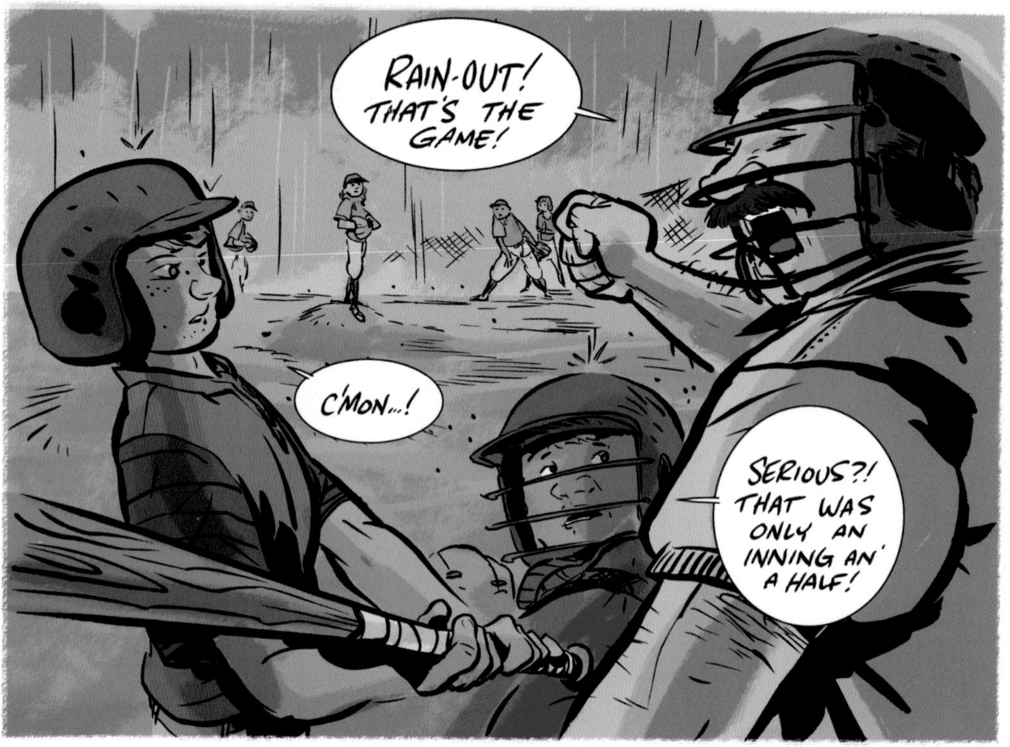
RAIN-OUT! THAT'S THE GAME!
C'MON...!
SERIOUS?! THAT WAS ONLY AN INNING AN' A HALF!

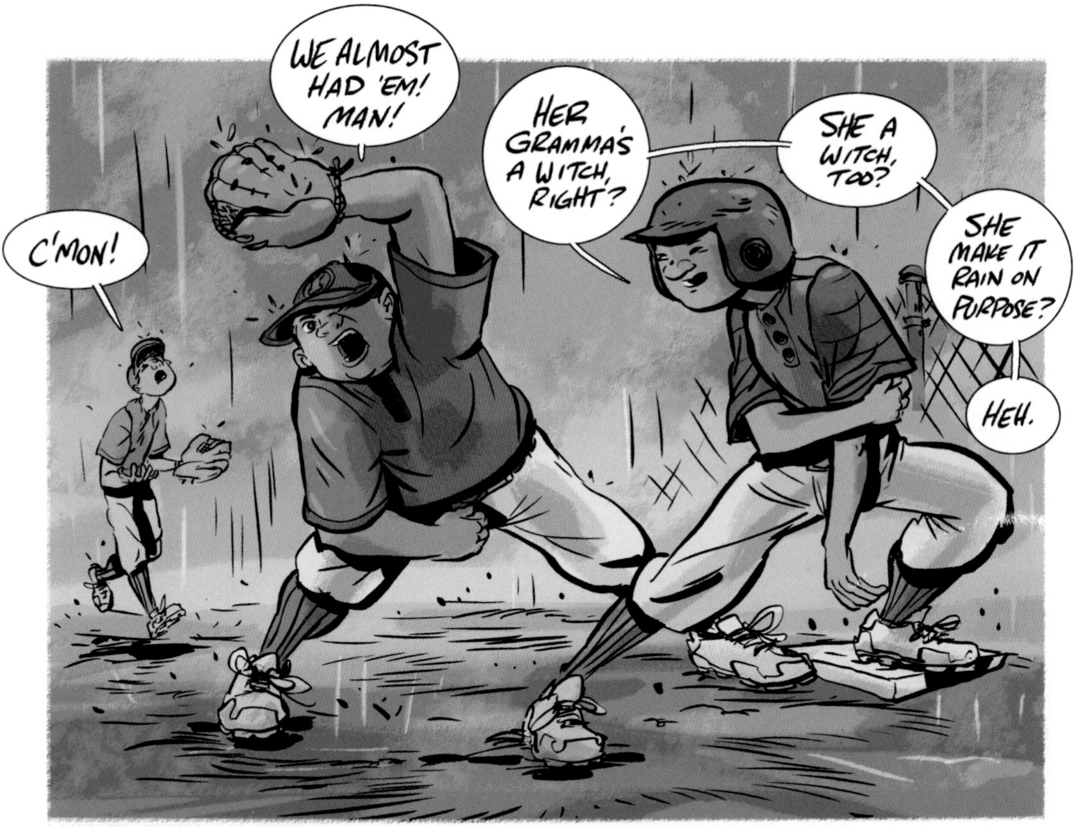
C'MON!
WE ALMOST HAD 'EM! MAN!
HER GRAMMA'S A WITCH, RIGHT?
SHE A WITCH, TOO?
SHE MAKE IT RAIN ON PURPOSE?
HEH.

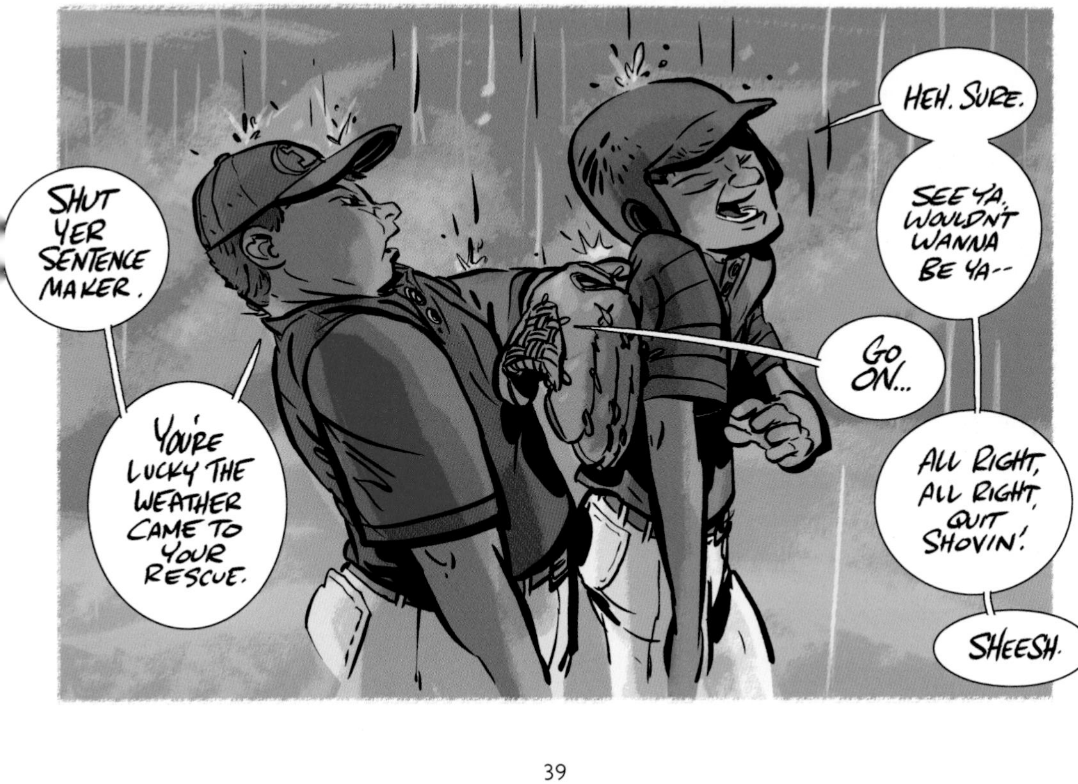
SHUT YER SENTENCE MAKER.
YOU'RE LUCKY THE WEATHER CAME TO YOUR RESCUE.
HEH. SURE.
SEE YA, WOULDN'T WANNA BE YA--
GO ON...
ALL RIGHT, ALL RIGHT, QUIT SHOVIN'.
SHEESH.

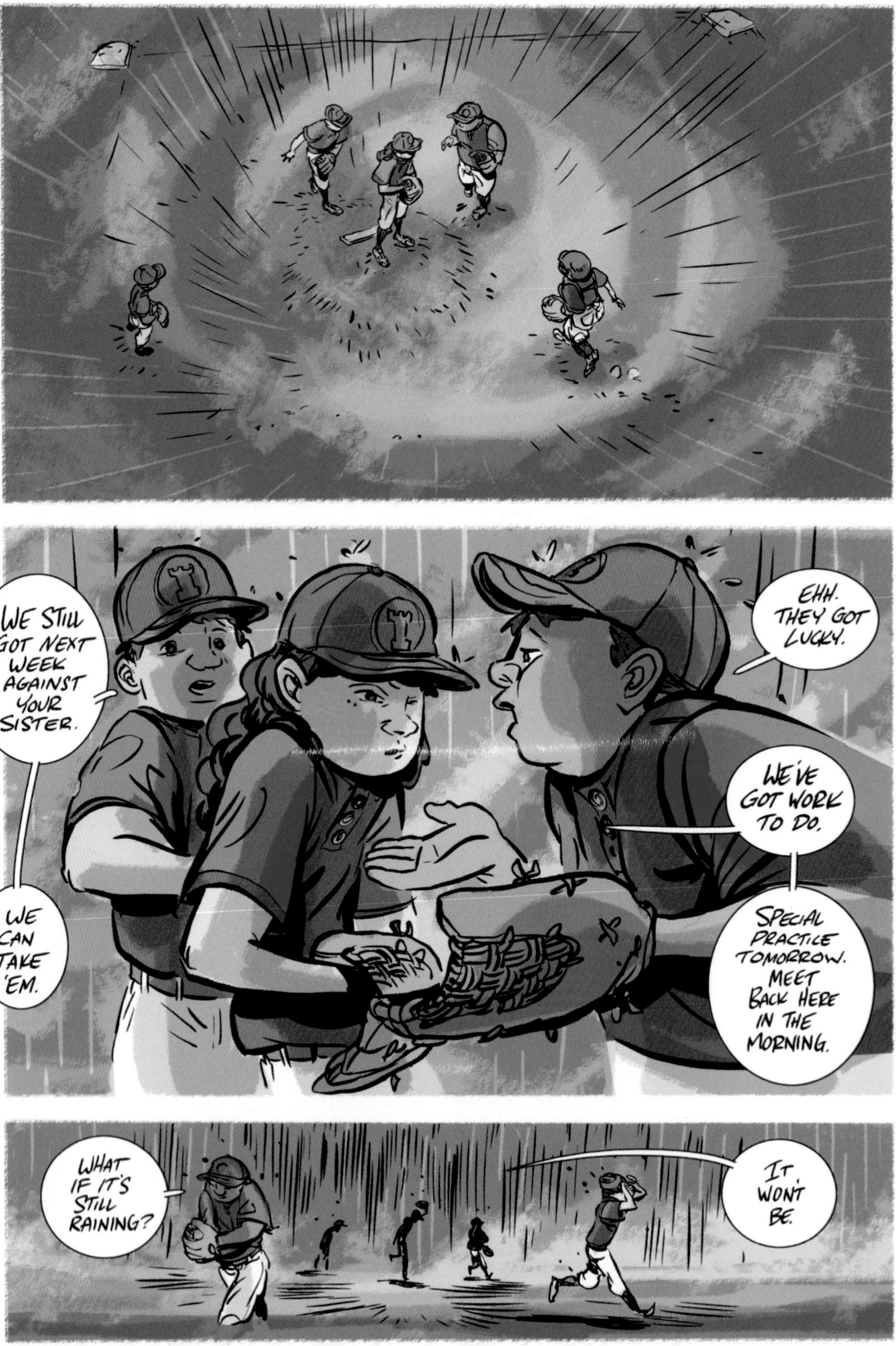
WE STILL GOT NEXT WEEK AGAINST YOUR SISTER.
WE CAN TAKE 'EM.
EHH. THEY GOT LUCKY.
WE'VE GOT WORK TO DO.
SPECIAL PRACTICE TOMORROW. MEET BACK HERE IN THE MORNING.
WHAT IF IT'S STILL RAINING?
IT WON'T BE.

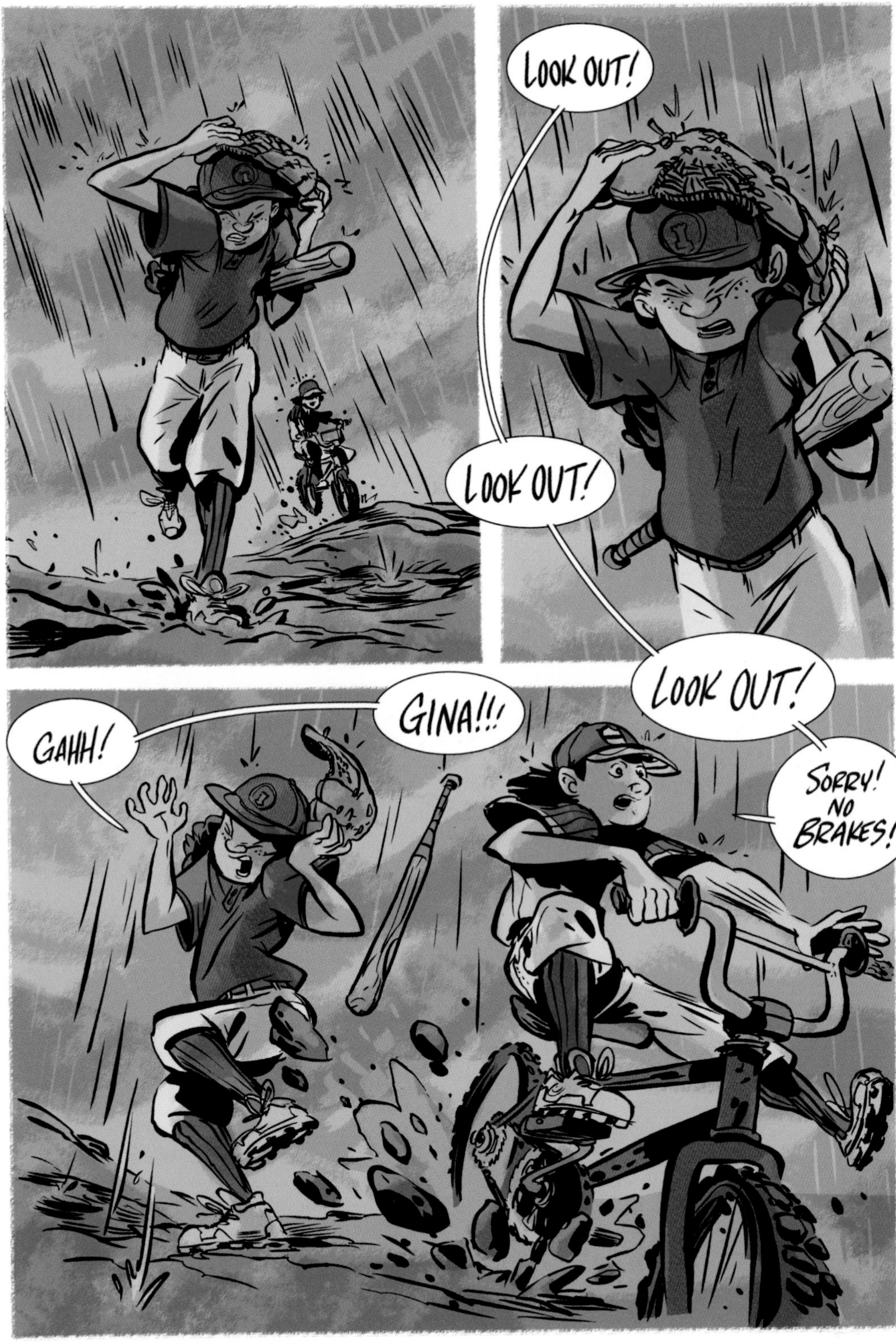
LOOK OUT!
LOOK OUT!
LOOK OUT!
GAHH!
GINA!!!
SORRY! NO BRAKES!

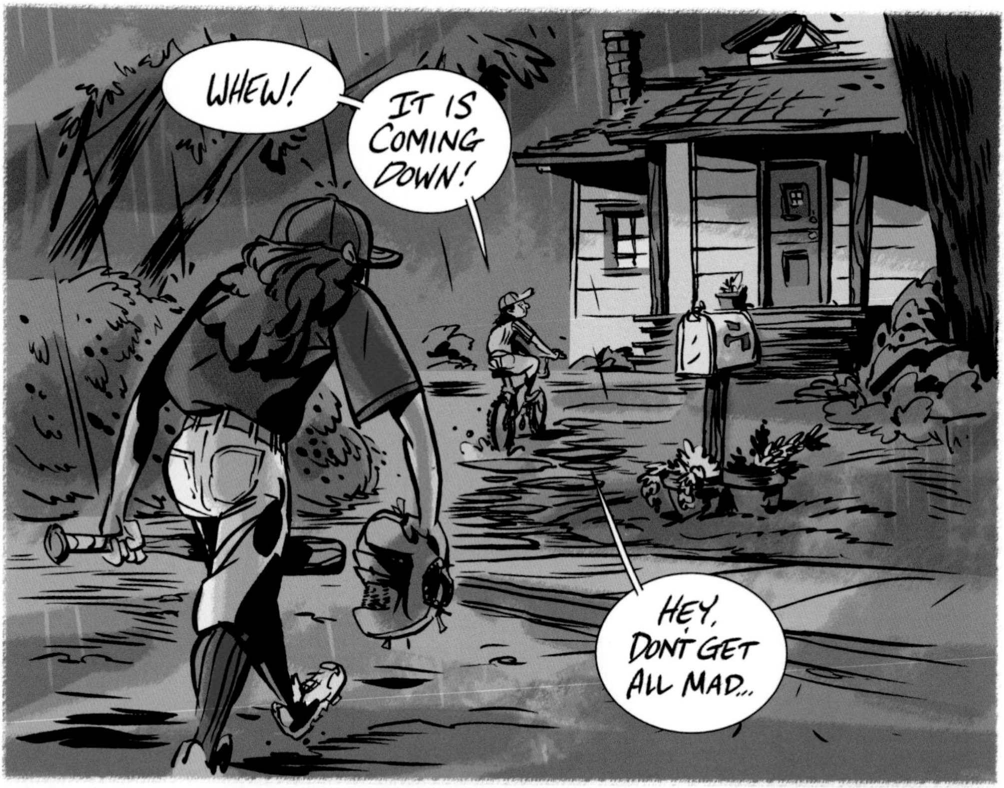
WHEW!
IT IS COMING DOWN!
HEY, DON'T GET ALL MAD...

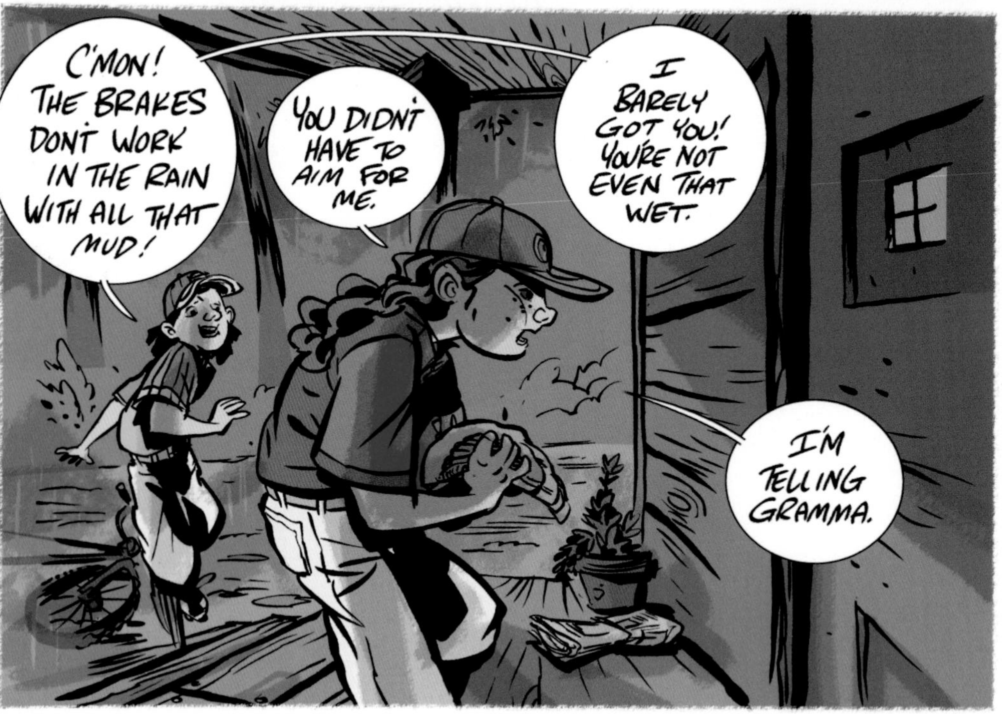
I BARELY GOT YOU! YOU'RE NOT EVEN THAT WET.
C'MON! THE BRAKES DON'T WORK IN THE RAIN WITH ALL THAT MUD!
YOU DIDN'T HAVE TO AIM FOR ME.
I'M TELLING GRAMMA.

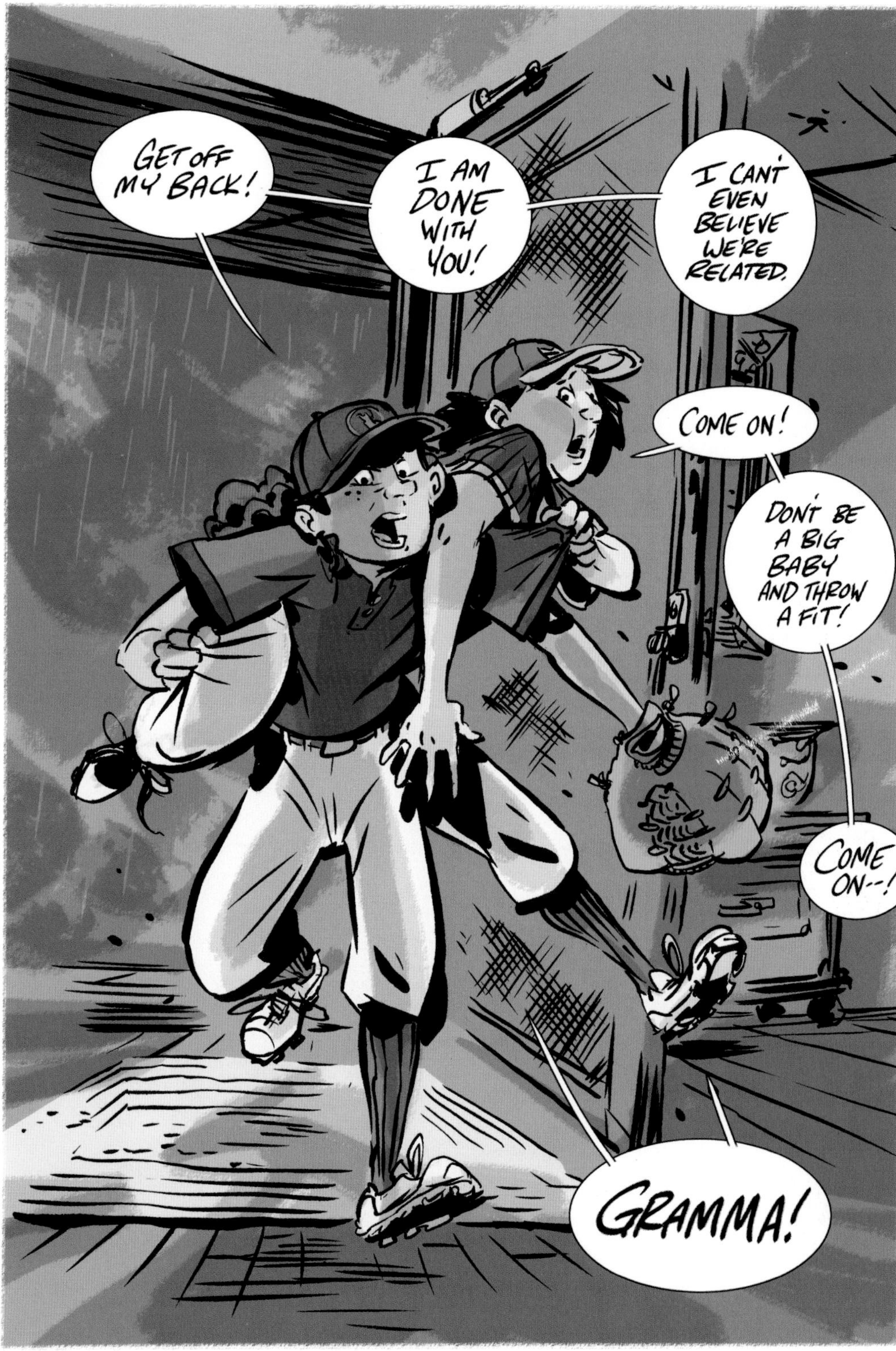
GET OFF MY BACK!
I AM DONE WITH YOU!
I CAN'T EVEN BELIEVE WE'RE RELATED.
COME ON!
DON'T BE A BIG BABY AND THROW A FIT!
COME ON--!
GRAMMA!

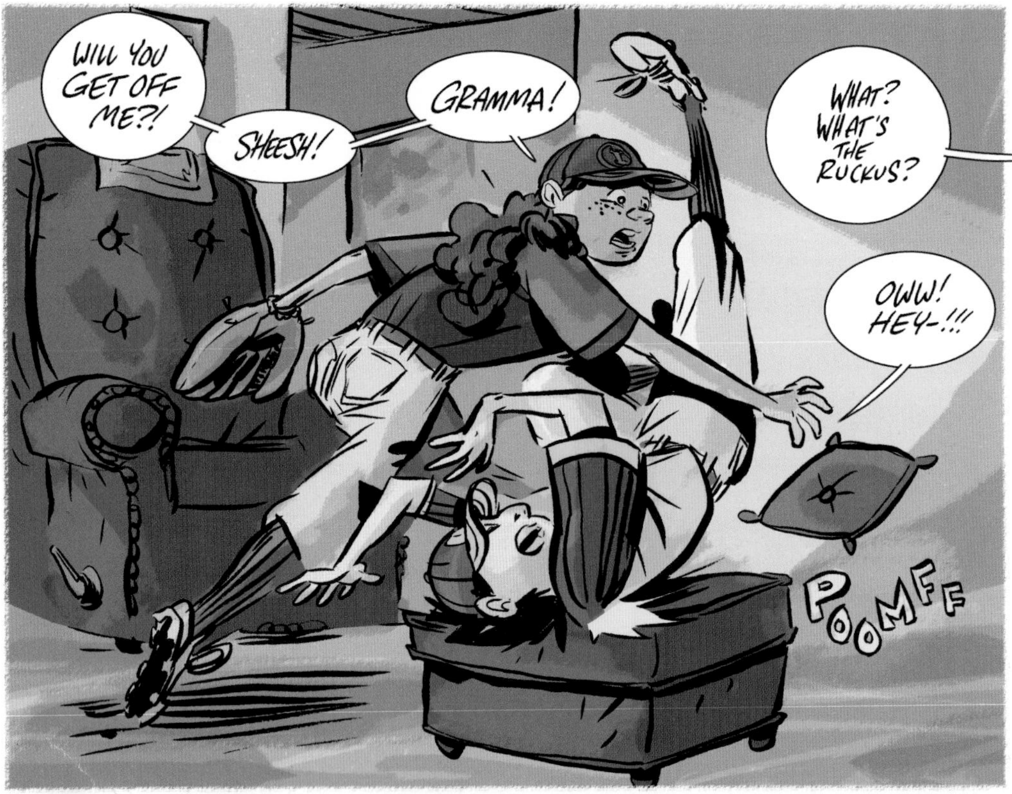
WILL YOU GET OFF ME?!
SHEESH!
GRAMMA!
WHAT? WHAT'S THE RUCKUS?
OWW! HEY-!!!
POOMFF

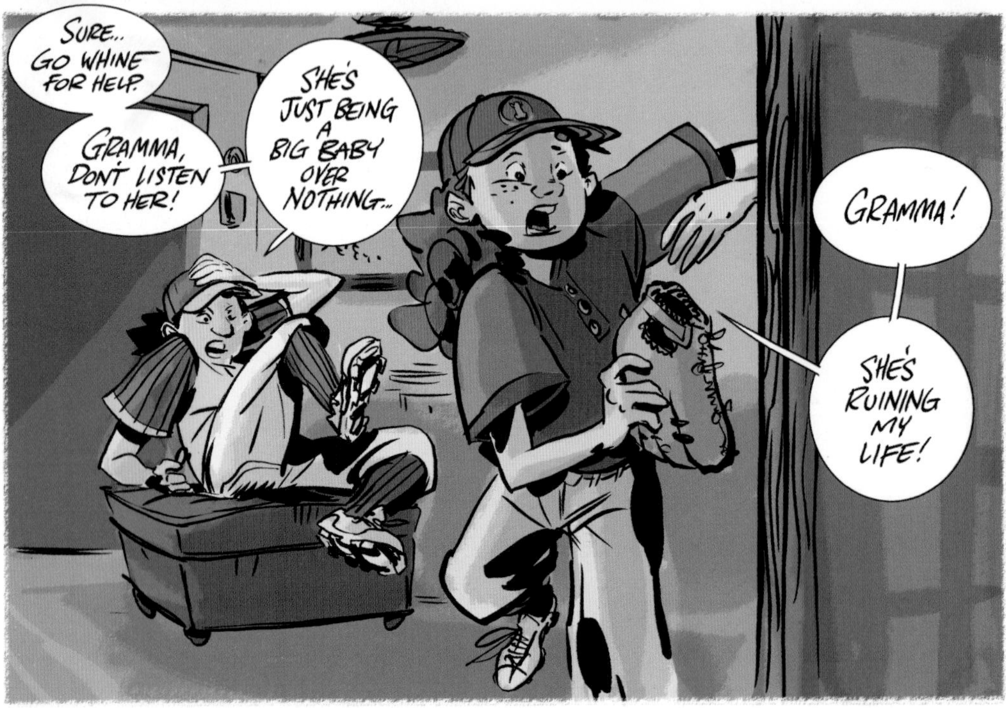
SURE... GO WHINE FOR HELP.
GRAMMA, DON'T LISTEN TO HER!
SHE'S JUST BEING A BIG BABY OVER NOTHING...
GRAMMA!
SHE'S RUINING MY LIFE!

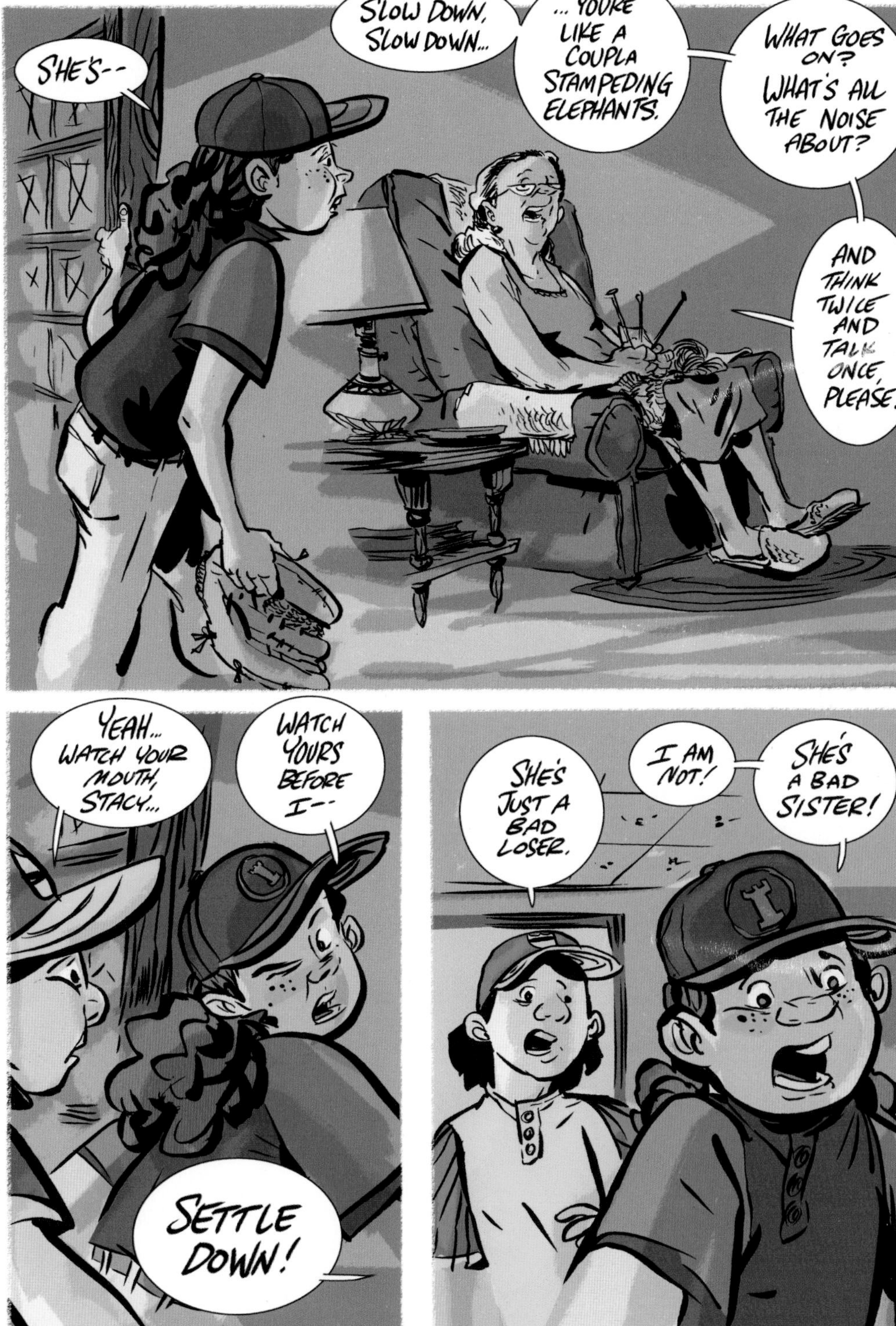
SHE'S--
SLOW DOWN, SLOW DOWN...
...YOU'RE LIKE A COUPLA STAMPEDING ELEPHANTS.
WHAT GOES ON? WHAT'S ALL THE NOISE ABOUT?
AND THINK TWICE AND TALK ONCE, PLEASE.
YEAH... WATCH YOUR MOUTH, STACY...
WATCH YOURS BEFORE I--
SETTLE DOWN!
SHE'S JUST A BAD LOSER.
I AM NOT!
SHE'S A BAD SISTER!

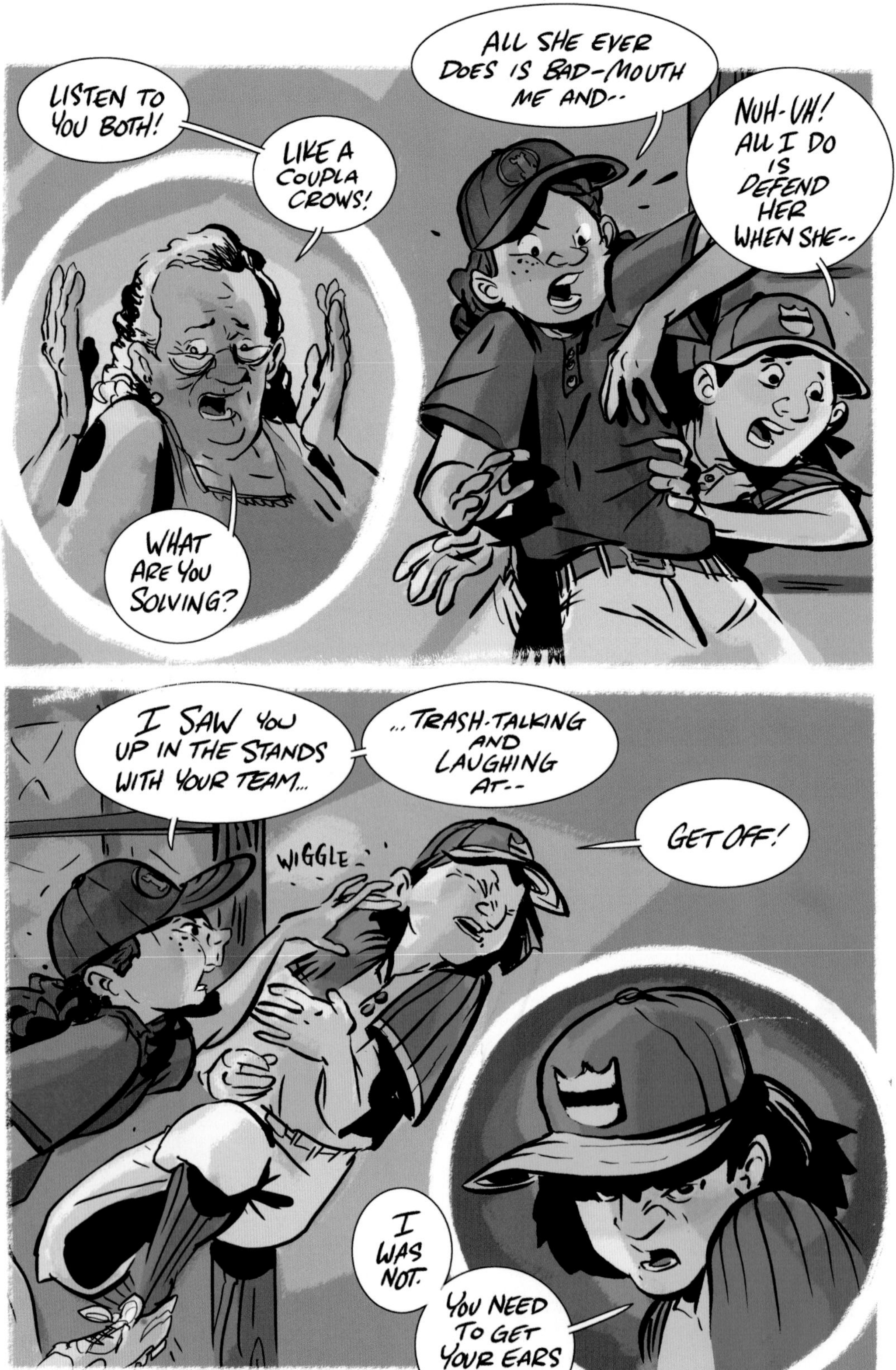
LISTEN TO YOU BOTH!
LIKE A COUPLA CROWS!
WHAT ARE YOU SOLVING?
ALL SHE EVER DOES IS BAD-MOUTH ME AND--
NUH-UH! ALL I DO IS DEFEND HER WHEN SHE--
I SAW YOU UP IN THE STANDS WITH YOUR TEAM...
...TRASH-TALKING AND LAUGHING AT--
WIGGLE
GET OFF!
I WAS NOT.
YOU NEED TO GET YOUR EARS CHECKED.

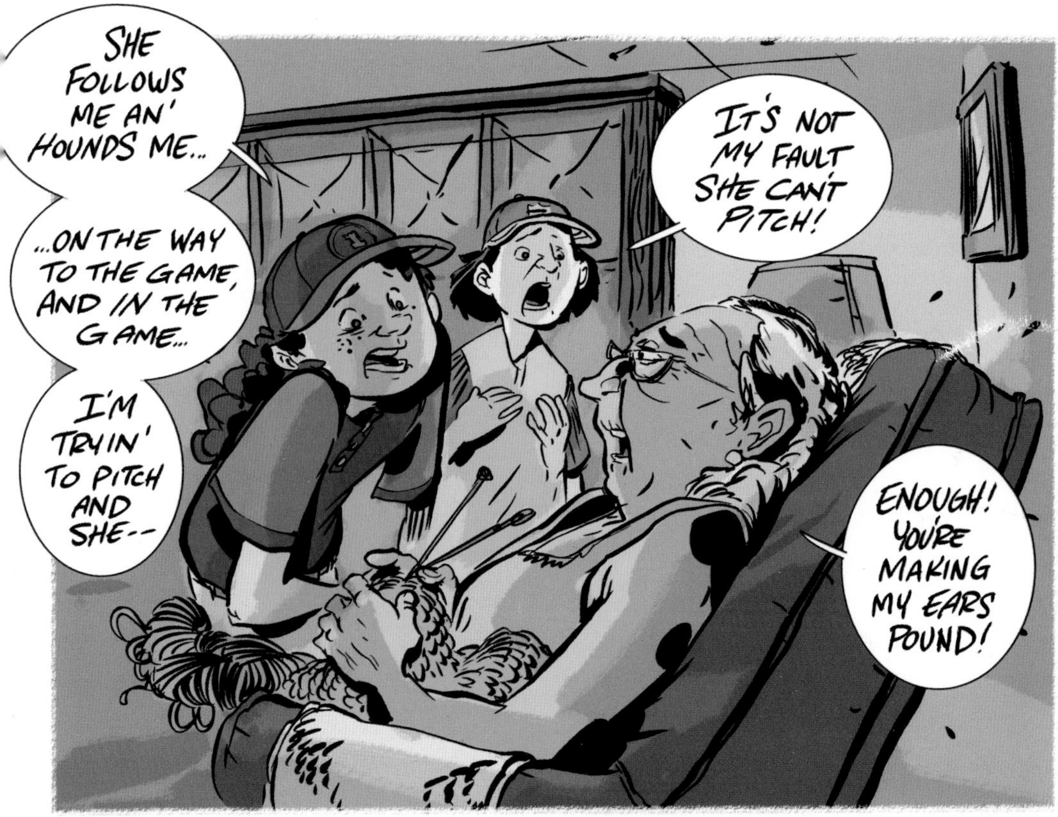
SHE FOLLOWS ME AN' HOUNDS ME...
...ON THE WAY TO THE GAME, AND IN THE GAME...
I'M TRYIN' TO PITCH AND SHE--
IT'S NOT MY FAULT SHE CAN'T PITCH!
ENOUGH! YOU'RE MAKING MY EARS POUND!

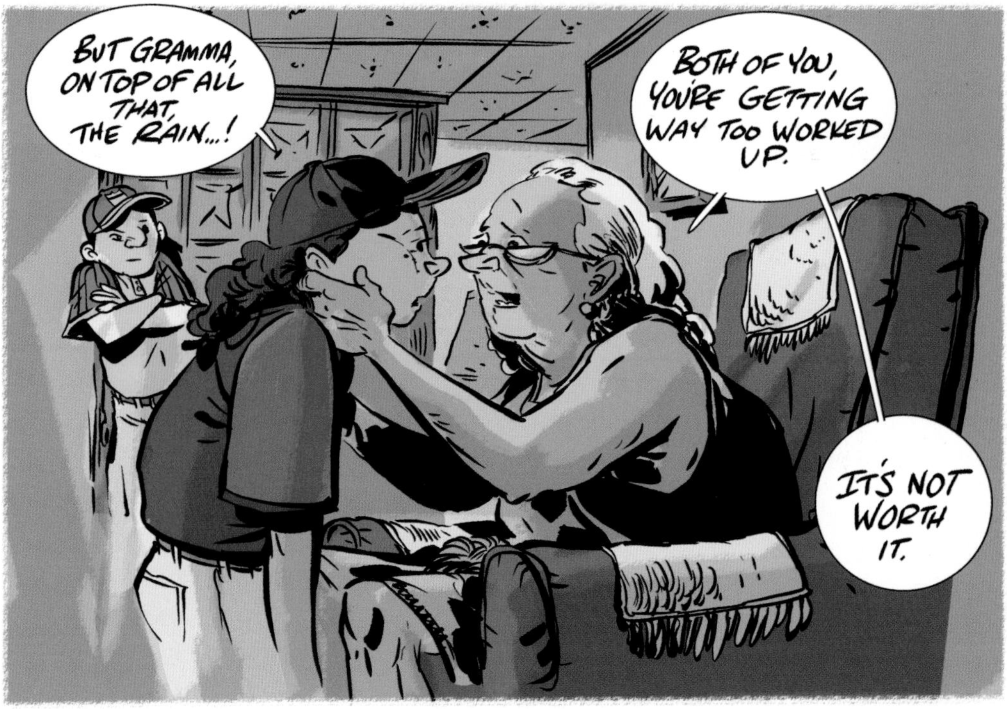
BUT GRAMMA, ON TOP OF ALL THAT, THE RAIN...!
BOTH OF YOU, YOU'RE GETTING WAY TOO WORKED UP.
IT'S NOT WORTH IT.

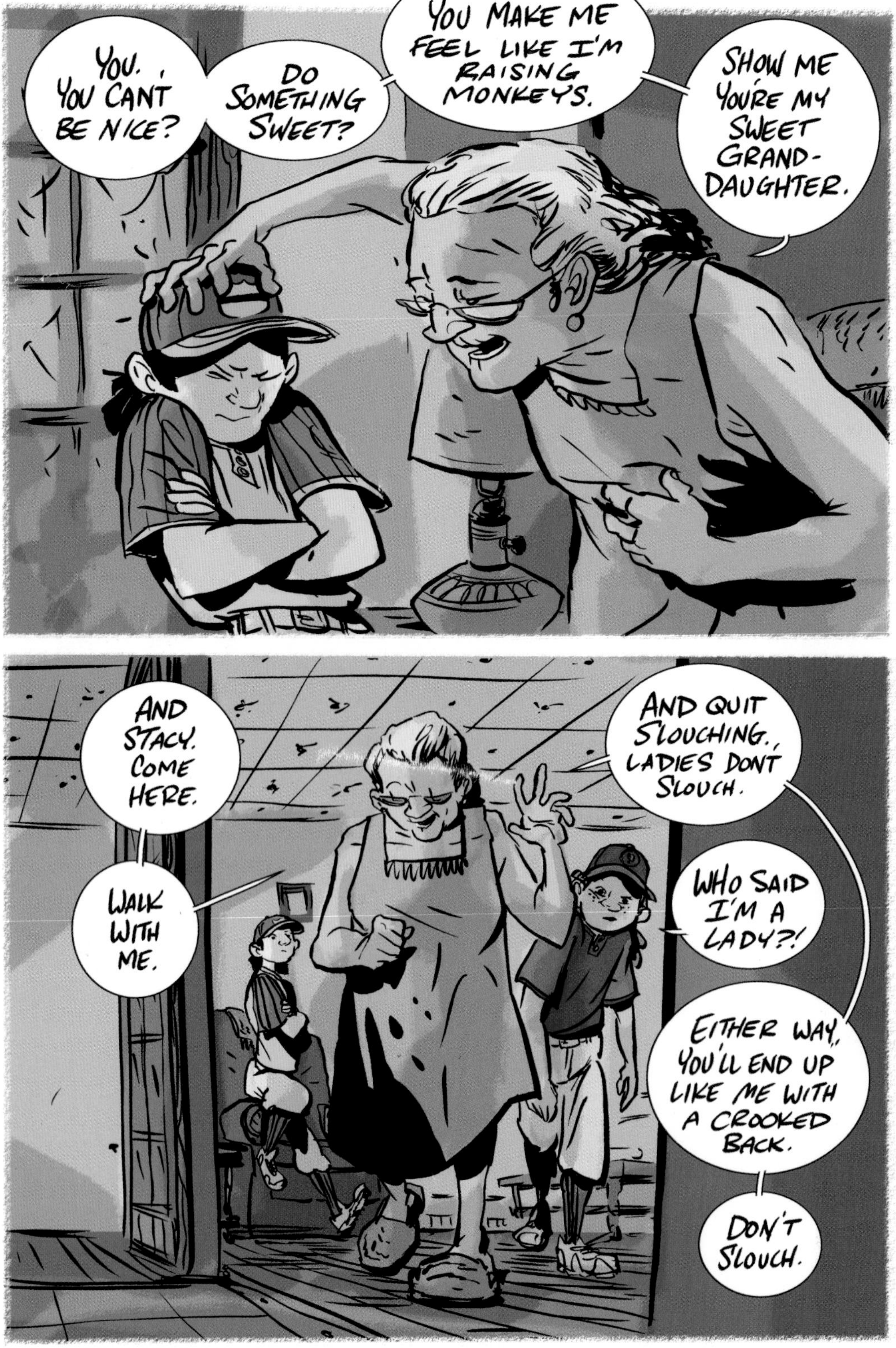

YOU. YOU CAN'T BE NICE?
DO SOMETHING SWEET?
YOU MAKE ME FEEL LIKE I'M RAISING MONKEYS.
SHOW ME YOU'RE MY SWEET GRAND-DAUGHTER.
AND STACY. COME HERE.
WALK WITH ME.
AND QUIT SLOUCHING. LADIES DON'T SLOUCH.
WHO SAID I'M A LADY?!
EITHER WAY, YOU'LL END UP LIKE ME WITH A CROOKED BACK.
DON'T SLOUCH.

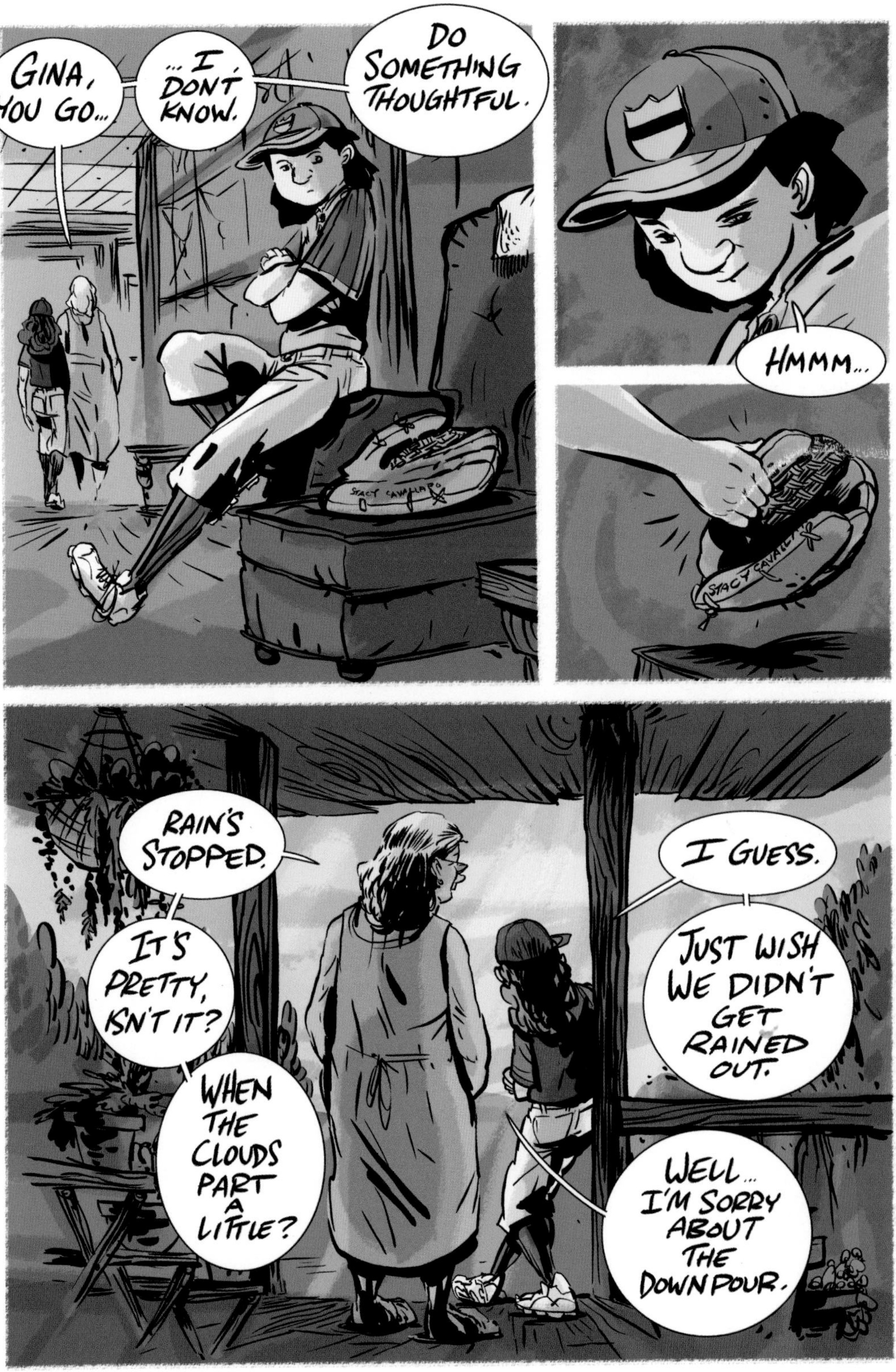

GINA, YOU GO...
...I DON'T KNOW.
DO SOMETHING THOUGHTFUL.
STACY CAVALLARO
HMMM...
STACY CAVALL
RAIN'S STOPPED.
IT'S PRETTY, ISN'T IT?
WHEN THE CLOUDS PART A LITTLE?
I GUESS.
JUST WISH WE DIDN'T GET RAINED OUT.
WELL... I'M SORRY ABOUT THE DOWNPOUR.

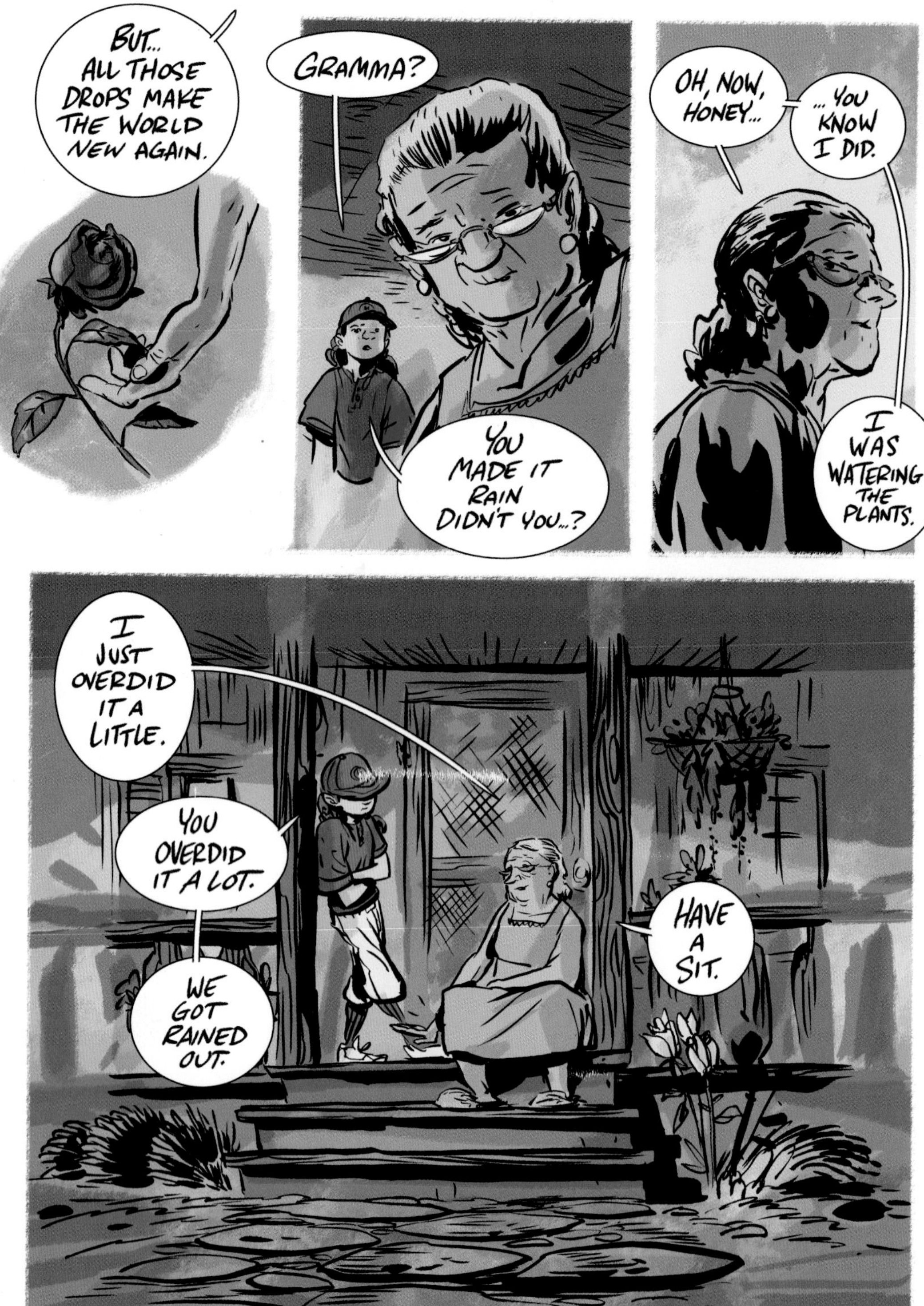
BUT... ALL THOSE DROPS MAKE THE WORLD NEW AGAIN.
GRAMMA?
YOU MADE IT RAIN DIDN'T YOU...?
OH, NOW, HONEY...
...YOU KNOW I DID.
I WAS WATERING THE PLANTS.
I JUST OVERDID IT A LITTLE.
YOU OVERDID IT A LOT.
WE GOT RAINED OUT.
HAVE A SIT.

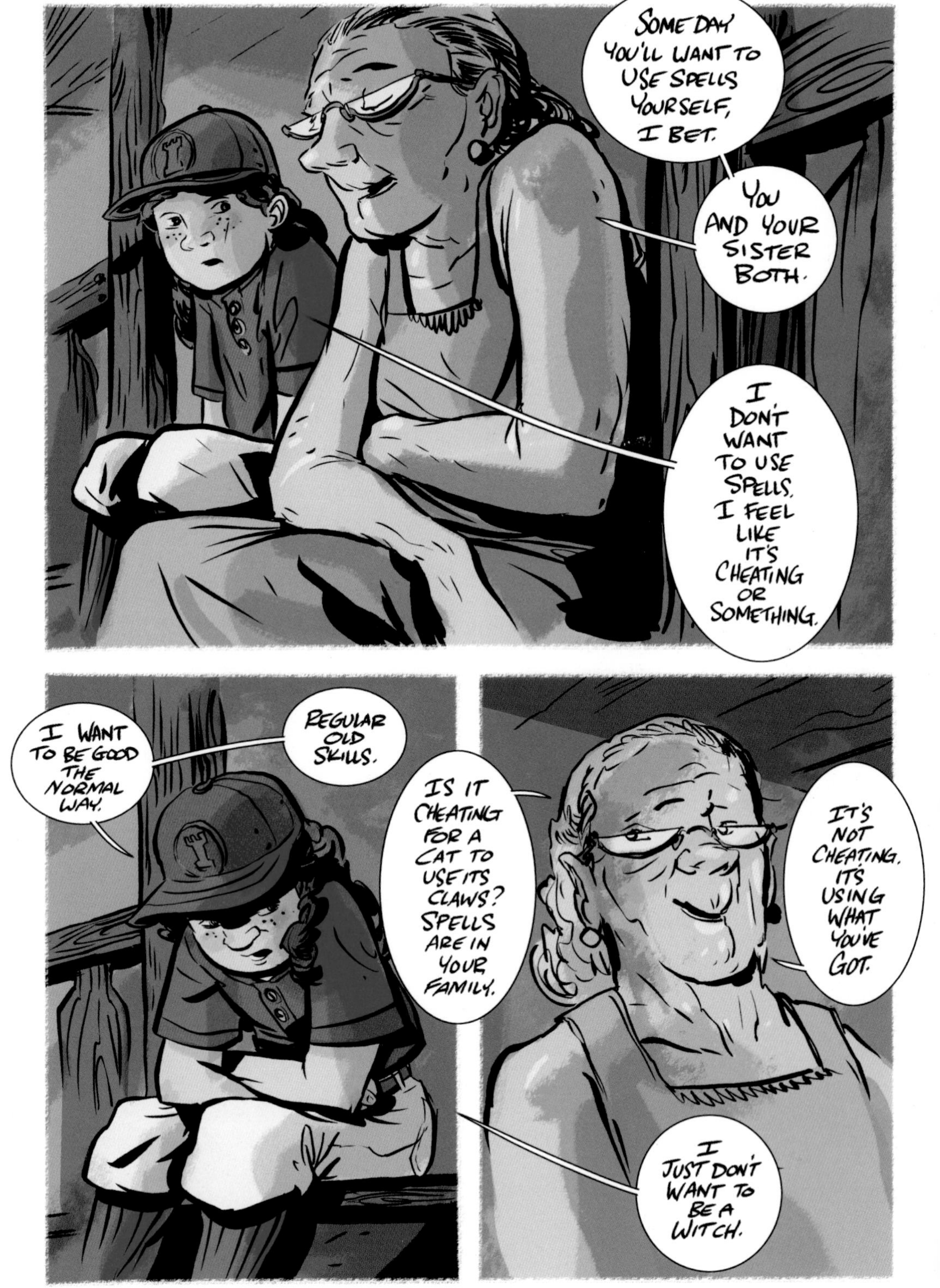
SOME DAY YOU'LL WANT TO USE SPELLS YOURSELF, I BET.
YOU AND YOUR SISTER BOTH.
I DON'T WANT TO USE SPELLS. I FEEL LIKE IT'S CHEATING OR SOMETHING.
I WANT TO BE GOOD THE NORMAL WAY.
REGULAR OLD SKILLS.
IS IT CHEATING FOR A CAT TO USE ITS CLAWS? SPELLS ARE IN YOUR FAMILY.
IT'S NOT CHEATING. IT'S USING WHAT YOU'VE GOT.
I JUST DON'T WANT TO BE A WITCH.

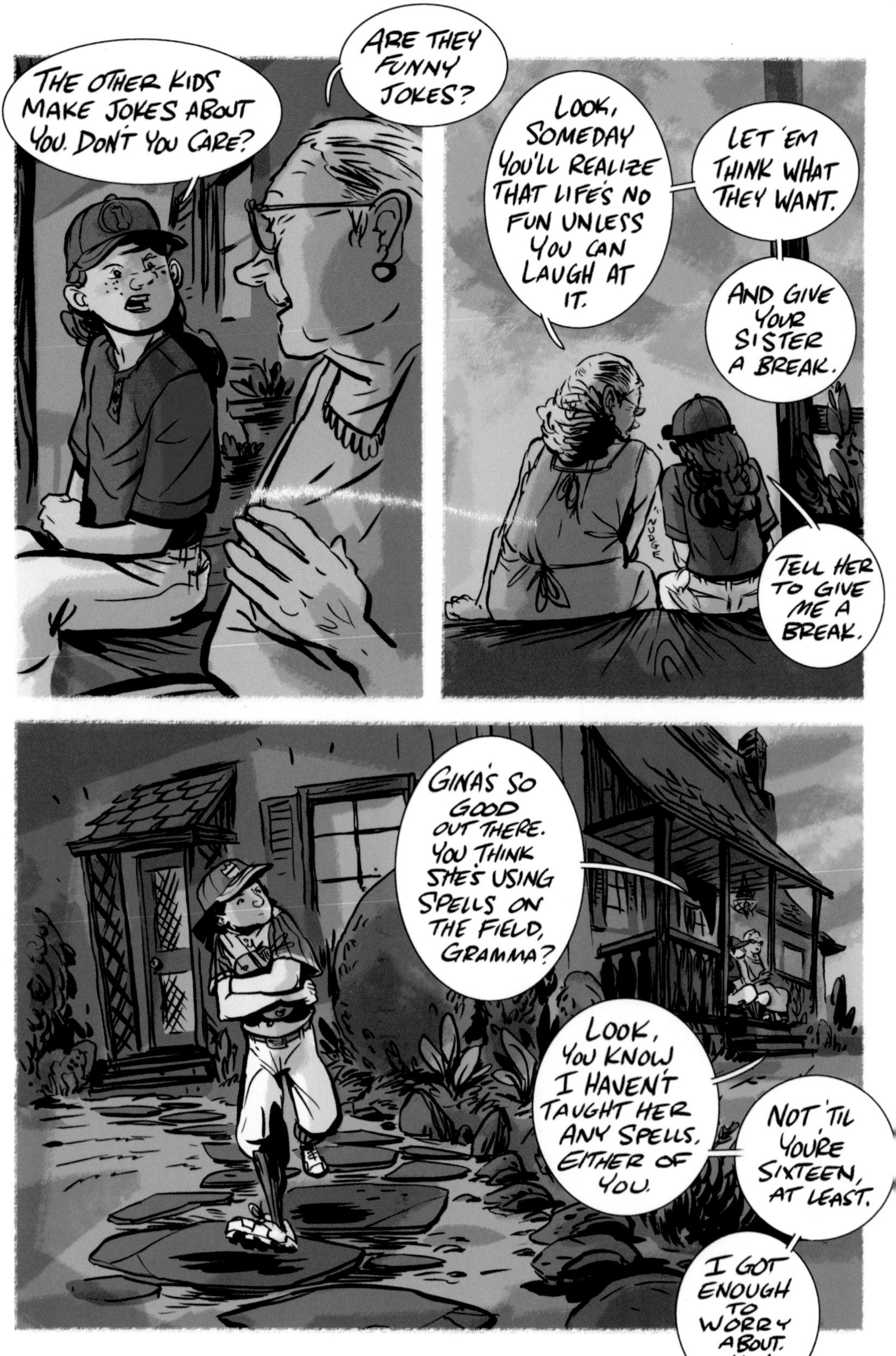
THE OTHER KIDS MAKE JOKES ABOUT YOU. DON'T YOU CARE?
ARE THEY FUNNY JOKES?
LOOK, SOMEDAY YOU'LL REALIZE THAT LIFE'S NO FUN UNLESS YOU CAN LAUGH AT IT.
LET 'EM THINK WHAT THEY WANT.
AND GIVE YOUR SISTER A BREAK.
NUDGE
TELL HER TO GIVE ME A BREAK.
GINA'S SO GOOD OUT THERE. YOU THINK SHE'S USING SPELLS ON THE FIELD, GRAMMA?
LOOK, YOU KNOW I HAVEN'T TAUGHT HER ANY SPELLS. EITHER OF YOU.
NOT 'TIL YOU'RE SIXTEEN, AT LEAST.
I GOT ENOUGH TO WORRY ABOUT. HEH!

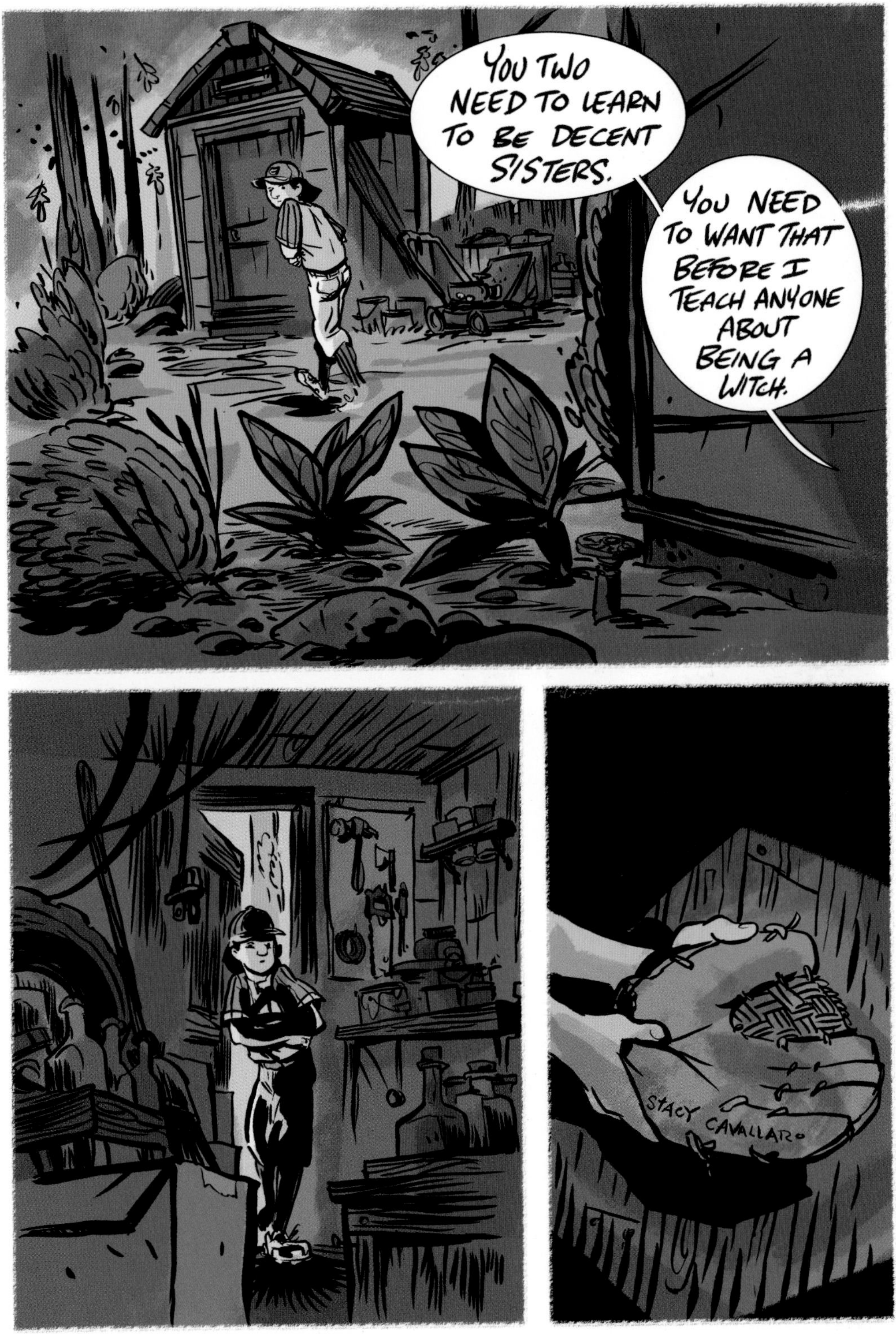
YOU TWO NEED TO LEARN TO BE DECENT SISTERS.
YOU NEED TO WANT THAT BEFORE I TEACH ANYONE ABOUT BEING A WITCH.
STACY CAVALLARO

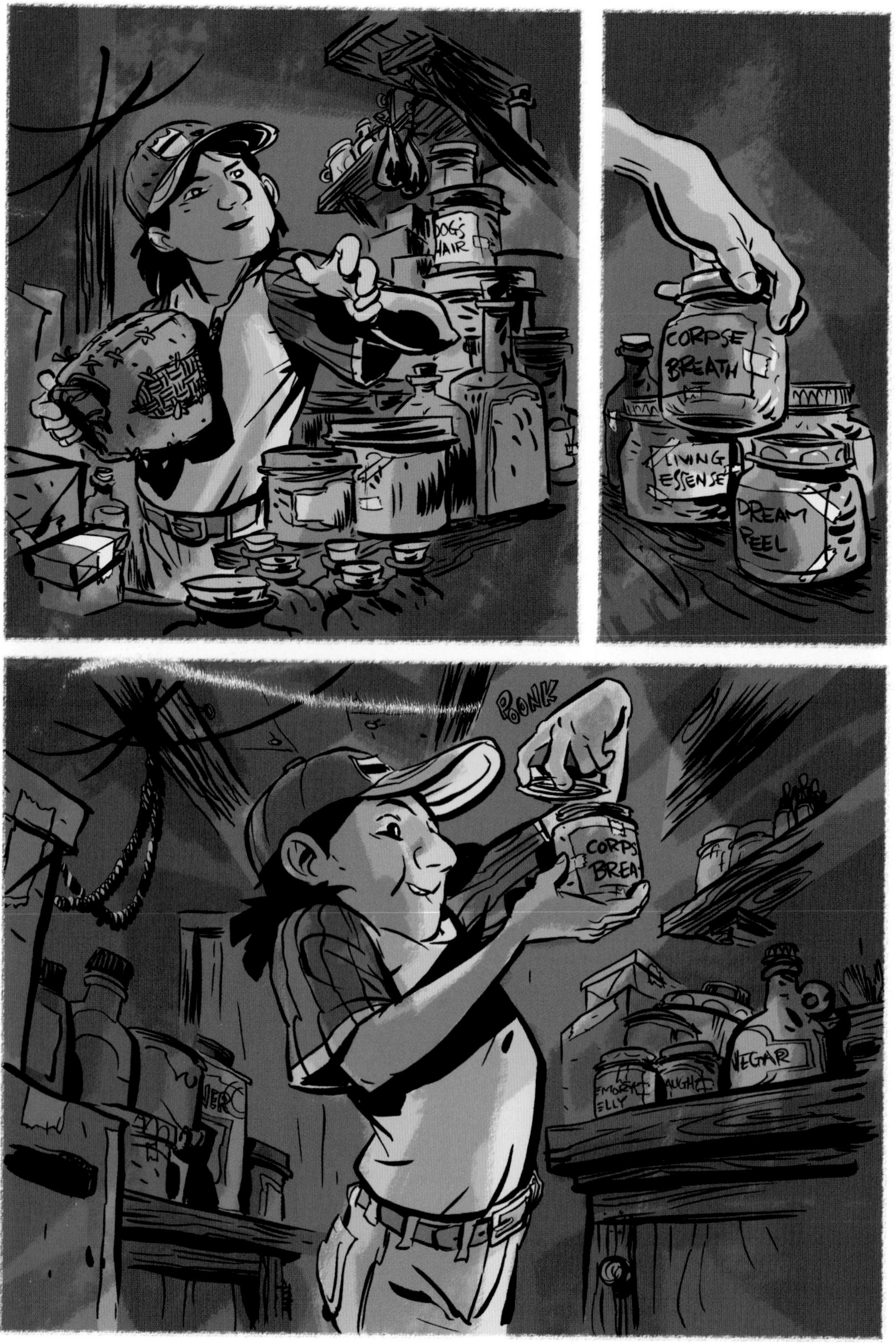
DOG'S HAIR
CORPSE BREATH
LIVING ESSENSE
DREAM PEEL
POONK
CORPS BREA

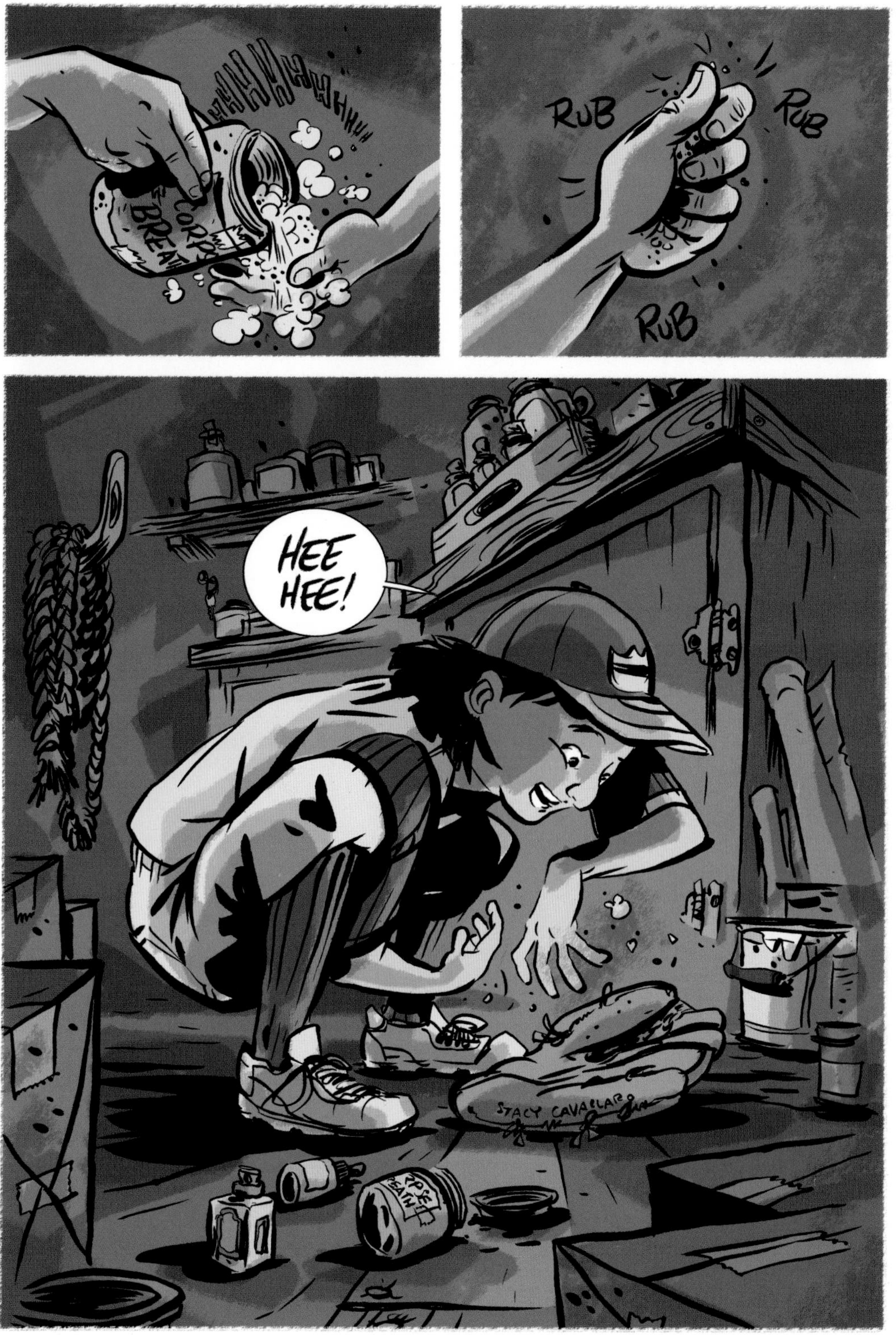
RUB
RUB
RUB
HEE HEE!
STACY CAVALLARO

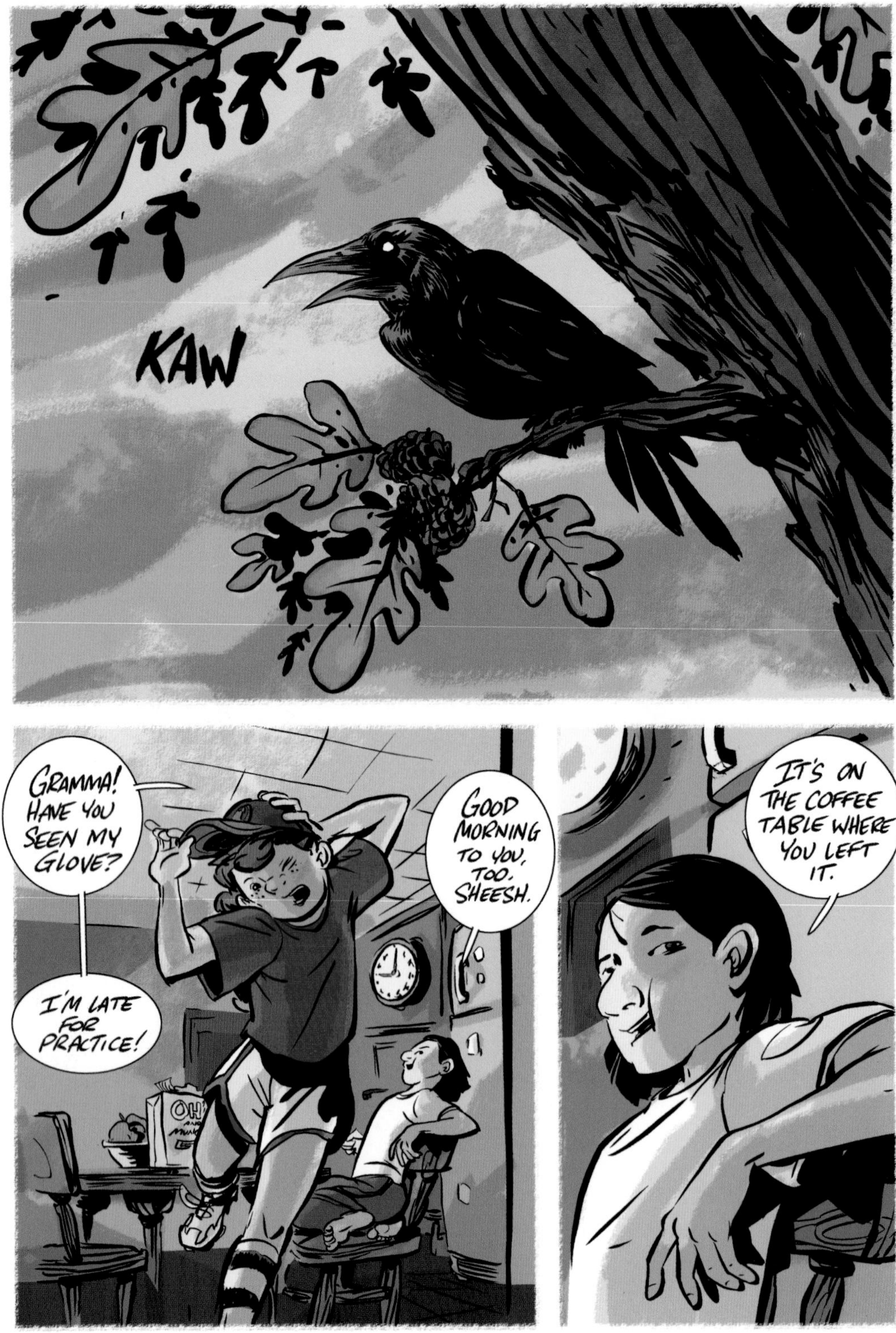
KAW
GRAMMA! HAVE YOU SEEN MY GLOVE?
I'M LATE FOR PRACTICE!
GOOD MORNING TO YOU, TOO. SHEESH.
IT'S ON THE COFFEE TABLE WHERE YOU LEFT IT.

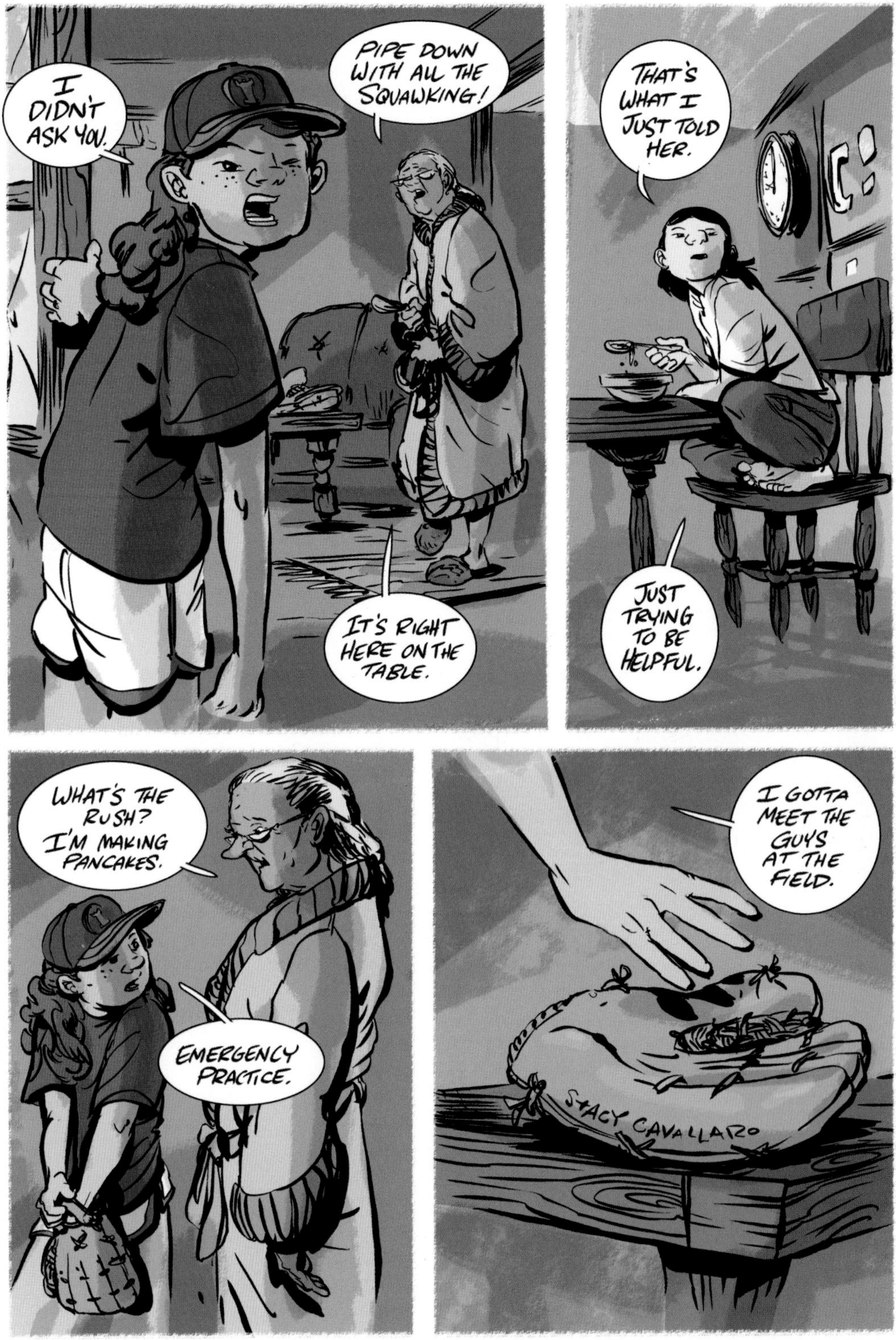
I DIDN'T ASK YOU.
PIPE DOWN WITH ALL THE SQUAWKING!
IT'S RIGHT HERE ON THE TABLE.
THAT'S WHAT I JUST TOLD HER.
JUST TRYING TO BE HELPFUL.
WHAT'S THE RUSH? I'M MAKING PANCAKES.
EMERGENCY PRACTICE.
I GOTTA MEET THE GUYS AT THE FIELD.
STACY CAVALLARO

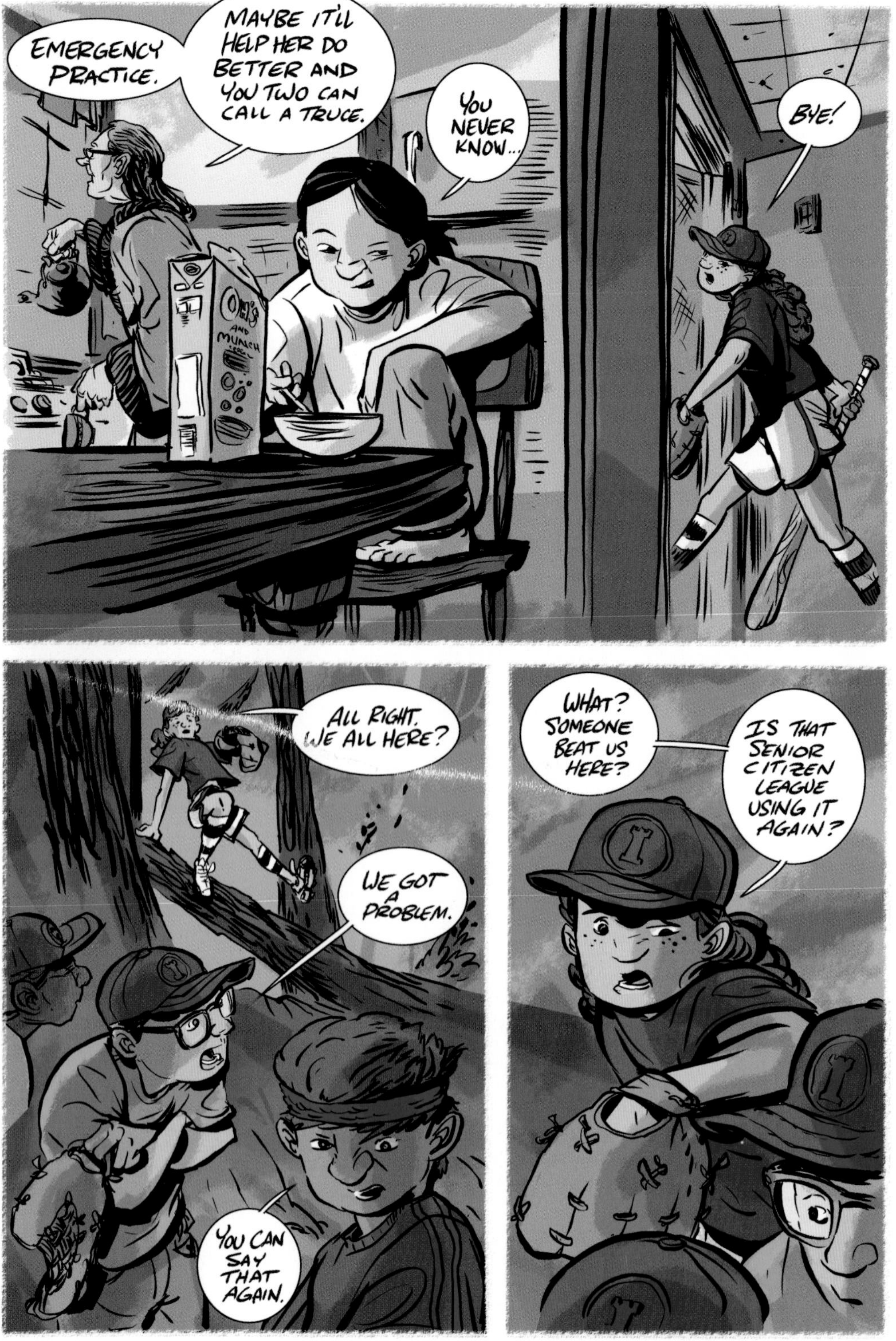
EMERGENCY PRACTICE.
MAYBE IT'LL HELP HER DO BETTER AND YOU TWO CAN CALL A TRUCE.
YOU NEVER KNOW...
BYE!
ALL RIGHT. WE ALL HERE?
WE GOT A PROBLEM.
YOU CAN SAY THAT AGAIN.
WHAT? SOMEONE BEAT US HERE?
IS THAT SENIOR CITIZEN LEAGUE USING IT AGAIN?

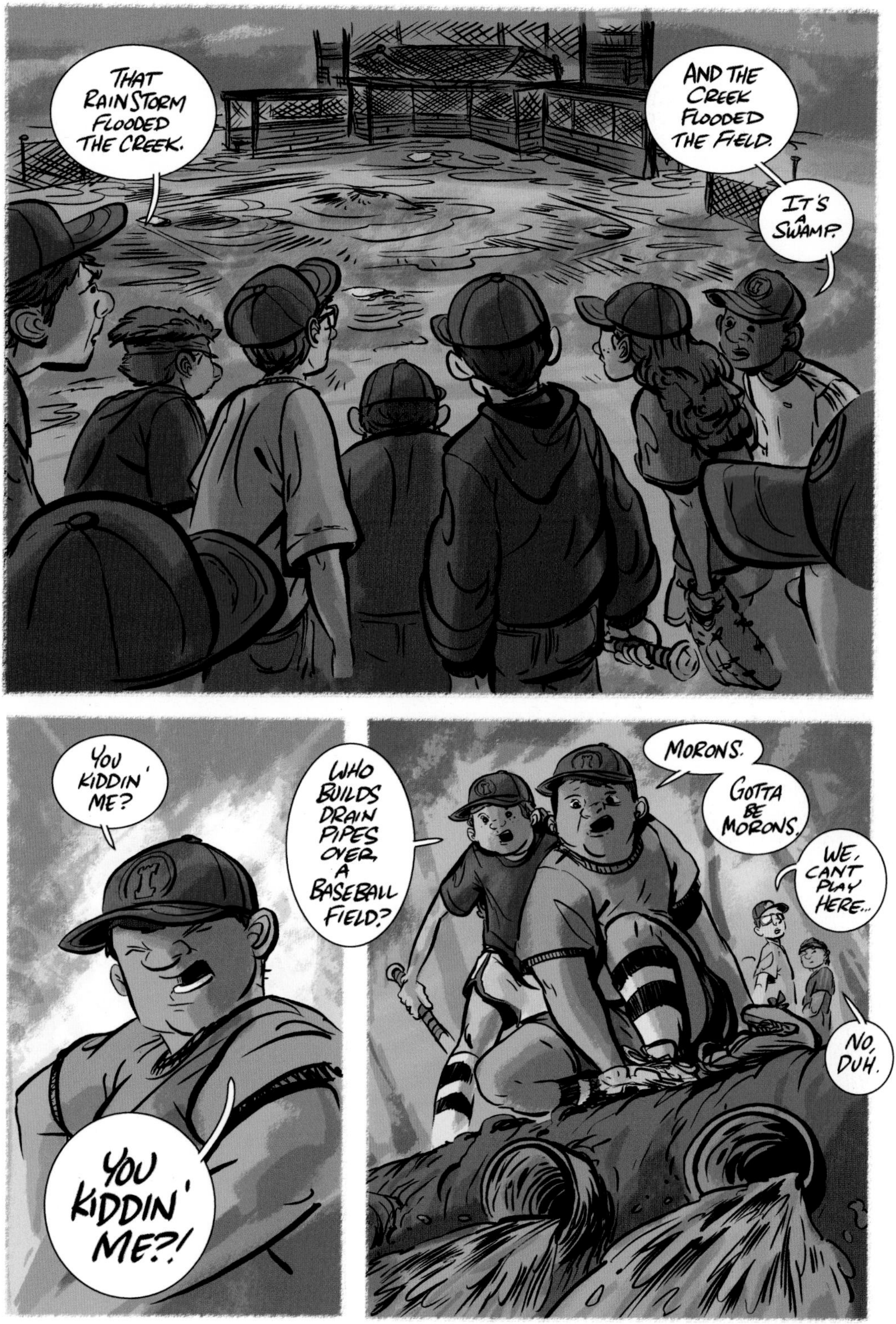
THAT RAINSTORM FLOODED THE CREEK.
AND THE CREEK FLOODED THE FIELD.
IT'S A SWAMP.
YOU KIDDIN' ME?
YOU KIDDIN' ME?!
WHO BUILDS DRAIN PIPES OVER A BASEBALL FIELD?
MORONS.
GOTTA BE MORONS.
WE CANT PLAY HERE...
NO, DUH.

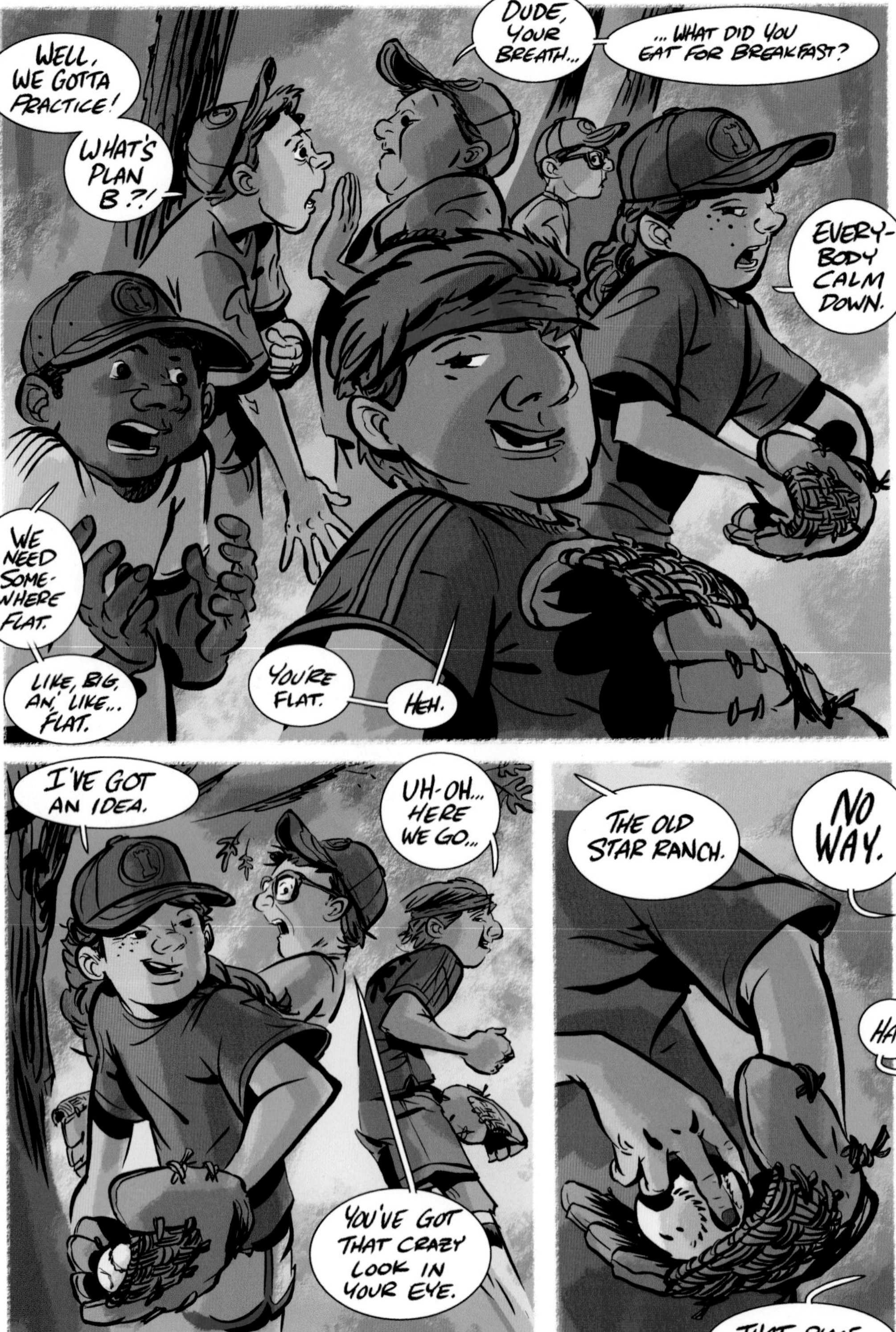
WELL, WE GOTTA PRACTICE!
WHAT'S PLAN B?!
DUDE, YOUR BREATH...
...WHAT DID YOU EAT FOR BREAKFAST?
EVERY-BODY CALM DOWN.
WE NEED SOME-WHERE FLAT.
LIKE, BIG, AN' LIKE... FLAT.
YOU'RE FLAT.
HEH.
I'VE GOT AN IDEA.
UH-OH... HERE WE GO...
YOU'VE GOT THAT CRAZY LOOK IN YOUR EYE.
THE OLD STAR RANCH.
NO WAY.
HA!
THAT PLACE IS HAUNTED!

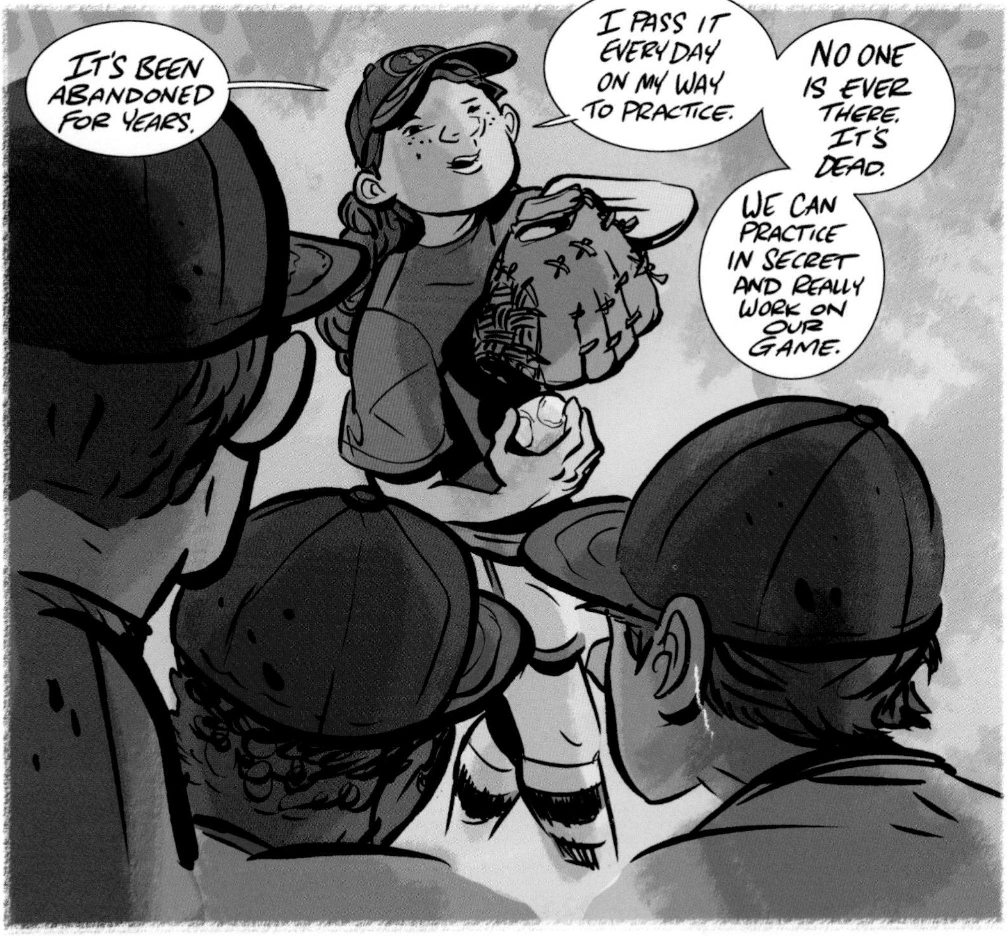
IT'S BEEN ABANDONED FOR YEARS.
I PASS IT EVERY DAY ON MY WAY TO PRACTICE.
NO ONE IS EVER THERE. IT'S DEAD.
WE CAN PRACTICE IN SECRET AND REALLY WORK ON OUR GAME.

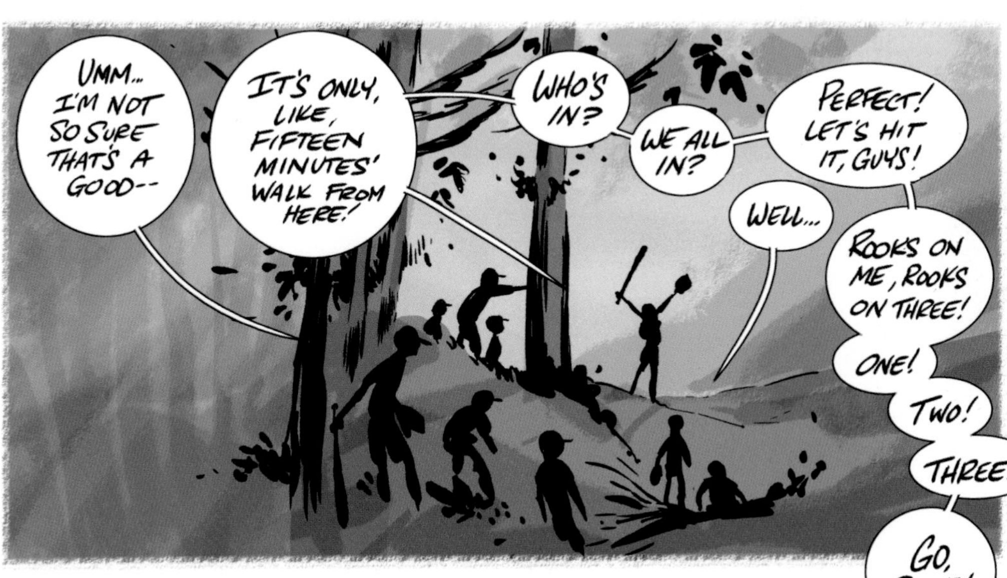
UMM... I'M NOT SO SURE THAT'S A GOOD--
IT'S ONLY, LIKE, FIFTEEN MINUTES' WALK FROM HERE!
WHO'S IN?
WE ALL IN?
PERFECT! LET'S HIT IT, GUYS!
WELL...
ROOKS ON ME, ROOKS ON THREE!
ONE!
TWO!
THREE!
GO, ROOKS!

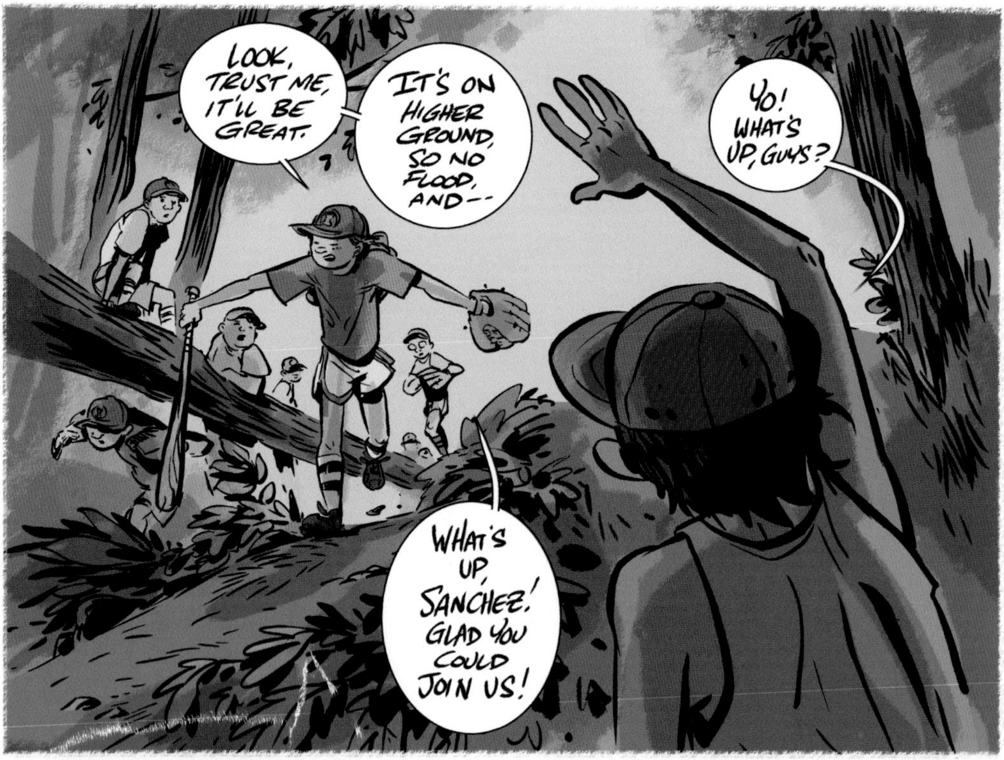
LOOK, TRUST ME, IT'LL BE GREAT.
IT'S ON HIGHER GROUND, SO NO FLOOD, AND--
YO! WHAT'S UP, GUYS?
WHAT'S UP, SANCHEZ! GLAD YOU COULD JOIN US!

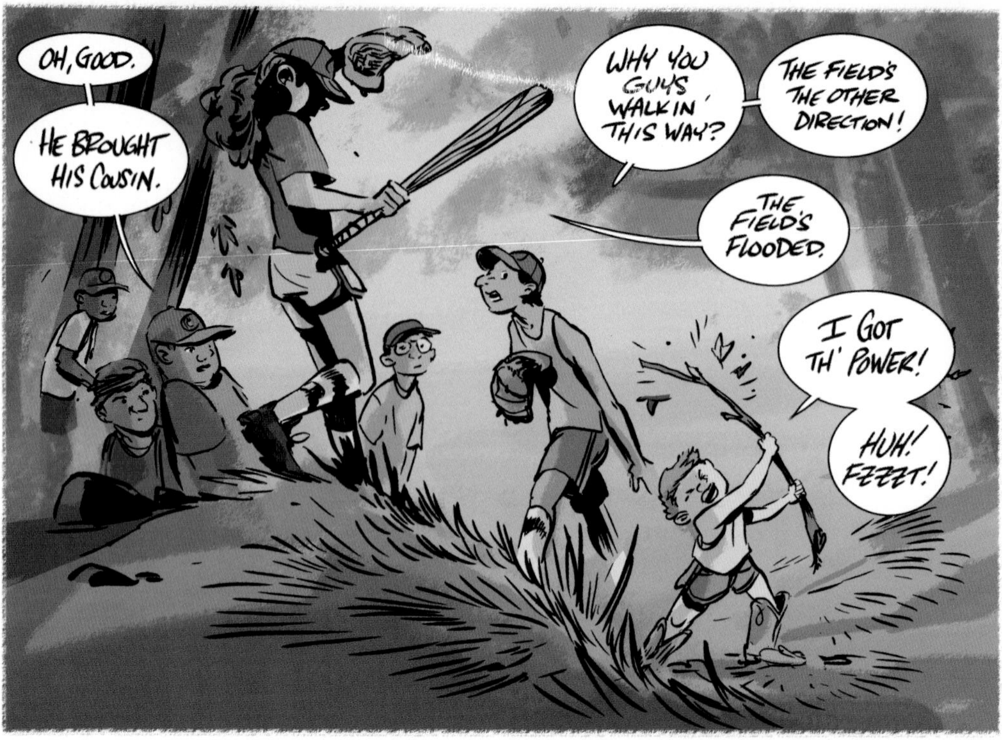
OH, GOOD.
HE BROUGHT HIS COUSIN.
WHY YOU GUYS WALKIN' THIS WAY?
THE FIELD'S THE OTHER DIRECTION!
THE FIELD'S FLOODED.
I GOT TH' POWER!
HUH! FZZZT!

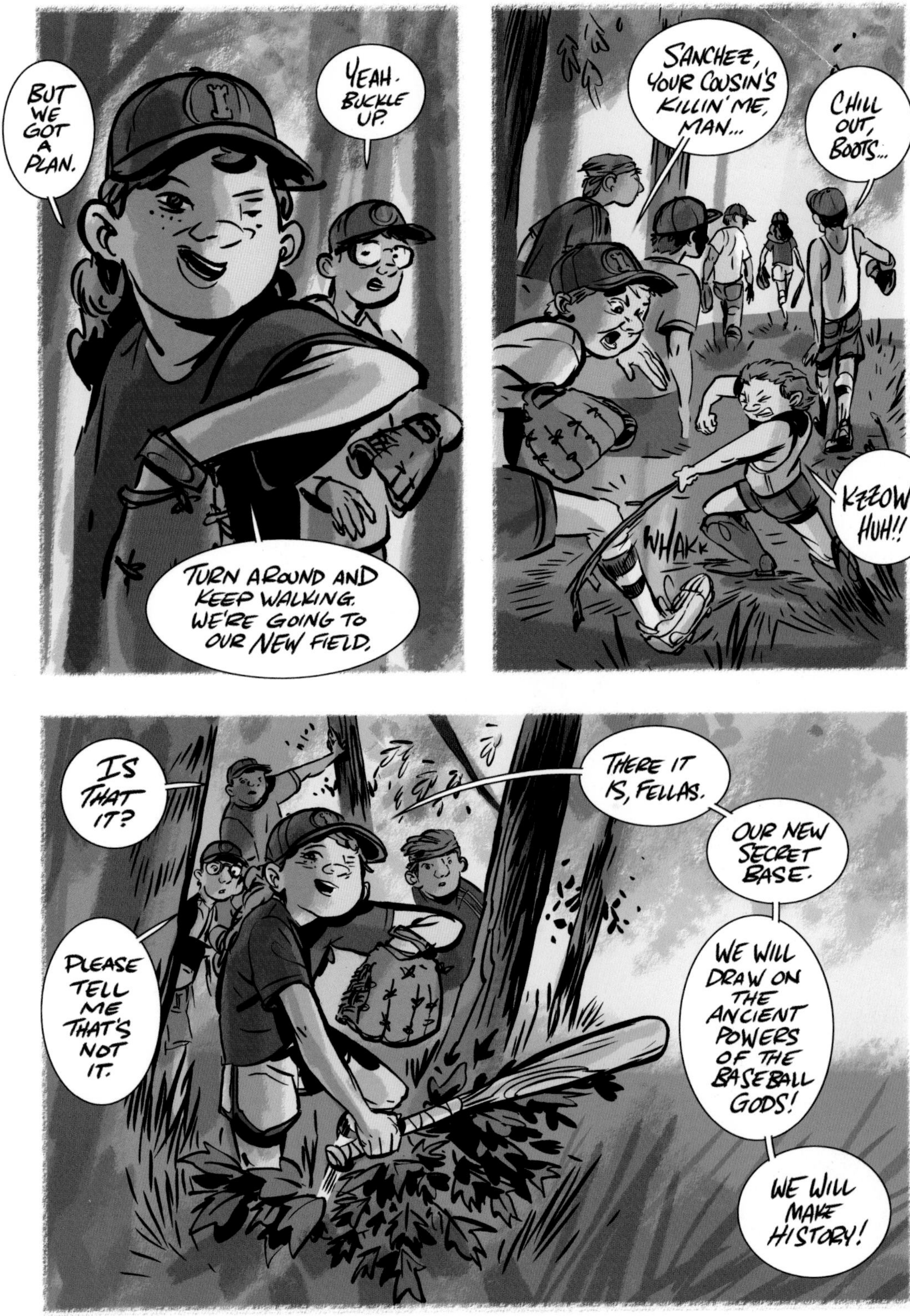
BUT WE GOT A PLAN.
YEAH. BUCKLE UP.
TURN AROUND AND KEEP WALKING. WE'RE GOING TO OUR NEW FIELD.
SANCHEZ, YOUR COUSIN'S KILLIN' ME, MAN...
CHILL OUT, BOOTS...
WHAKK
KEZOW! HUH!!
IS THAT IT?
THERE IT IS, FELLAS.
PLEASE TELL ME THAT'S NOT IT.
OUR NEW SECRET BASE.
WE WILL DRAW ON THE ANCIENT POWERS OF THE BASEBALL GODS!
WE WILL MAKE HISTORY!

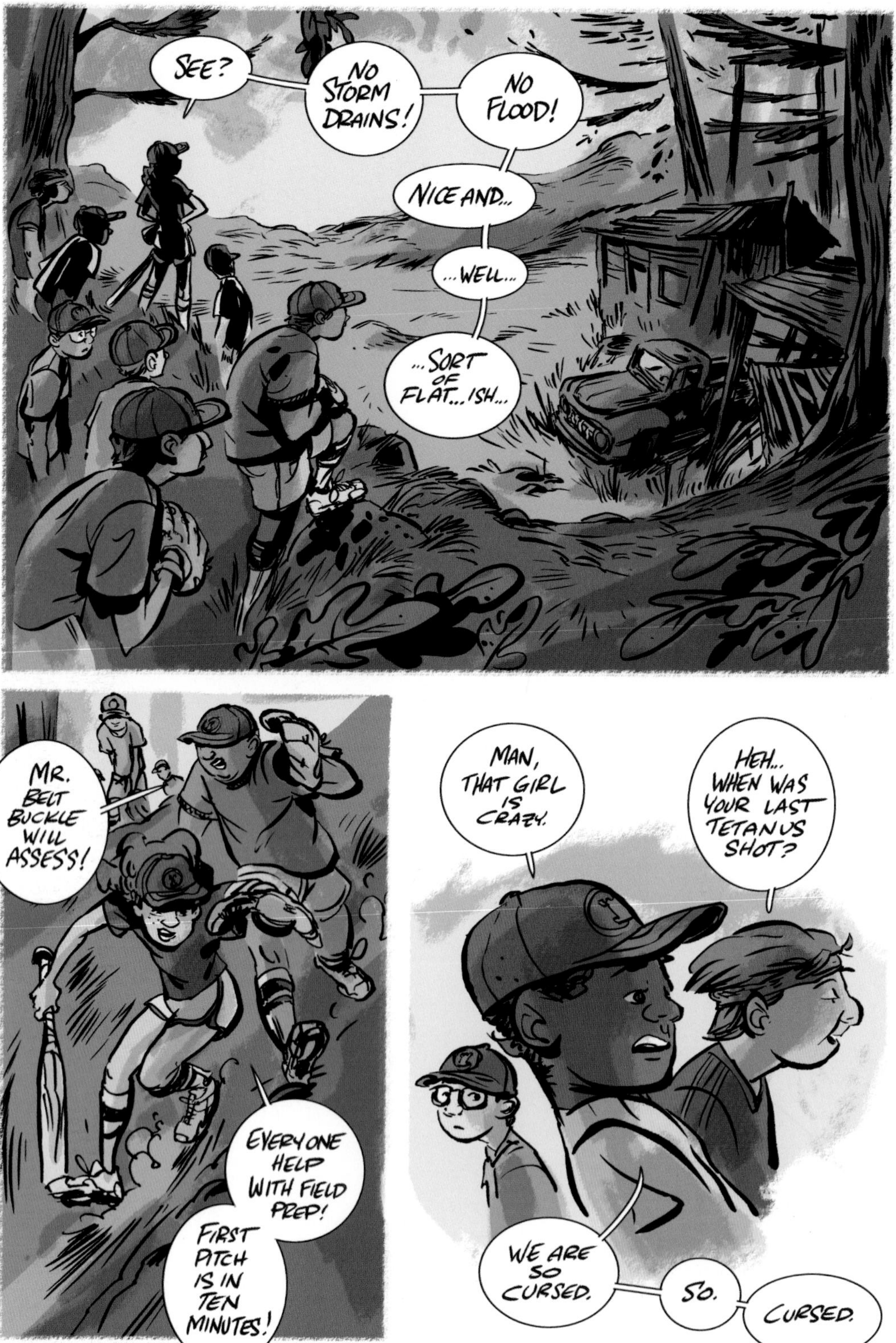
SEE?
NO STORM DRAINS!
NO FLOOD!
NICE AND...
...WELL...
...SORT OF FLAT...ISH...
MR. BELT BUCKLE WILL ASSESS!
EVERYONE HELP WITH FIELD PREP!
FIRST PITCH IS IN TEN MINUTES!
MAN, THAT GIRL IS CRAZY.
HEH... WHEN WAS YOUR LAST TETANUS SHOT?
WE ARE SO CURSED.
SO.
CURSED.

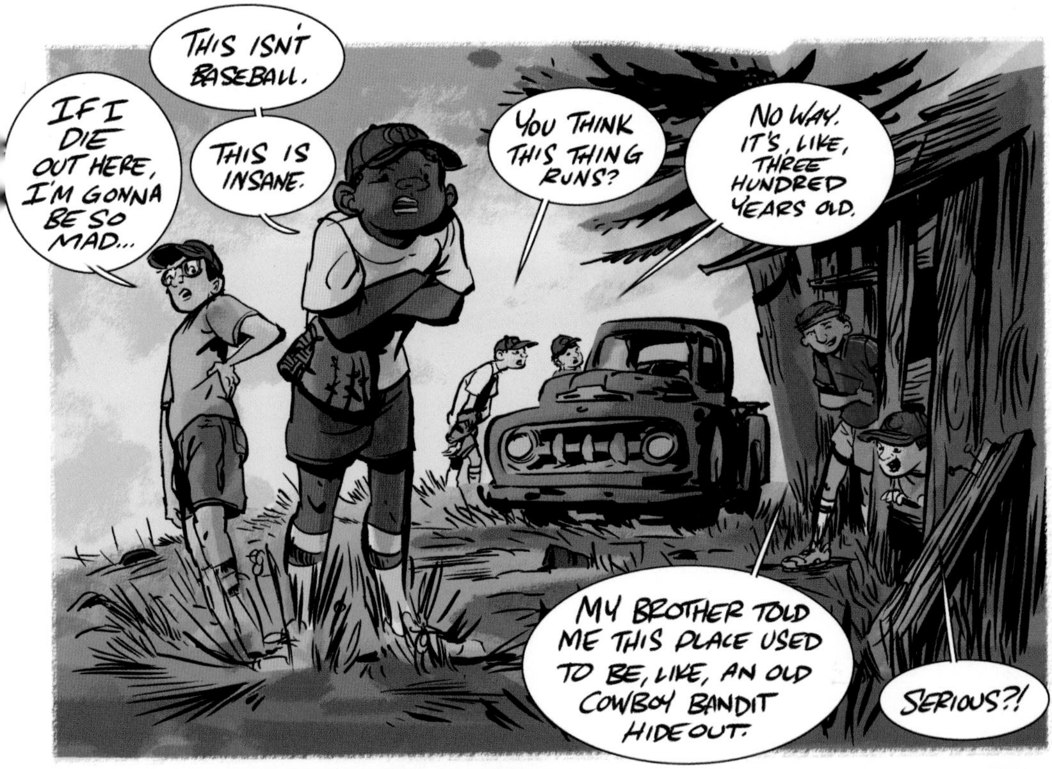
IF I DIE OUT HERE, I'M GONNA BE SO MAD...
THIS ISN'T BASEBALL.
THIS IS INSANE.
YOU THINK THIS THING RUNS?
NO WAY. IT'S, LIKE, THREE HUNDRED YEARS OLD.
MY BROTHER TOLD ME THIS PLACE USED TO BE, LIKE, AN OLD COWBOY BANDIT HIDEOUT.
SERIOUS?!

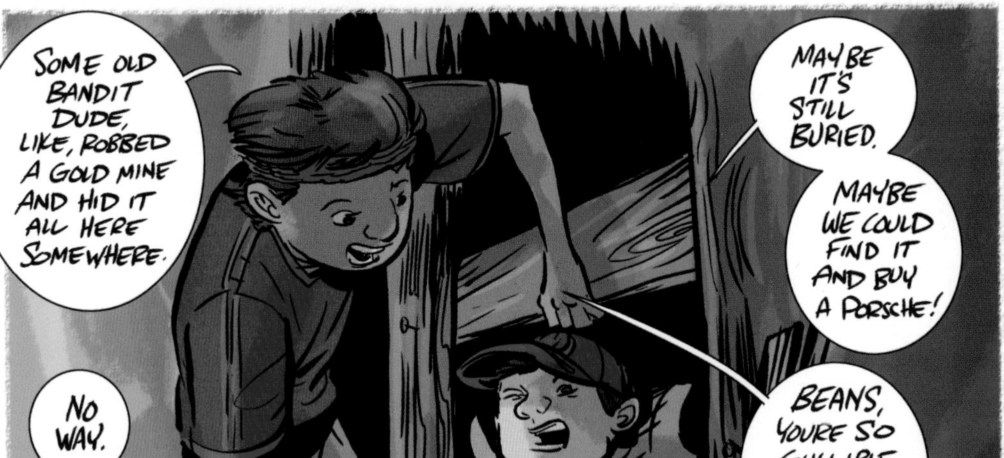
SOME OLD BANDIT DUDE, LIKE, ROBBED A GOLD MINE AND HID IT ALL HERE SOMEWHERE.
MAYBE IT'S STILL BURIED.
MAYBE WE COULD FIND IT AND BUY A PORSCHE!
NO WAY.
NO WAY!
BEANS, YOU'RE SO GULLIBLE. I MADE THAT UP! DUH!
THERE'S NOTHING BURIED OUT HERE!
PSSH. I KNEW THAT.

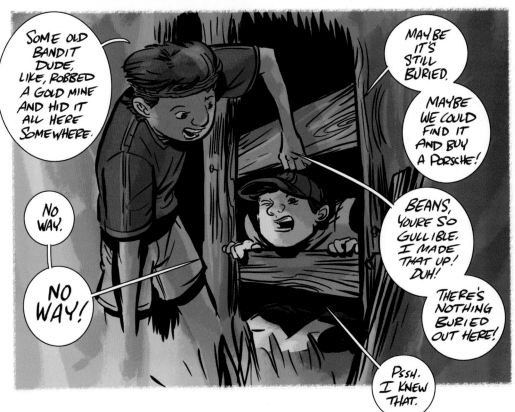

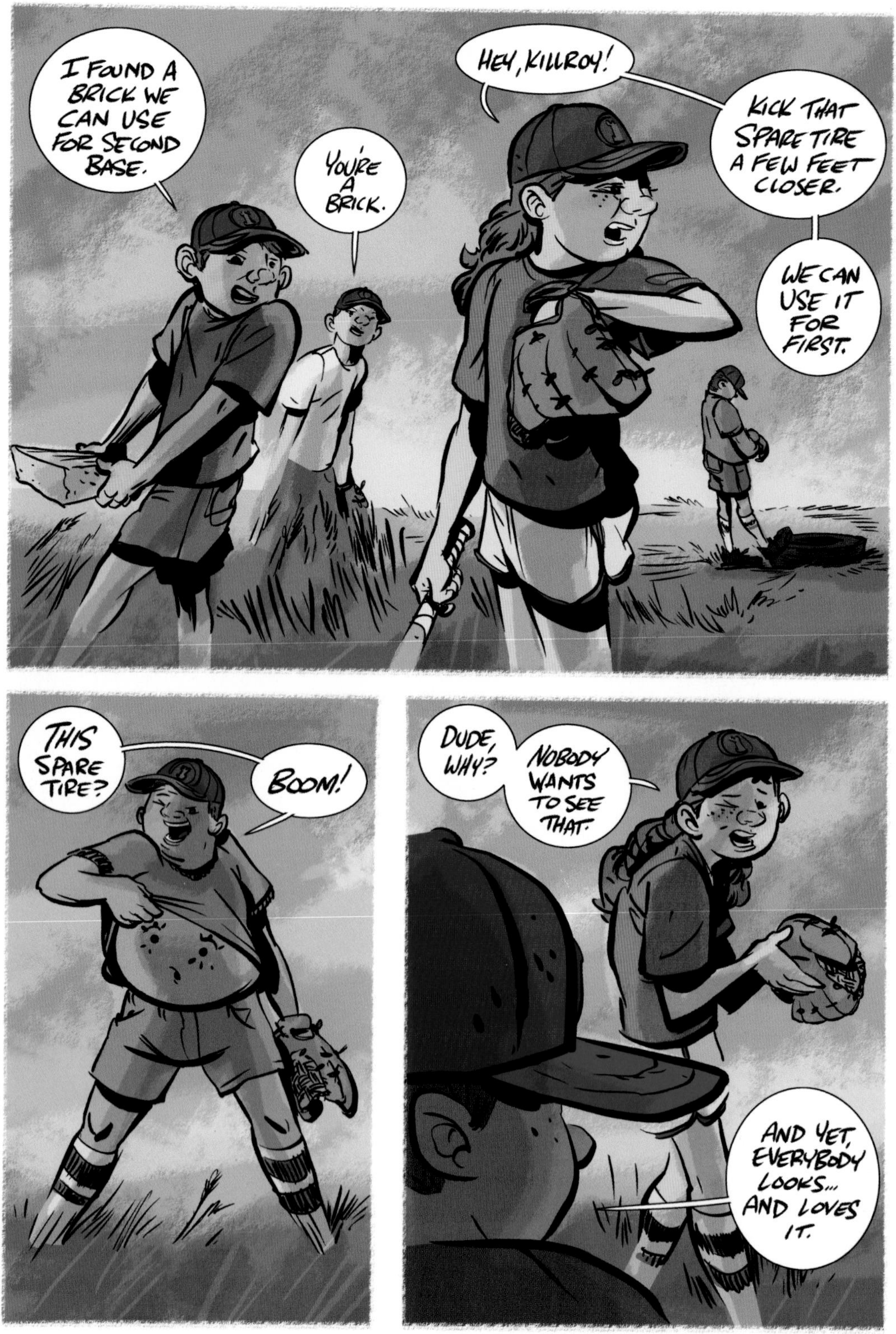
I FOUND A BRICK WE CAN USE FOR SECOND BASE.
YOU'RE A BRICK.
HEY, KILLROY!
KICK THAT SPARE TIRE A FEW FEET CLOSER.
WE CAN USE IT FOR FIRST.
THIS SPARE TIRE?
BOOM!
DUDE, WHY?
NOBODY WANTS TO SEE THAT.
AND YET, EVERYBODY LOOKS... AND LOVES IT.

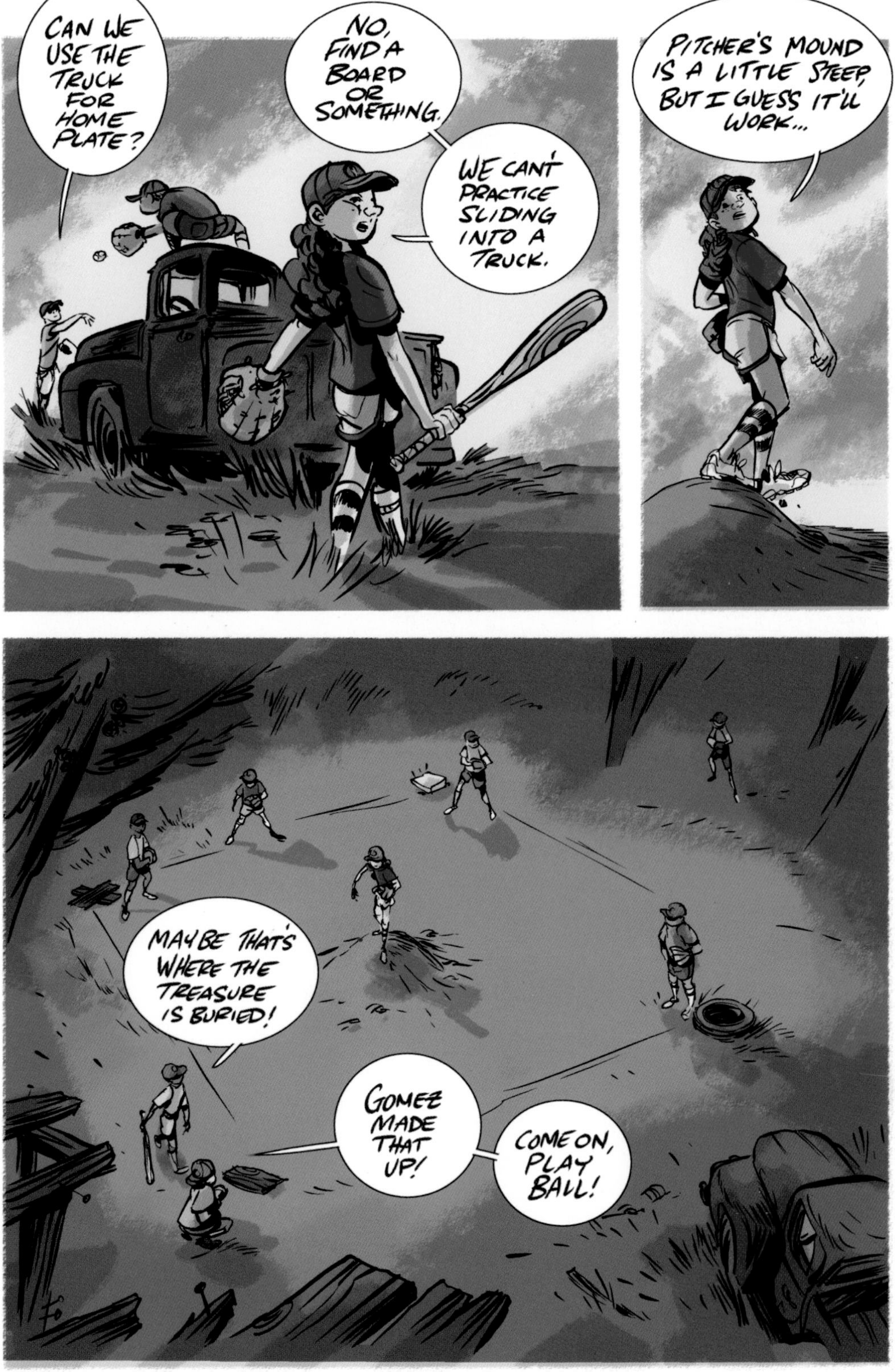
CAN WE USE THE TRUCK FOR HOME PLATE?
NO, FIND A BOARD OR SOMETHING.
WE CAN'T PRACTICE SLIDING INTO A TRUCK.
PITCHER'S MOUND IS A LITTLE STEEP, BUT I GUESS IT'LL WORK...
MAYBE THAT'S WHERE THE TREASURE IS BURIED!
GOMEZ MADE THAT UP!
COME ON, PLAY BALL!

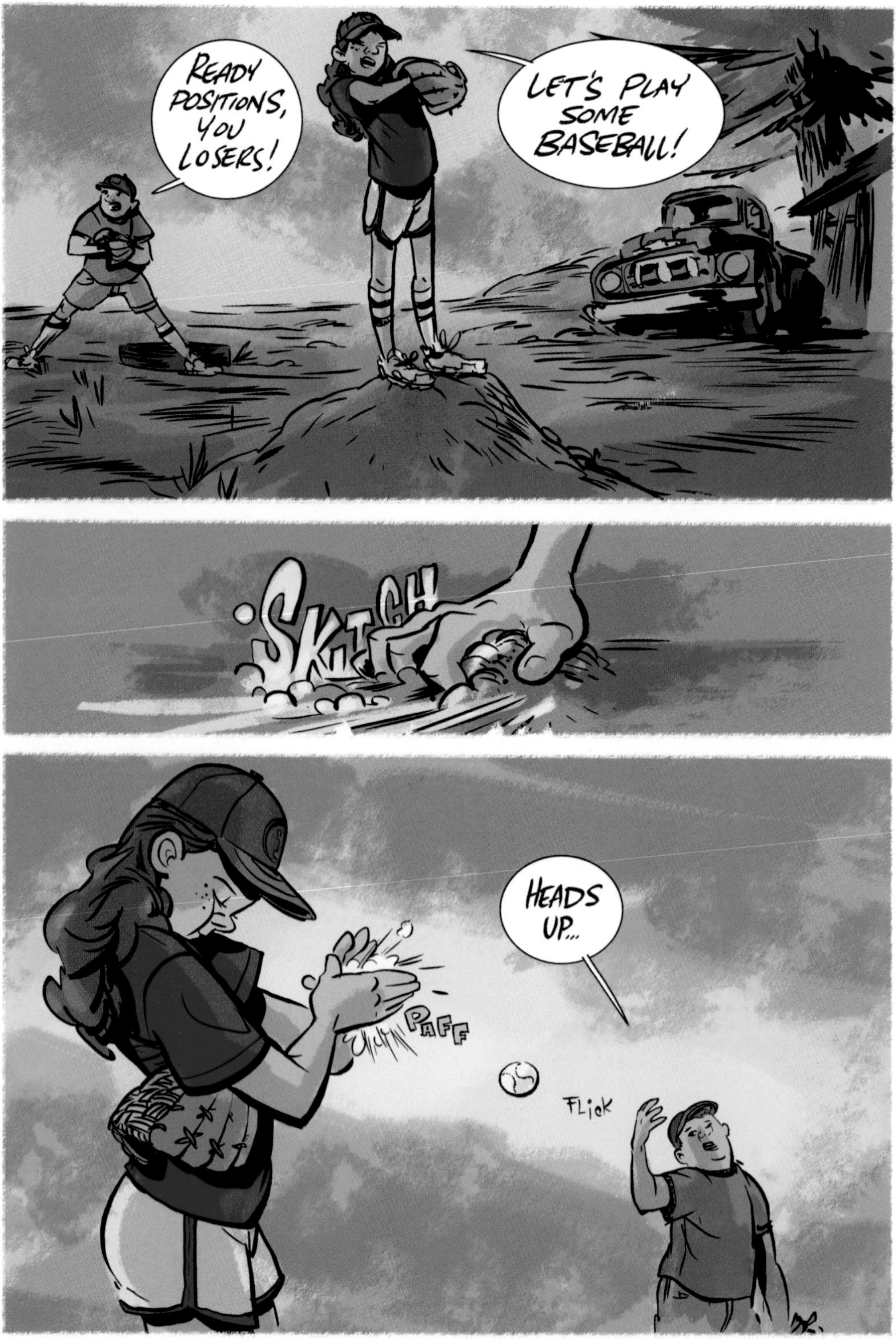
READY POSITIONS, YOU LOSERS!
LET'S PLAY SOME BASEBALL!
SKTCH
HEADS UP...
PAFF
FLICK

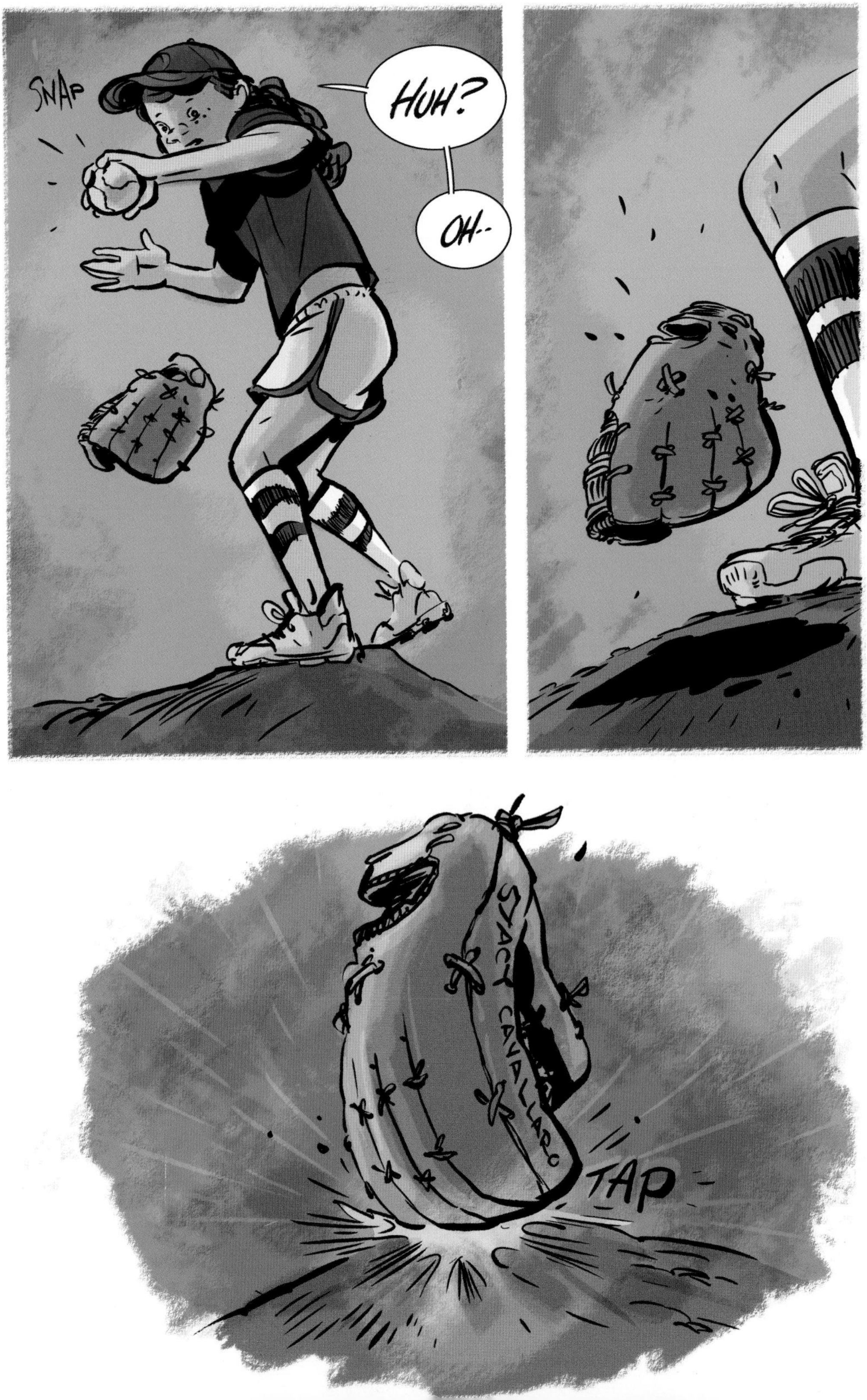
SNAP
HUH?
OH..
STACY CAVALLARO
TAP

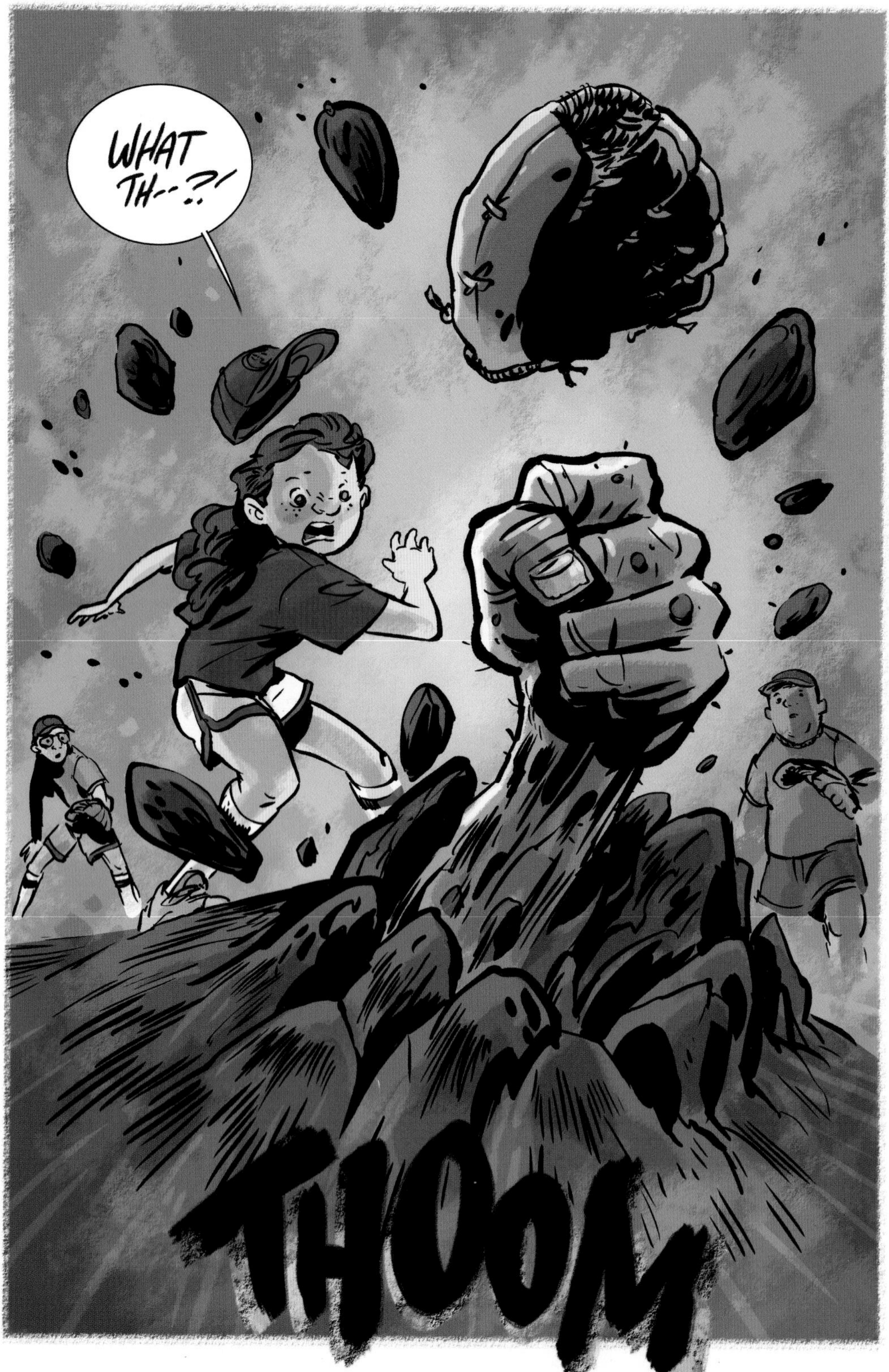
WHAT TH--?!
THOOM

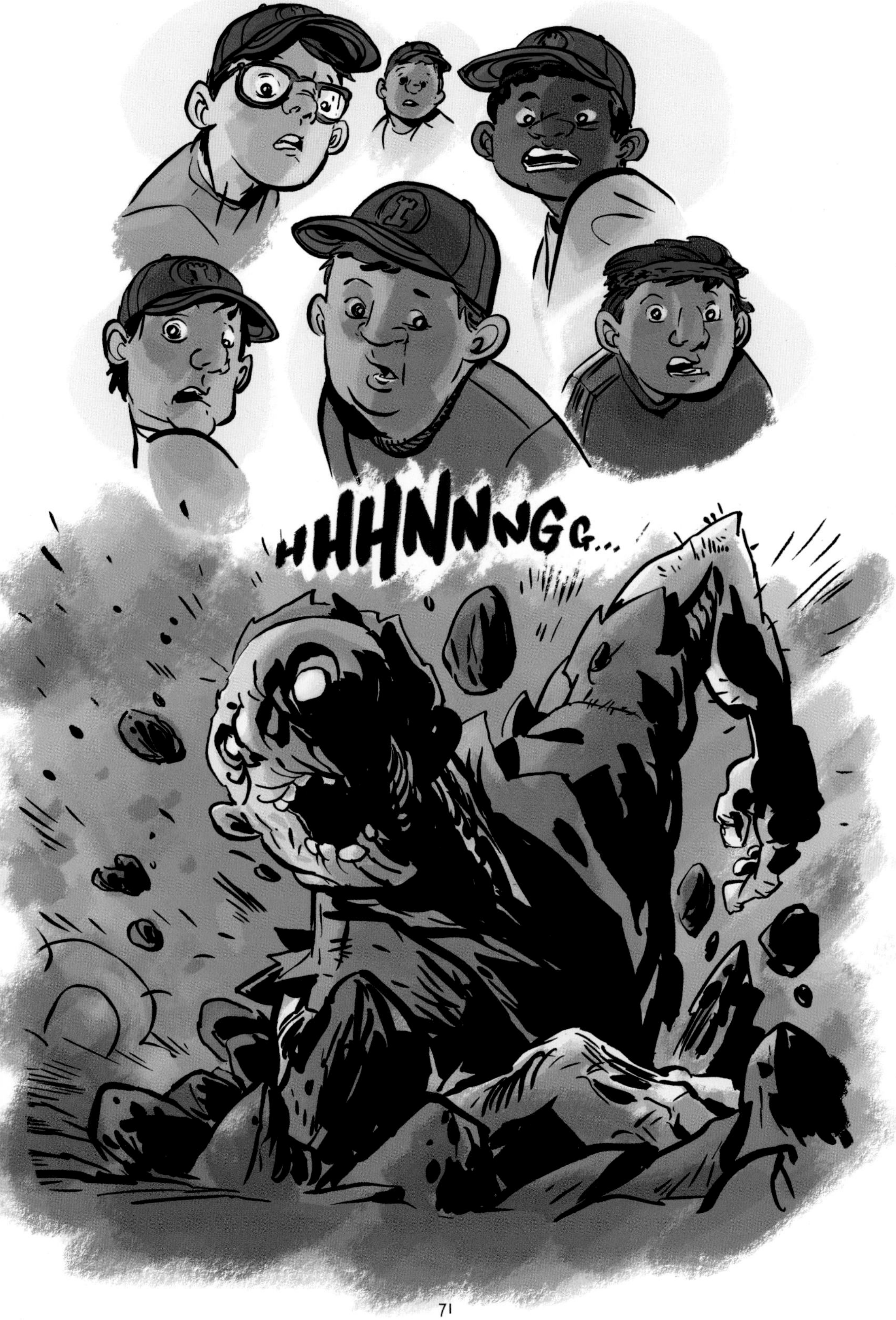
HHHNNNNGG...

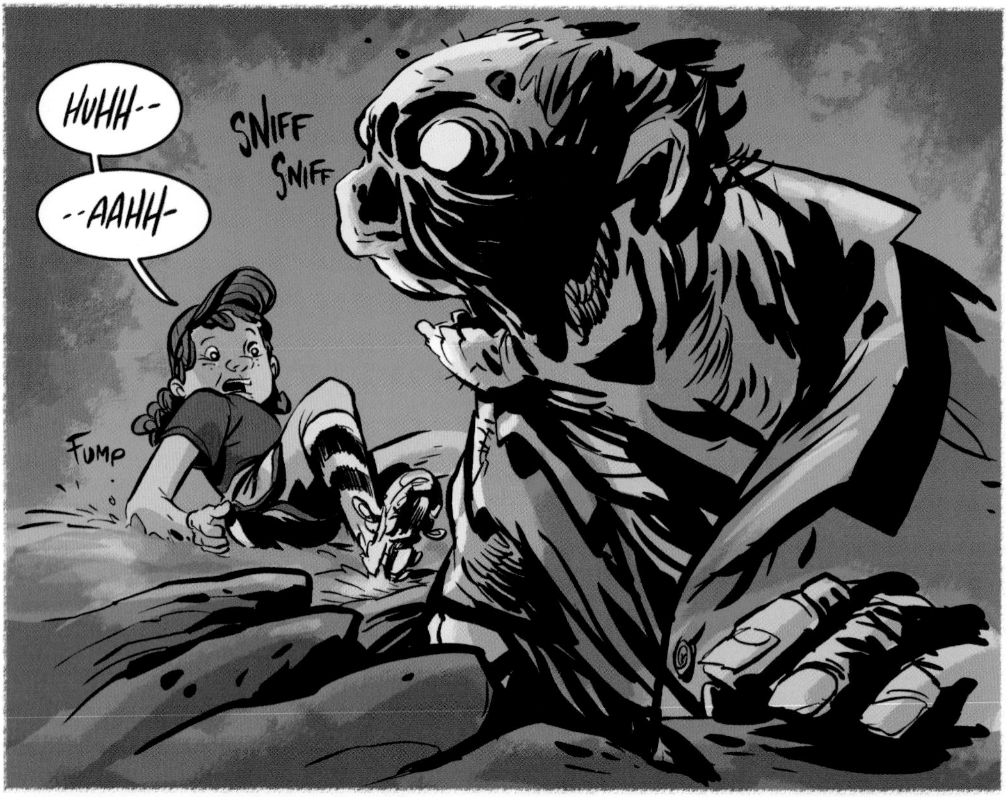
HUHH--
--AAHH-
SNIFF
SNIFF
FUMP

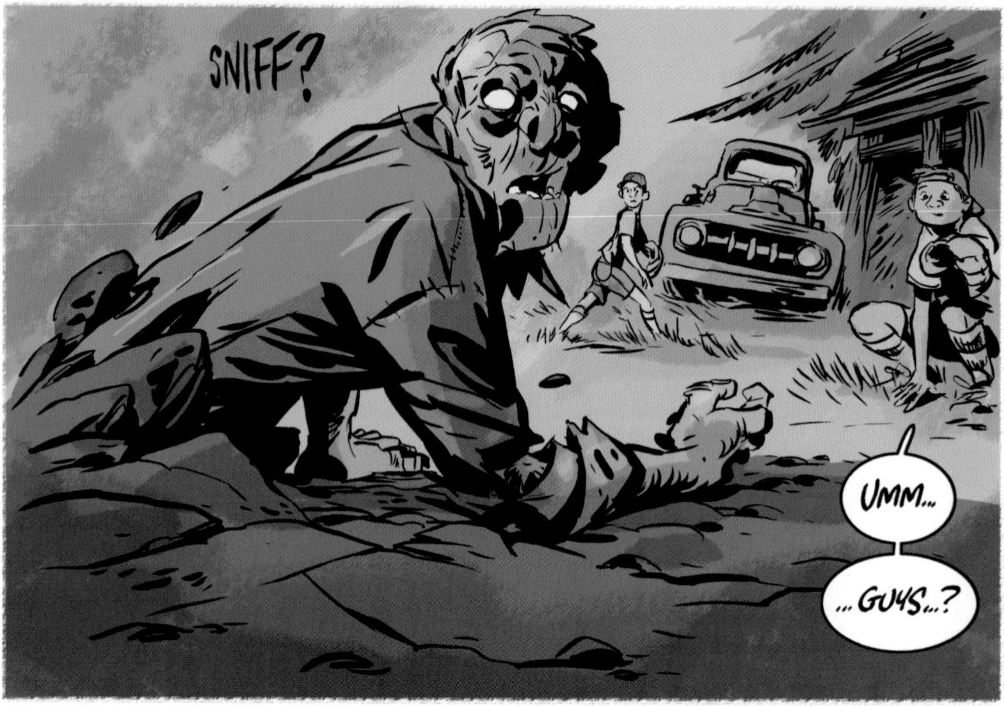
SNIFF?
UMM...
...GUYS...?

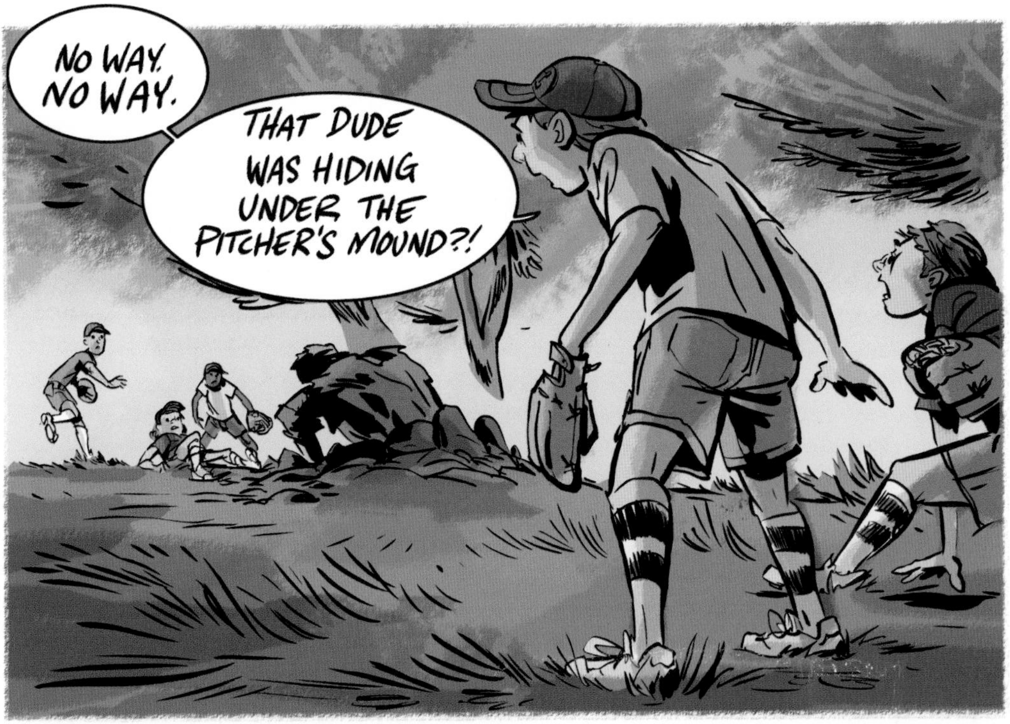
NO WAY. NO WAY.
THAT DUDE WAS HIDING UNDER THE PITCHER'S MOUND?!

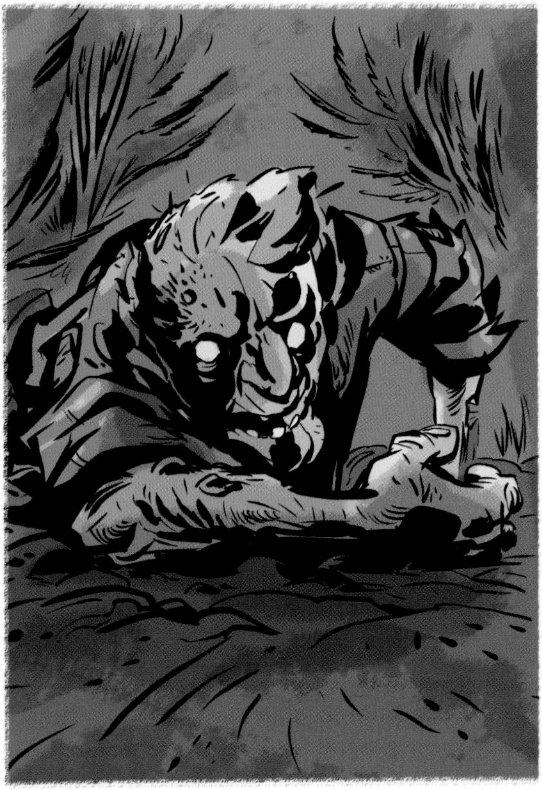

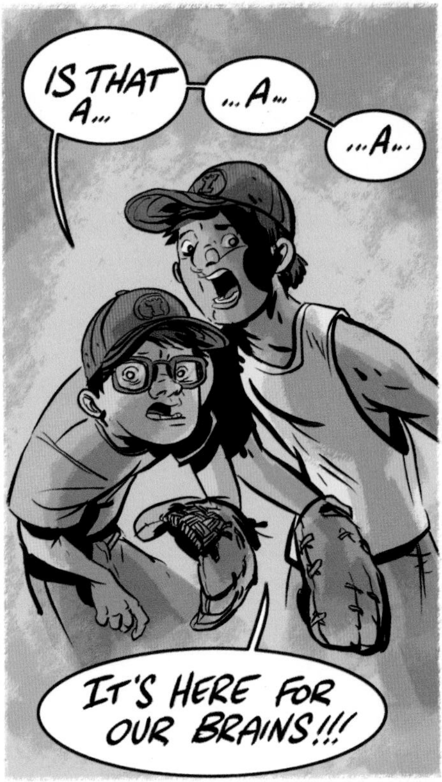
IS THAT A...
...A...
...A...
IT'S HERE FOR OUR BRAINS!!!

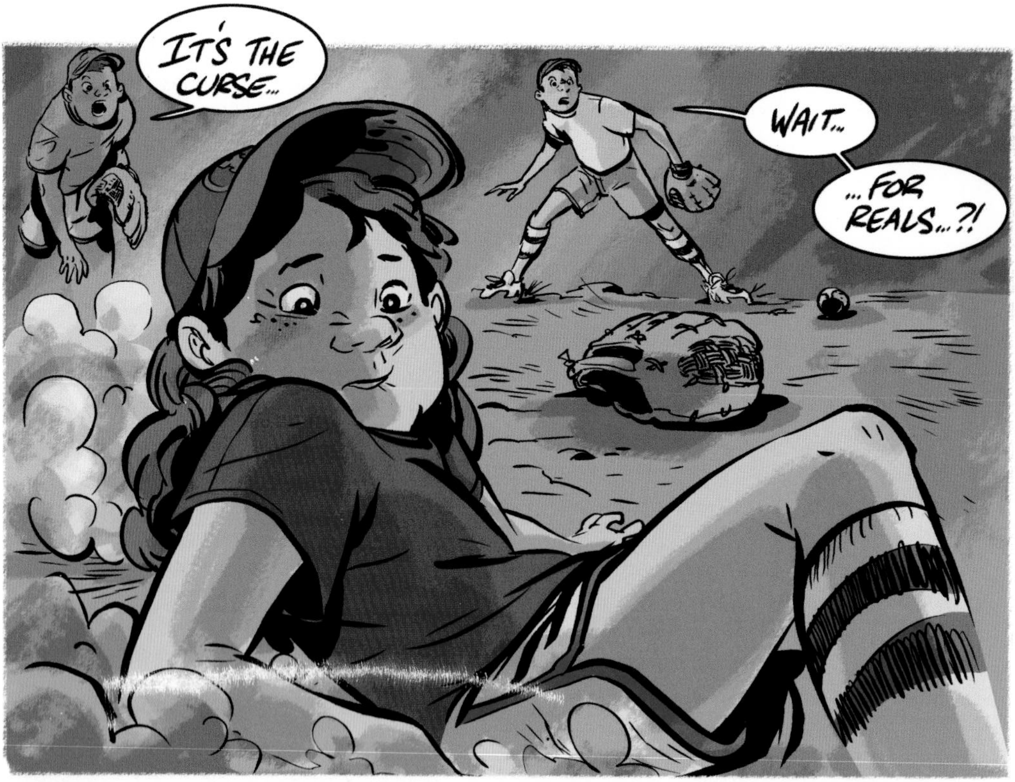
IT'S THE CURSE...
WAIT...
...FOR REALS...?!

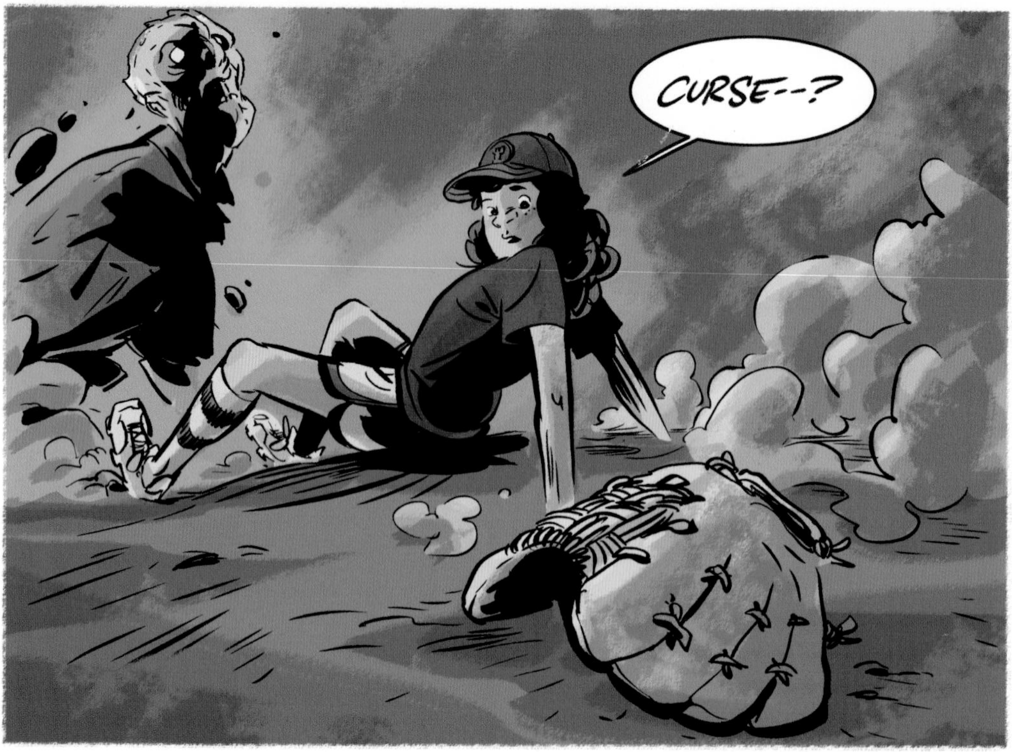
CURSE--?

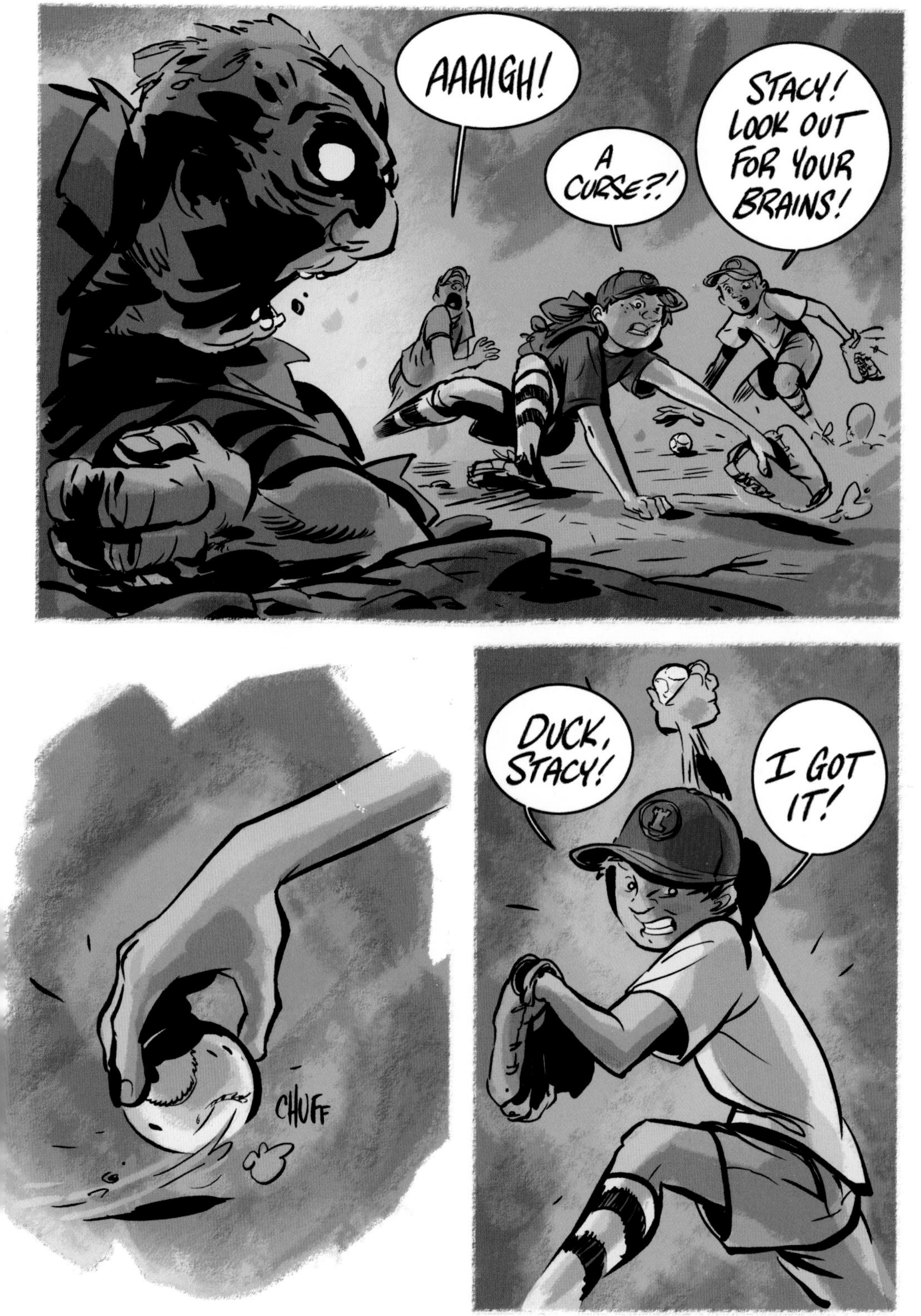
AAAIGH!
A CURSE?!
STACY! LOOK OUT FOR YOUR BRAINS!
CHUFF
DUCK, STACY!
I GOT IT!

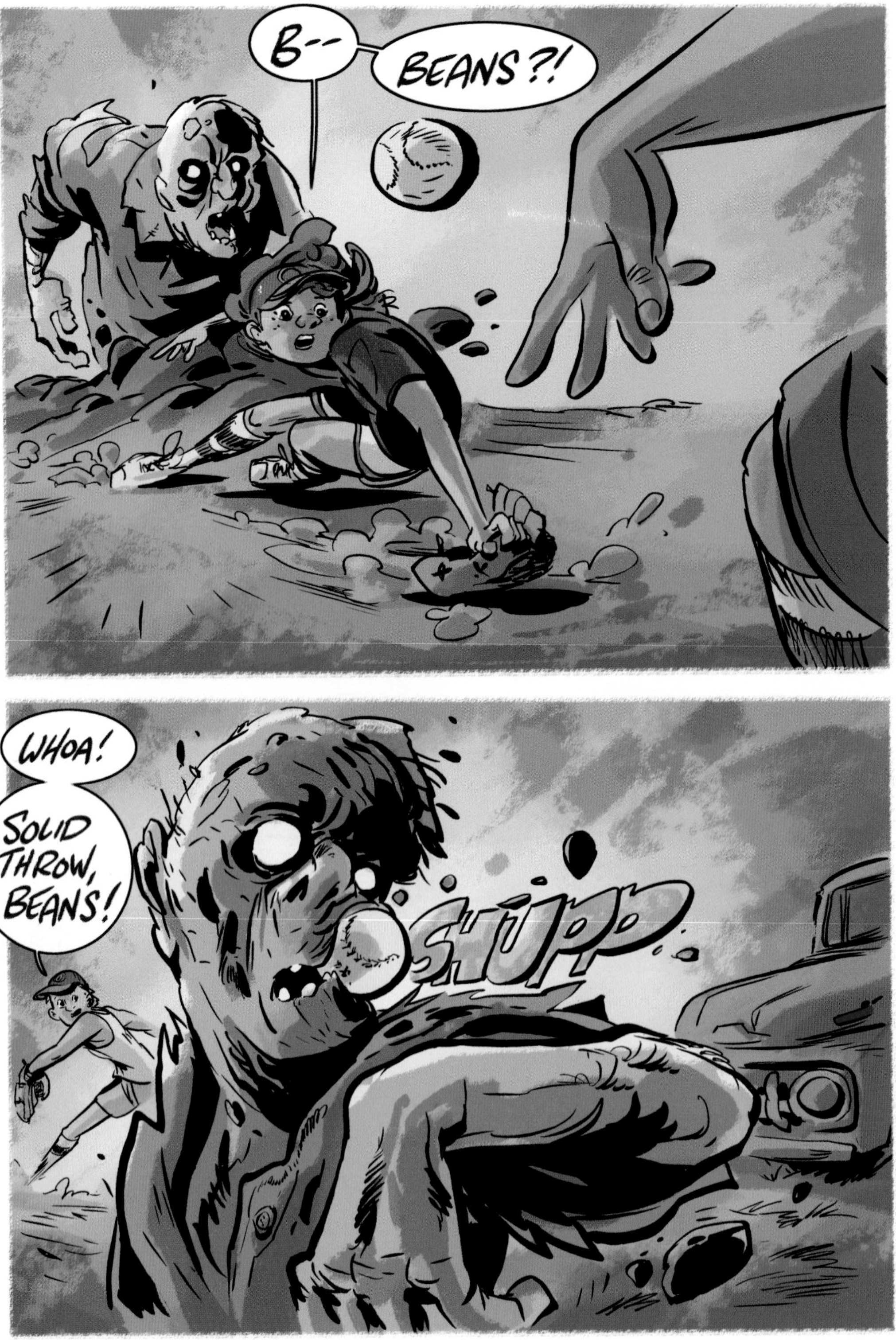
B--
BEANS?!
WHOA!
SOLID THROW, BEANS!
SHUPP

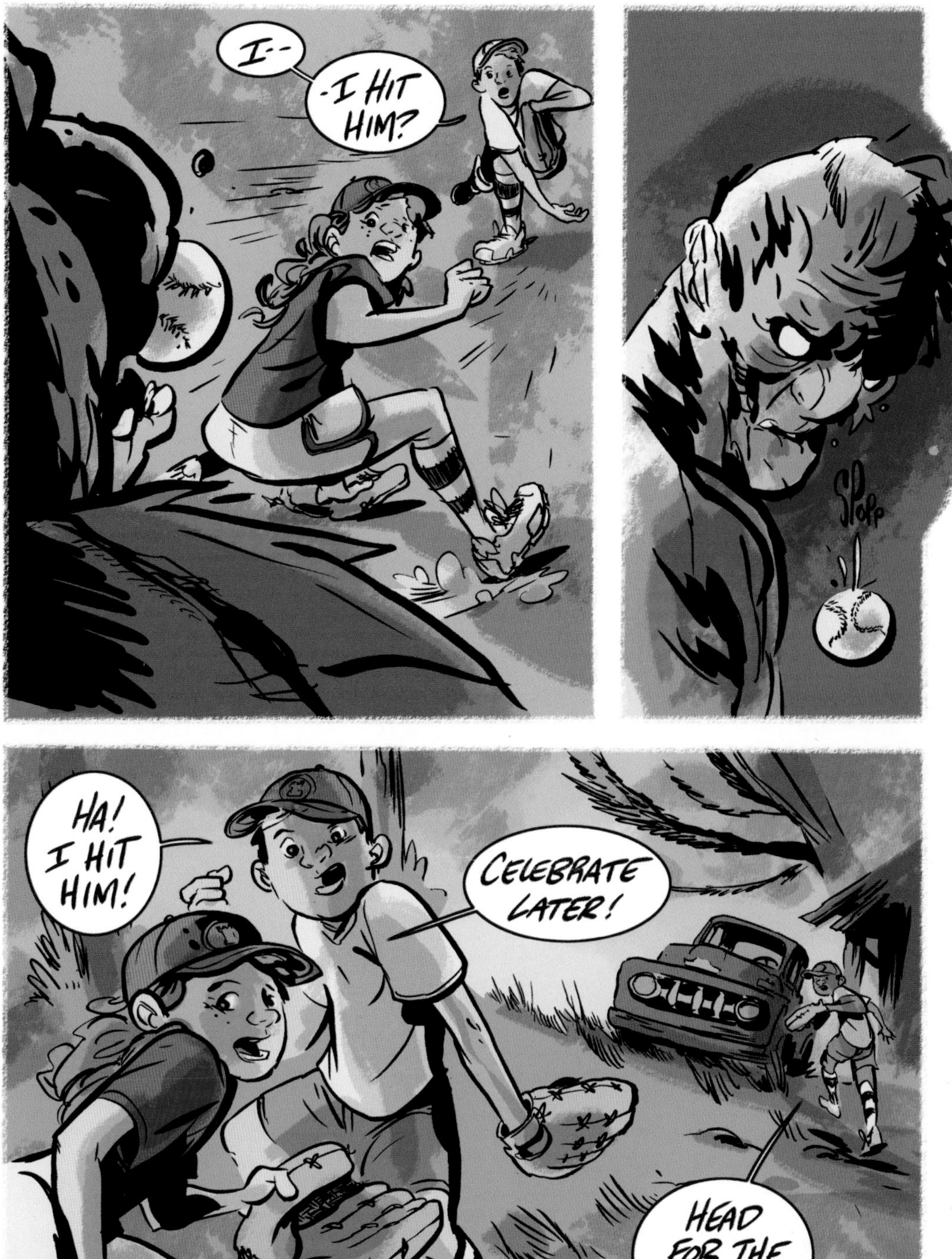
I--
-I HIT HIM?
SPOPP
HA! I HIT HIM!
CELEBRATE LATER!
HEAD FOR THE TRUCK!

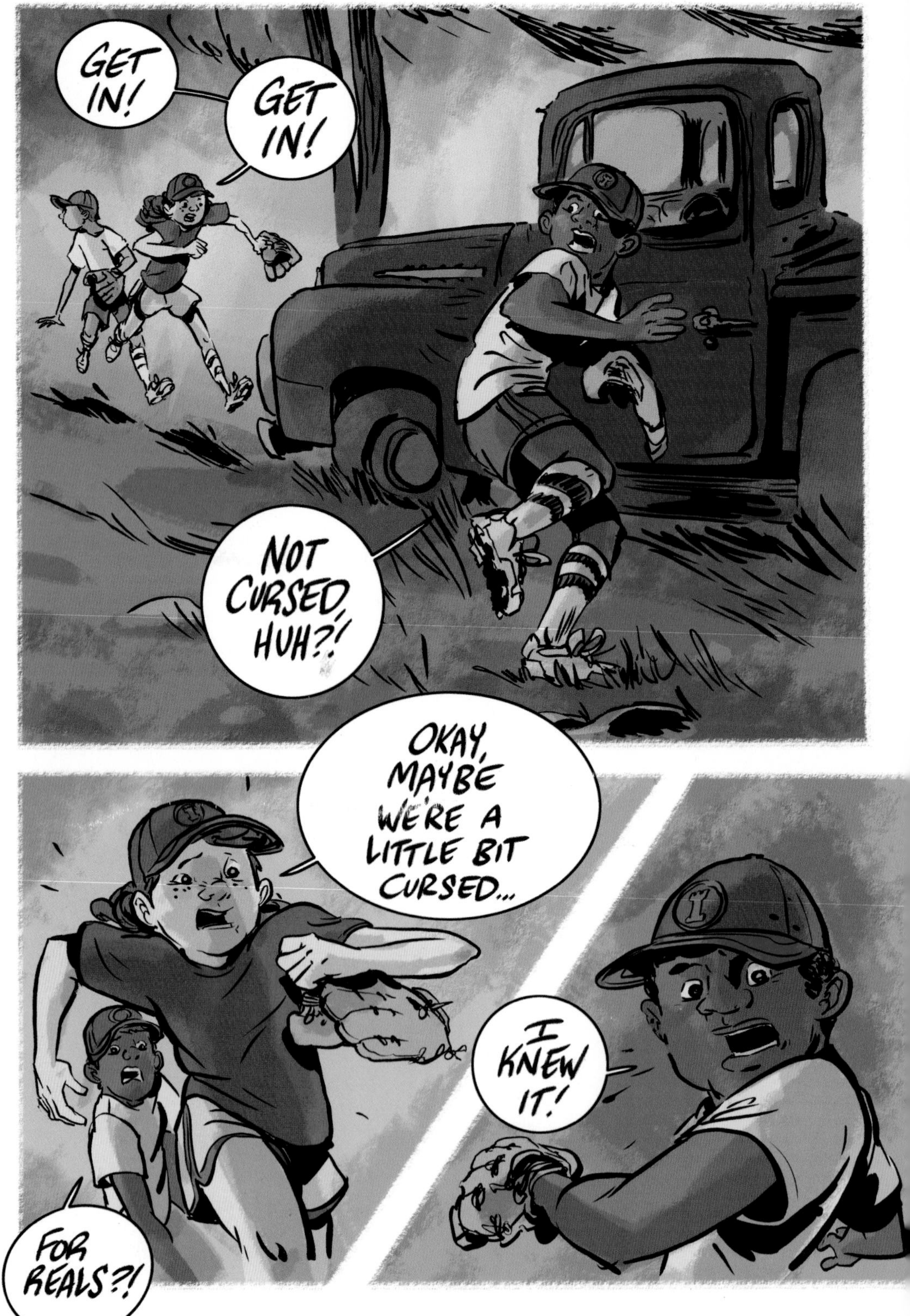
GET IN!
GET IN!
NOT CURSED, HUH?!
OKAY, MAYBE WE'RE A LITTLE BIT CURSED...
FOR REALS?!
I KNEW IT!

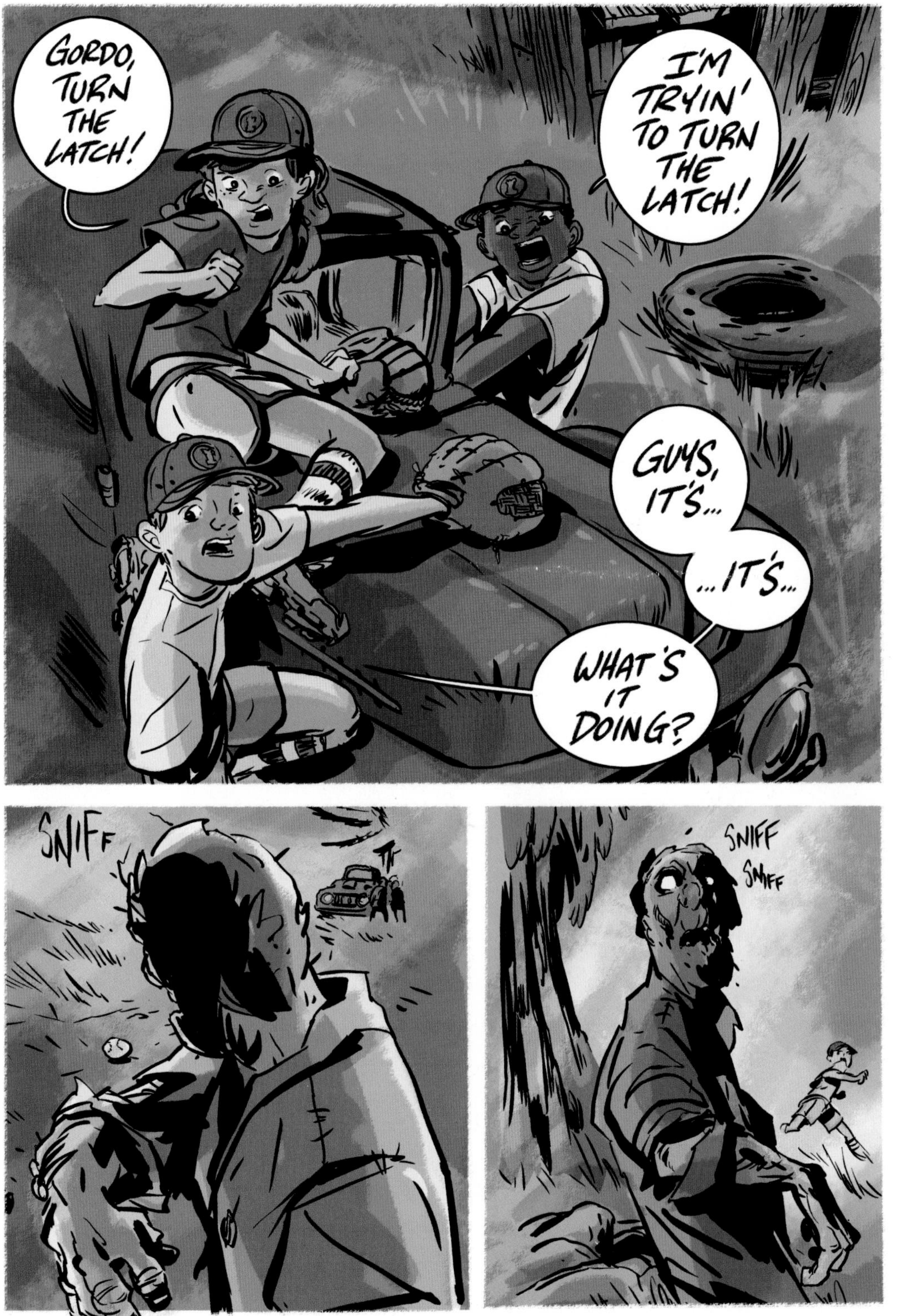
GORDO, TURN THE LATCH!
I'M TRYIN' TO TURN THE LATCH!
GUYS, IT'S...
...IT'S...
WHAT'S IT DOING?
SNIFF
SNIFF
SNIFF

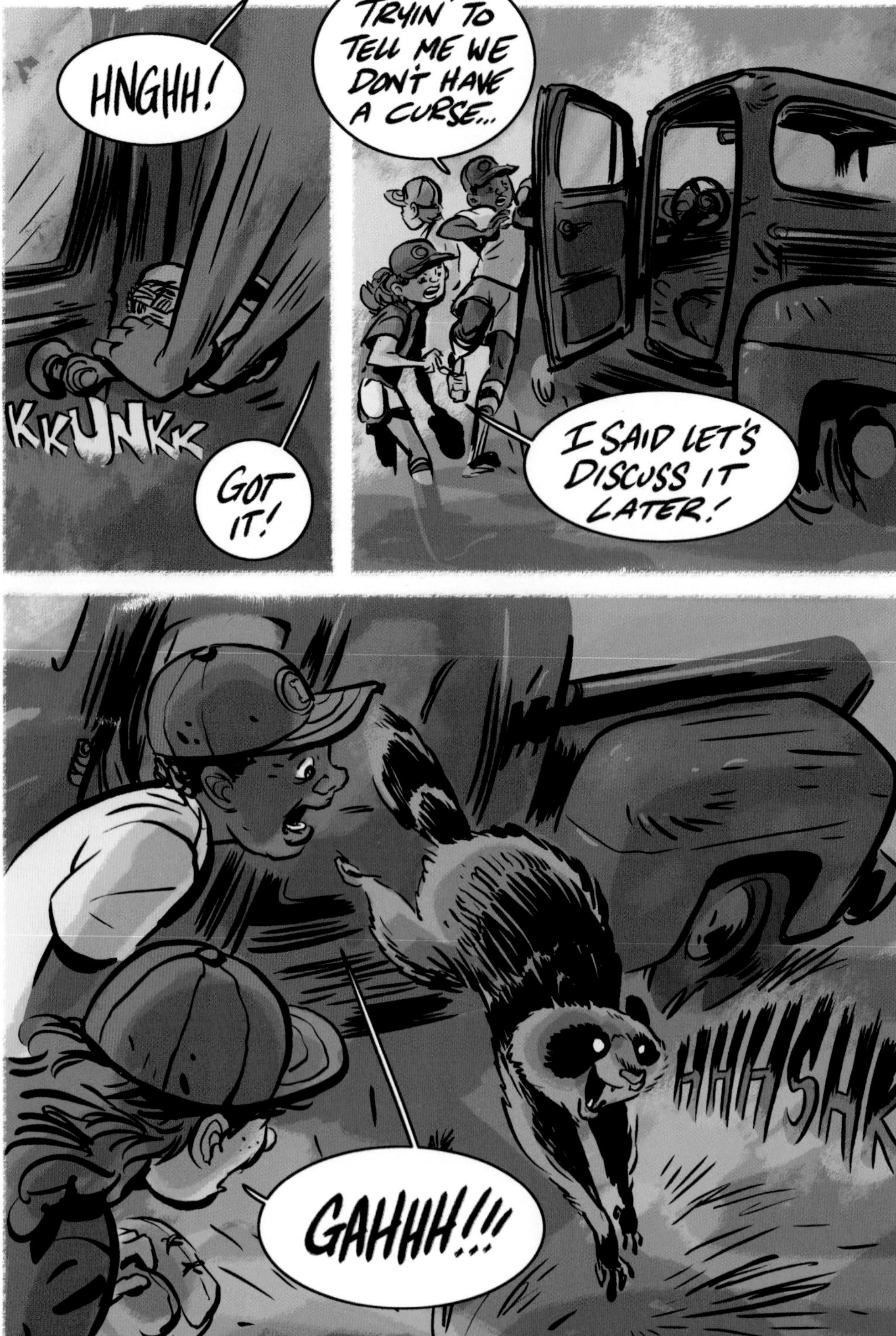
HNGHH!
KKUNKK
GOT IT!
TRYIN' TO TELL ME WE DON'T HAVE A CURSE...
I SAID LET'S DISCUSS IT LATER!
HHHSHK
GAHHH!!!

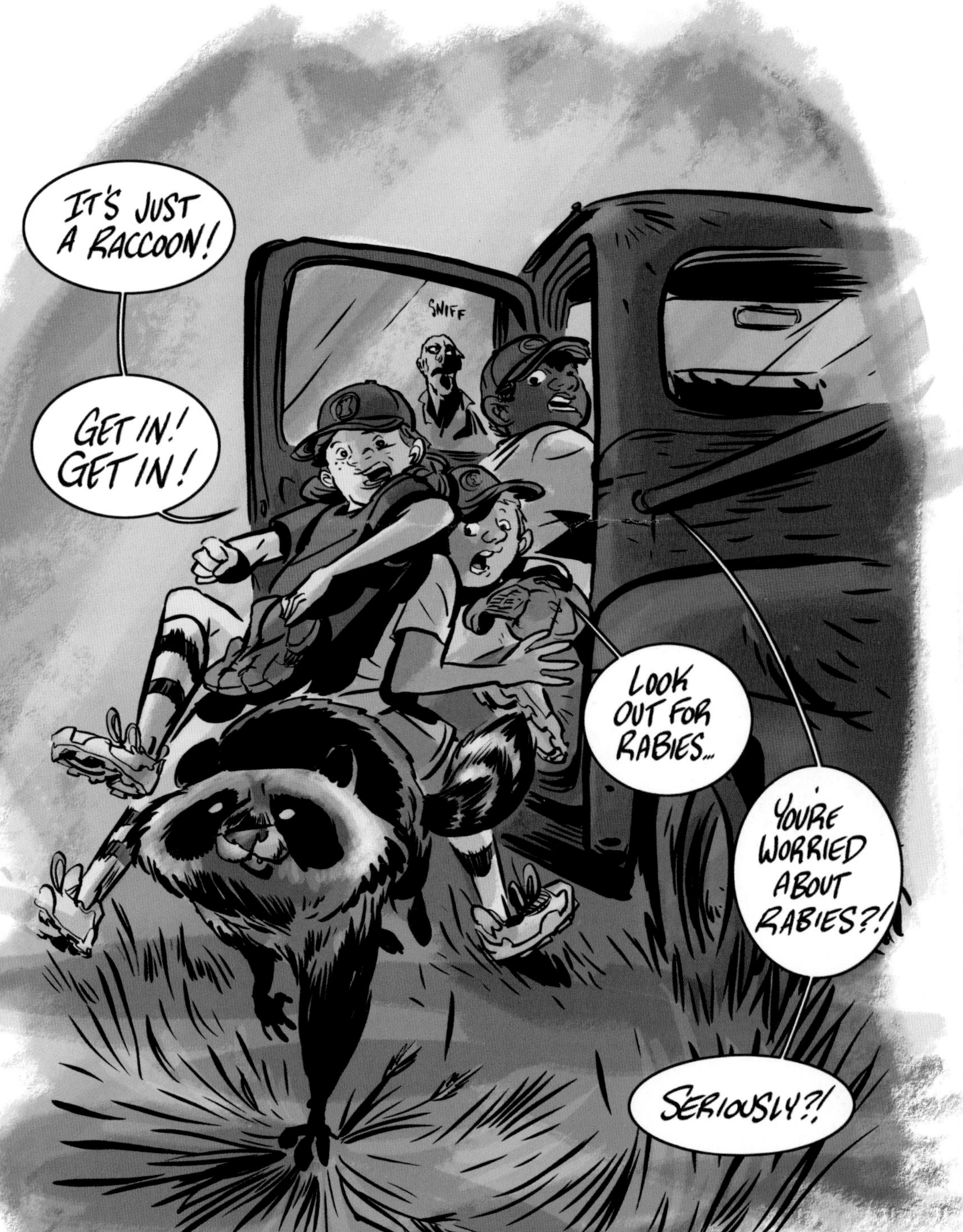
IT'S JUST A RACCOON!
GET IN! GET IN!
SNIFF
LOOK OUT FOR RABIES...
YOU'RE WORRIED ABOUT RABIES?!
SERIOUSLY?!

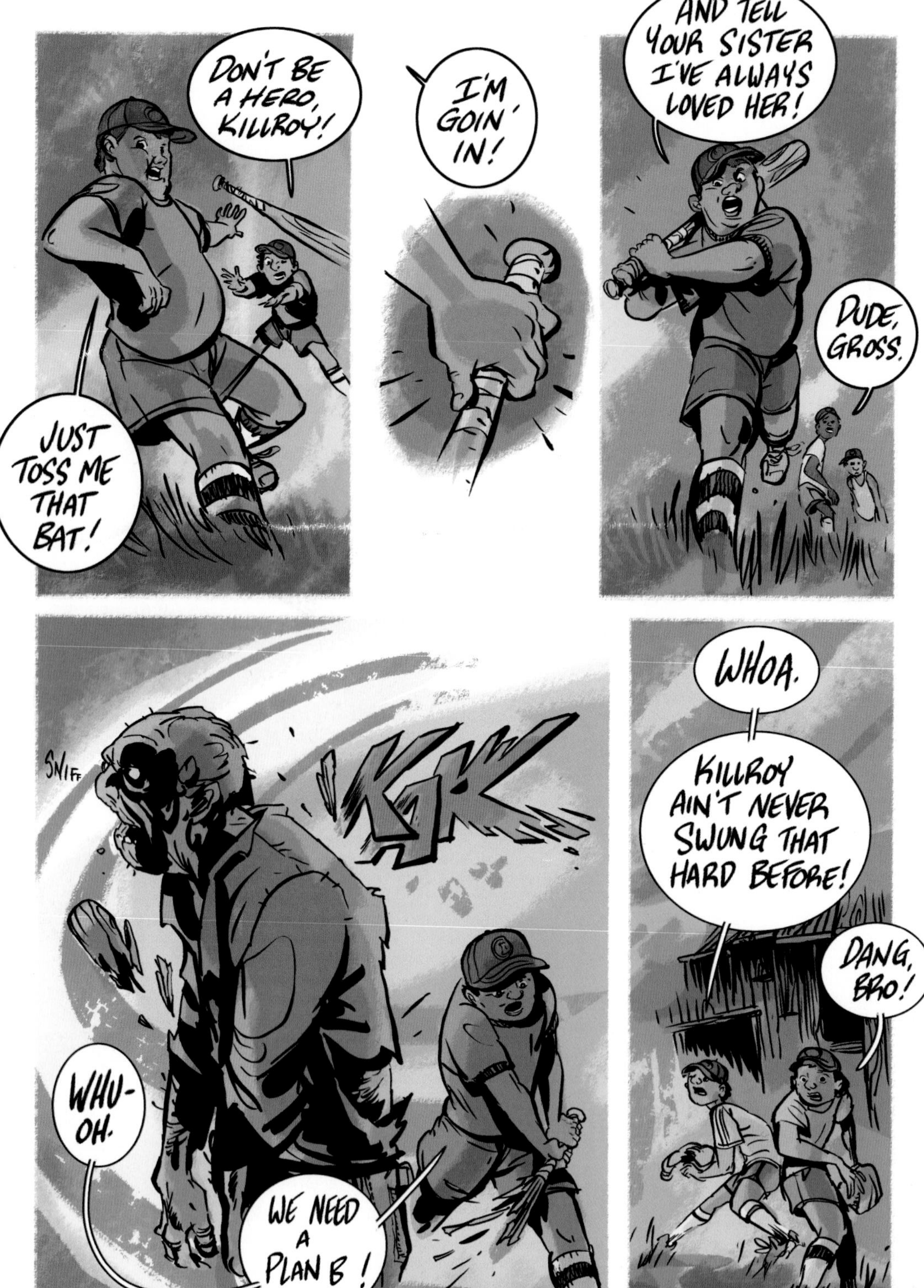
DON'T BE A HERO, KILLROY!
JUST TOSS ME THAT BAT!
I'M GOIN' IN!
AND TELL YOUR SISTER I'VE ALWAYS LOVED HER!
DUDE, GROSS.
SNIFF
KK
WHU-OH.
WE NEED A PLAN B!
WHOA.
KILLROY AIN'T NEVER SWUNG THAT HARD BEFORE!
DANG, BRO!

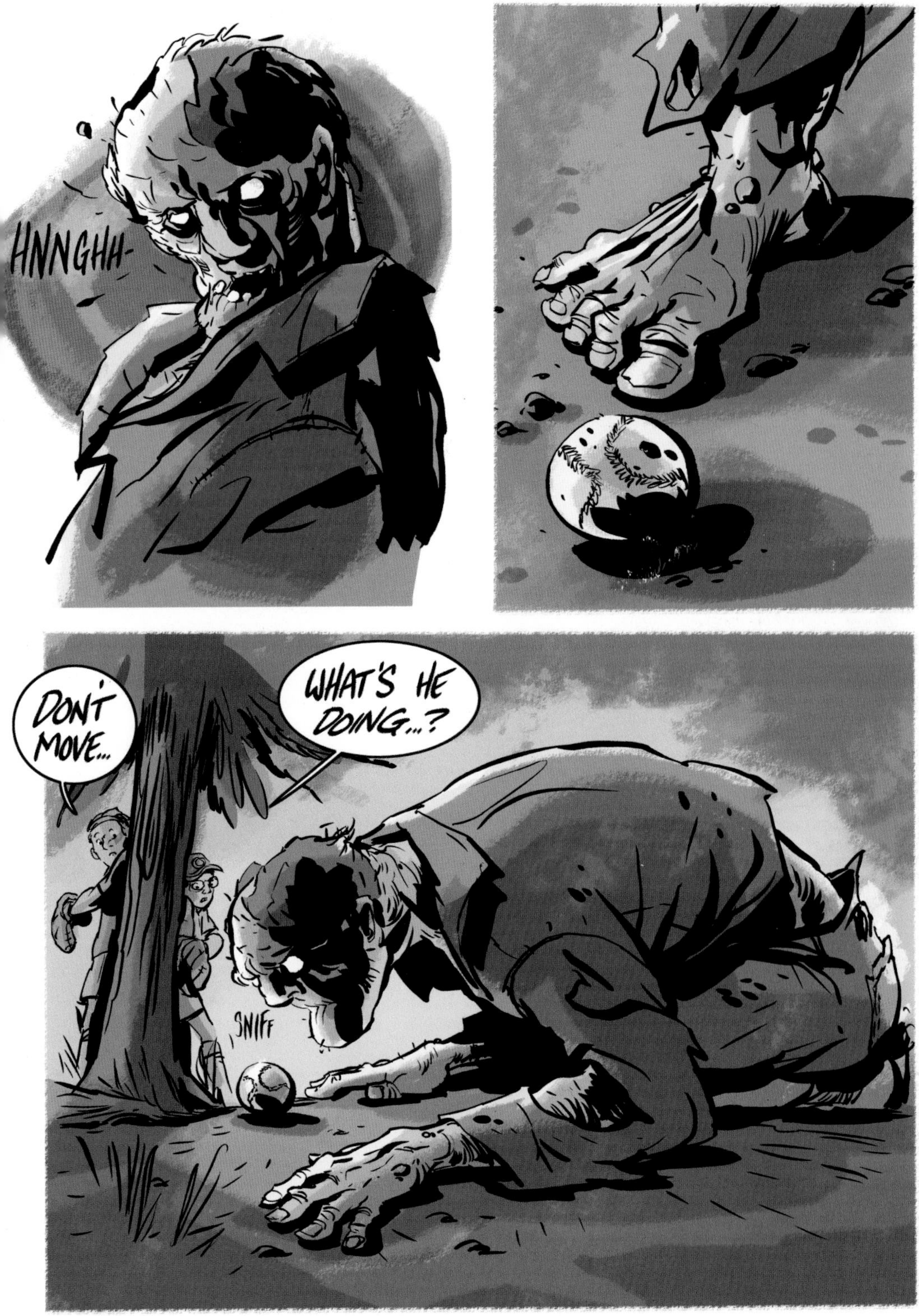
HNNGHH-
DON'T MOVE...
WHAT'S HE DOING...?
SNIFF

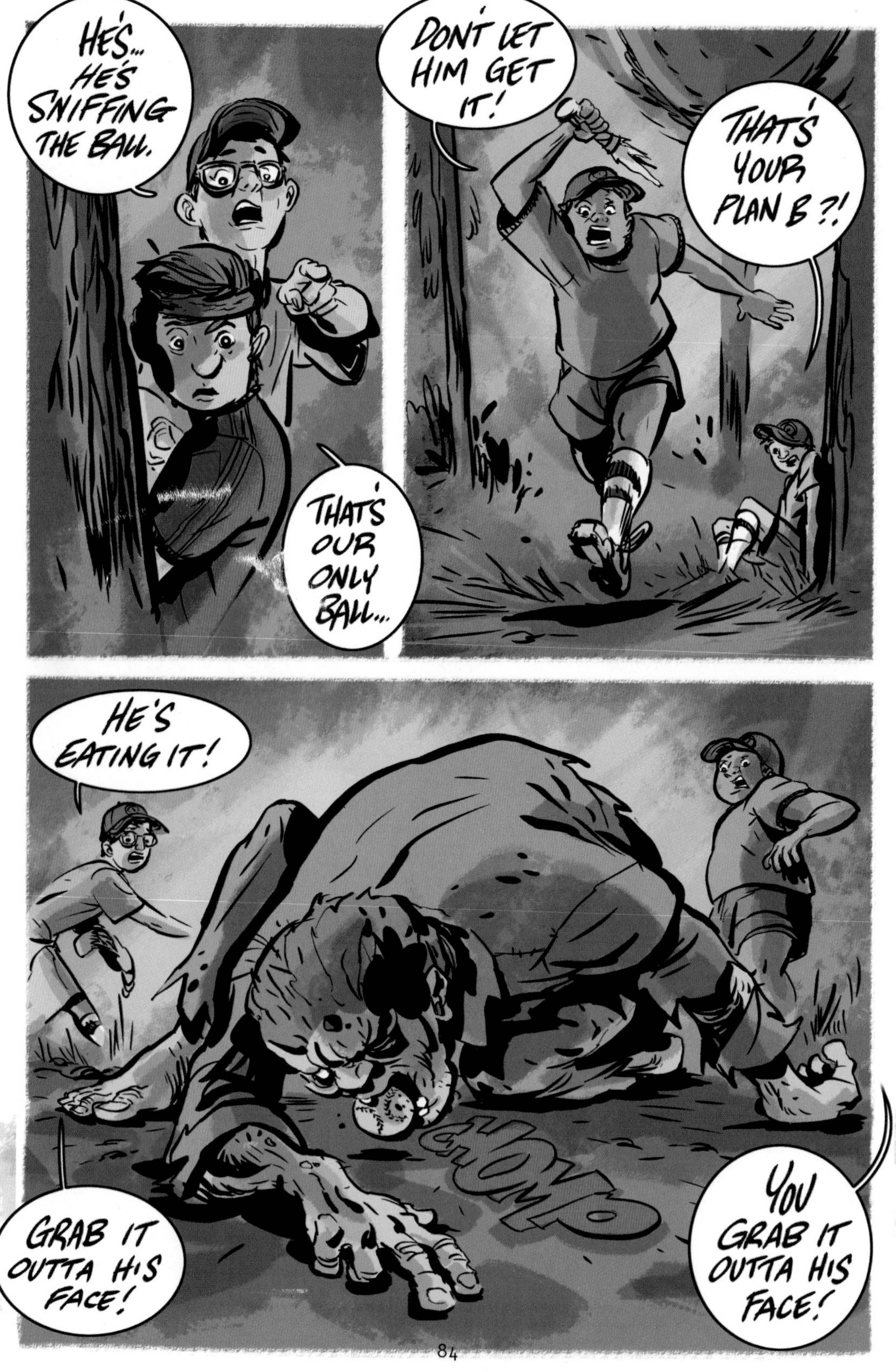
HE'S... HE'S SNIFFING THE BALL.
THAT'S OUR ONLY BALL...
DON'T LET HIM GET IT!
THAT'S YOUR PLAN B ?!
HE'S EATING IT!
CHOMP
GRAB IT OUTTA HIS FACE!
YOU GRAB IT OUTTA HIS FACE!

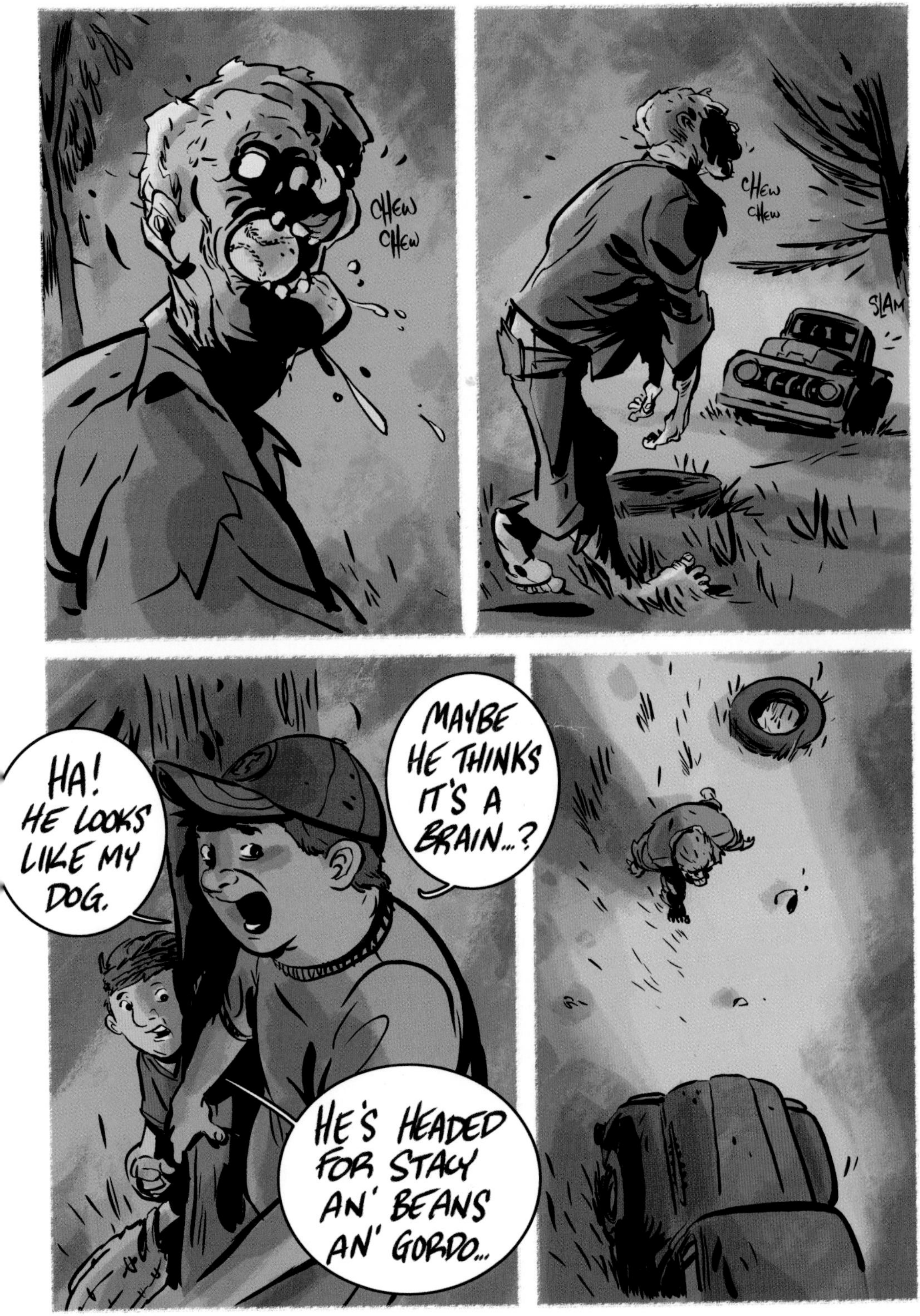
CHEW
CHEW
CHEW
CHEW
SLAM
HA! HE LOOKS LIKE MY DOG.
MAYBE HE THINKS IT'S A BRAIN...?
HE'S HEADED FOR STACY AN' BEANS AN' GORDO...

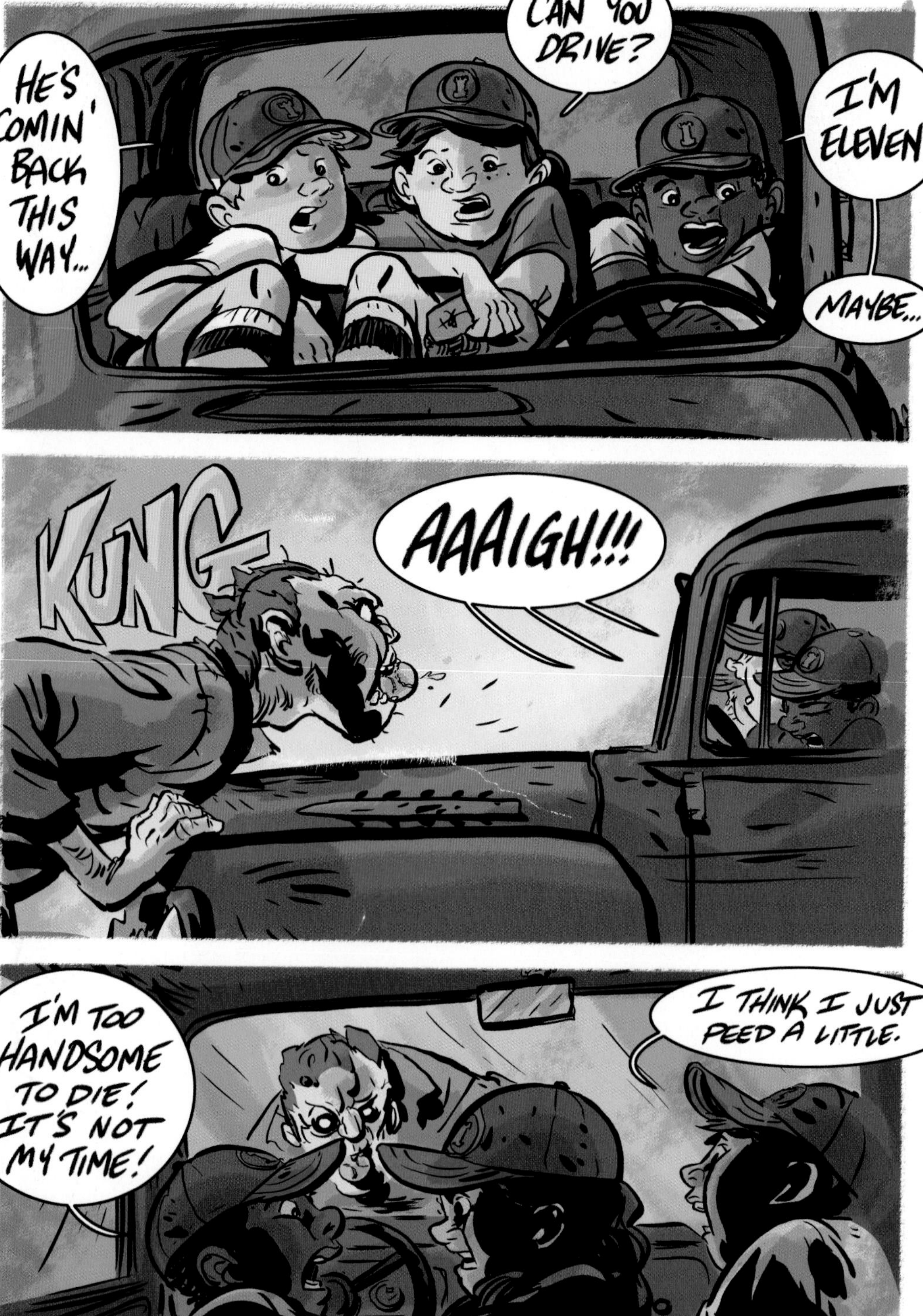
HE'S COMIN' BACK THIS WAY...
CAN YOU DRIVE?
I'M ELEVEN!
MAYBE...
KUNG
AAAIGH!!!
I'M TOO HANDSOME TO DIE! IT'S NOT MY TIME!
I THINK I JUST PEED A LITTLE.

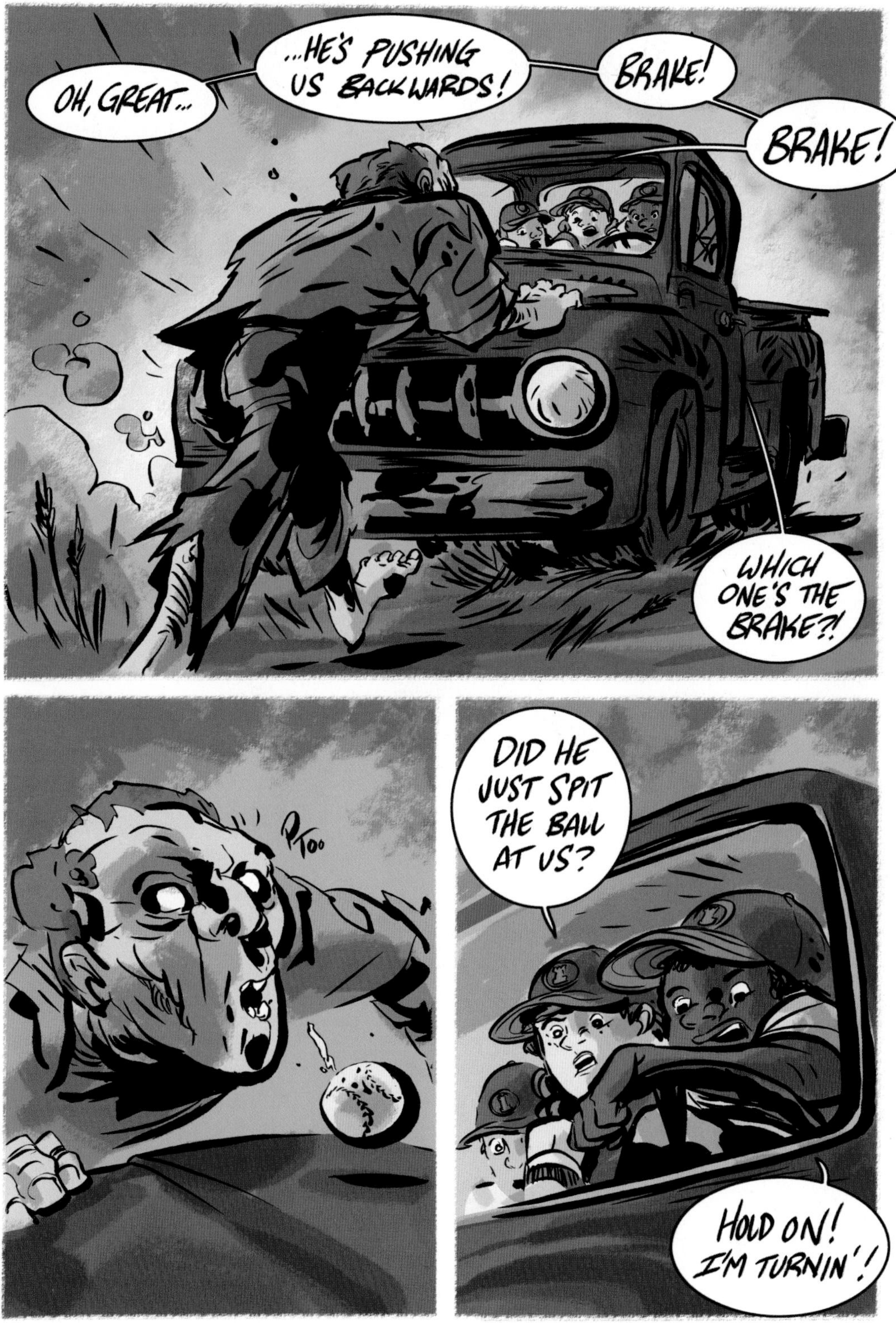
OH, GREAT...
...HE'S PUSHING US BACKWARDS!
BRAKE!
BRAKE!
WHICH ONE'S THE BRAKE?!
PTOO
DID HE JUST SPIT THE BALL AT US?
HOLD ON! I'M TURNIN'!

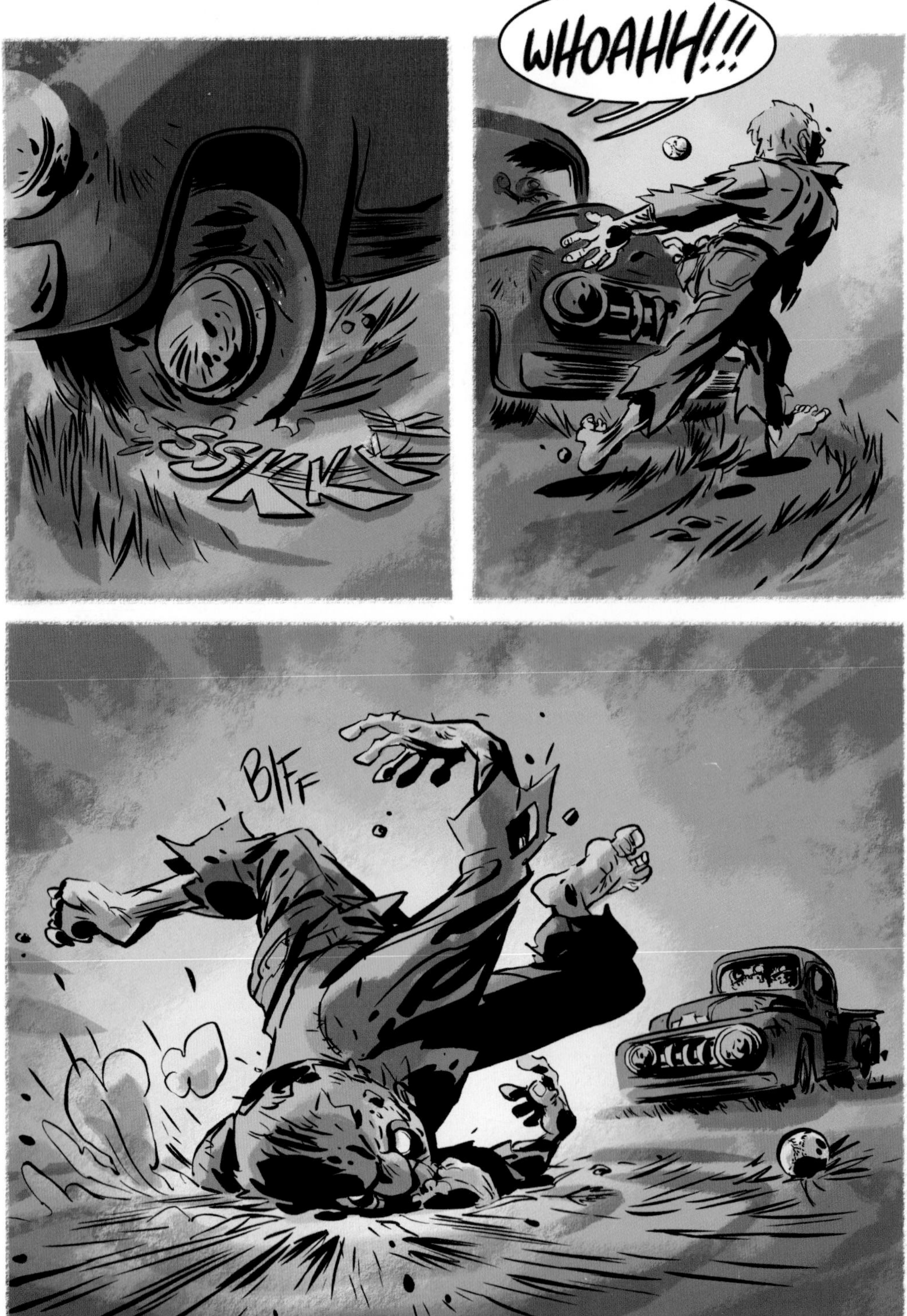
SSKKK
WHOAHH!!!
BIFF

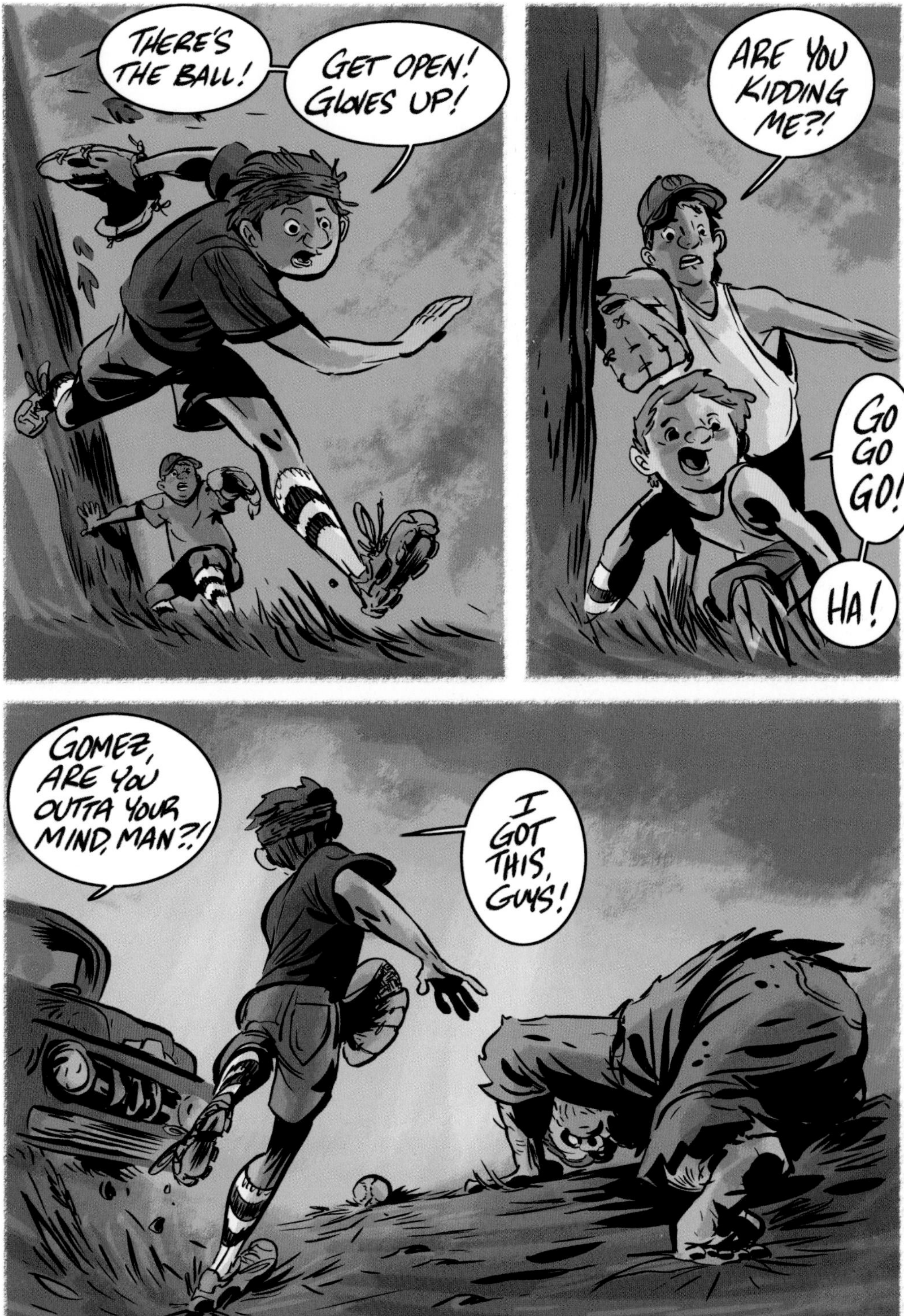
THERE'S THE BALL!
GET OPEN! GLOVES UP!
ARE YOU KIDDING ME?!
GO GO GO!
HA!
GOMEZ, ARE YOU OUTTA YOUR MIND, MAN?!
I GOT THIS, GUYS!

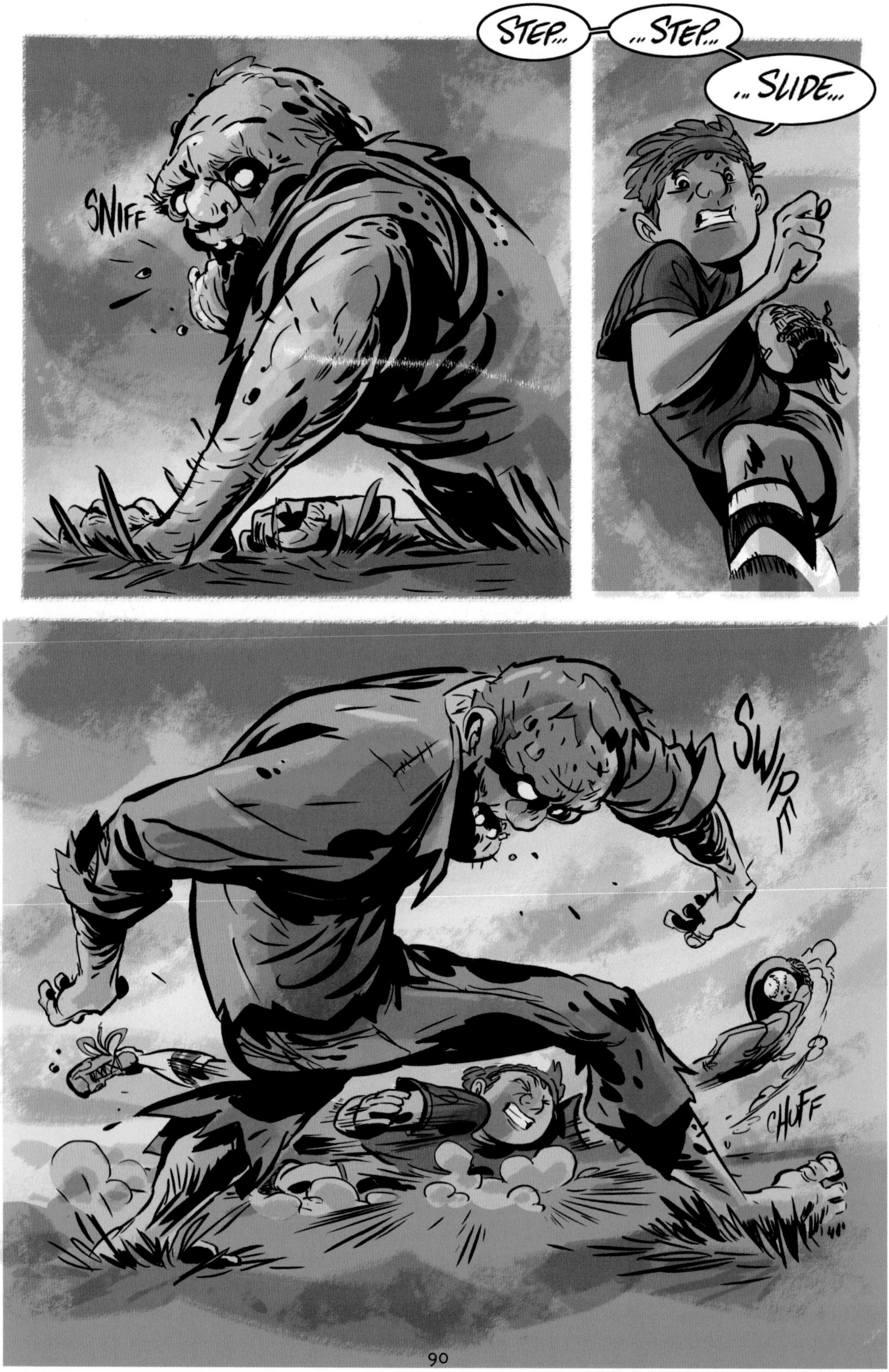
SNIFF
STEP...
...STEP...
...SLIDE...
SWIPE
CHUFF

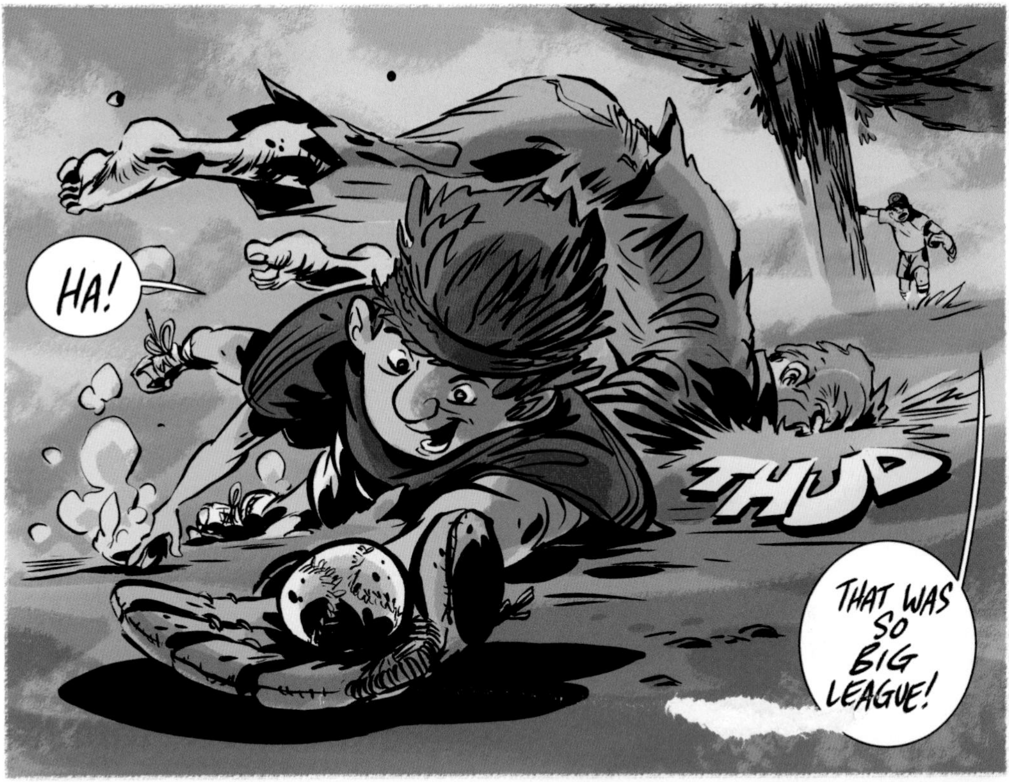
HA!
THUD
THAT WAS SO BIG LEAGUE!

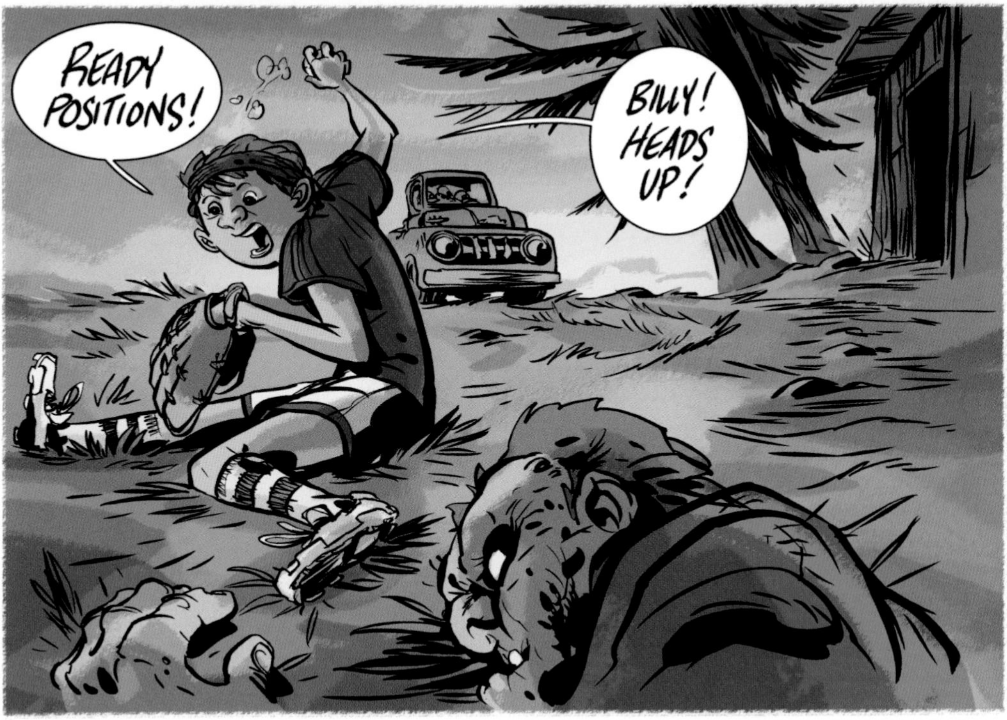
READY POSITIONS!
BILLY! HEADS UP!

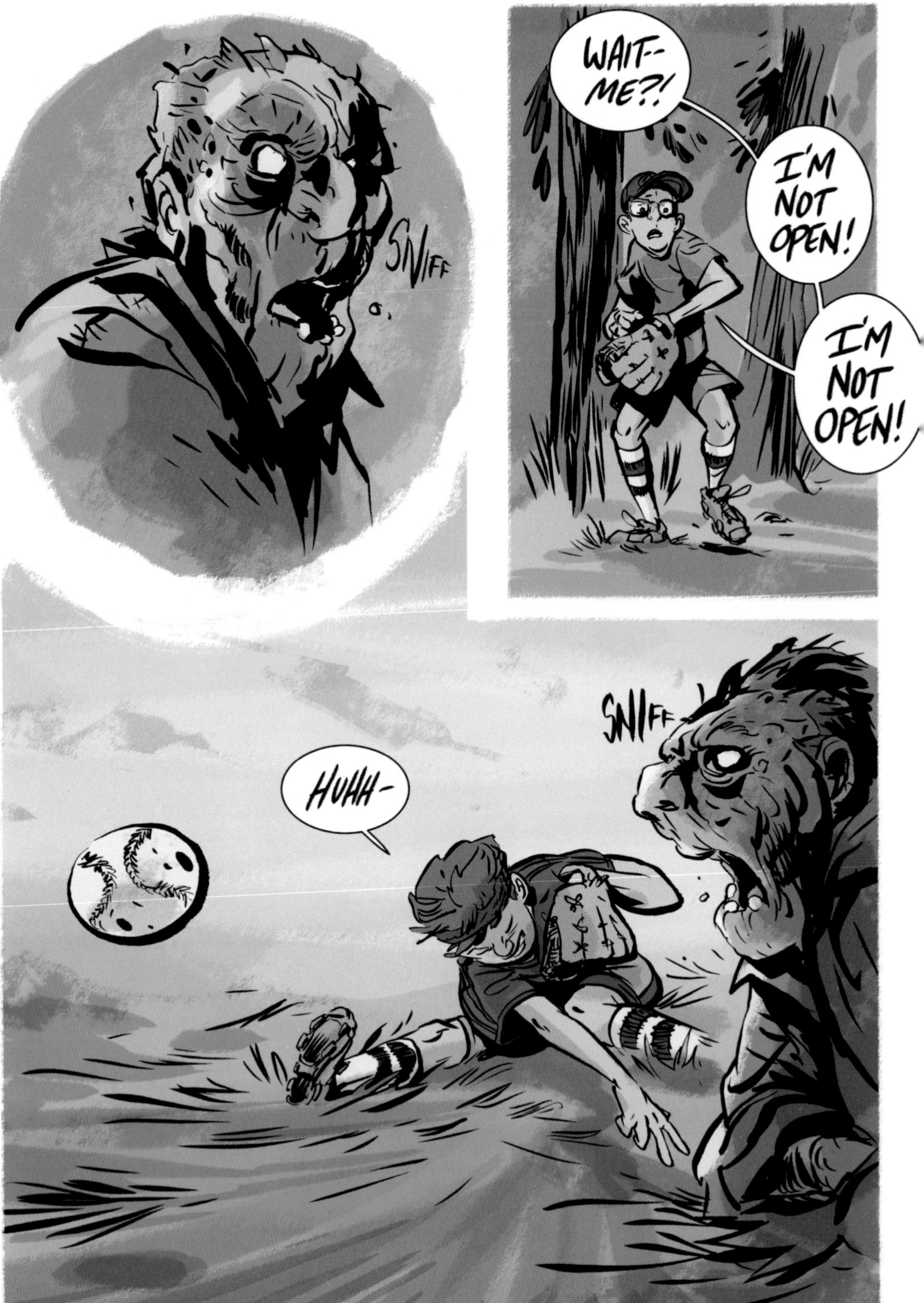
SNIFF
WAIT- ME?!
I'M NOT OPEN!
I'M NOT OPEN!
SNIFF
HUHH-

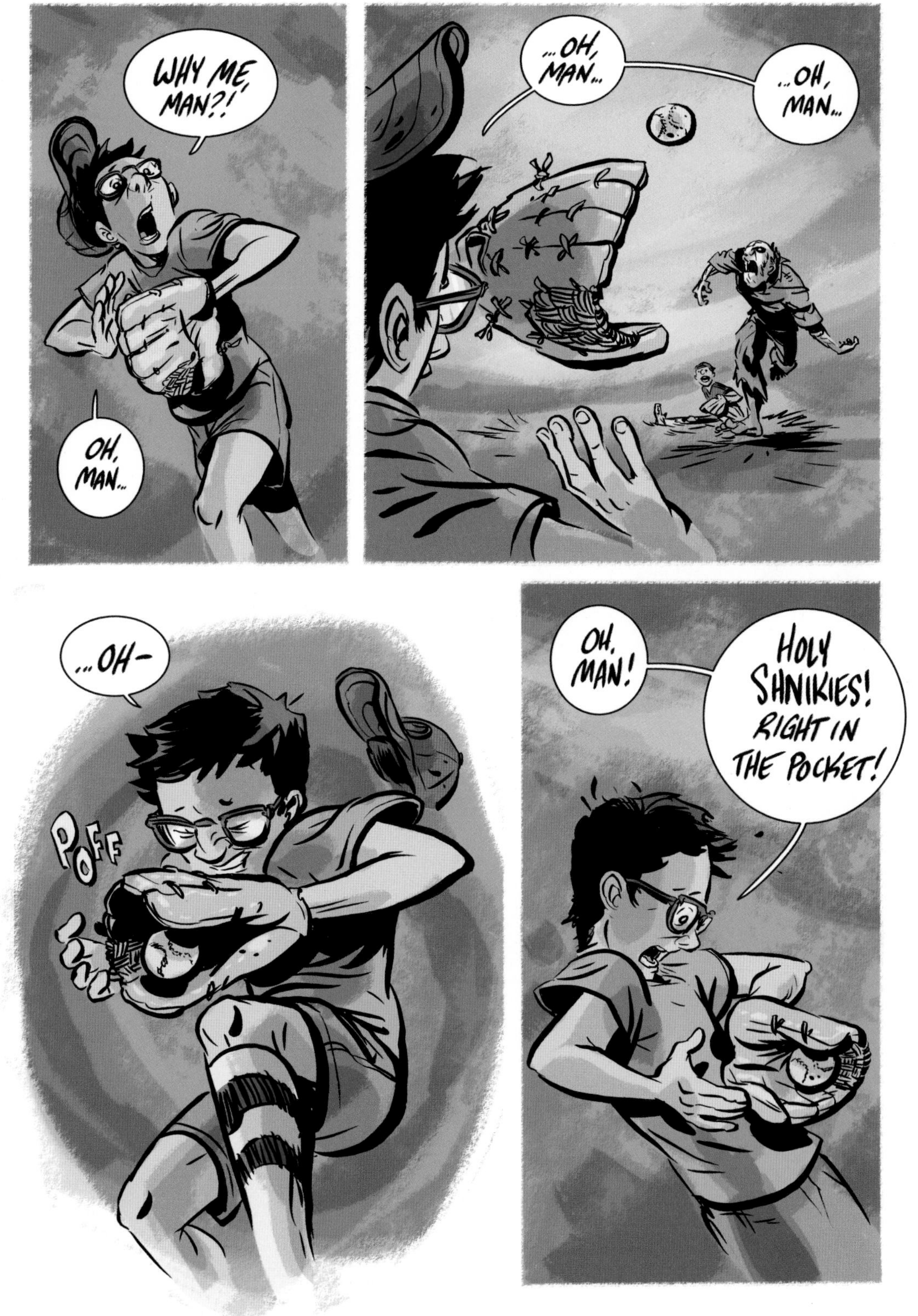
WHY ME, MAN?!
OH, MAN...
...OH, MAN...
...OH, MAN...
...OH-
POFF
OH, MAN!
HOLY SHNIKIES! RIGHT IN THE POCKET!

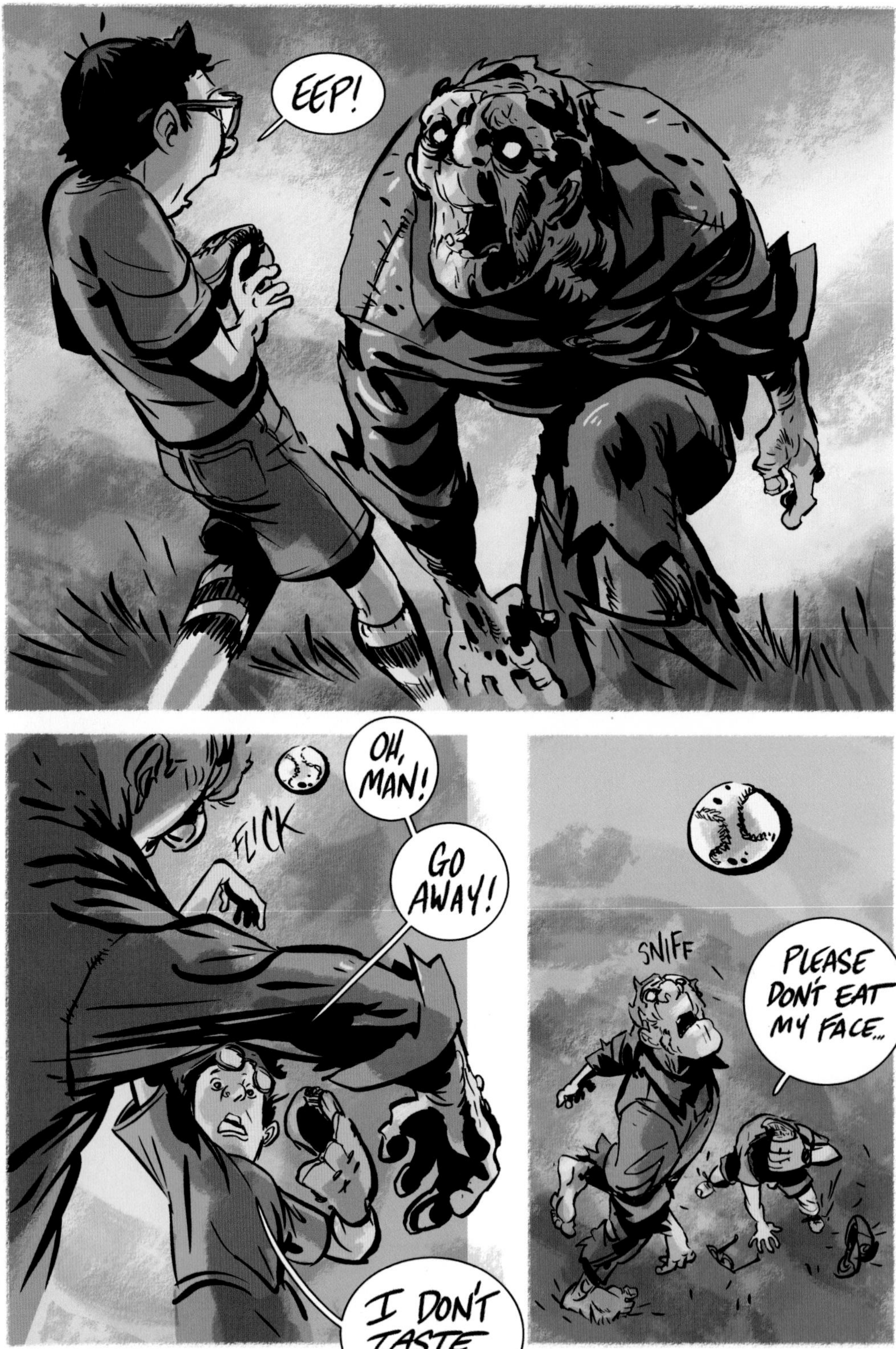
EEP!
OH, MAN!
FLICK
GO AWAY!
I DON'T TASTE GOOD!
SNIFF
PLEASE DON'T EAT MY FACE...

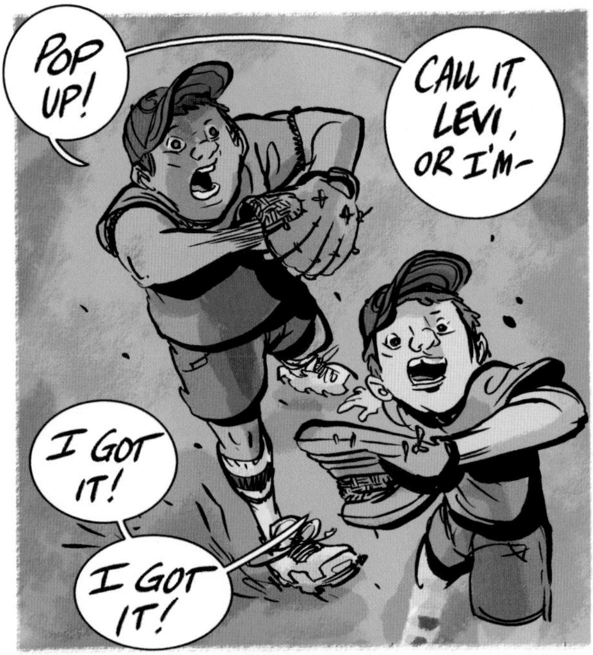
POP UP!
CALL IT, LEVI, OR I'M-
I GOT IT!
I GOT IT!

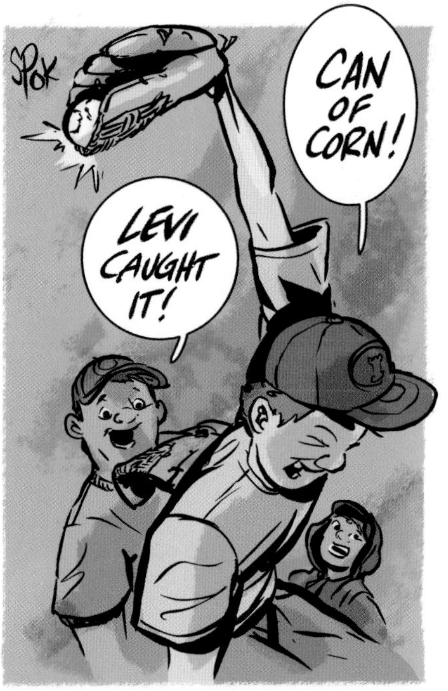
SPOK
CAN OF CORN!
LEVI CAUGHT IT!

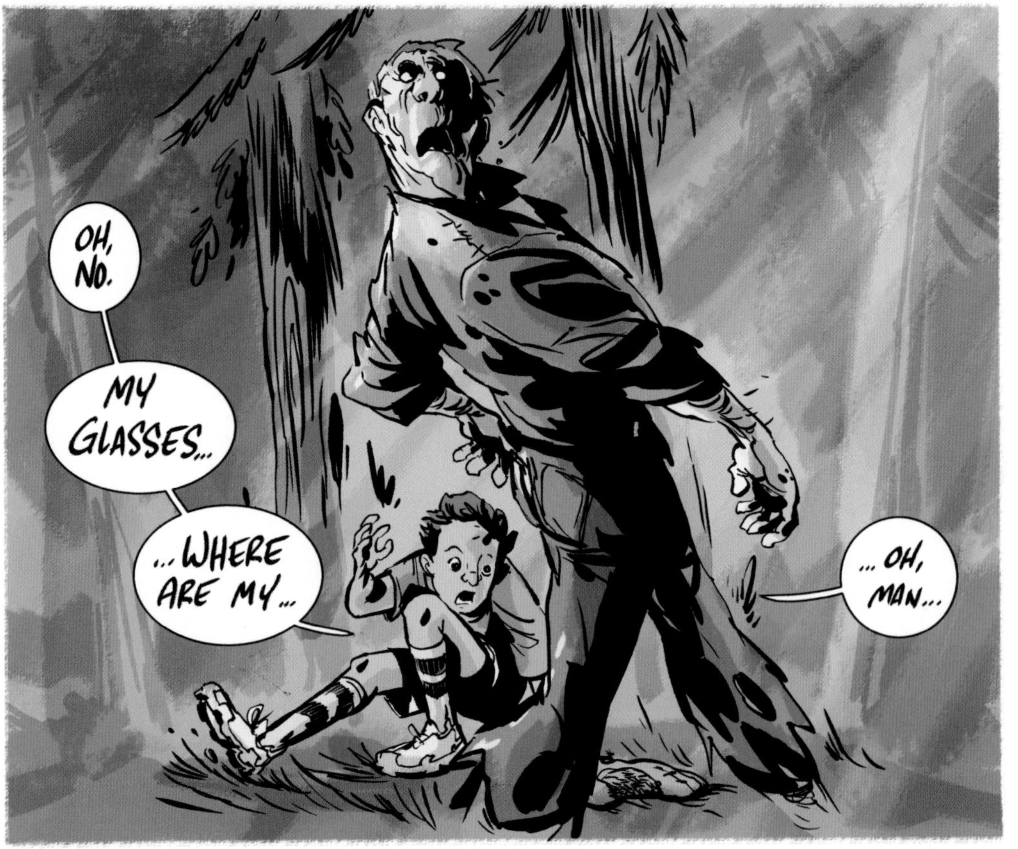
OH, NO.
MY GLASSES...
...WHERE ARE MY...
...OH, MAN...

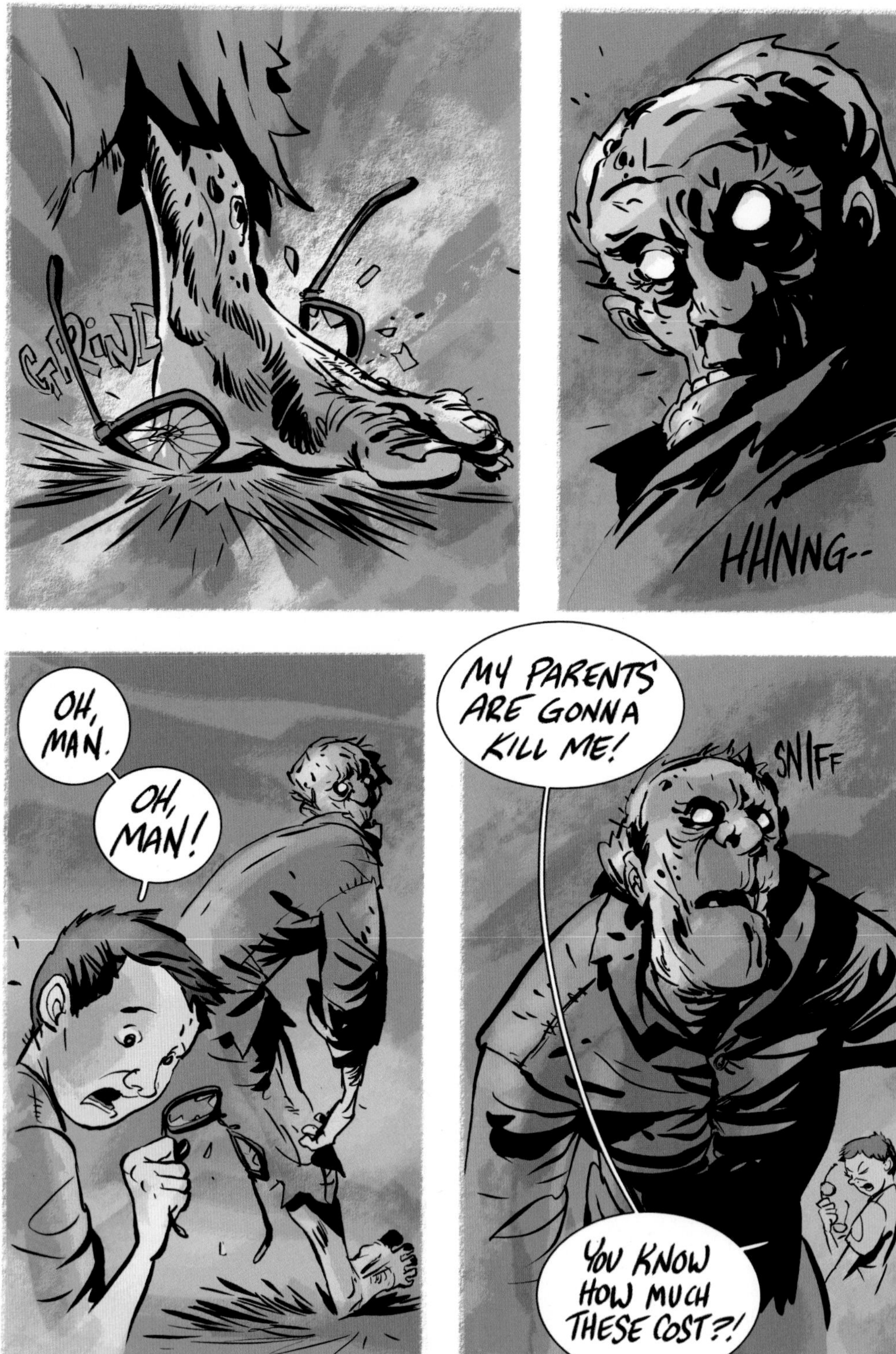
GRIND
HHNNG--
OH, MAN.
OH, MAN!
MY PARENTS ARE GONNA KILL ME!
SNIFF
YOU KNOW HOW MUCH THESE COST?!

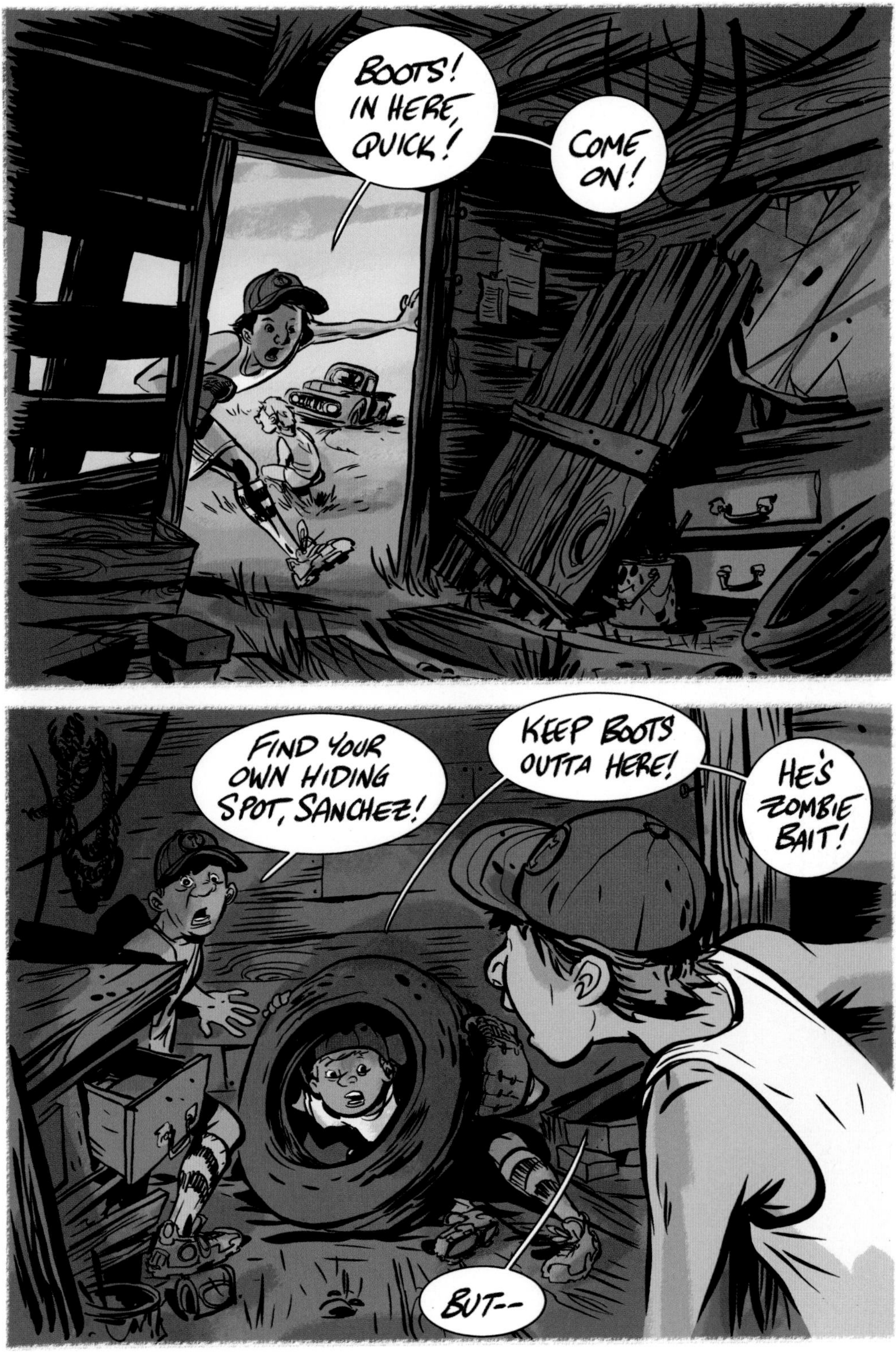

BOOTS! IN HERE, QUICK!
COME ON!
FIND YOUR OWN HIDING SPOT, SANCHEZ!
KEEP BOOTS OUTTA HERE!
HE'S ZOMBIE BAIT!
BUT--

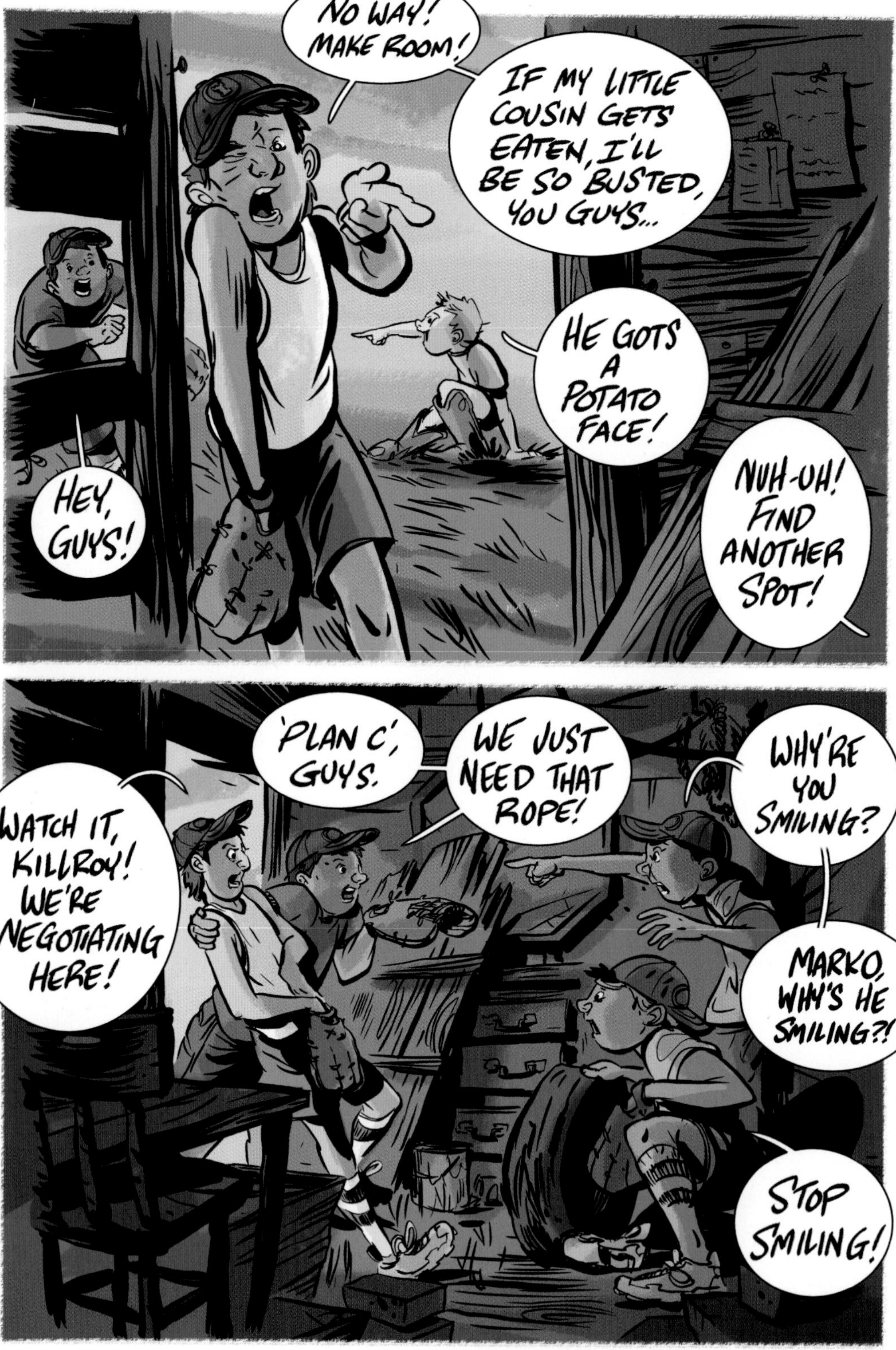

NO WAY! MAKE ROOM!
IF MY LITTLE COUSIN GETS EATEN, I'LL BE SO BUSTED, YOU GUYS...
HEY, GUYS!
HE GOTS A POTATO FACE!
NUH-UH! FIND ANOTHER SPOT!
WATCH IT, KILLROY! WE'RE NEGOTIATING HERE!
'PLAN C', GUYS.
WE JUST NEED THAT ROPE!
WHY'RE YOU SMILING?
MARKO, WHY'S HE SMILING?!
STOP SMILING!

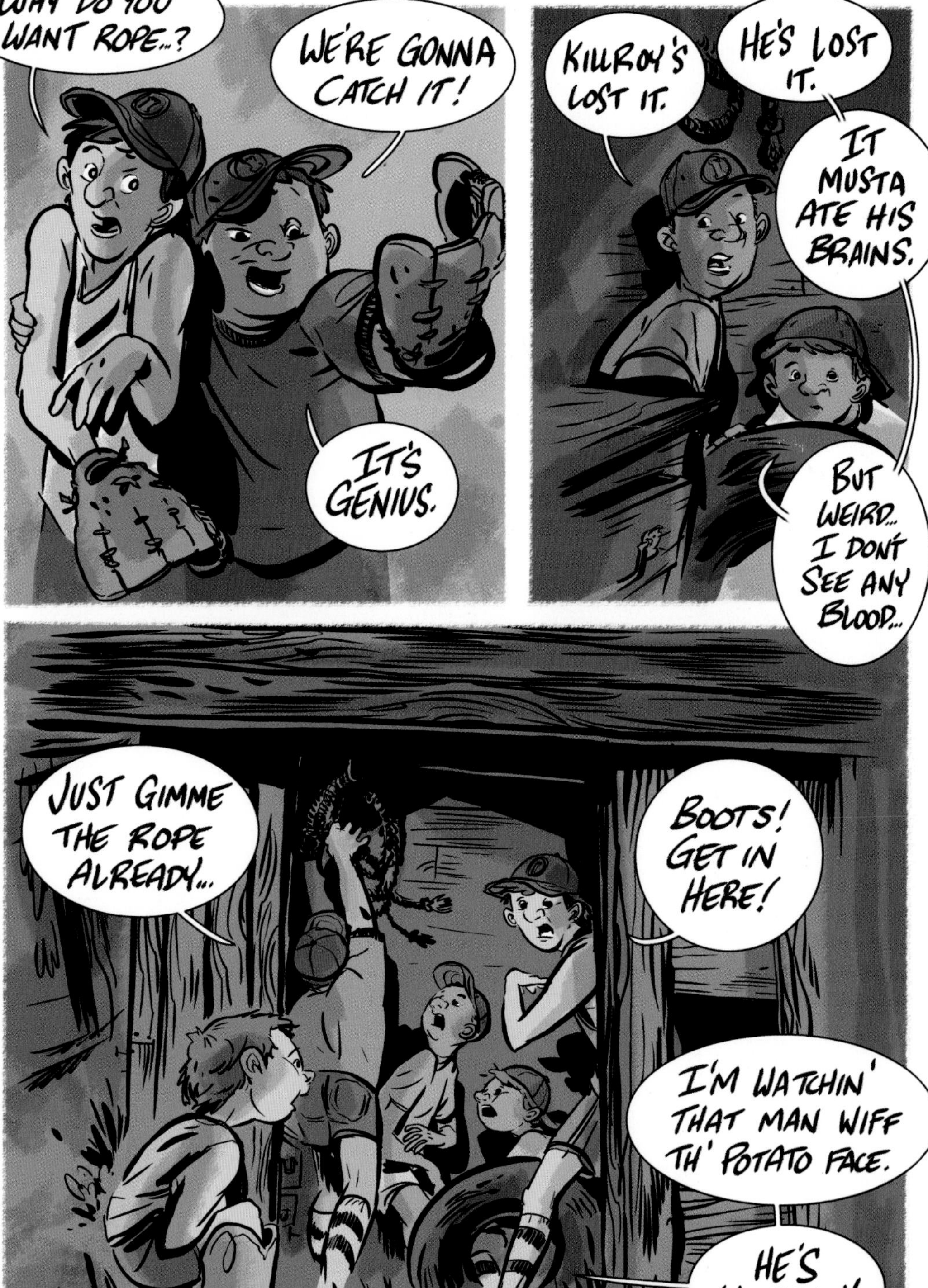
WHY DO YOU WANT ROPE...?
WE'RE GONNA CATCH IT!
IT'S GENIUS.
KILLROY'S LOST IT.
HE'S LOST IT.
IT MUSTA ATE HIS BRAINS.
BUT WEIRD... I DON'T SEE ANY BLOOD...
JUST GIMME THE ROPE ALREADY...
BOOTS! GET IN HERE!
I'M WATCHIN' THAT MAN WIFF TH' POTATO FACE.
HE'S WOBBLY!

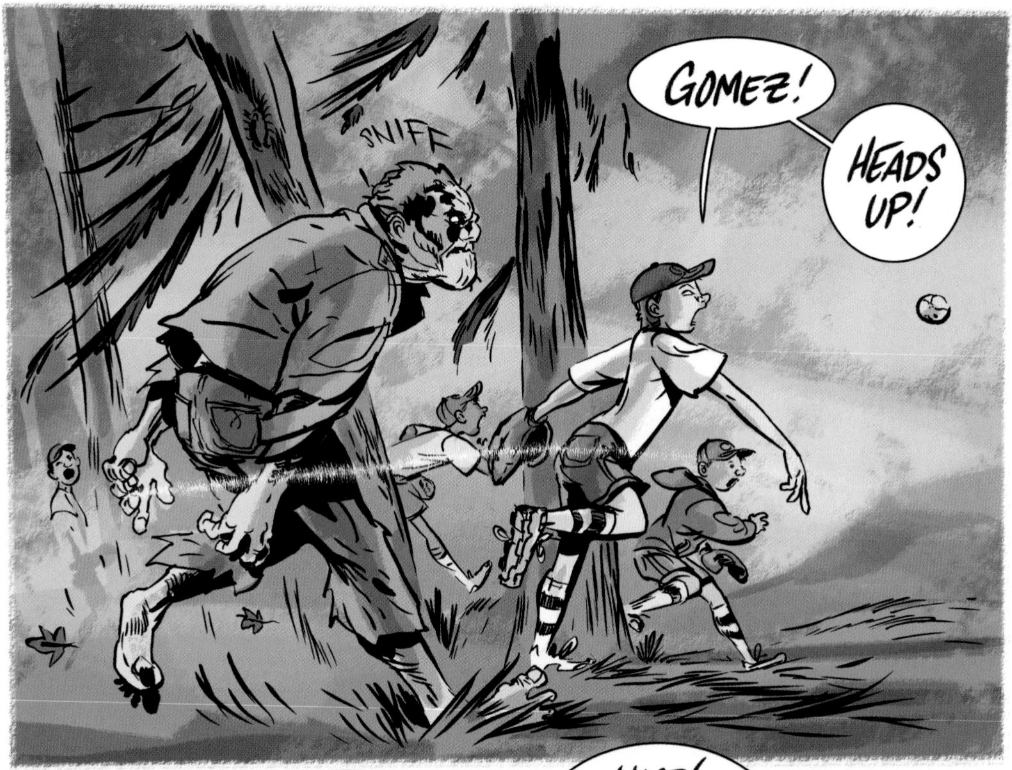
SNIFF
GOMEZ!
HEADS UP!

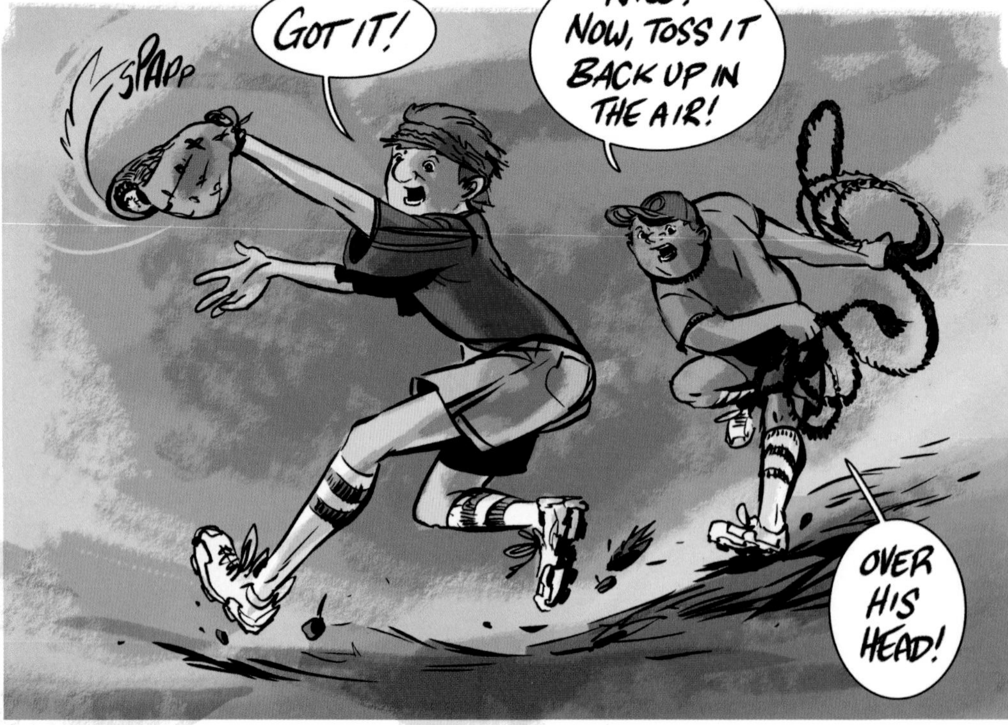
SPAPP
GOT IT!
NICE! NOW, TOSS IT BACK UP IN THE AIR!
OVER HIS HEAD!

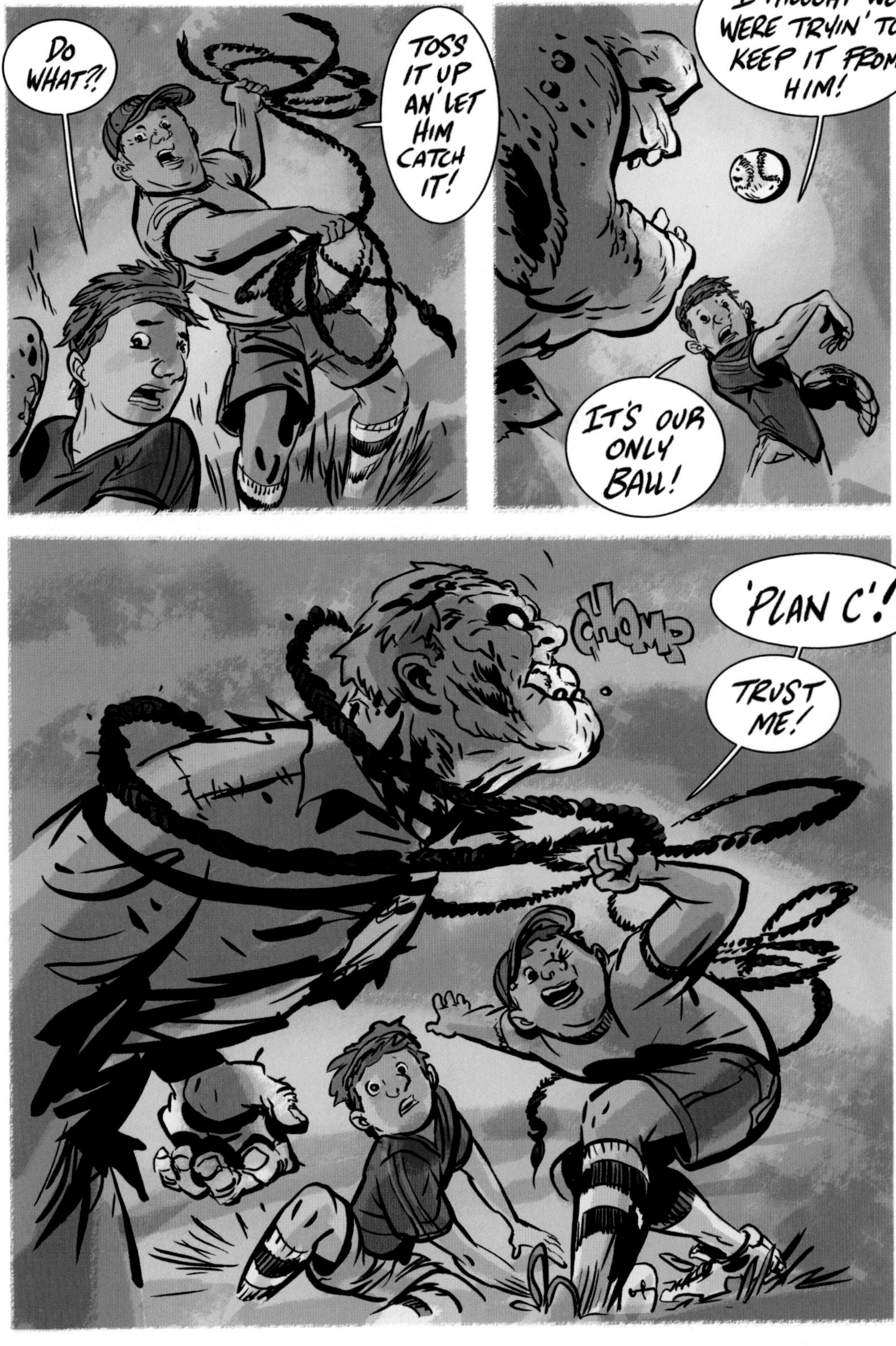
DO WHAT?!
TOSS IT UP AN' LET HIM CATCH IT!
I THOUGHT WE WERE TRYIN' TO KEEP IT FROM HIM!
IT'S OUR ONLY BALL!
CHOMP
'PLAN C'!
TRUST ME!

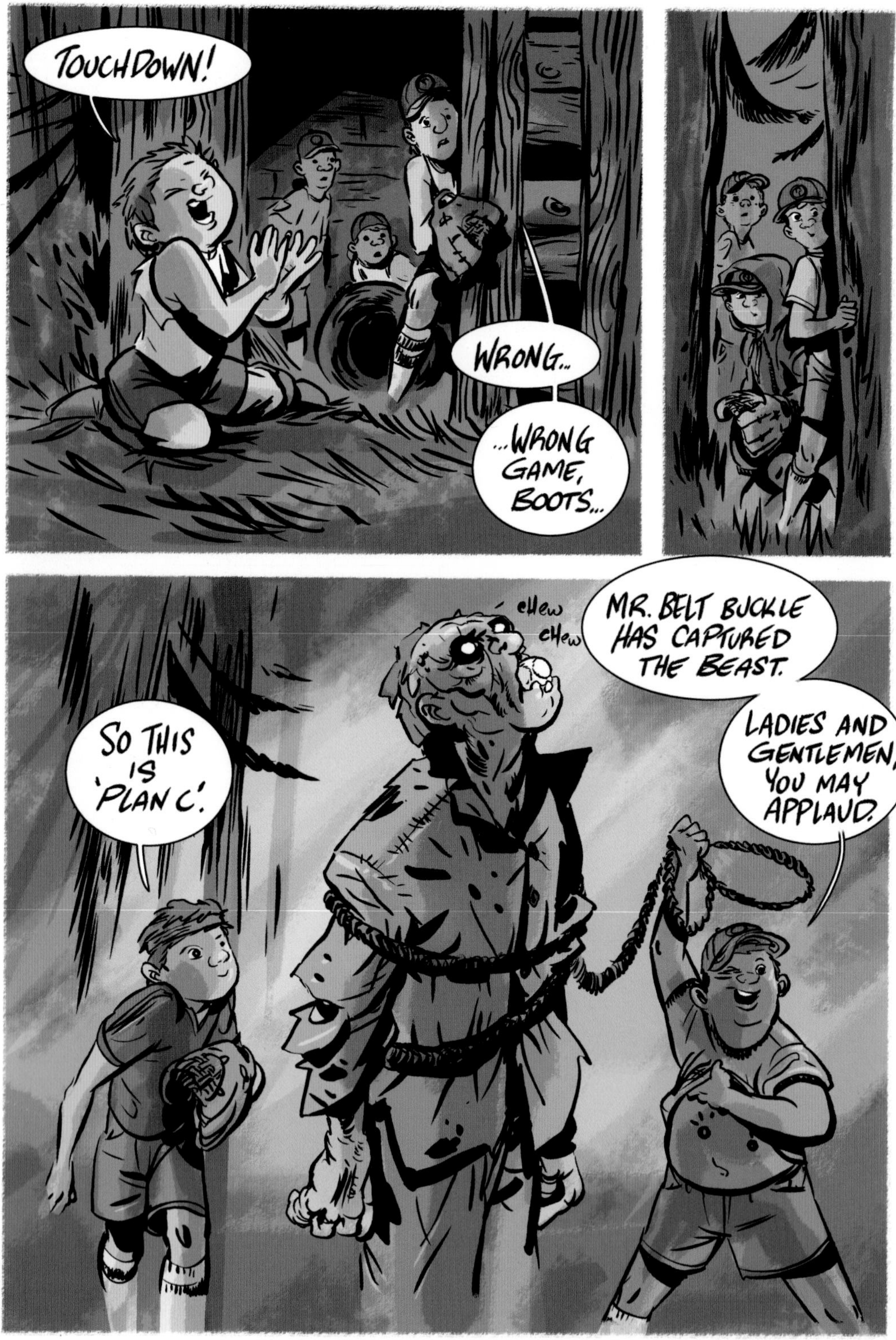
TOUCHDOWN!
WRONG...
...WRONG GAME, BOOTS...
chew chew
MR. BELT BUCKLE HAS CAPTURED THE BEAST.
LADIES AND GENTLEMEN, YOU MAY APPLAUD.
SO THIS IS 'PLAN C'.

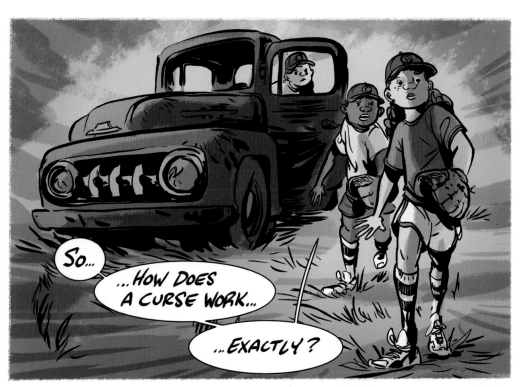

So...

...HOW DOES A CURSE WORK...

...EXACTLY?

FAMILY SECRET.

HE STINKS.

LIKE, OFFICIALLY. THE WORST STINK.

CHEW CHEW

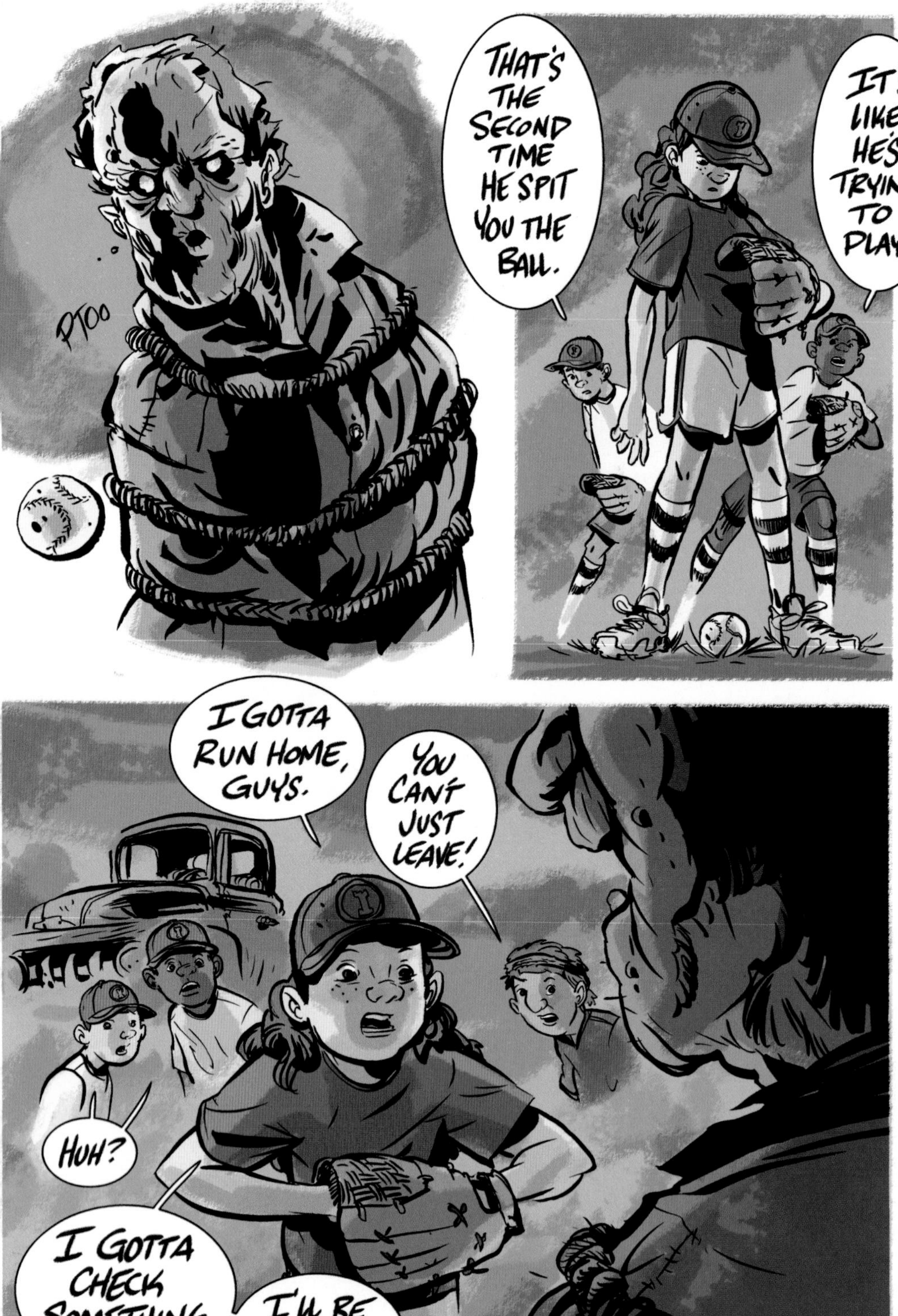
PTOO
THAT'S THE SECOND TIME HE SPIT YOU THE BALL.
IT'S LIKE HE'S TRYIN' TO PLAY.
I GOTTA RUN HOME, GUYS.
YOU CAN'T JUST LEAVE!
HUH?
I GOTTA CHECK SOMETHING.
I'LL BE BACK IN AN HOUR.

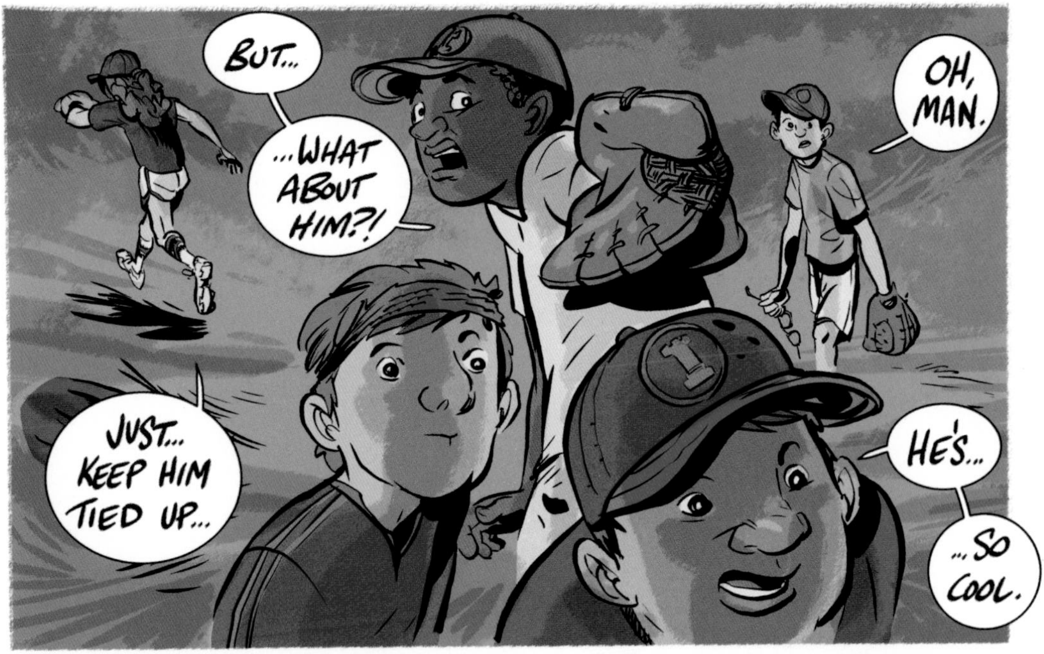
BUT...
...WHAT ABOUT HIM?!
OH, MAN.
JUST... KEEP HIM TIED UP...
HE'S...
...SO COOL.

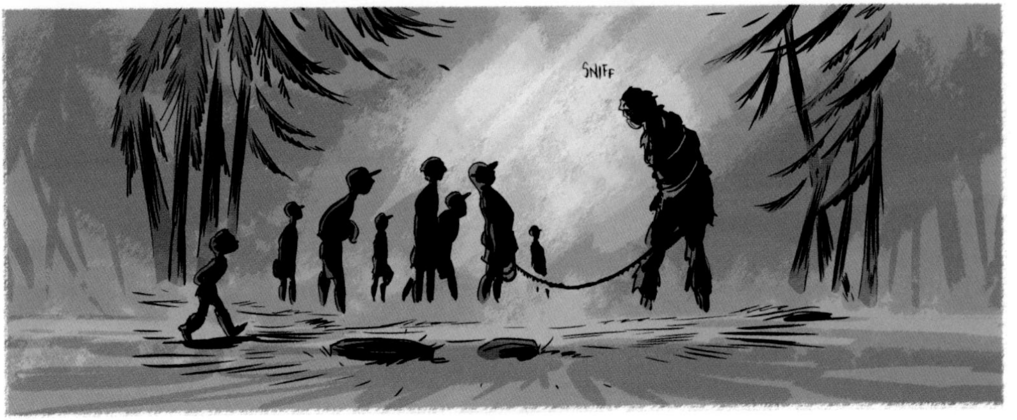
SNIFF

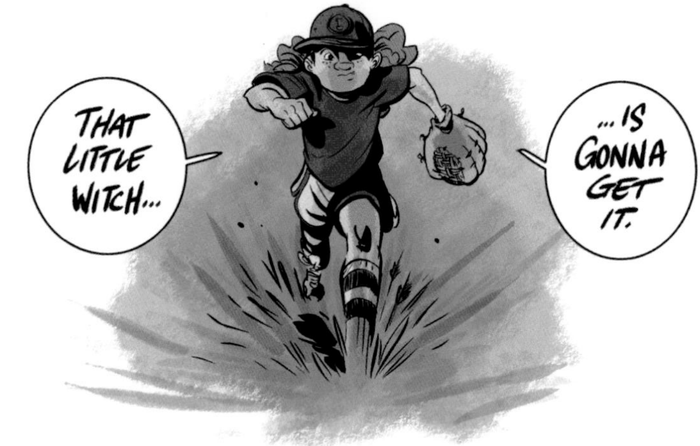
THAT LITTLE WITCH...
...IS GONNA GET IT.

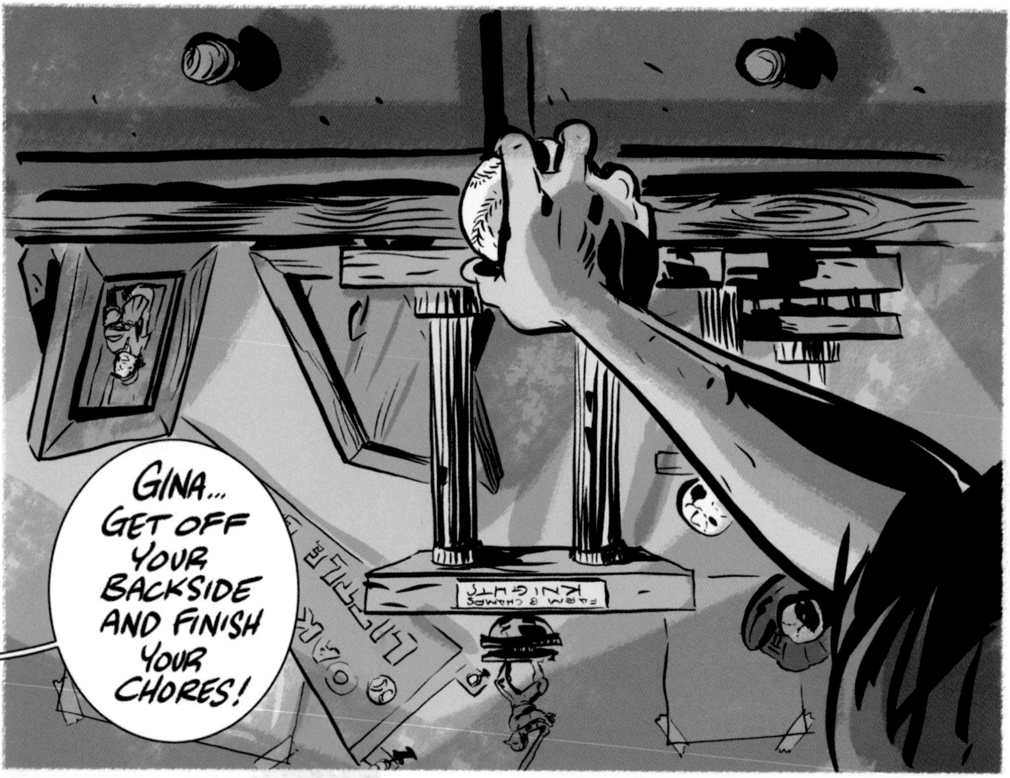
GINA... GET OFF YOUR BACKSIDE AND FINISH YOUR CHORES!

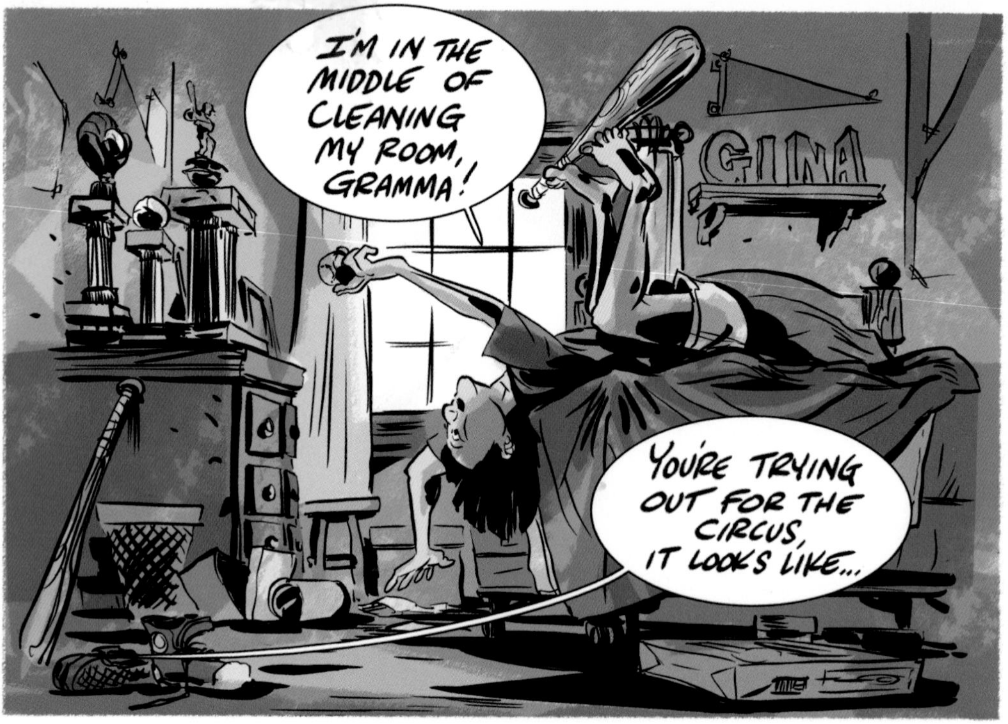
GINA
I'M IN THE MIDDLE OF CLEANING MY ROOM, GRAMMA!
YOU'RE TRYING OUT FOR THE CIRCUS, IT LOOKS LIKE...

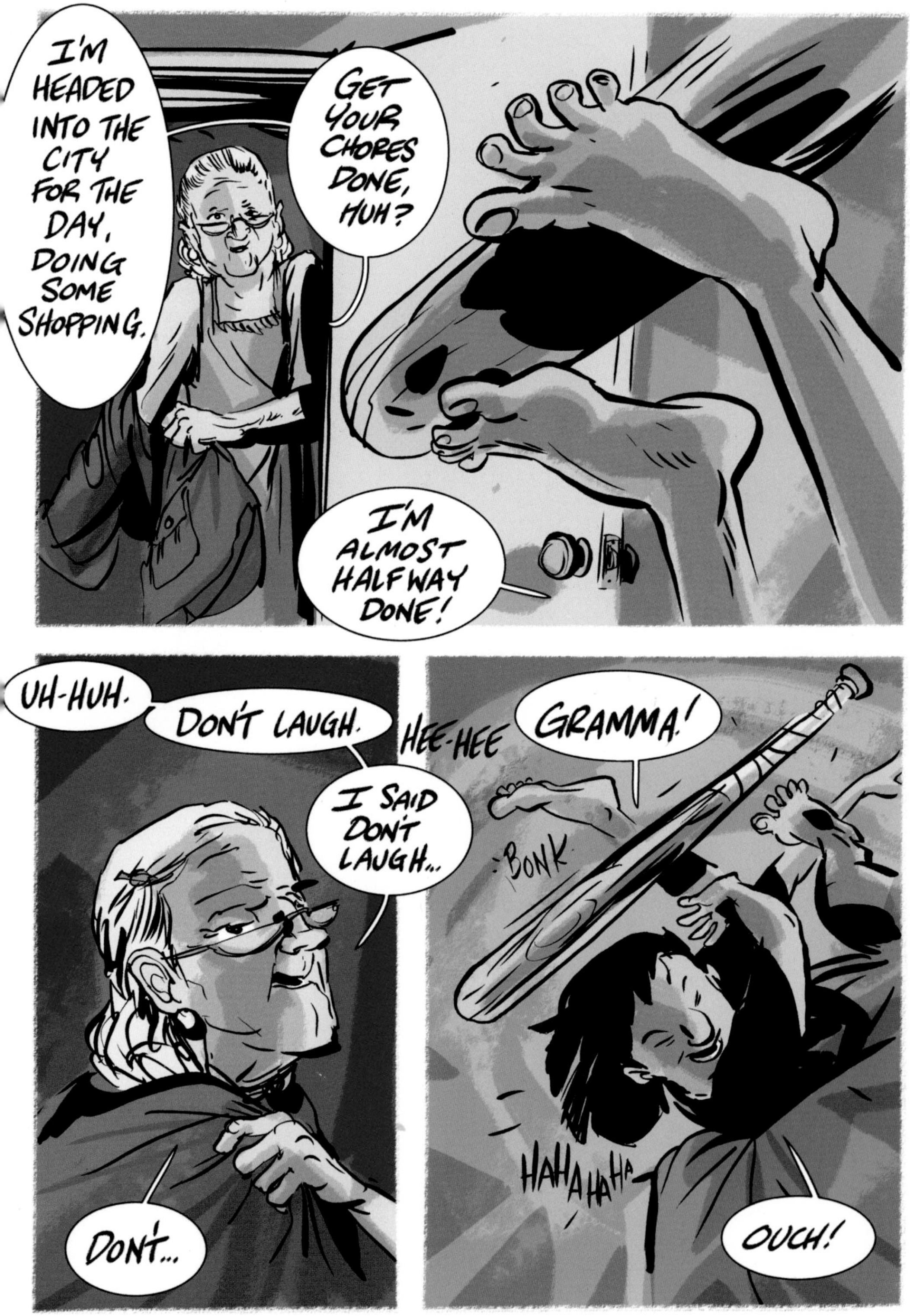
I'M HEADED INTO THE CITY FOR THE DAY, DOING SOME SHOPPING.
GET YOUR CHORES DONE, HUH?
I'M ALMOST HALFWAY DONE!
UH-HUH.
DON'T LAUGH.
I SAID DON'T LAUGH...
DON'T...
HEE-HEE
GRAMMA!
BONK
HAHAHAHAHA
OUCH!

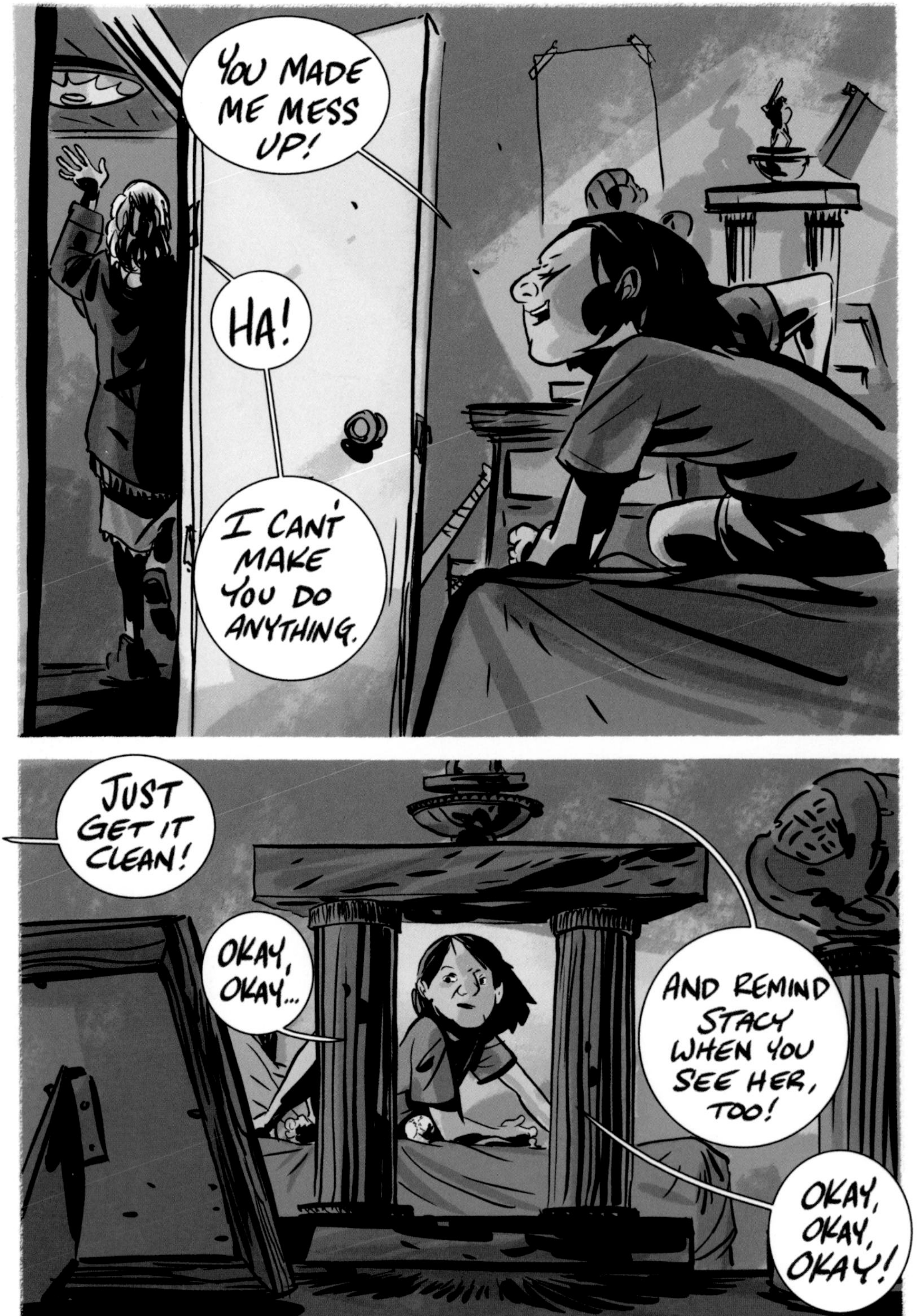
YOU MADE ME MESS UP!
HA!
I CAN'T MAKE YOU DO ANYTHING.
JUST GET IT CLEAN!
OKAY, OKAY...
AND REMIND STACY WHEN YOU SEE HER, TOO!
OKAY, OKAY, OKAY!

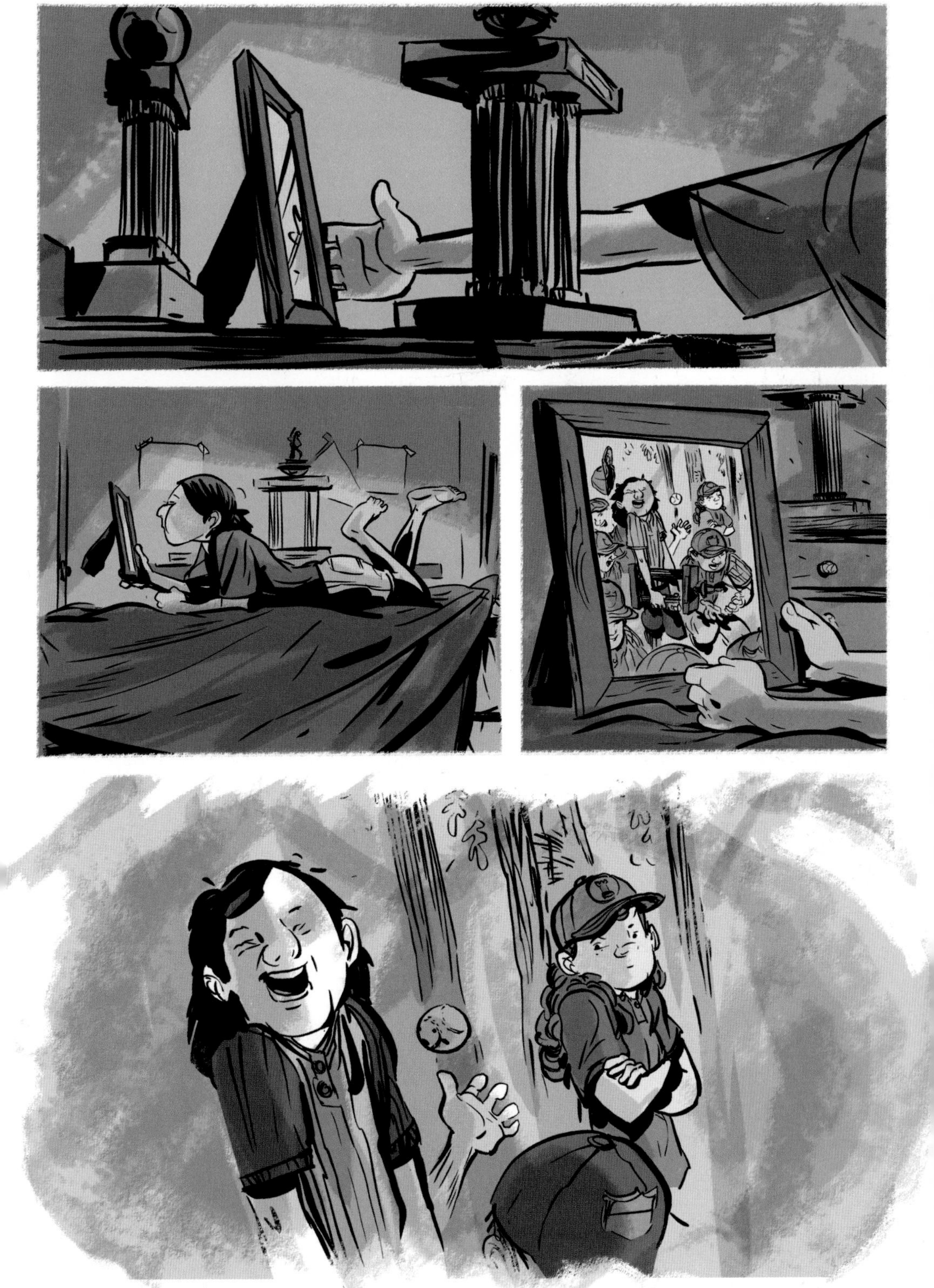

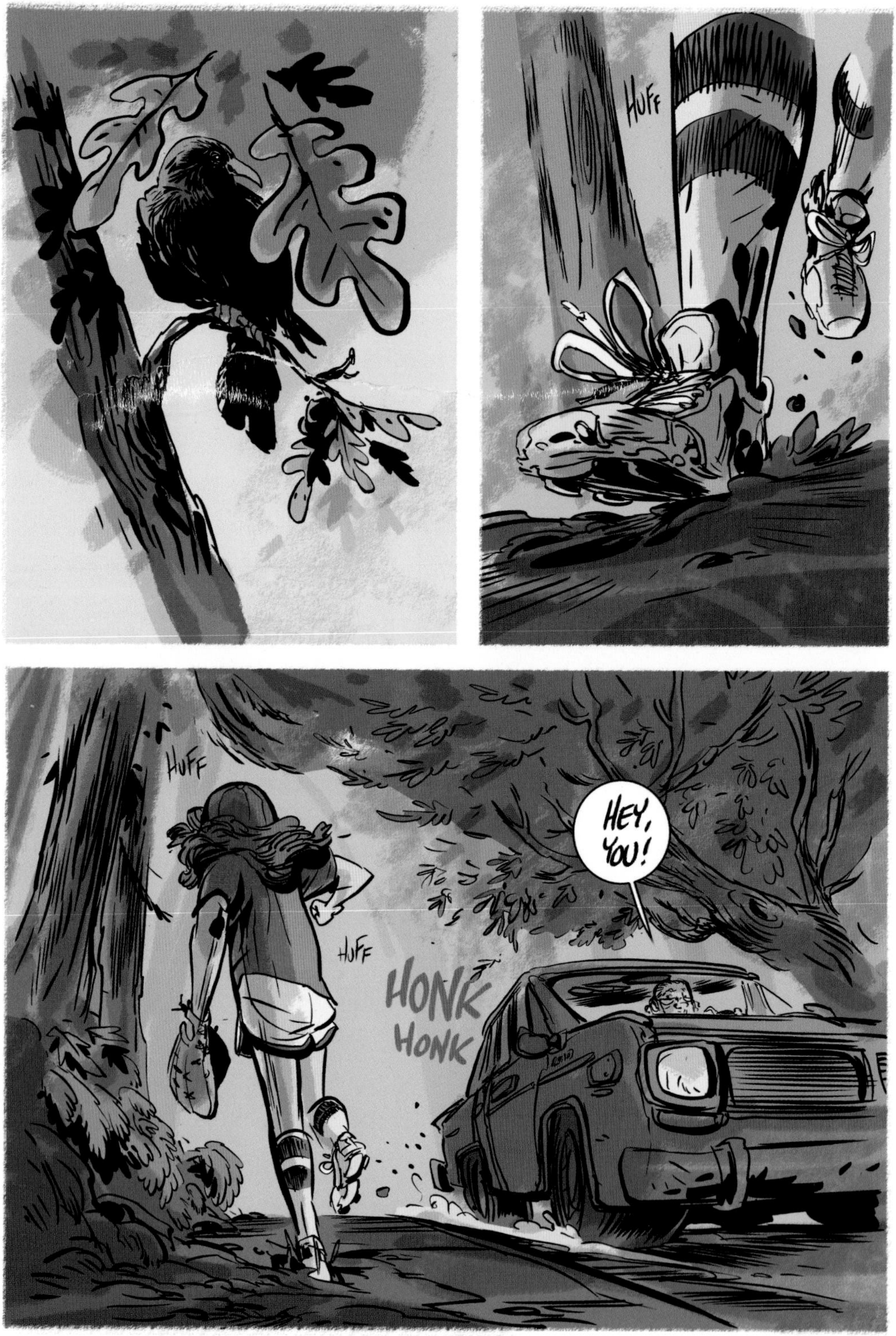
HUFF
HUFF
HUFF
HEY, YOU!
HONK
HONK

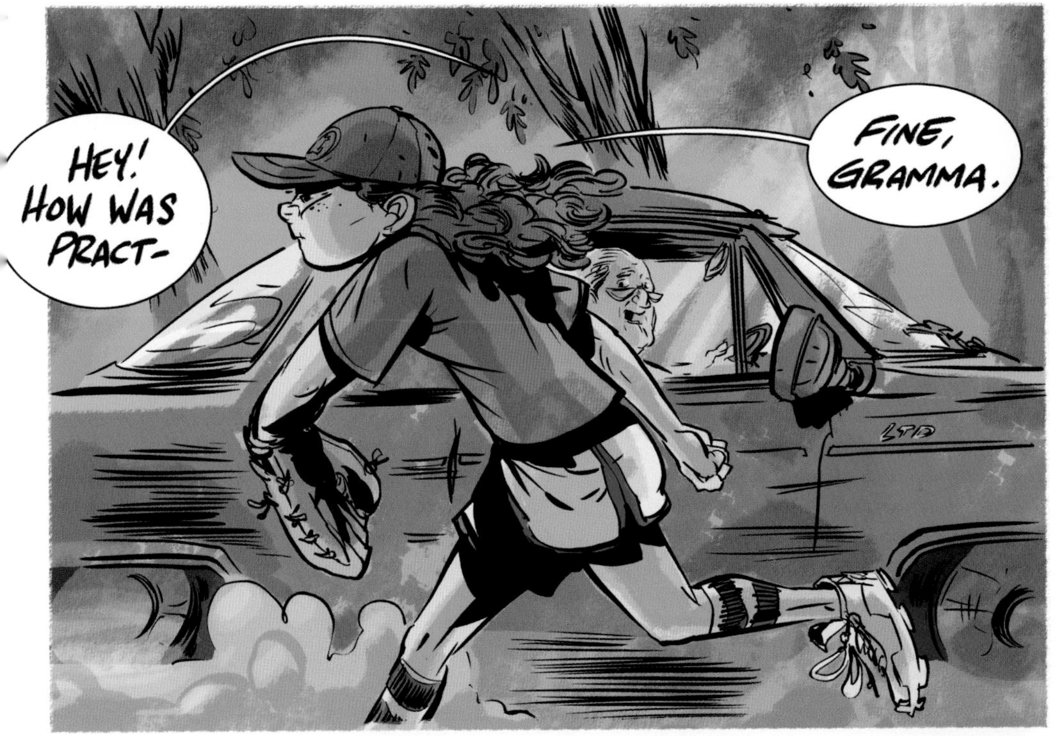
HEY! HOW WAS PRACT-
FINE, GRAMMA.
LTD

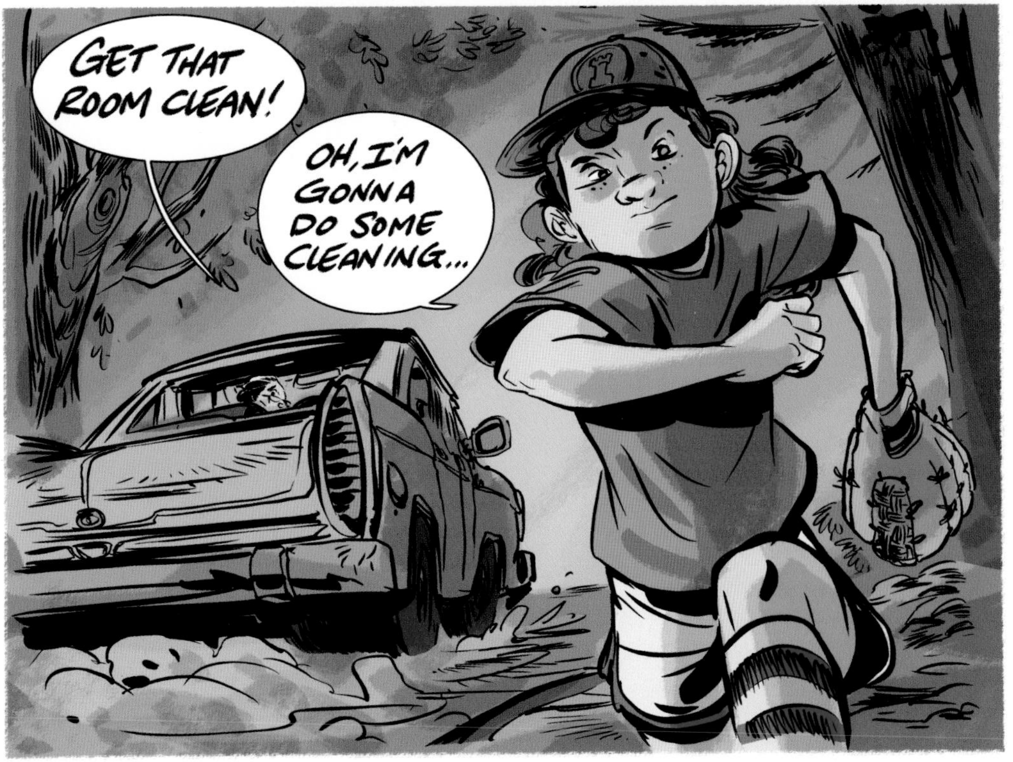
GET THAT ROOM CLEAN!
OH, I'M GONNA DO SOME CLEANING...

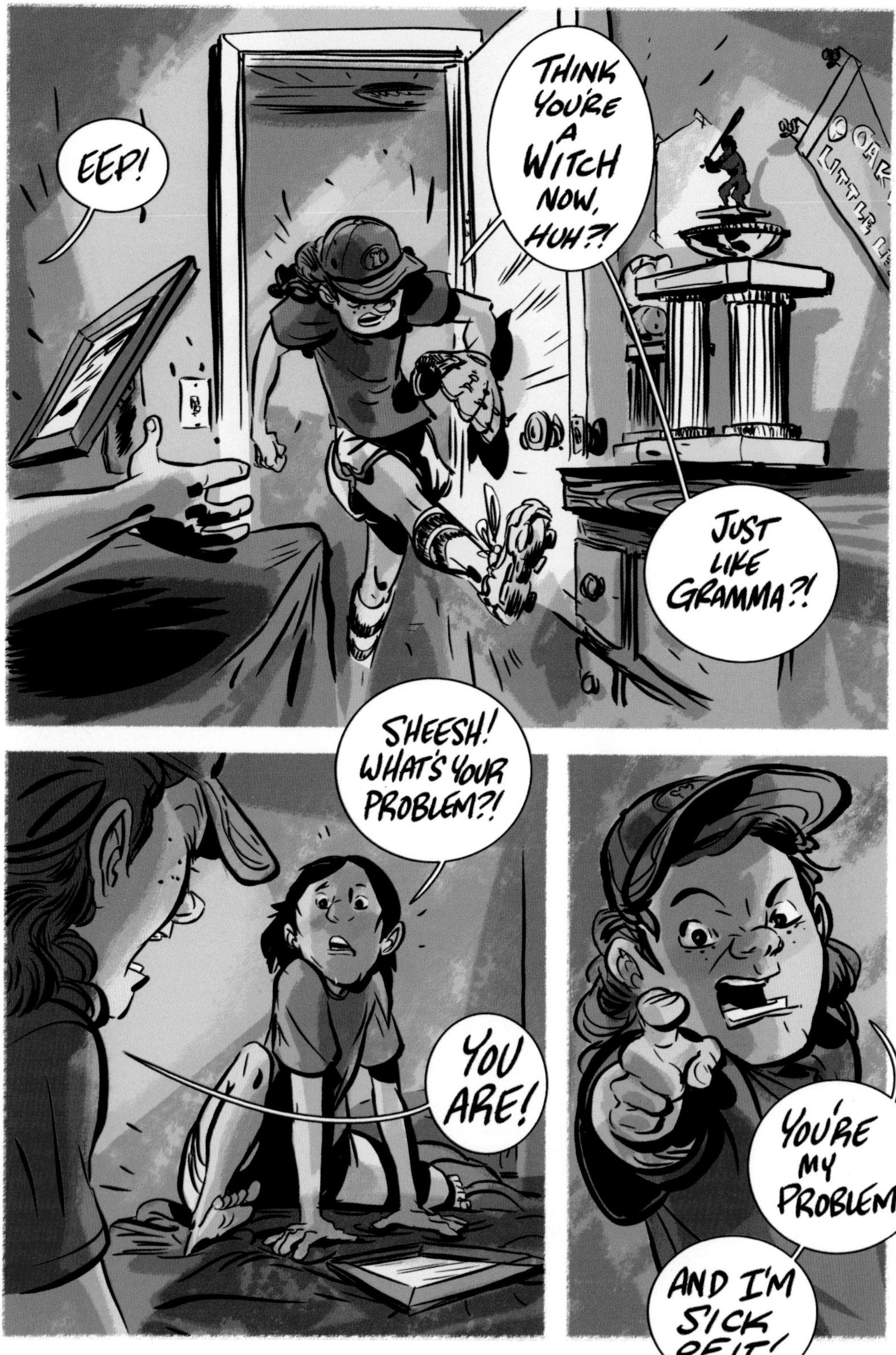
EEP!
THINK YOU'RE A WITCH NOW, HUH?!
JUST LIKE GRAMMA?!
SHEESH! WHAT'S YOUR PROBLEM?!
YOU ARE!
YOU'RE MY PROBLEM!
AND I'M SICK OF IT!

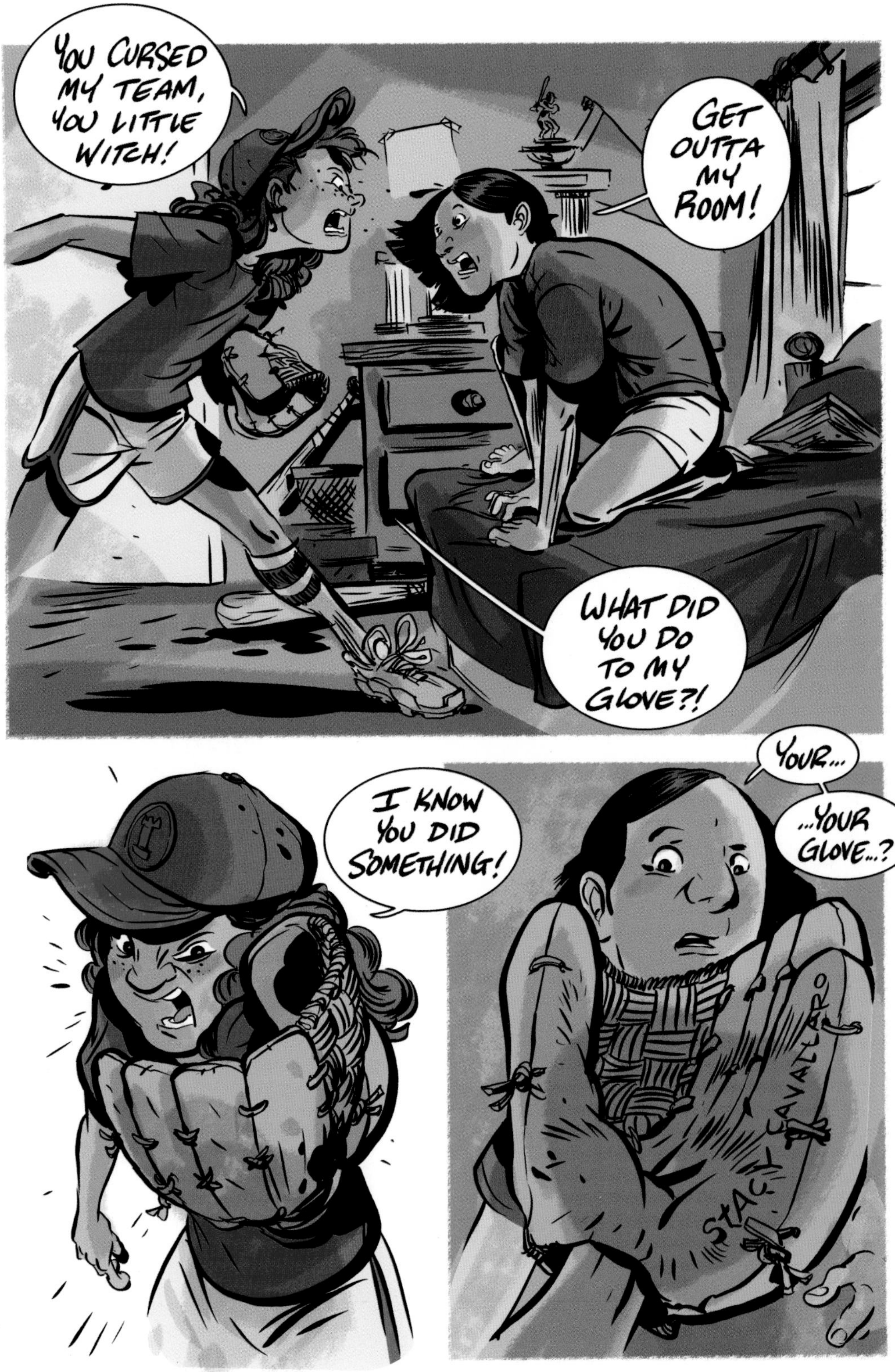
YOU CURSED MY TEAM, YOU LITTLE WITCH!
GET OUTTA MY ROOM!
WHAT DID YOU DO TO MY GLOVE?!
I KNOW YOU DID SOMETHING!
YOUR...
...YOUR GLOVE...?
STACY CAVALLARO

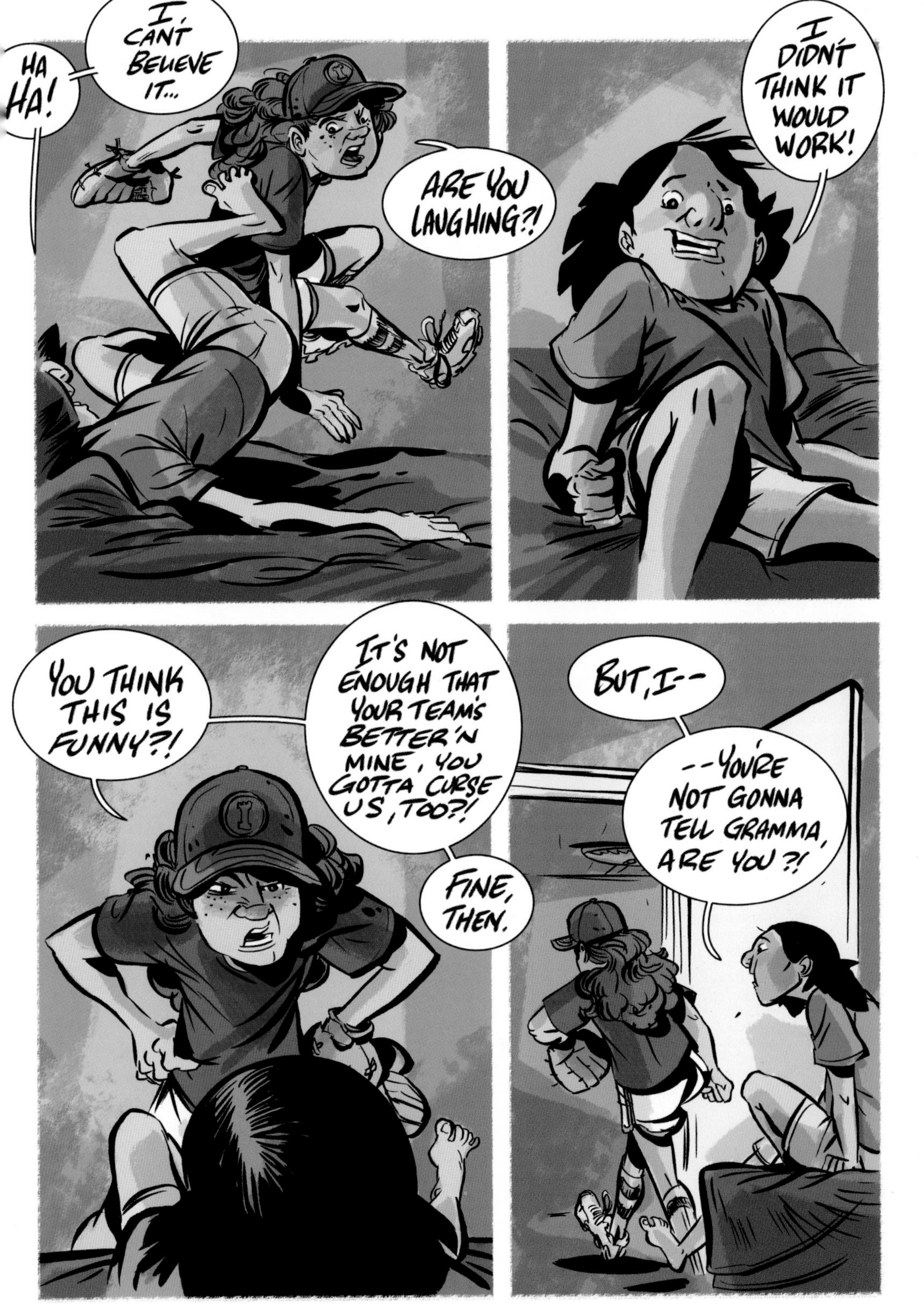
HA HA!
I, CAN'T BELIEVE IT...
ARE YOU LAUGHING?!
I DIDN'T THINK IT WOULD WORK!
YOU THINK THIS IS FUNNY?!
IT'S NOT ENOUGH THAT YOUR TEAM'S BETTER'N MINE, YOU GOTTA CURSE US, TOO?!
FINE, THEN.
BUT, I--
--YOU'RE NOT GONNA TELL GRAMMA, ARE YOU?!

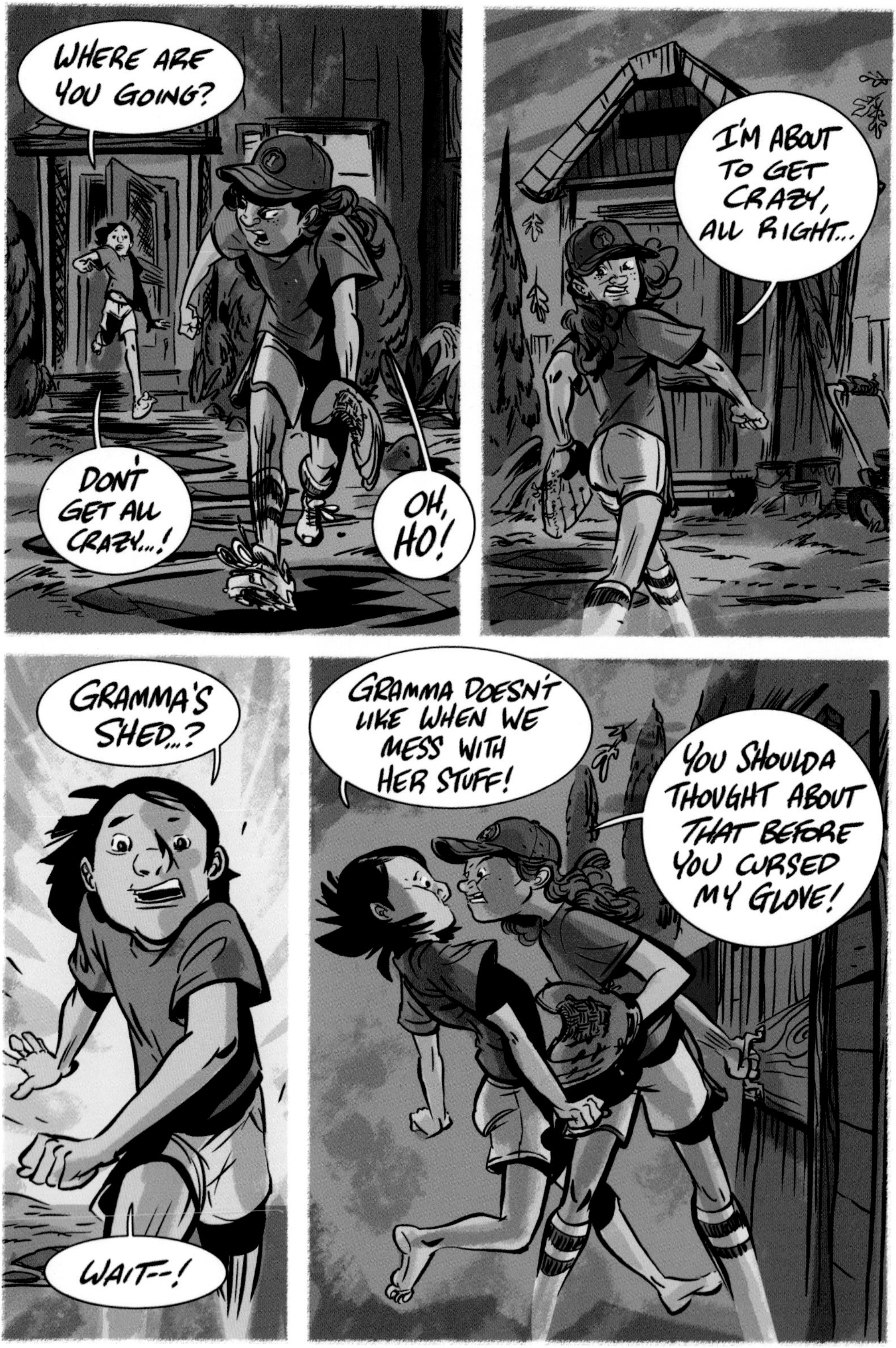
WHERE ARE YOU GOING?
DON'T GET ALL CRAZY...!
OH, HO!
I'M ABOUT TO GET CRAZY, ALL RIGHT...
GRAMMA'S SHED...?
WAIT--!
GRAMMA DOESN'T LIKE WHEN WE MESS WITH HER STUFF!
YOU SHOULDA THOUGHT ABOUT THAT BEFORE YOU CURSED MY GLOVE!

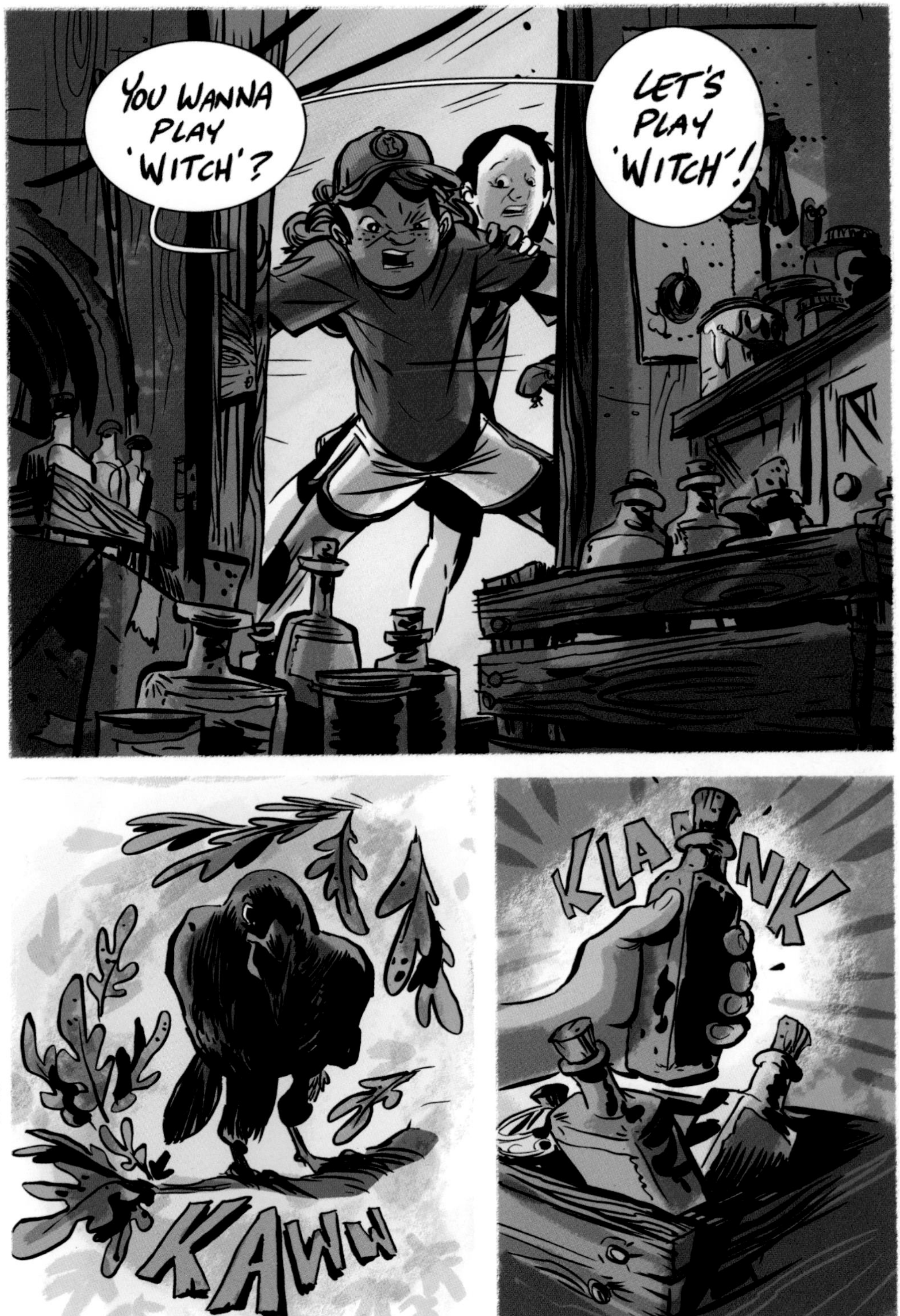
YOU WANNA PLAY 'WITCH'?
LET'S PLAY 'WITCH'!
KAWW
KLANNK

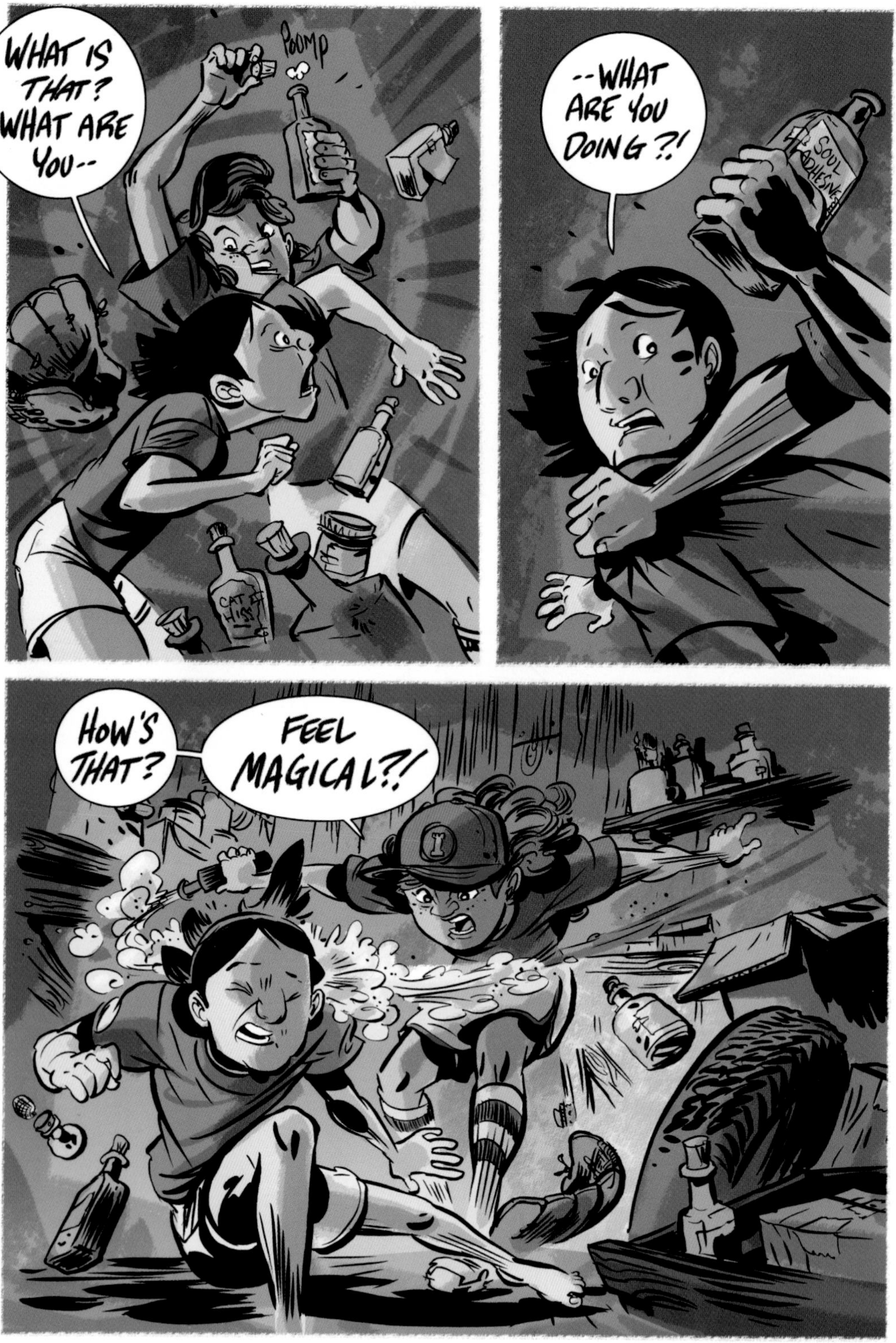
WHAT IS THAT? WHAT ARE YOU--
POOMP
--WHAT ARE YOU DOING?!
SOUL ADHESIVE
CAT HISS
HOW'S THAT?
FEEL MAGICAL?!

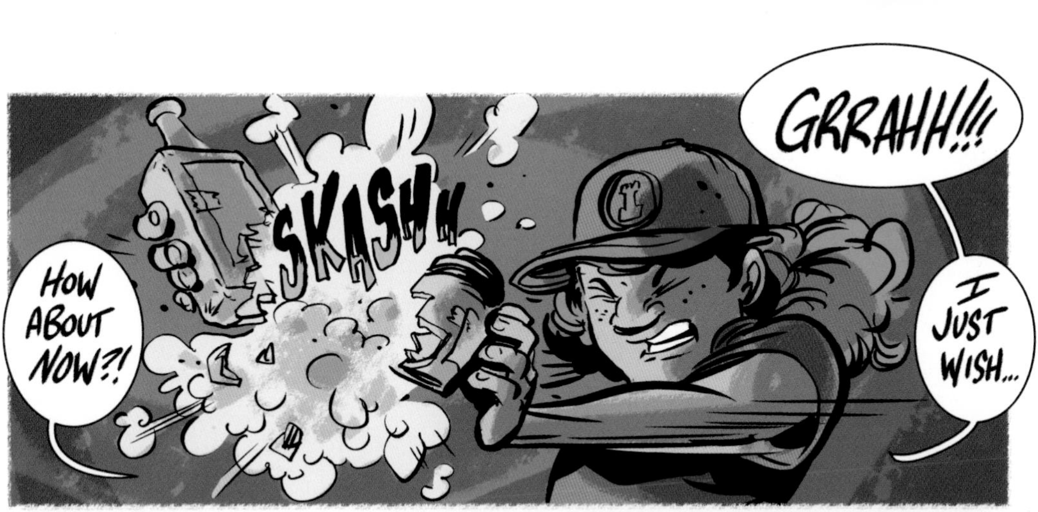
GRRAHH!!!
I JUST WISH...
SKASHH
HOW ABOUT NOW?!

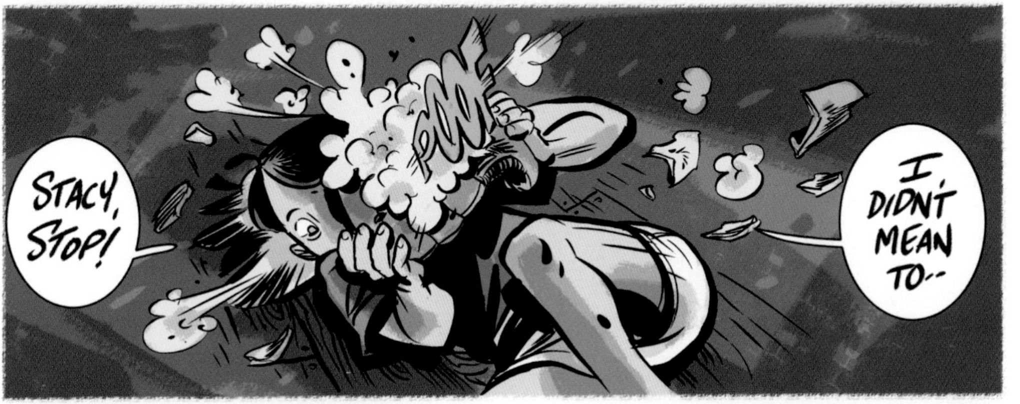
I, DIDN'T MEAN TO--
STACY, STOP!

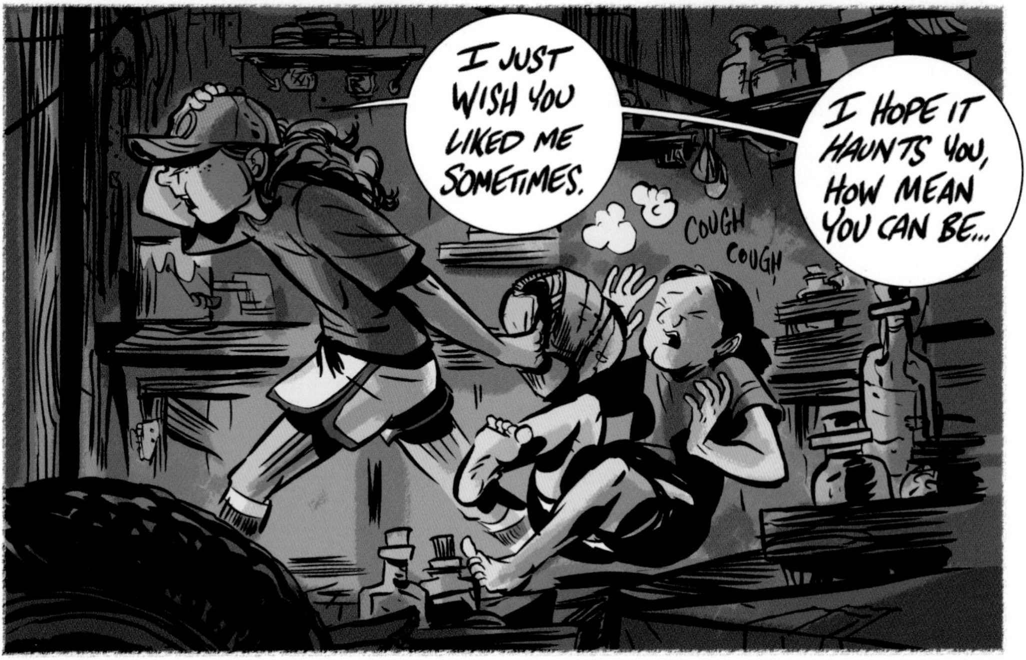
I JUST WISH YOU LIKED ME SOMETIMES.
I HOPE IT HAUNTS YOU, HOW MEAN YOU CAN BE...
COUGH COUGH

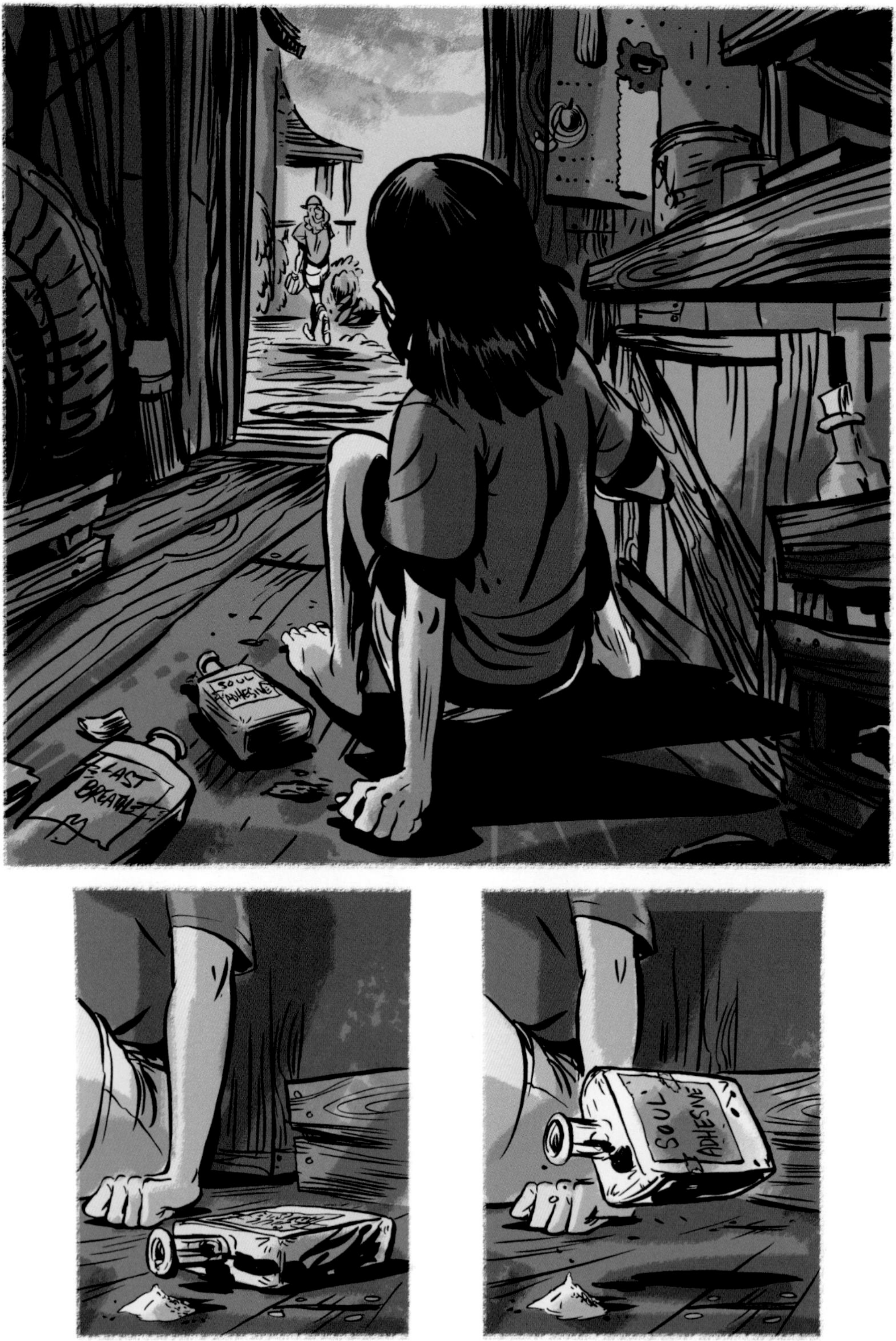
SOUL ADHESIVE
LAST BREATH
SOUL ADHESIVE

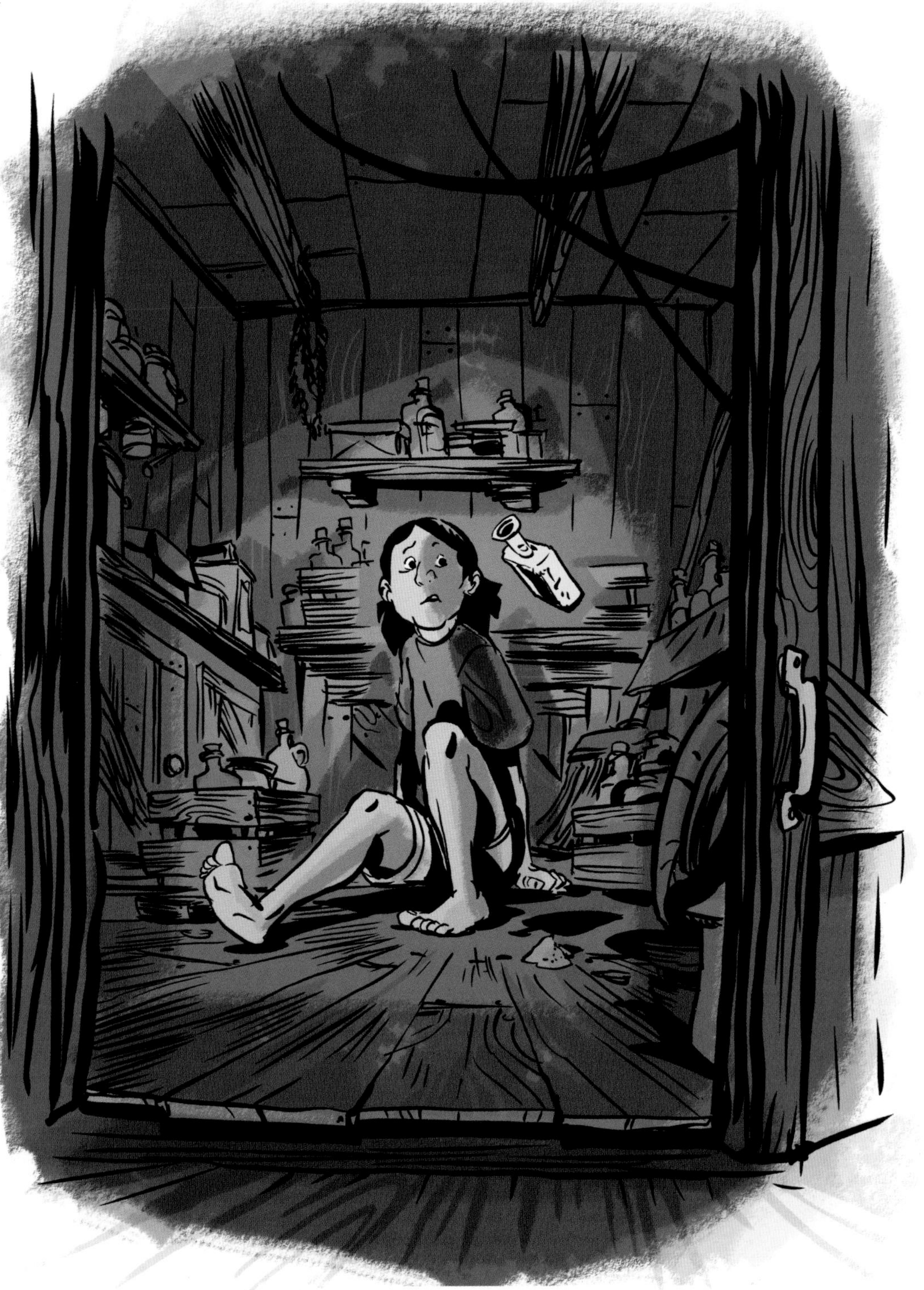

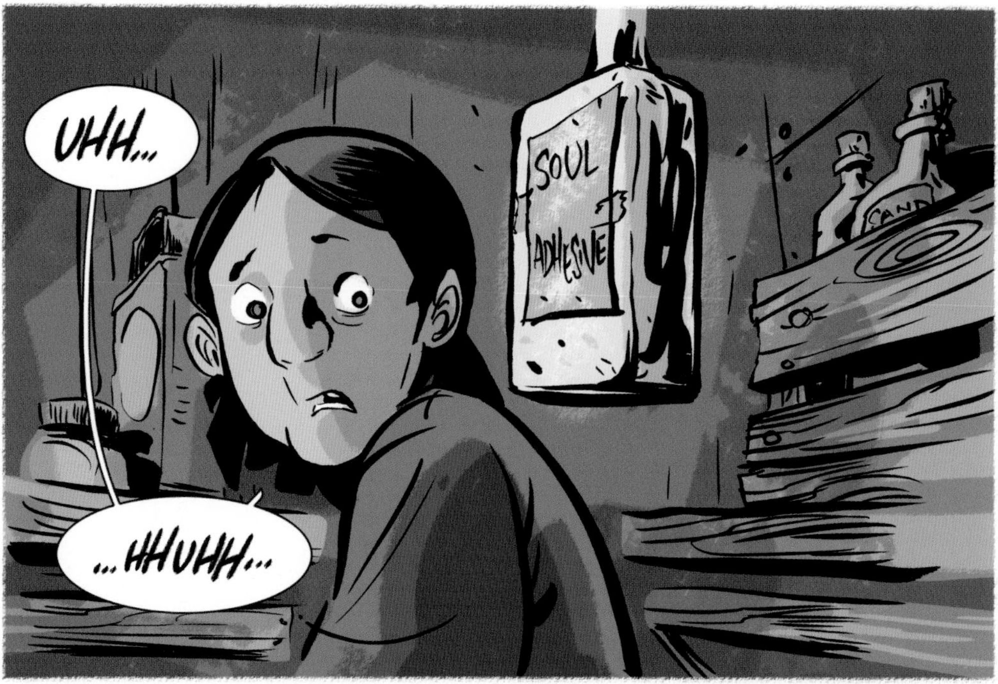
UHH...
...HHUHH...
SOUL ADHESIVE

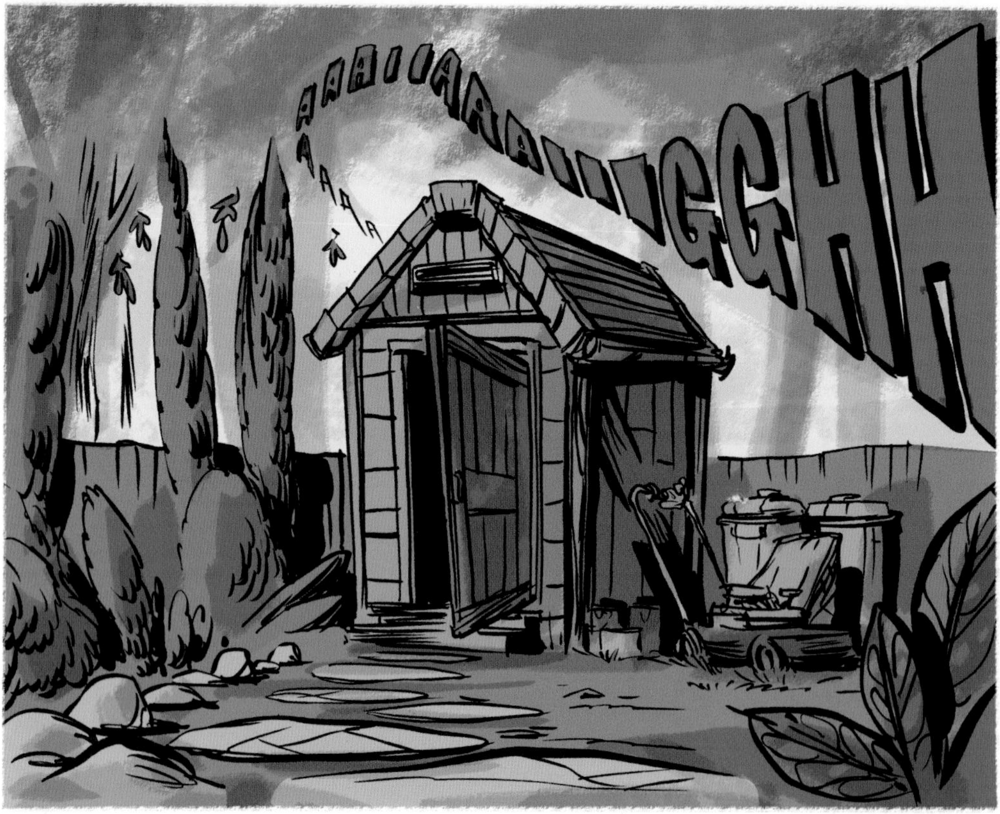
AAAIIAAAAAA...GGHH

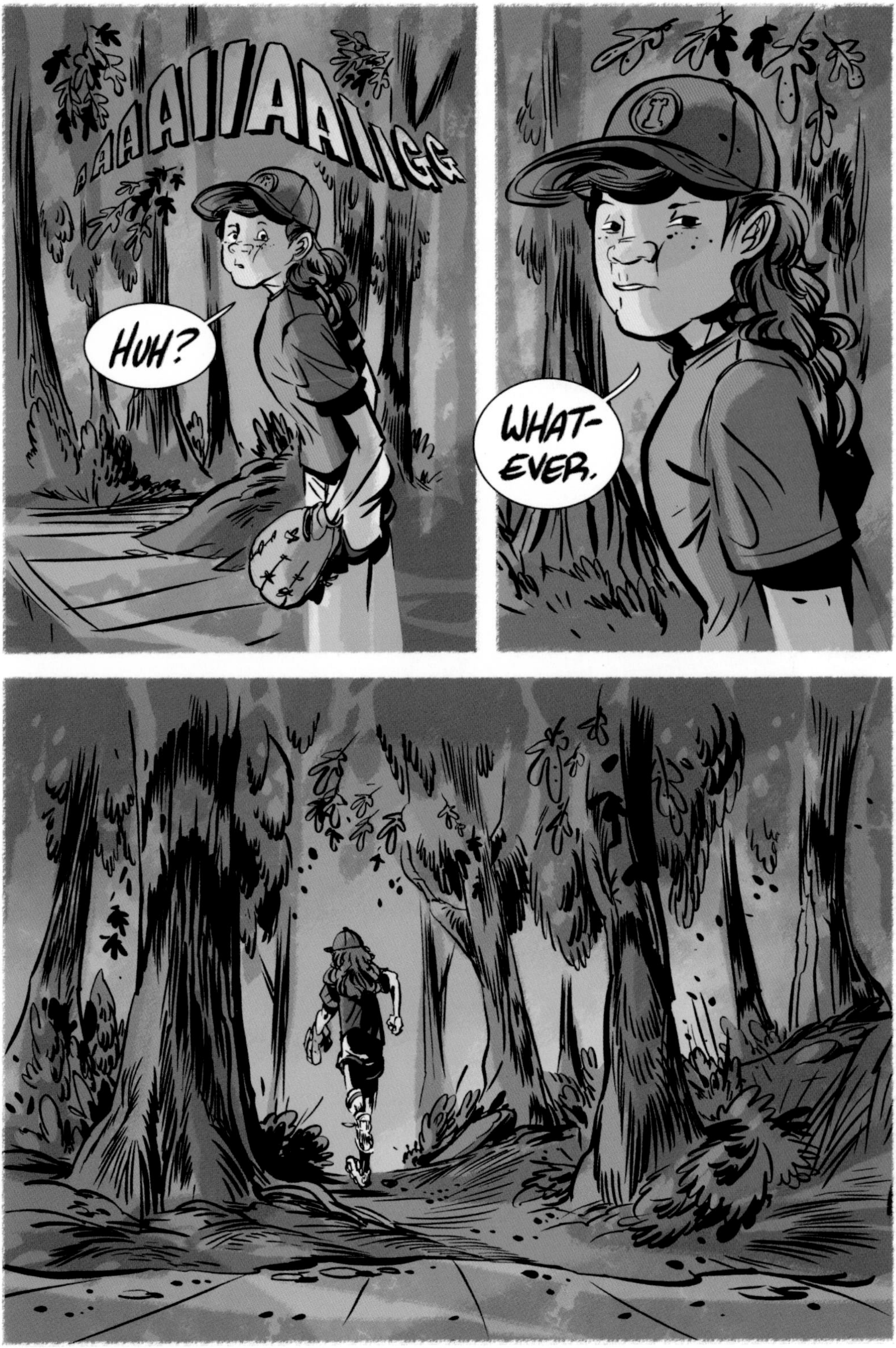
AAAIIIAAIIGG
HUH?
WHAT-EVER.

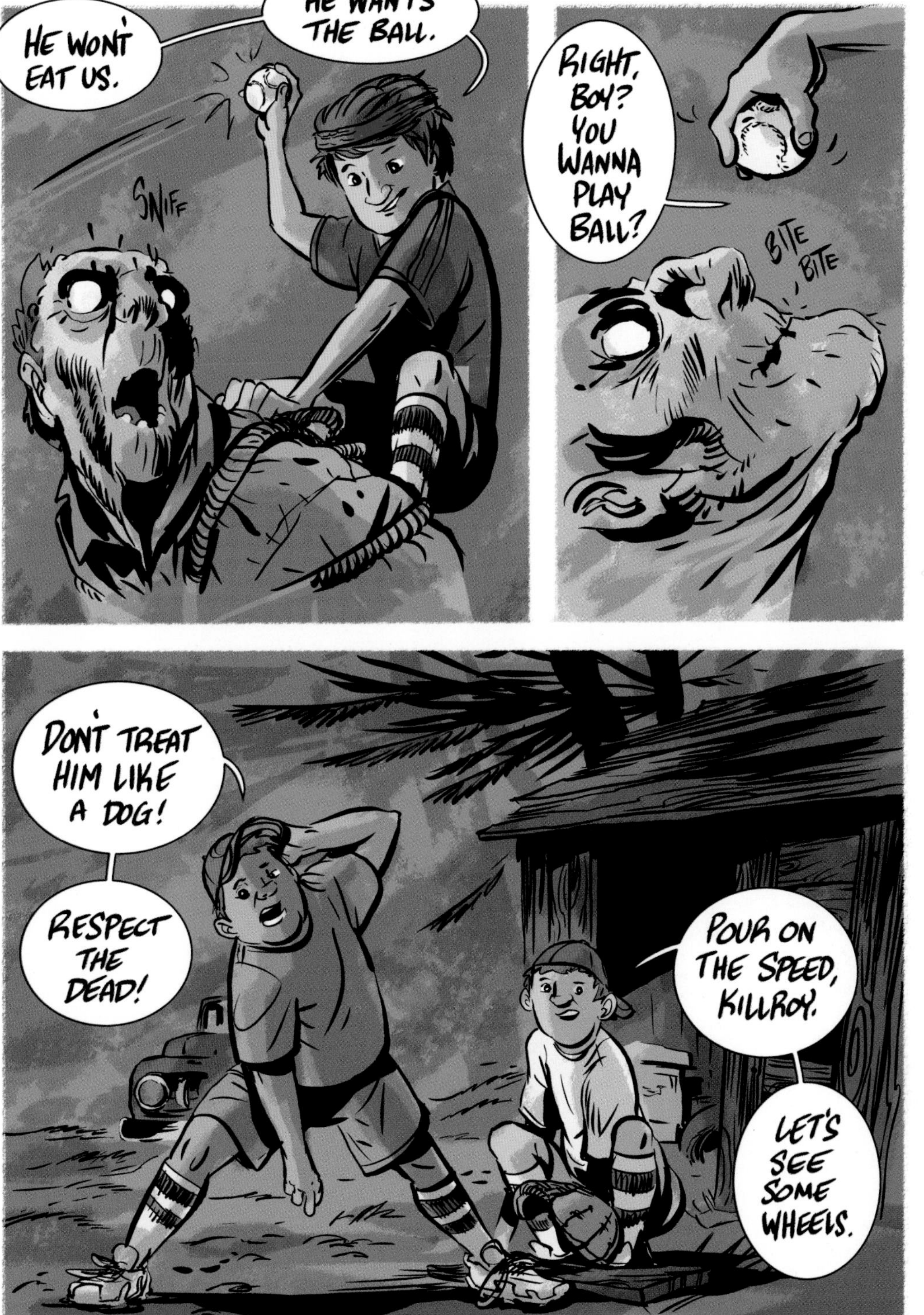
HE WANTS THE BALL.
HE WON'T EAT US.
SNIFF
RIGHT, BOY? YOU WANNA PLAY BALL?
BITE BITE
DON'T TREAT HIM LIKE A DOG!
RESPECT THE DEAD!
POUR ON THE SPEED, KILLROY.
LET'S SEE SOME WHEELS.

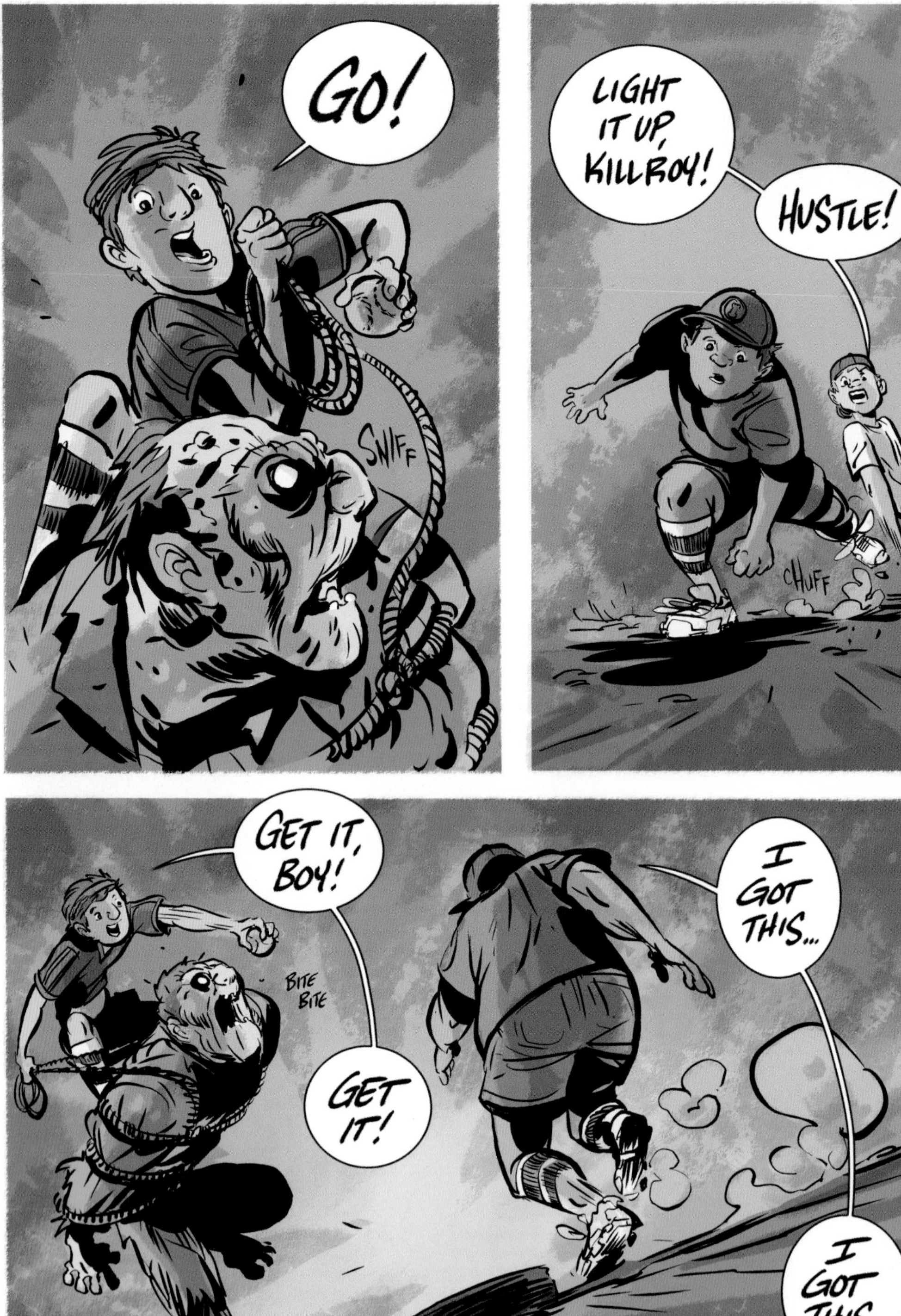
GO!
SNIFF
LIGHT IT UP, KILLBOY!
HUSTLE!
CHUFF
GET IT, BOY!
BITE BITE
GET IT!
I GOT THIS...
I GOT THIS...

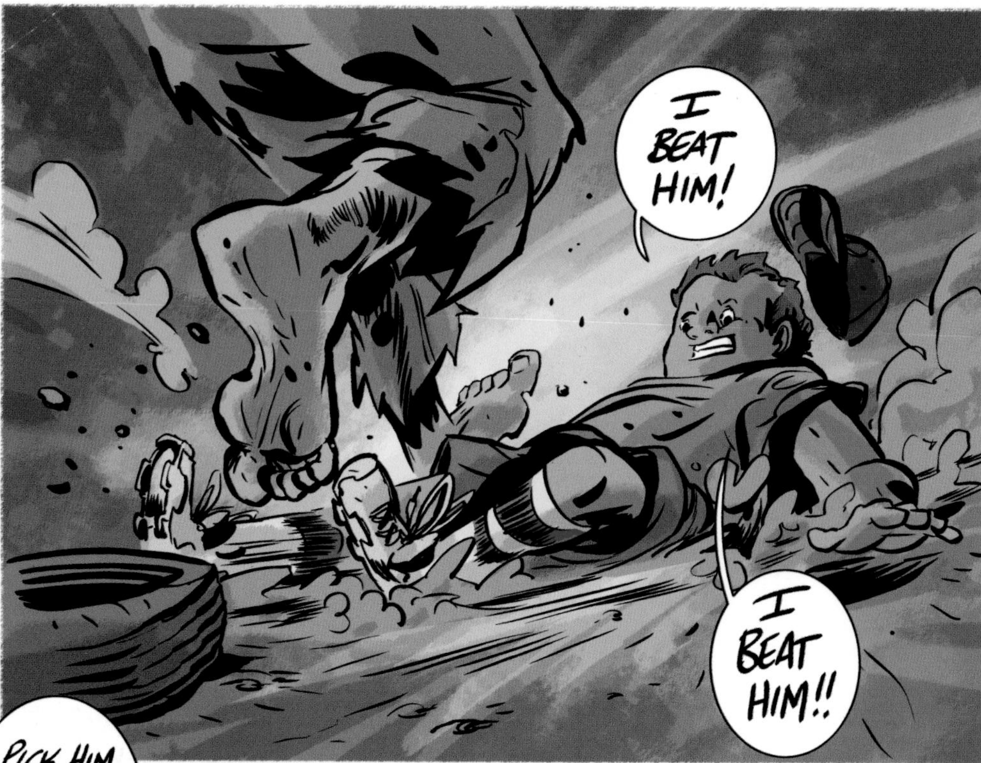
I BEAT HIM!
I BEAT HIM!!

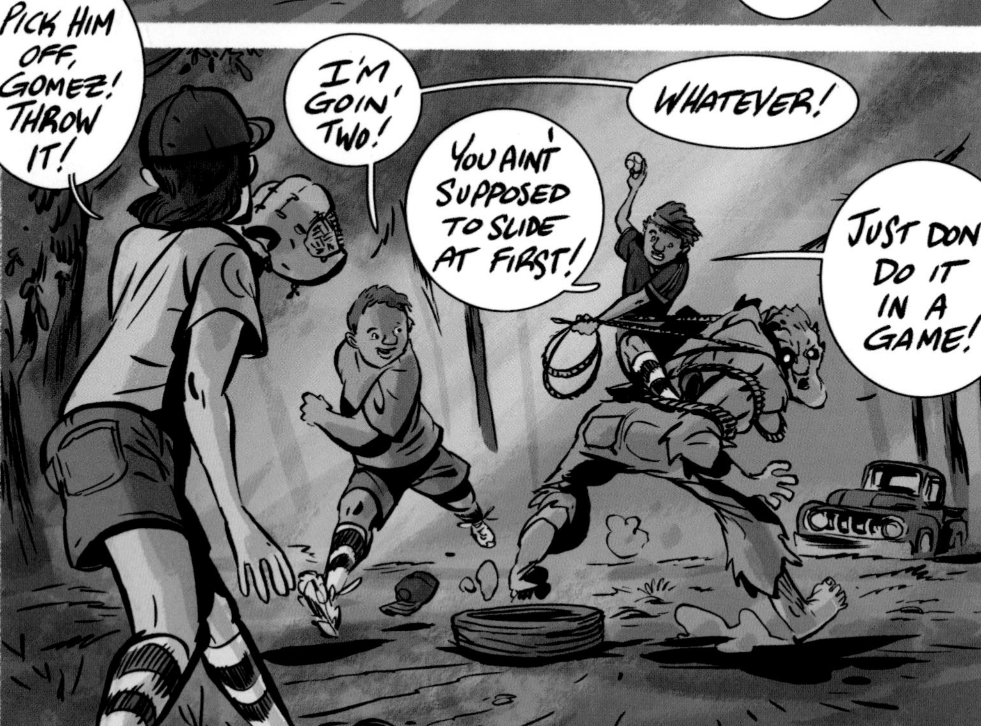
PICK HIM OFF, GOMEZ! THROW IT!
I'M GOIN' TWO!
WHATEVER!
YOU AIN'T SUPPOSED TO SLIDE AT FIRST!
JUST DON'T DO IT IN A GAME!

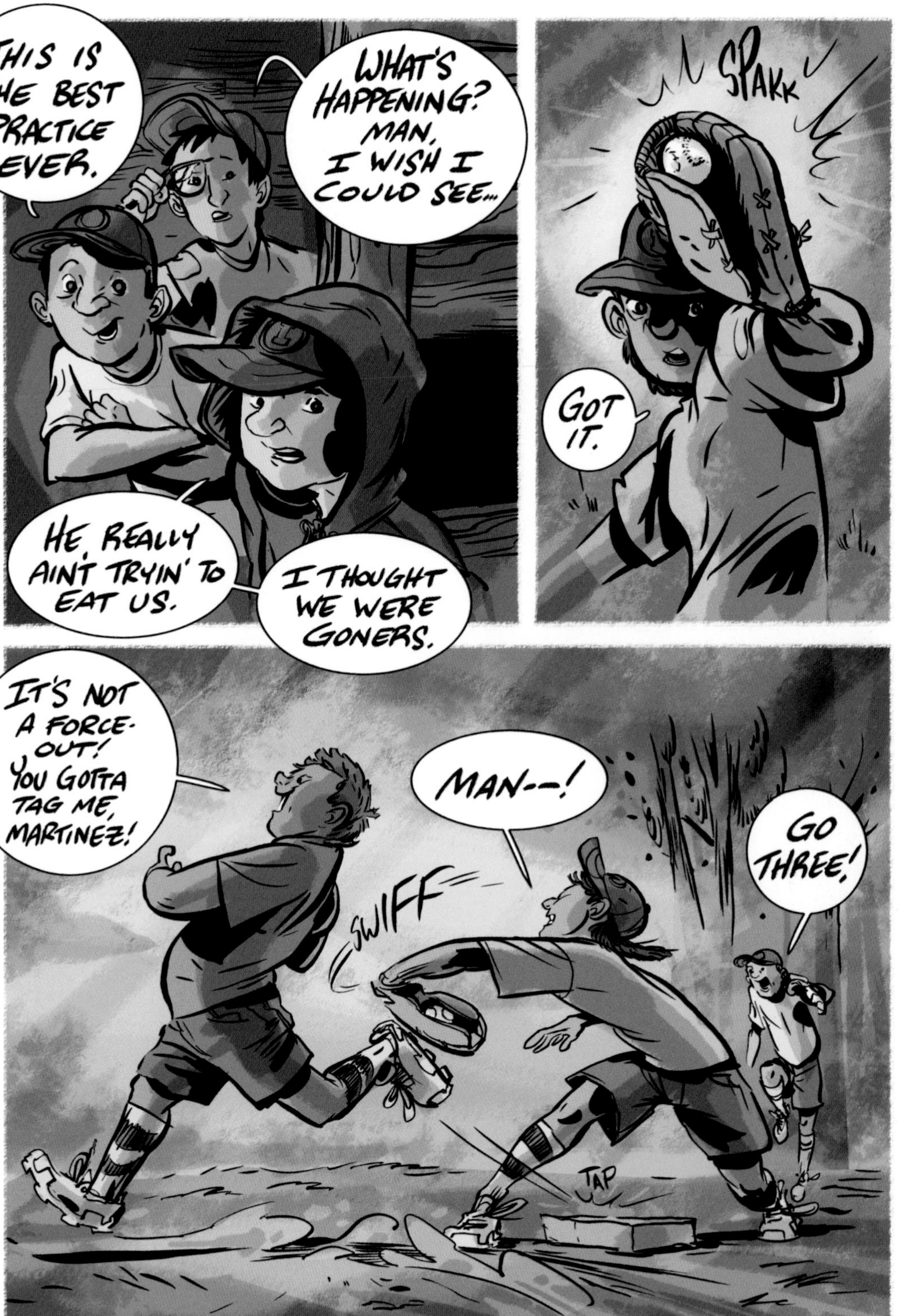

THIS IS THE BEST PRACTICE EVER.
WHAT'S HAPPENING? MAN, I WISH I COULD SEE...
HE REALLY AIN'T TRYIN' TO EAT US.
I THOUGHT WE WERE GONERS.
SPAKK
GOT IT.
IT'S NOT A FORCE-OUT! YOU GOTTA TAG ME, MARTINEZ!
MAN--!
GO THREE!
SWIFF
TAP

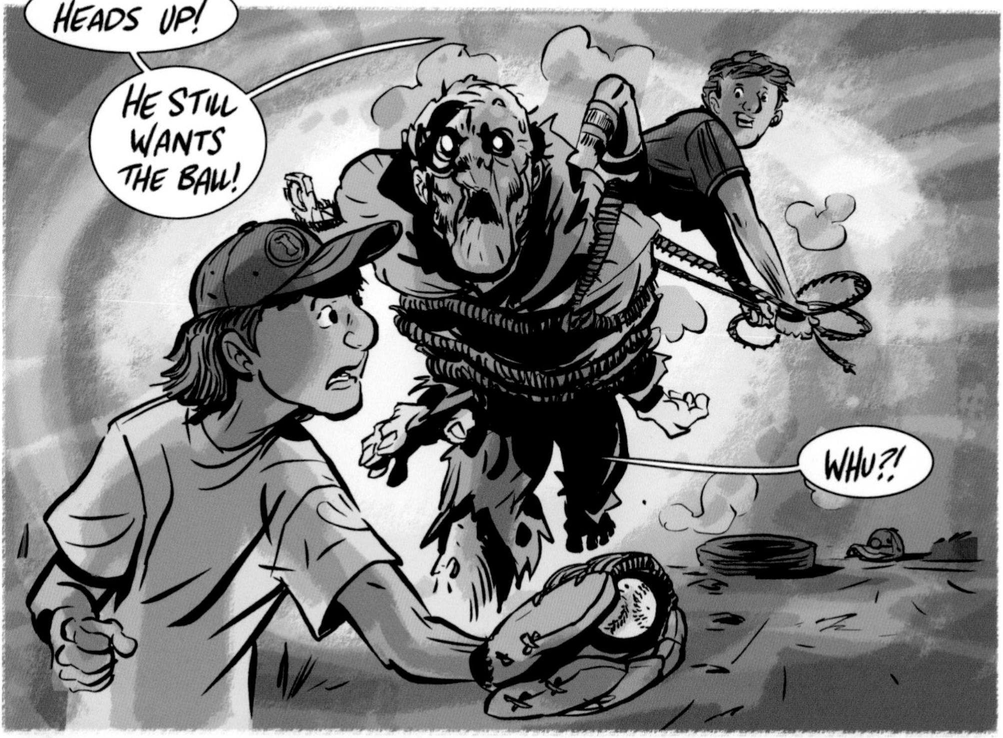
HEADS UP!
HE STILL WANTS THE BALL!
WHU?!

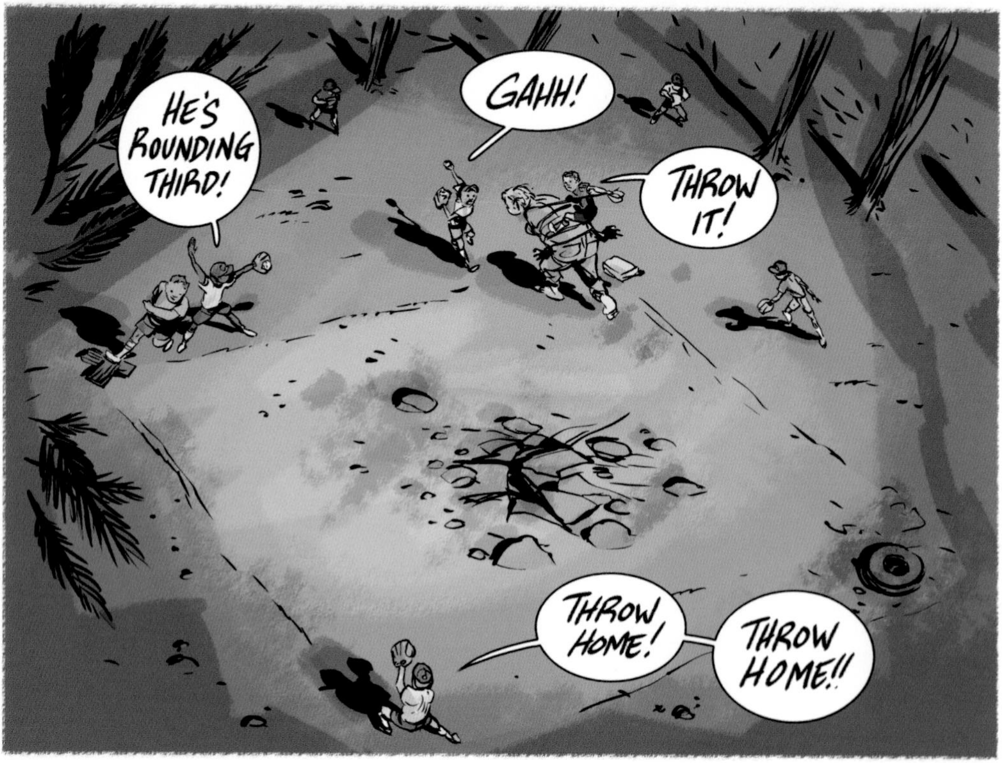
HE'S ROUNDING THIRD!
GAHH!
THROW IT!
THROW HOME!
THROW HOME!!

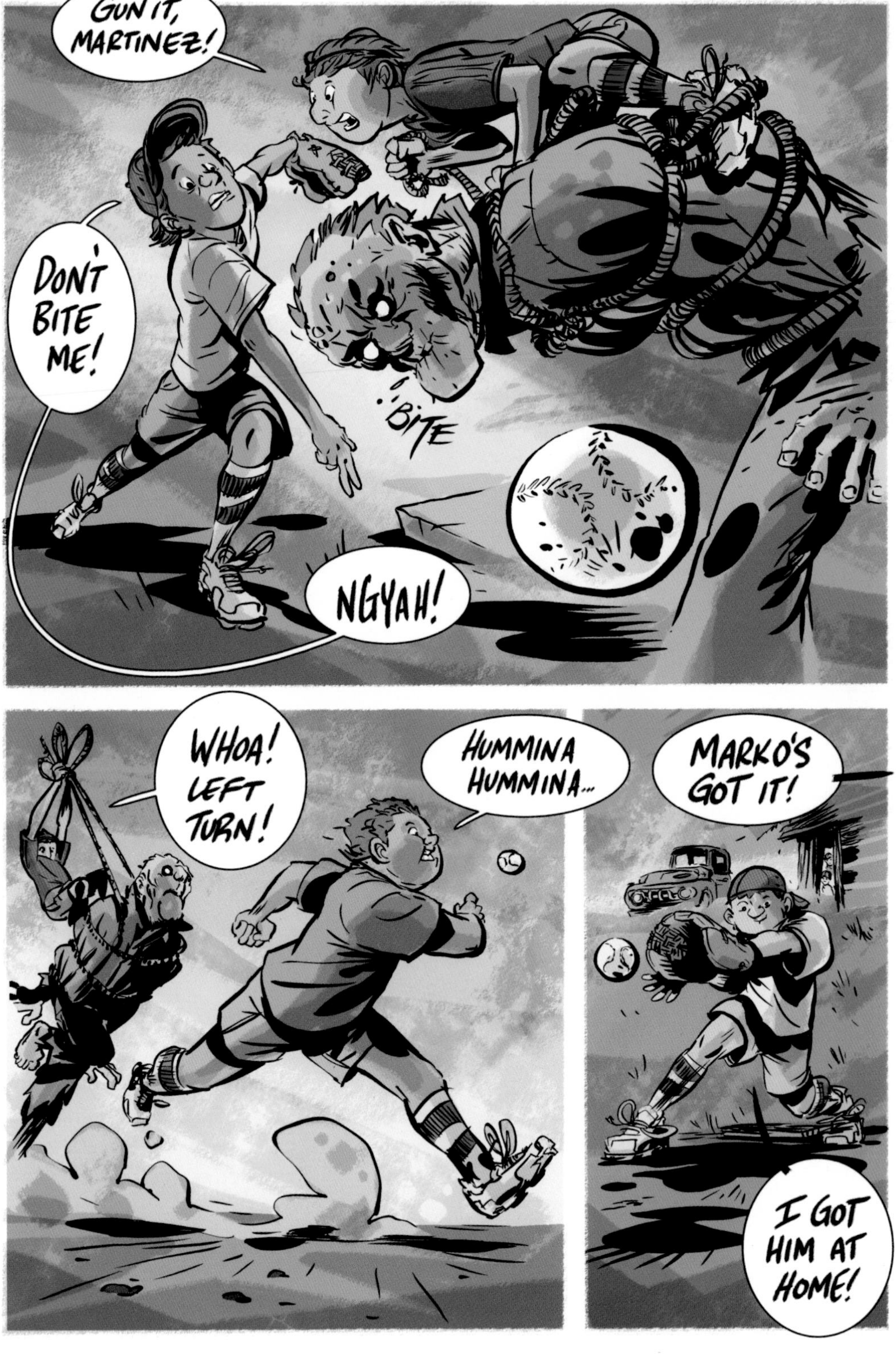
GUN IT, MARTINEZ!
DON'T BITE ME!
BITE
NGYAH!
WHOA! LEFT TURN!
HUMMINA HUMMINA...
MARKO'S GOT IT!
I GOT HIM AT HOME!

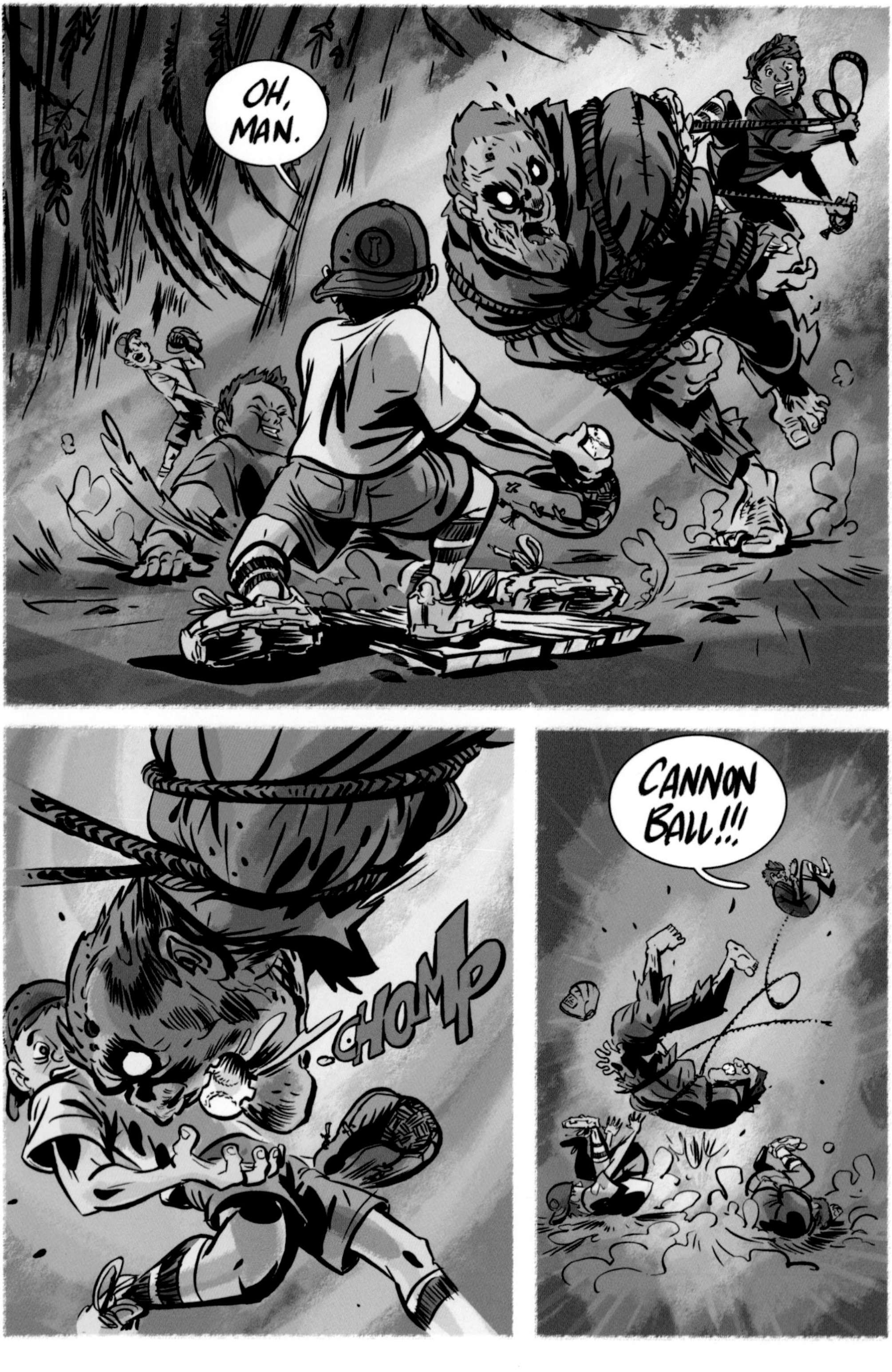
OH, MAN.
CHOMP
CANNON BALL!!!

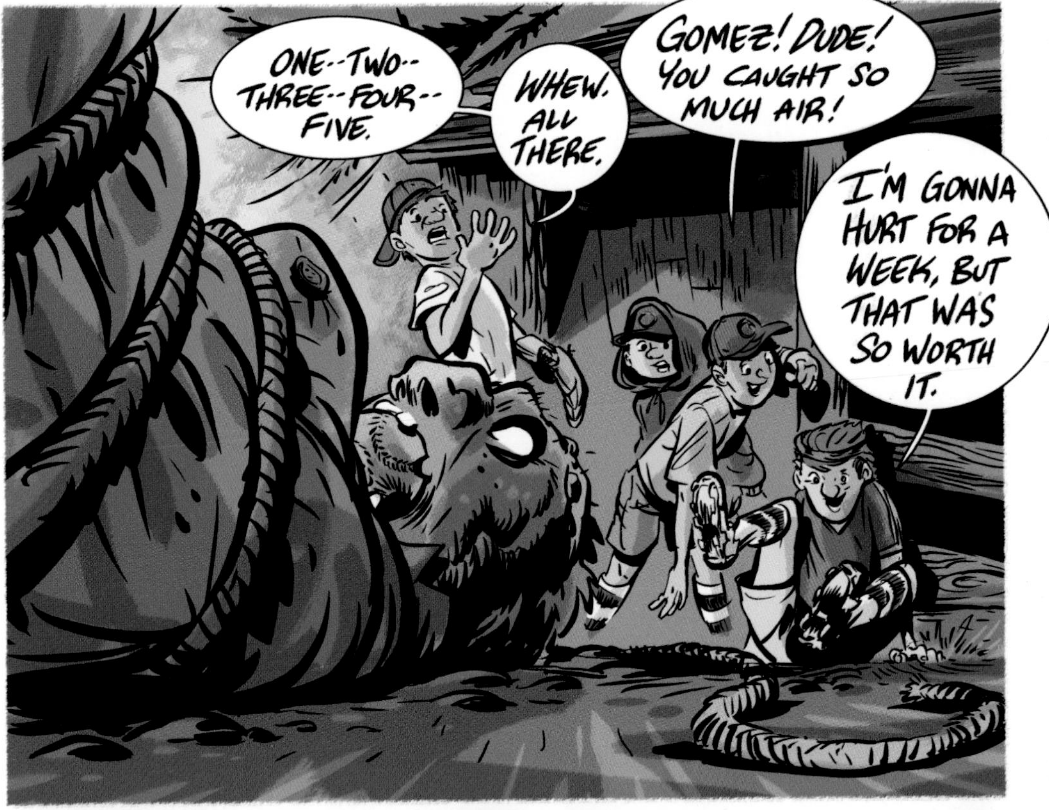
ONE--TWO--THREE--FOUR--FIVE.
WHEW. ALL THERE.
GOMEZ! DUDE! YOU CAUGHT SO MUCH AIR!
I'M GONNA HURT FOR A WEEK, BUT THAT WAS SO WORTH IT.

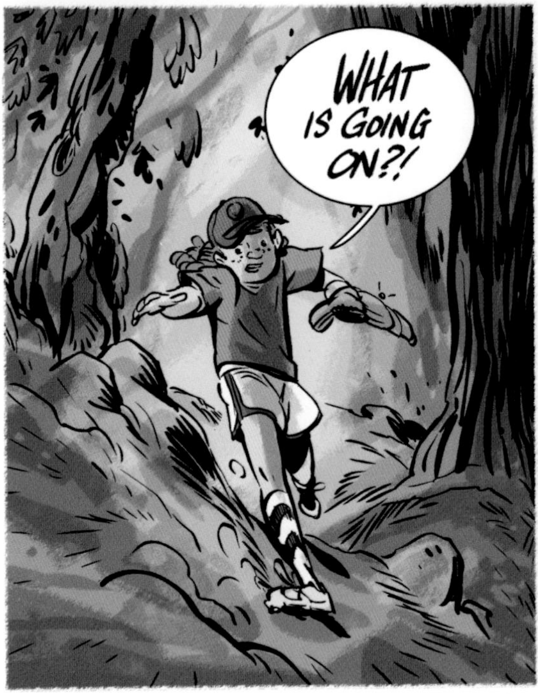
WHAT IS GOING ON?!

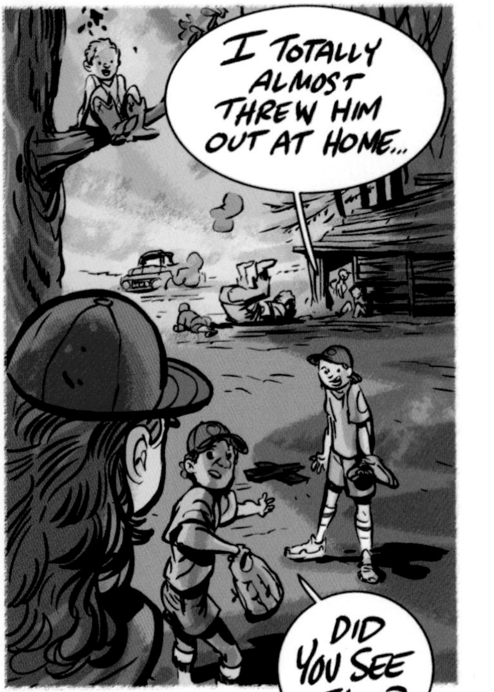
I TOTALLY ALMOST THREW HIM OUT AT HOME...
DID YOU SEE THAT?

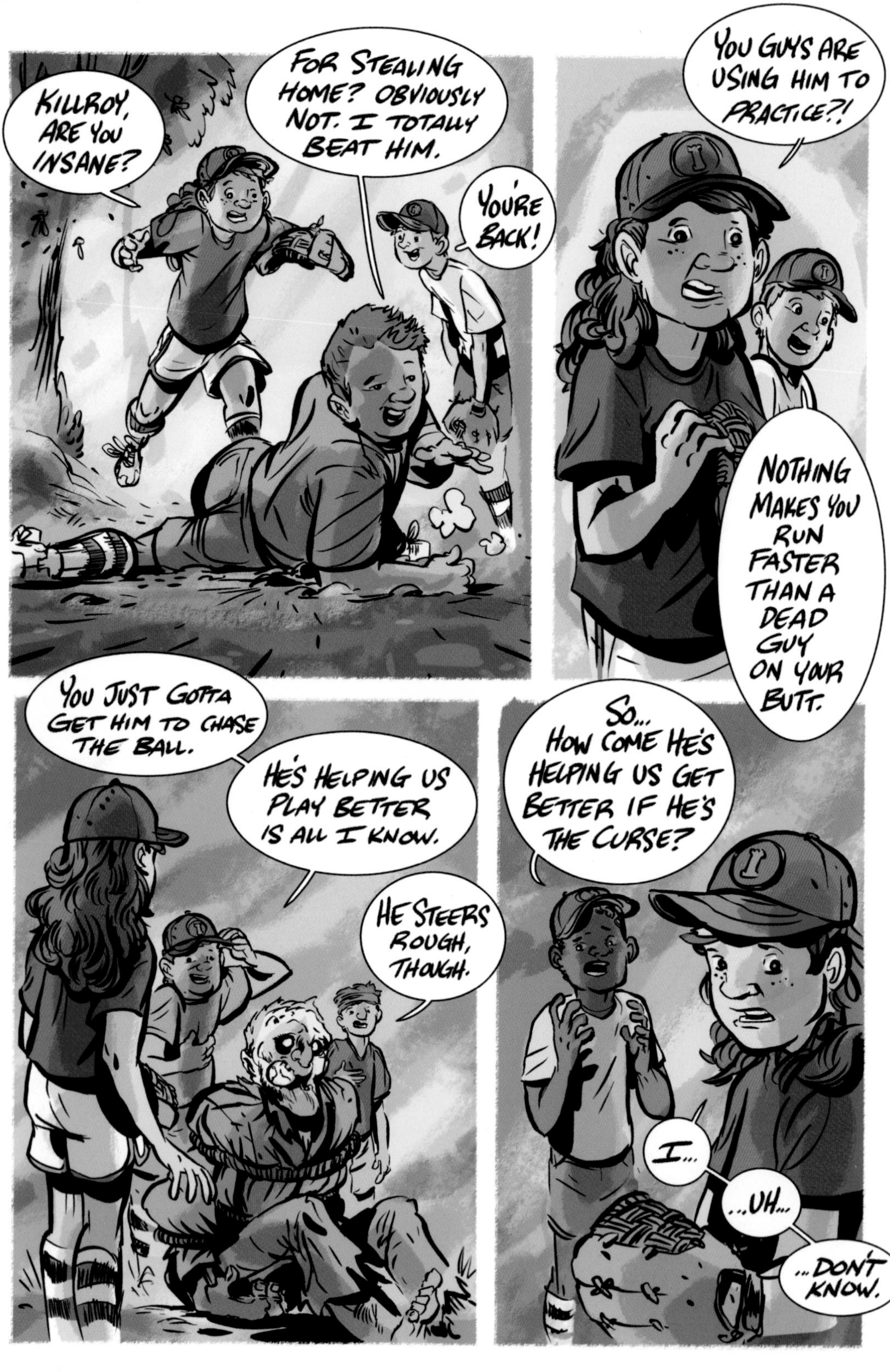

KILLROY, ARE YOU INSANE?
FOR STEALING HOME? OBVIOUSLY NOT. I TOTALLY BEAT HIM.
YOU'RE BACK!
YOU GUYS ARE USING HIM TO PRACTICE?!
NOTHING MAKES YOU RUN FASTER THAN A DEAD GUY ON YOUR BUTT.
YOU JUST GOTTA GET HIM TO CHASE THE BALL.
HE'S HELPING US PLAY BETTER IS ALL I KNOW.
HE STEERS ROUGH, THOUGH.
SO... HOW COME HE'S HELPING US GET BETTER IF HE'S THE CURSE?
I...
...UH...
...DON'T KNOW.

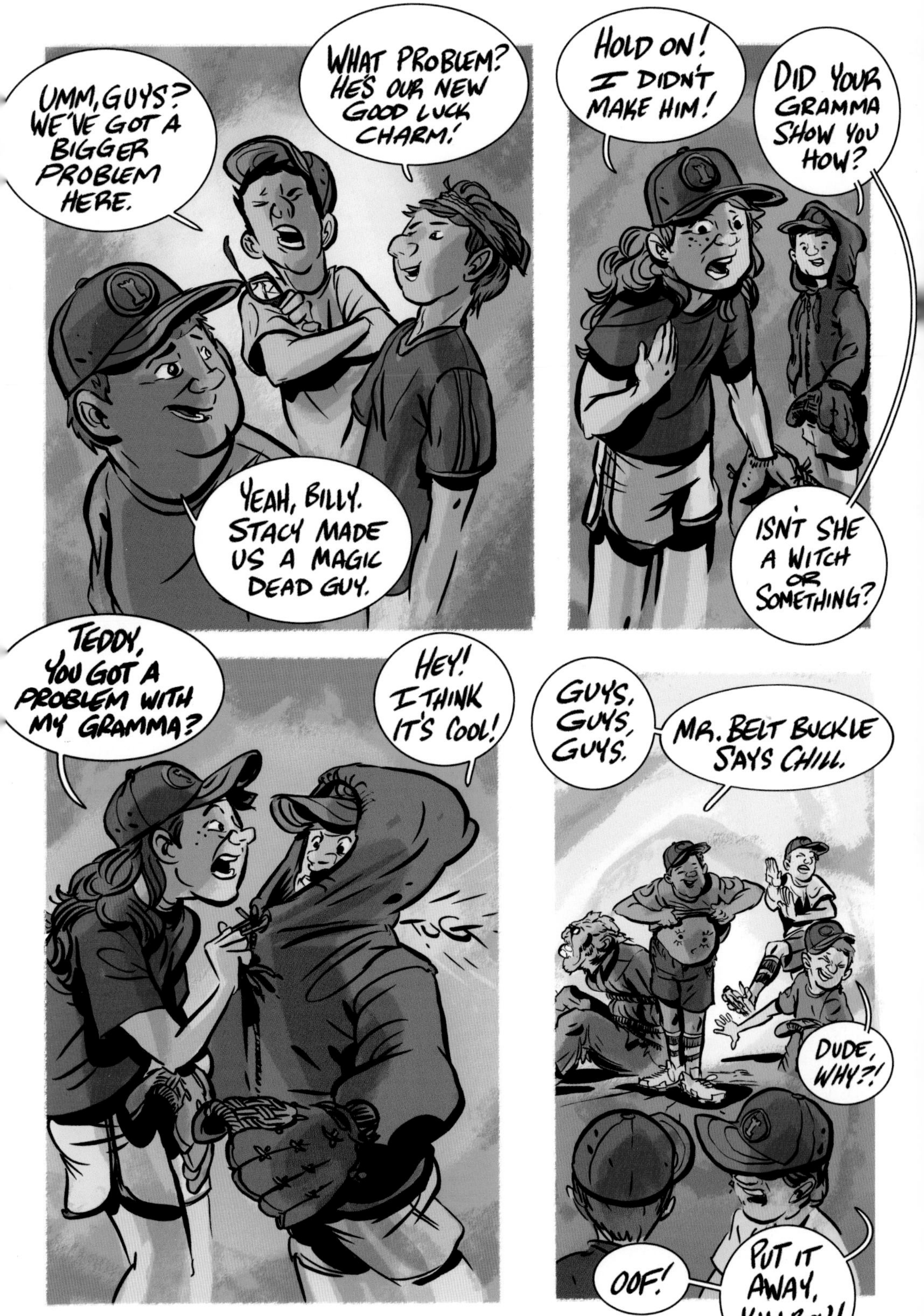
UMM, GUYS? WE'VE GOT A BIGGER PROBLEM HERE.
WHAT PROBLEM? HE'S OUR NEW GOOD LUCK CHARM!
YEAH, BILLY. STACY MADE US A MAGIC DEAD GUY.
HOLD ON! I DIDN'T MAKE HIM!
DID YOUR GRAMMA SHOW YOU HOW?
ISN'T SHE A WITCH OR SOMETHING?
TEDDY, YOU GOT A PROBLEM WITH MY GRAMMA?
HEY! I THINK IT'S COOL!
TUG
GUYS, GUYS, GUYS.
MR. BELT BUCKLE SAYS CHILL.
DUDE, WHY?!
OOF!
PUT IT AWAY, KILLROY!

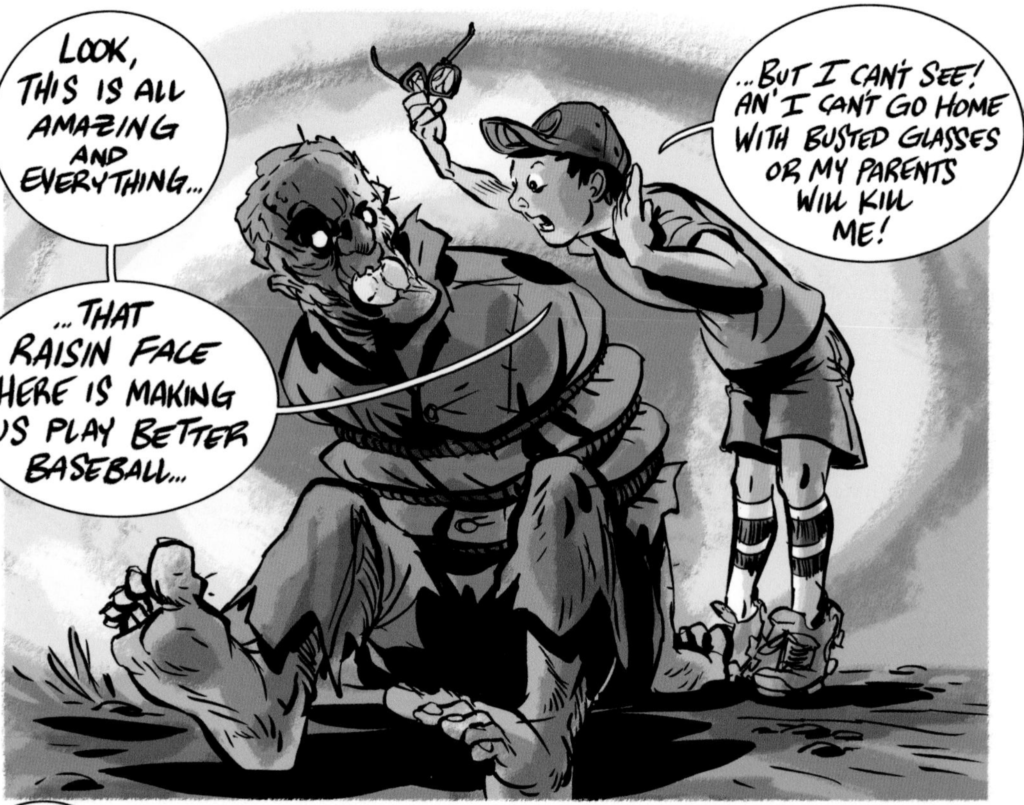
LOOK, THIS IS ALL AMAZING AND EVERYTHING...
...THAT RAISIN FACE HERE IS MAKING US PLAY BETTER BASEBALL...
...BUT I CAN'T SEE! AN' I CAN'T GO HOME WITH BUSTED GLASSES OR MY PARENTS WILL KILL ME!

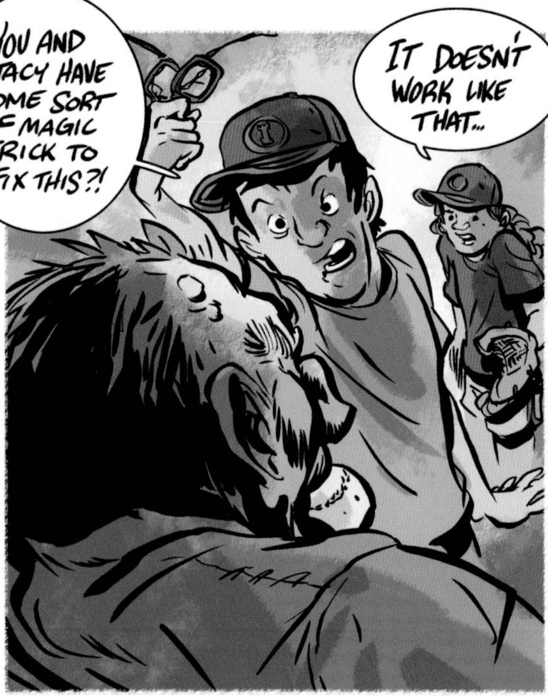
YOU AND STACY HAVE SOME SORT OF MAGIC TRICK TO FIX THIS?!
IT DOESN'T WORK LIKE THAT...

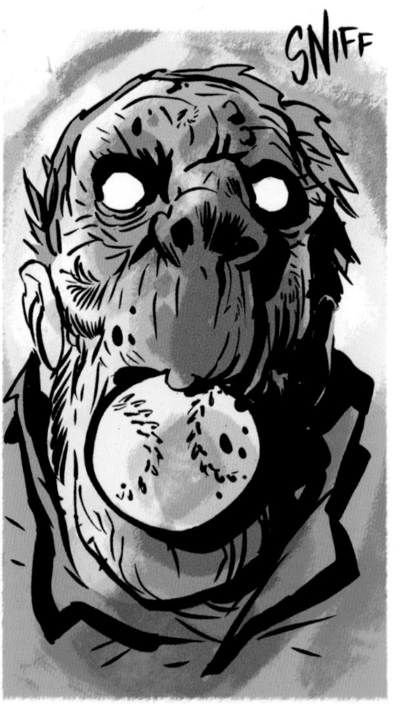
SNIFF

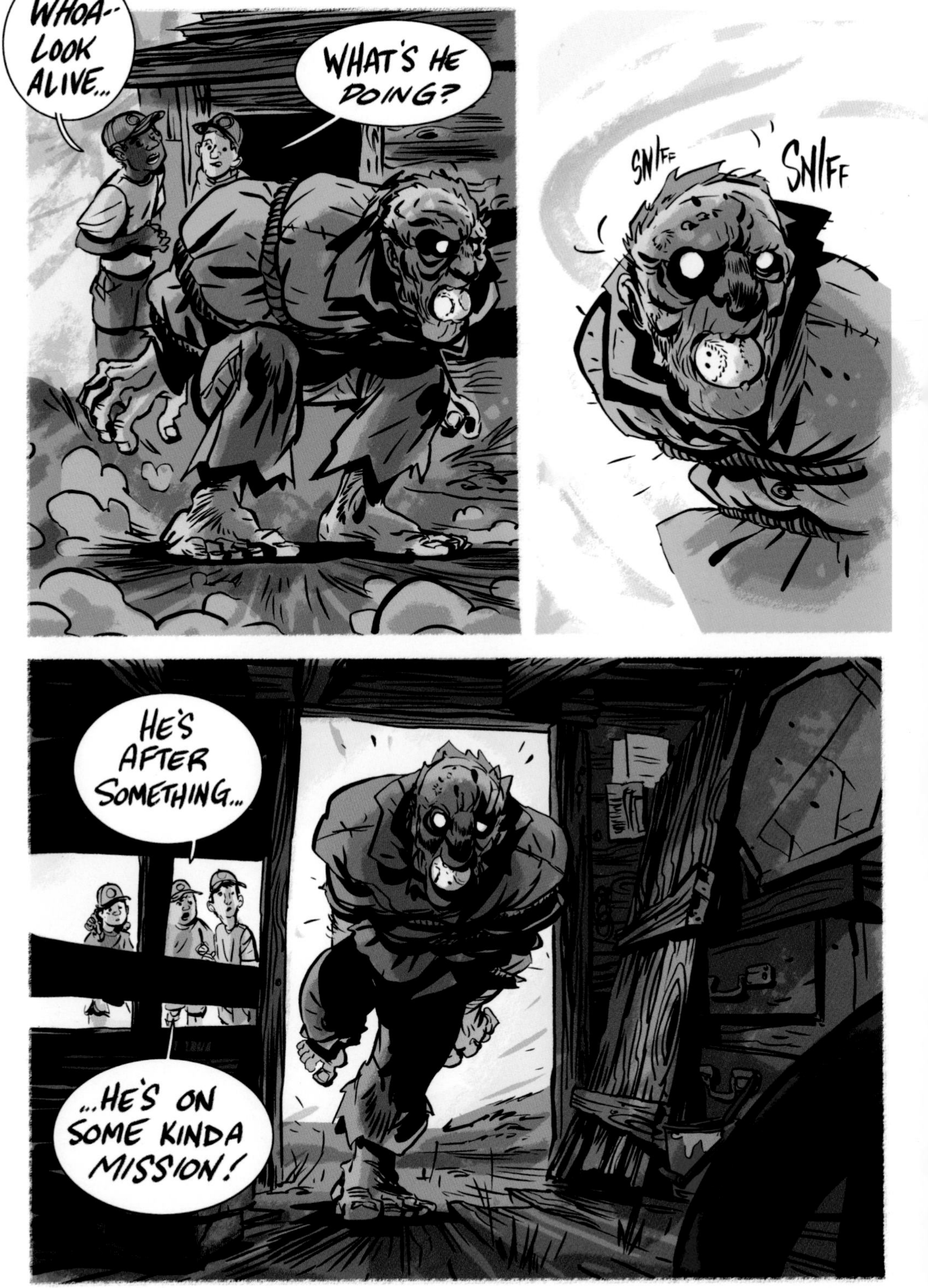
WHOA-- LOOK ALIVE...
WHAT'S HE DOING?
SNIFF
SNIFF
HE'S AFTER SOMETHING...
...HE'S ON SOME KINDA MISSION!

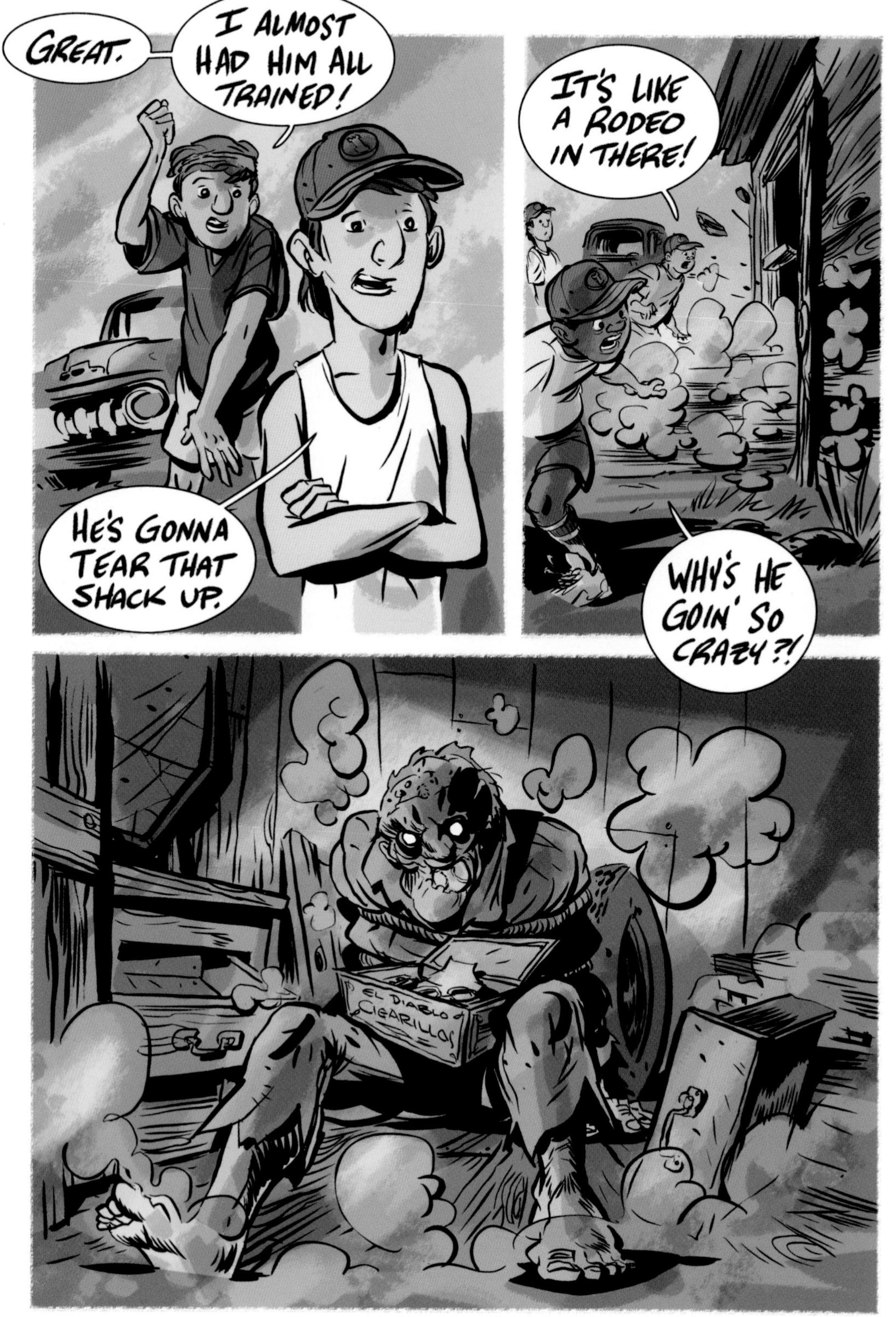
GREAT.
I ALMOST HAD HIM ALL TRAINED!
HE'S GONNA TEAR THAT SHACK UP.
IT'S LIKE A RODEO IN THERE!
WHY'S HE GOIN' SO CRAZY?!
EL DIABLO CIGARILLOS

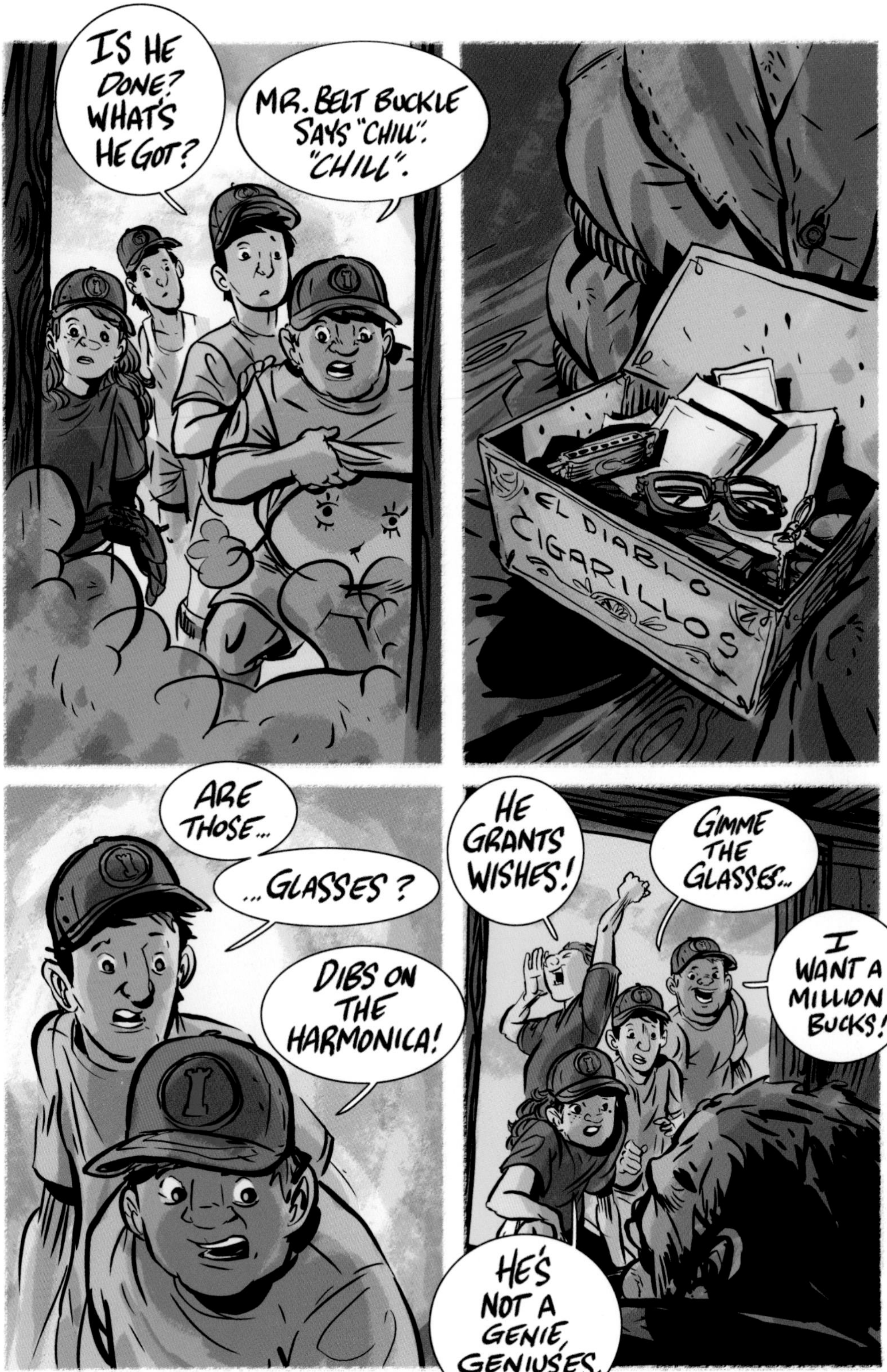
IS HE DONE? WHAT'S HE GOT?
MR. BELT BUCKLE SAYS "CHILL". "CHILL".
EL DIABLO CIGARILLOS
ARE THOSE...
...GLASSES?
DIBS ON THE HARMONICA!
HE GRANTS WISHES!
GIMME THE GLASSES...
I WANT A MILLION BUCKS!
HE'S NOT A GENIE, GENIUSES.

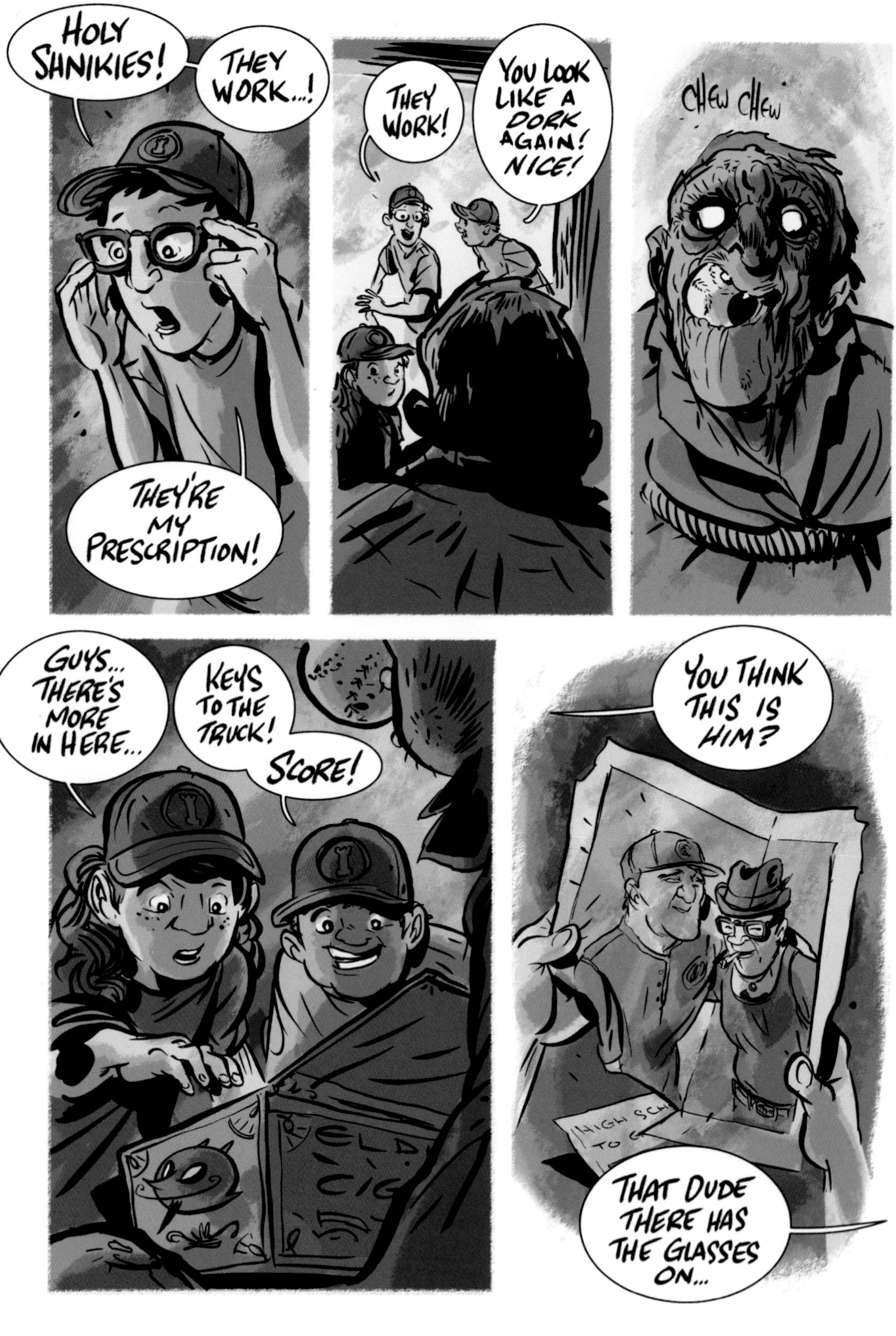
HOLY SHNIKIES!
THEY WORK...!
THEY'RE MY PRESCRIPTION!
THEY WORK!
YOU LOOK LIKE A DORK AGAIN! NICE!
CHEW CHEW
GUYS... THERE'S MORE IN HERE...
KEYS TO THE TRUCK!
SCORE!
YOU THINK THIS IS HIM?
THAT DUDE THERE HAS THE GLASSES ON...

THERE'S AN OLD ARTICLE HERE.

LET'S SEE WHAT'S IN THE NEWS...

CAREFUL... THAT'S SO OLD IT'S FALLING APART.

HYEAH. JUST LIKE HIM!

GOMEZ! DUDE! HE CAN HEAR YOU...!

HE CAN TAKE A JOKE.

CHECK IT OUT...

...HE WAS A ROOKIE SHORTSTOP!

THIS SAYS IT WAS FOUL PLAY.

SHORT STO
CUT SHORT

BASEBALL HOPEFUL
PRESUMED DEAD

...his rookie year
...akvale native then
...ar short stop with
...of .410. After a

...hasn't been seen.
...s last game ended
...urprise upset due
...icide squeeze in
...ninth inning.

...brother has
...isappeared as
...ll. Foul play
...s suspected and
...but the missing

HEH HEH... 'FOUL PLAY'.

GET IT?

I GET THAT IT MAYBE MEANS MURDER.

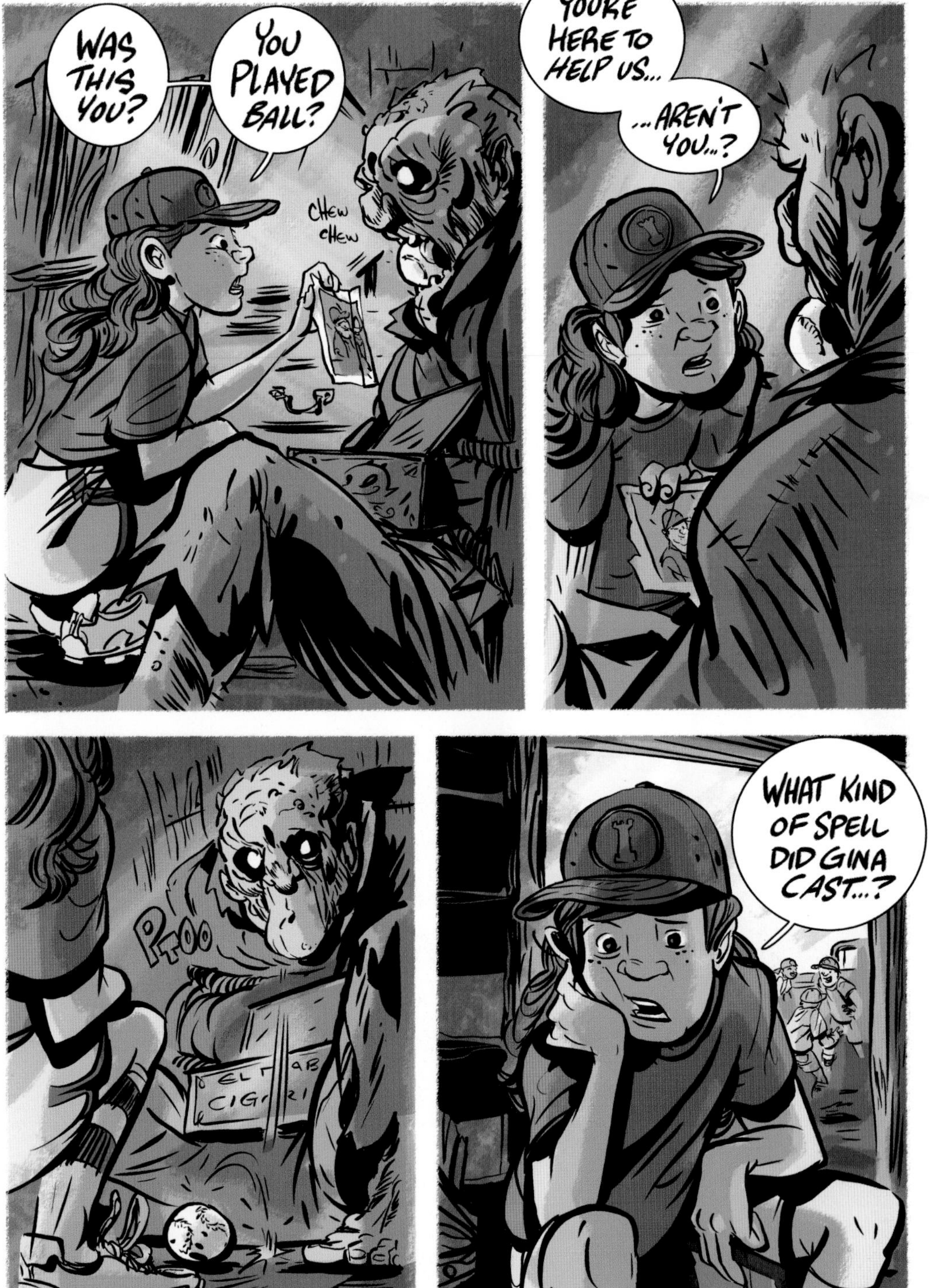
WAS THIS YOU?
YOU PLAYED BALL?
CHEW CHEW
YOU'RE HERE TO HELP US...
...AREN'T YOU...?
PTOO
WHAT KIND OF SPELL DID GINA CAST...?

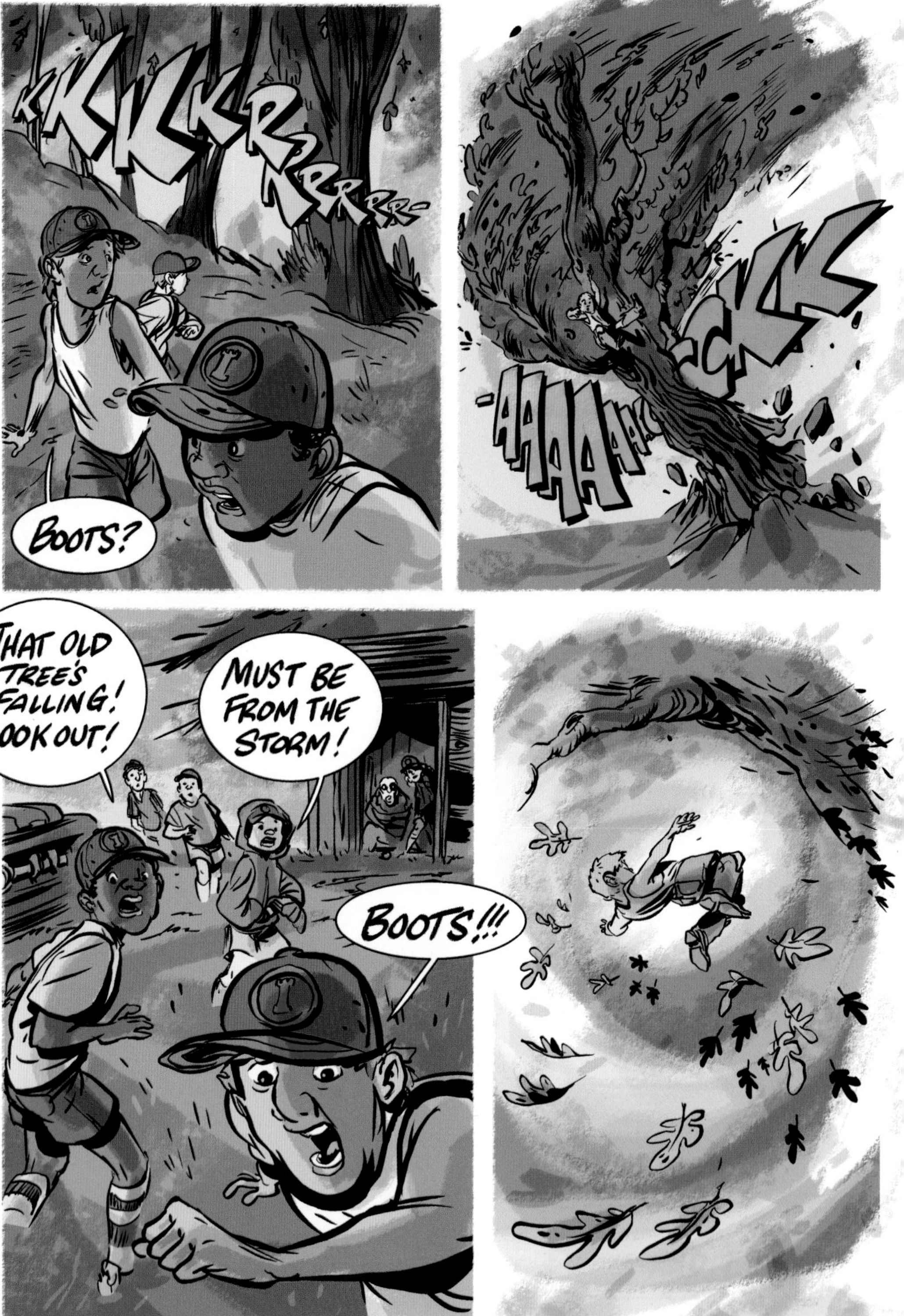
KKKKRRRRRR
BOOTS?
AAAAA
CCKK
THAT OLD TREE'S FALLING! LOOK OUT!
MUST BE FROM THE STORM!
BOOTS!!!

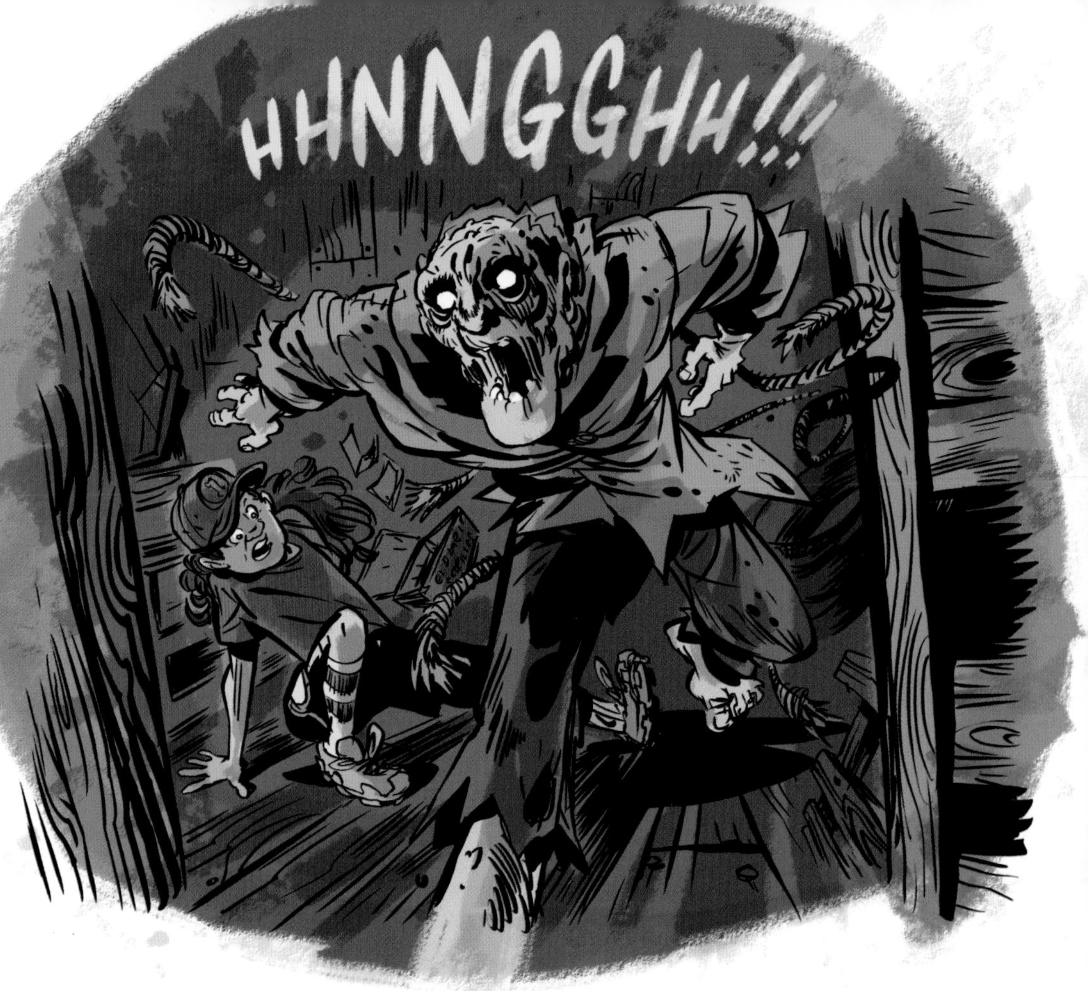
HHNNGGHH!!!

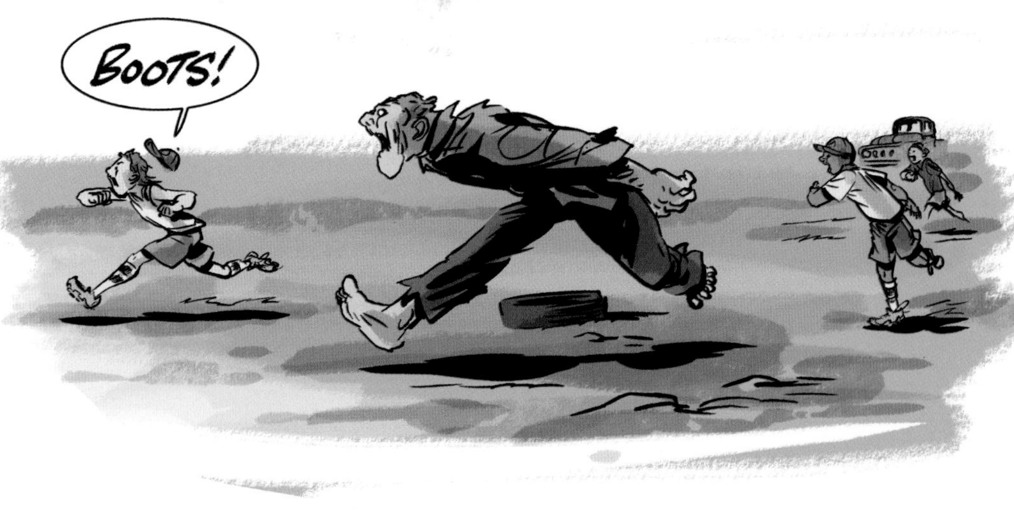
BOOTS!

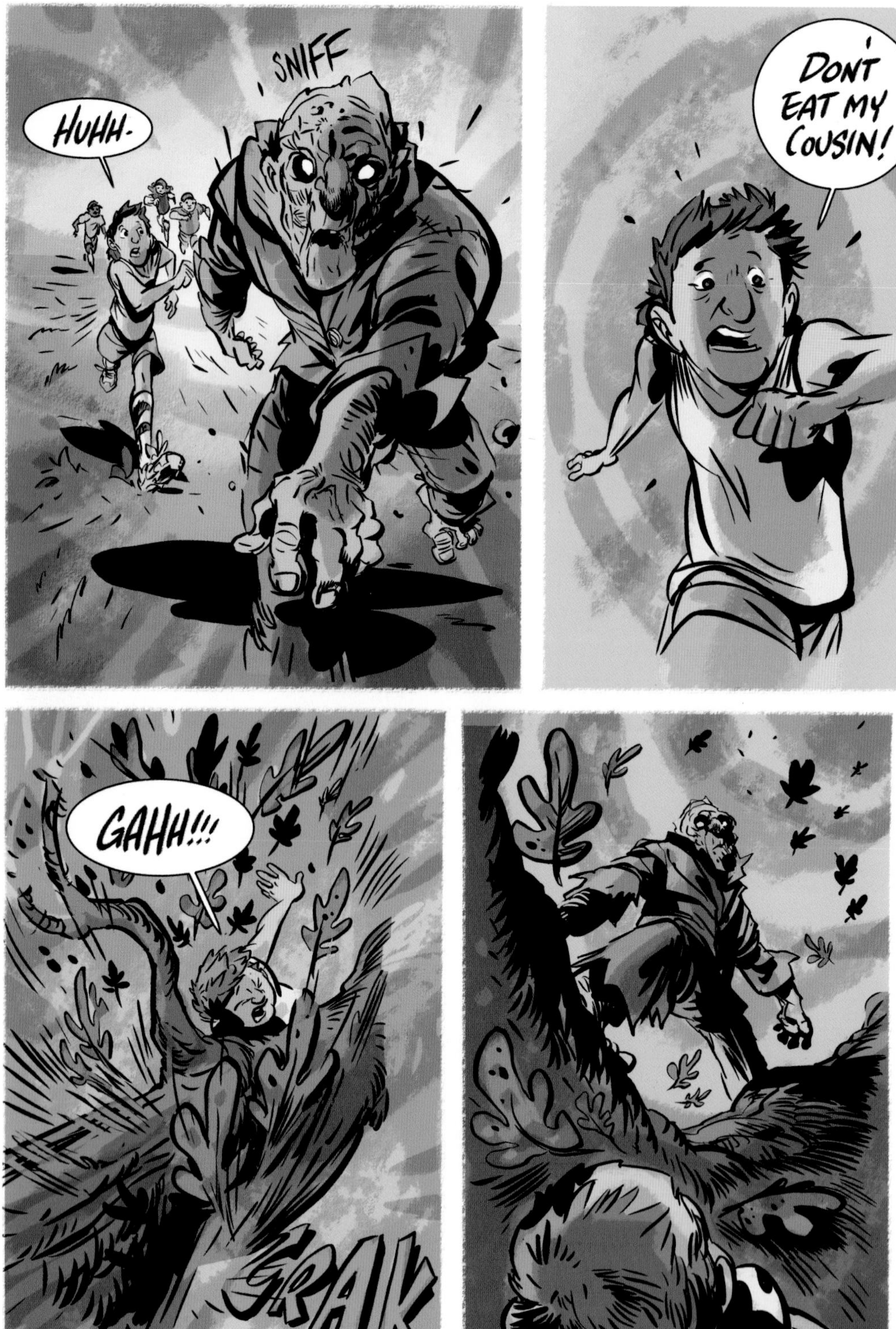
SNIFF
HUHH-
DON'T EAT MY COUSIN!
GAHH!!!
GRAK

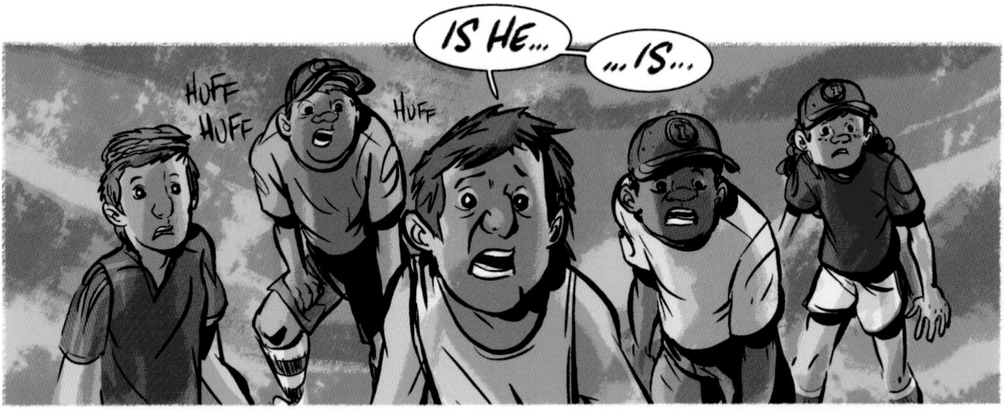
IS HE...
...IS...
HUFF
HUFF
HUFF

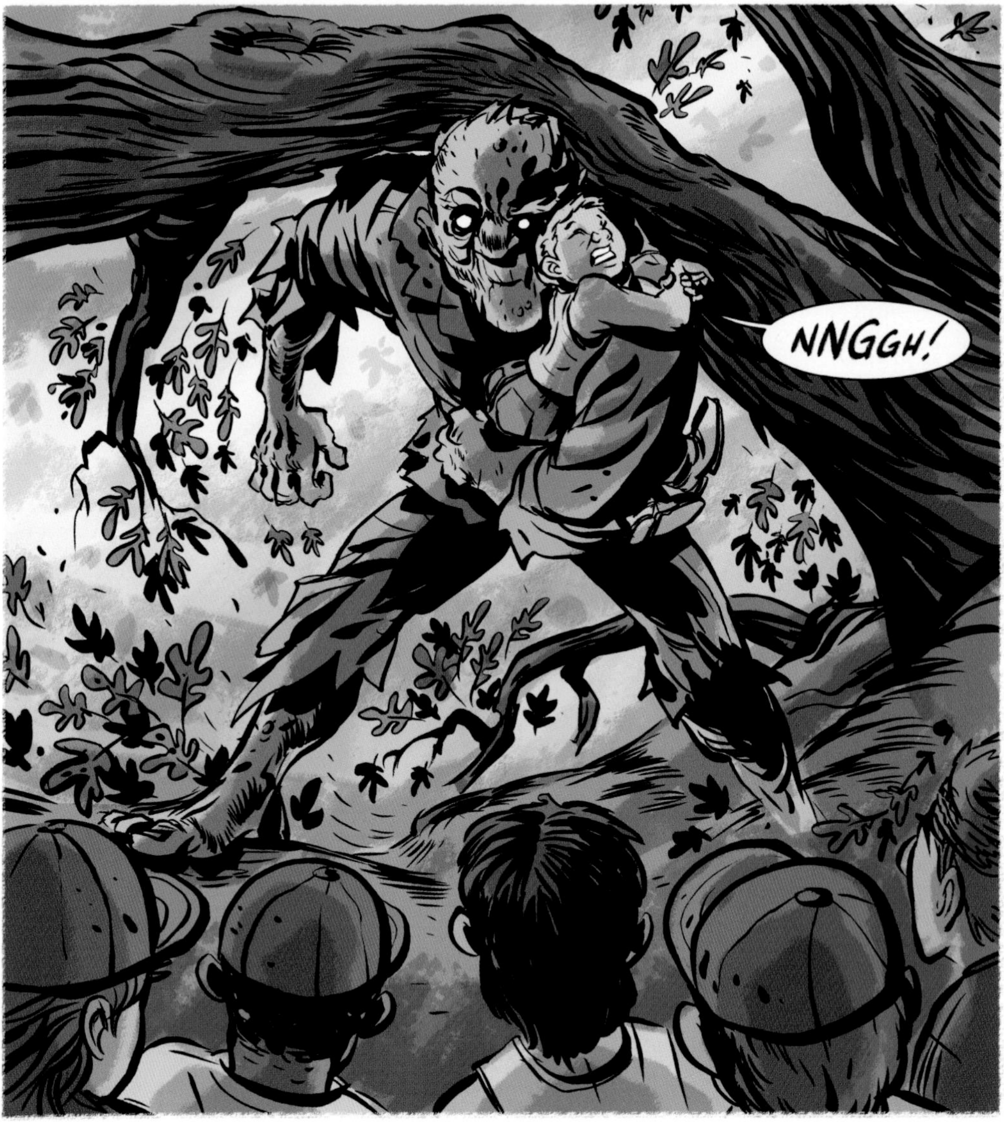
NNGGH!

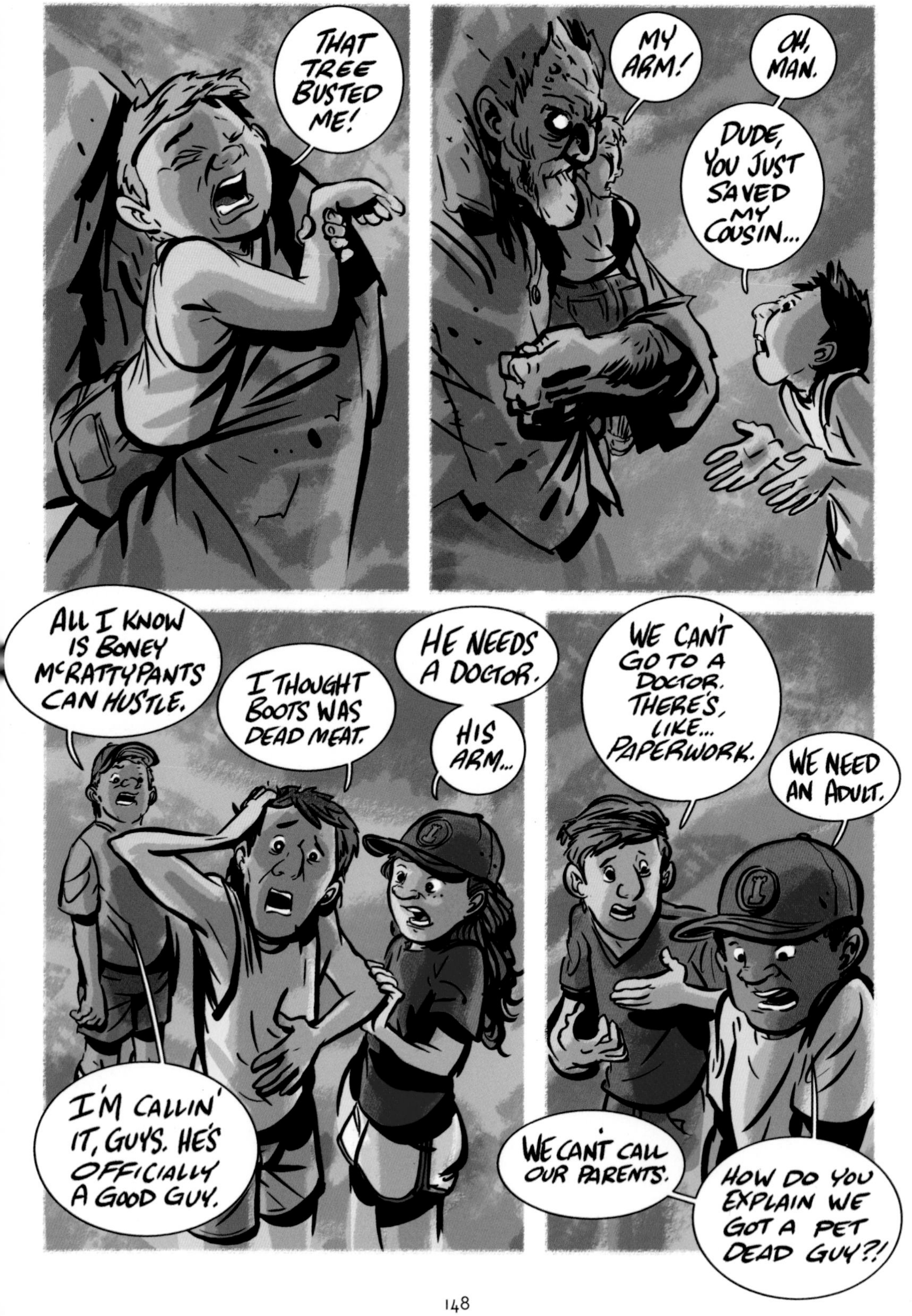
THAT TREE BUSTED ME!
MY ARM!
OH, MAN.
DUDE, YOU JUST SAVED MY COUSIN...
ALL I KNOW IS BONEY MCRATTYPANTS CAN HUSTLE.
I THOUGHT BOOTS WAS DEAD MEAT.
HE NEEDS A DOCTOR.
HIS ARM...
I'M CALLIN' IT, GUYS. HE'S OFFICIALLY A GOOD GUY.
WE CAN'T GO TO A DOCTOR. THERE'S, LIKE... PAPERWORK.
WE NEED AN ADULT.
WE CAN'T CALL OUR PARENTS.
HOW DO YOU EXPLAIN WE GOT A PET DEAD GUY?!

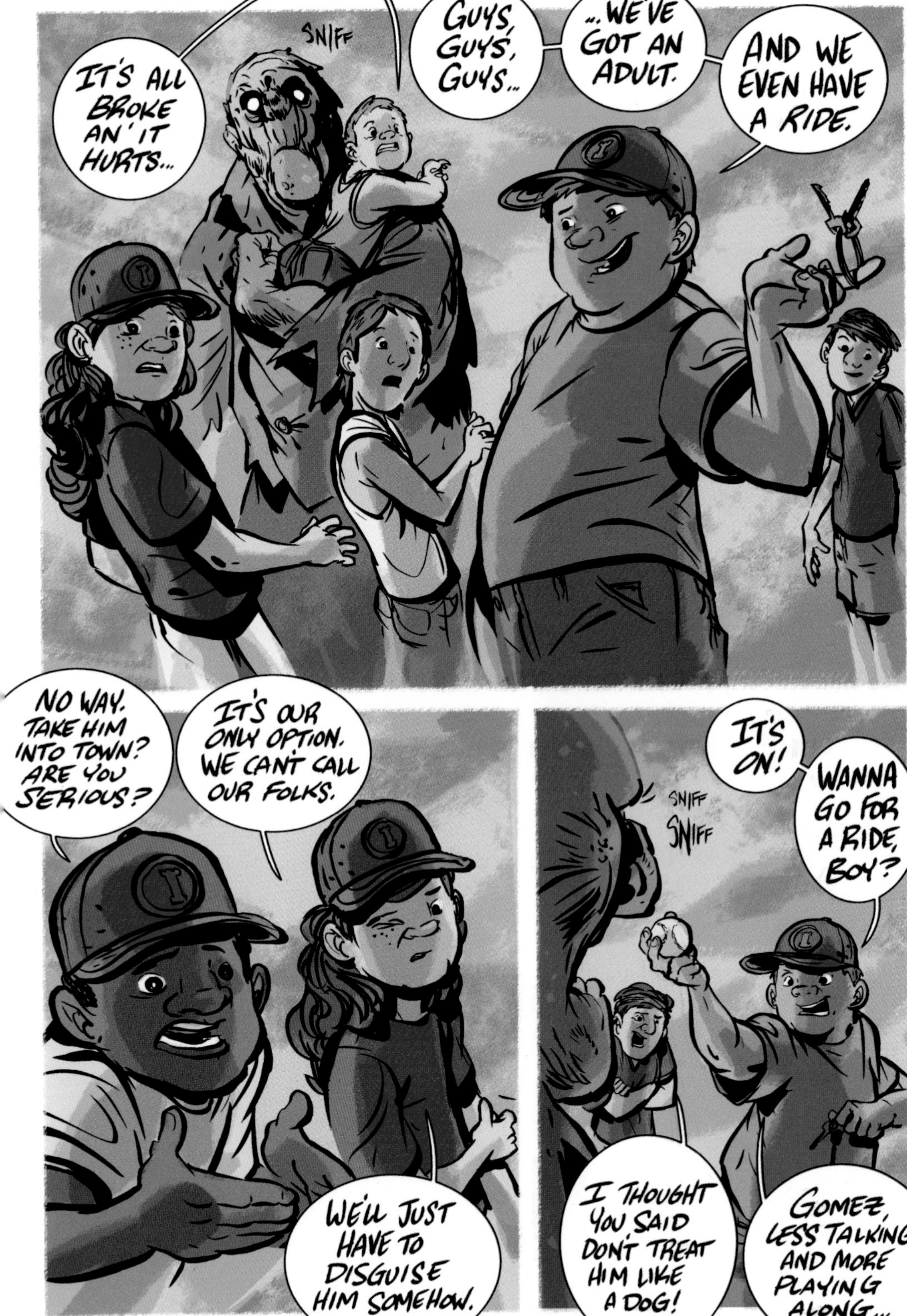
SNIFF
IT'S ALL BROKE AN' IT HURTS...
GUYS, GUYS, GUYS...
...WE'VE GOT AN ADULT.
AND WE EVEN HAVE A RIDE.
NO WAY. TAKE HIM INTO TOWN? ARE YOU SERIOUS?
IT'S OUR ONLY OPTION. WE CAN'T CALL OUR FOLKS.
WE'LL JUST HAVE TO DISGUISE HIM SOMEHOW.
IT'S ON!
SNIFF SNIFF
WANNA GO FOR A RIDE, BOY?
I THOUGHT YOU SAID DON'T TREAT HIM LIKE A DOG!
GOMEZ, LESS TALKING AND MORE PLAYING ALONG...

168

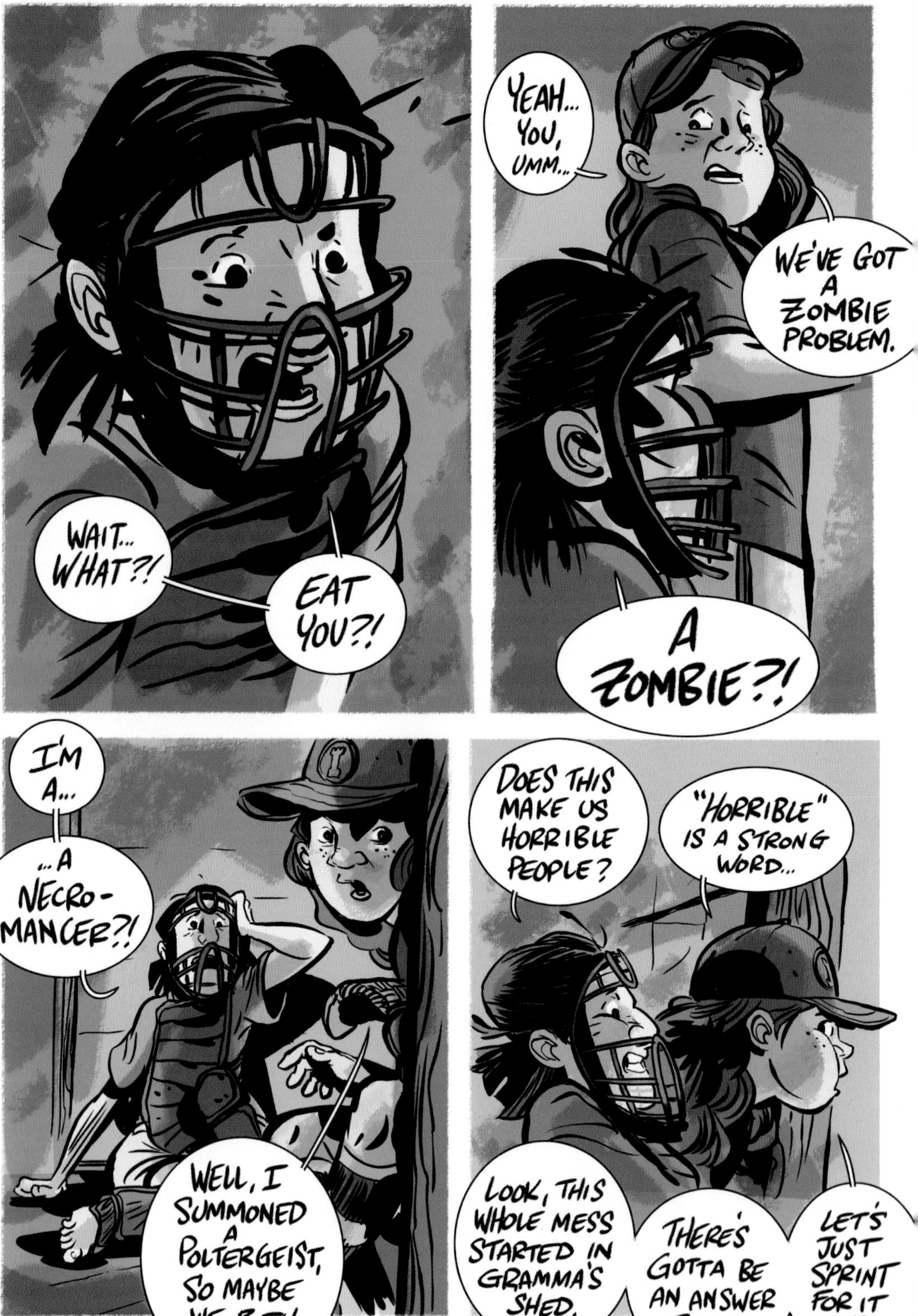
WAIT... WHAT?!
EAT YOU?!
YEAH... YOU, UMM...
WE'VE GOT A ZOMBIE PROBLEM.
A ZOMBIE?!
I'M A...
...A NECRO-MANCER?!
WELL, I SUMMONED A POLTERGEIST, SO MAYBE WE BOTH ARE?
DOES THIS MAKE US HORRIBLE PEOPLE?
"HORRIBLE" IS A STRONG WORD...
LOOK, THIS WHOLE MESS STARTED IN GRAMMA'S SHED.
THERE'S GOTTA BE AN ANSWER THERE.
LET'S JUST SPRINT FOR IT AND--

183

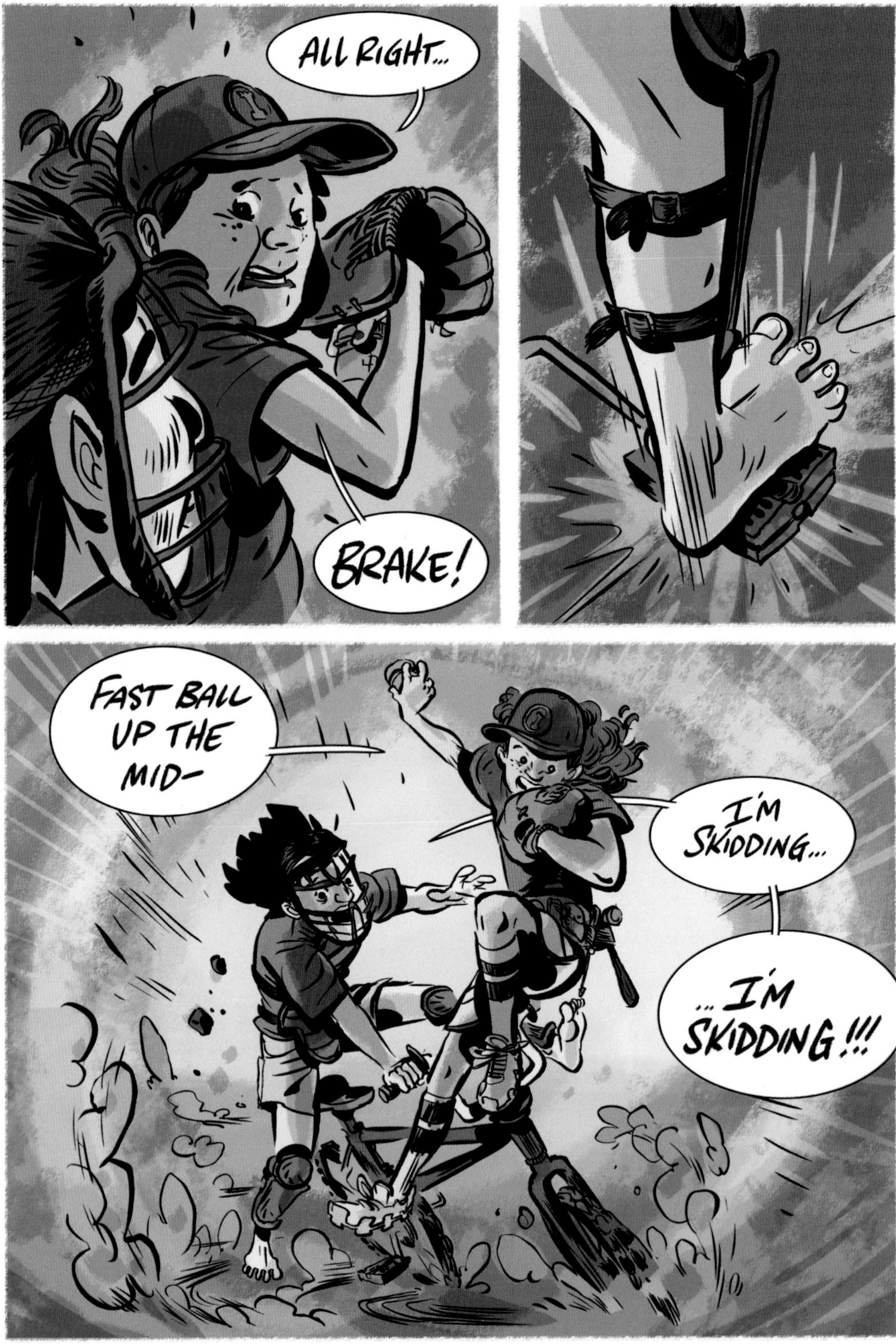
ALL RIGHT...
BRAKE!
FAST BALL UP THE MID-
I'M SKIDDING...
...I'M SKIDDING!!!

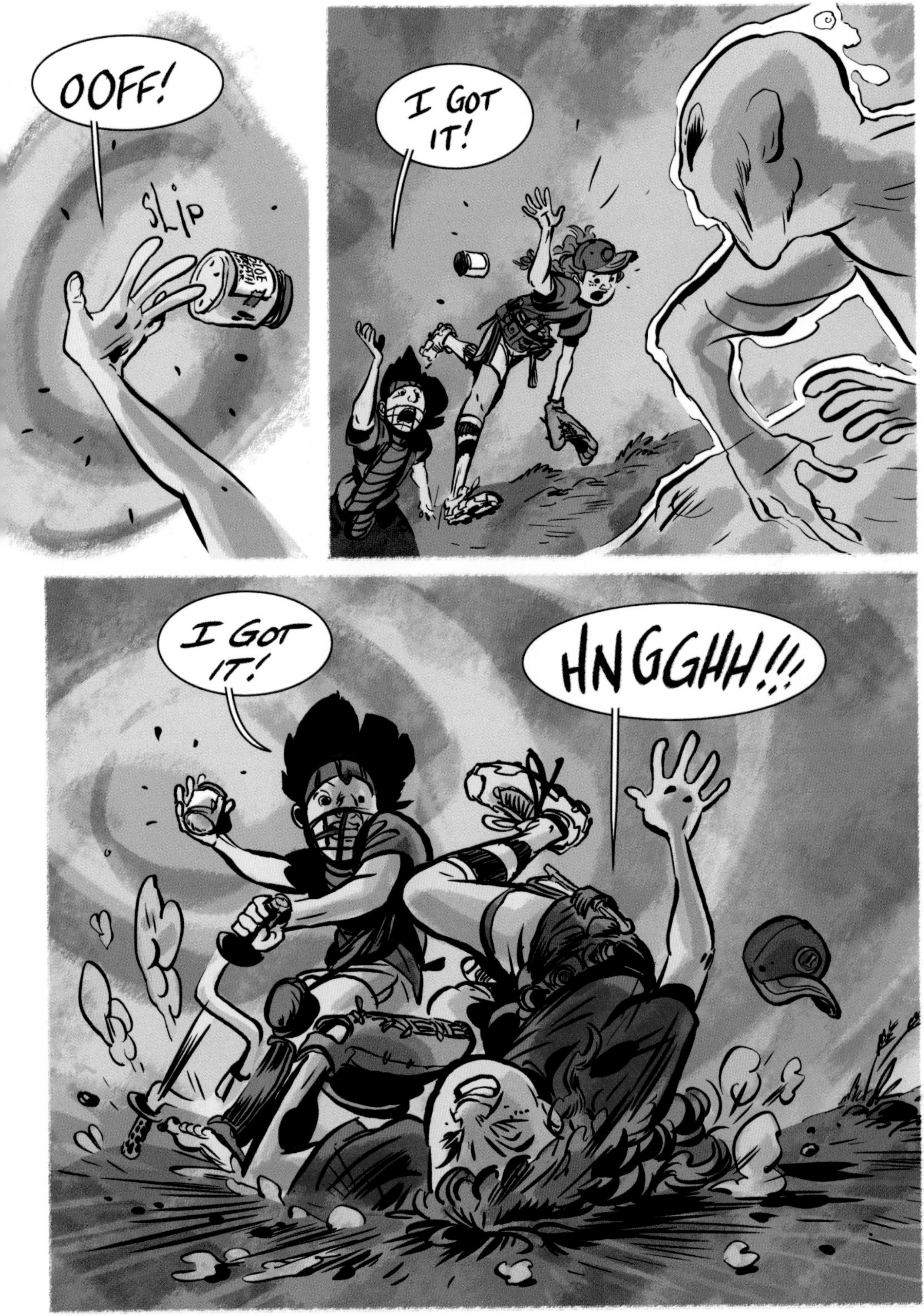
OOFF!
SLIP
I GOT IT!
I GOT IT!
HNGGHH!!!

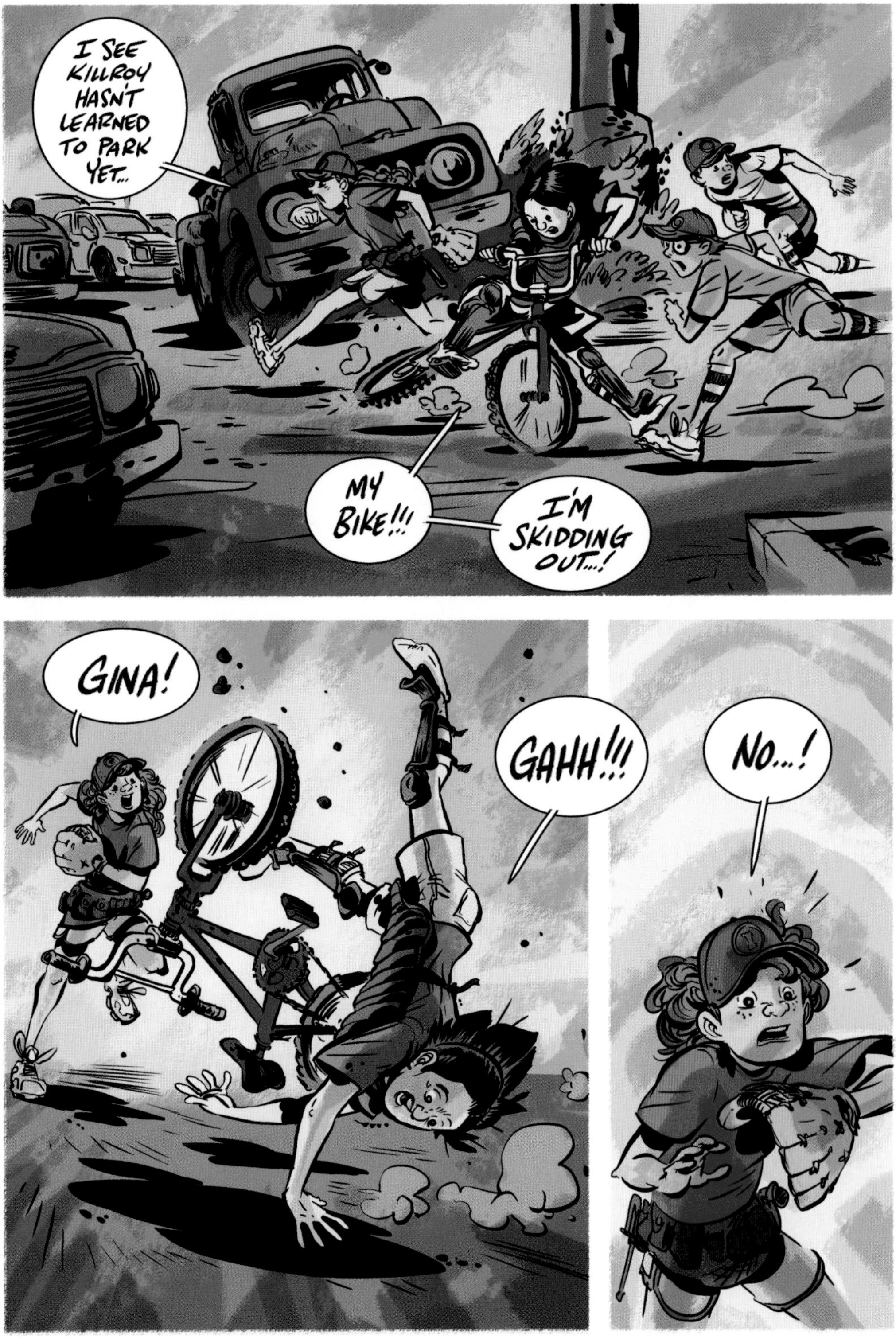
I SEE KILLROY HASN'T LEARNED TO PARK YET...
MY BIKE!!!
I'M SKIDDING OUT...!
GINA!
GAHH!!!
NO...!

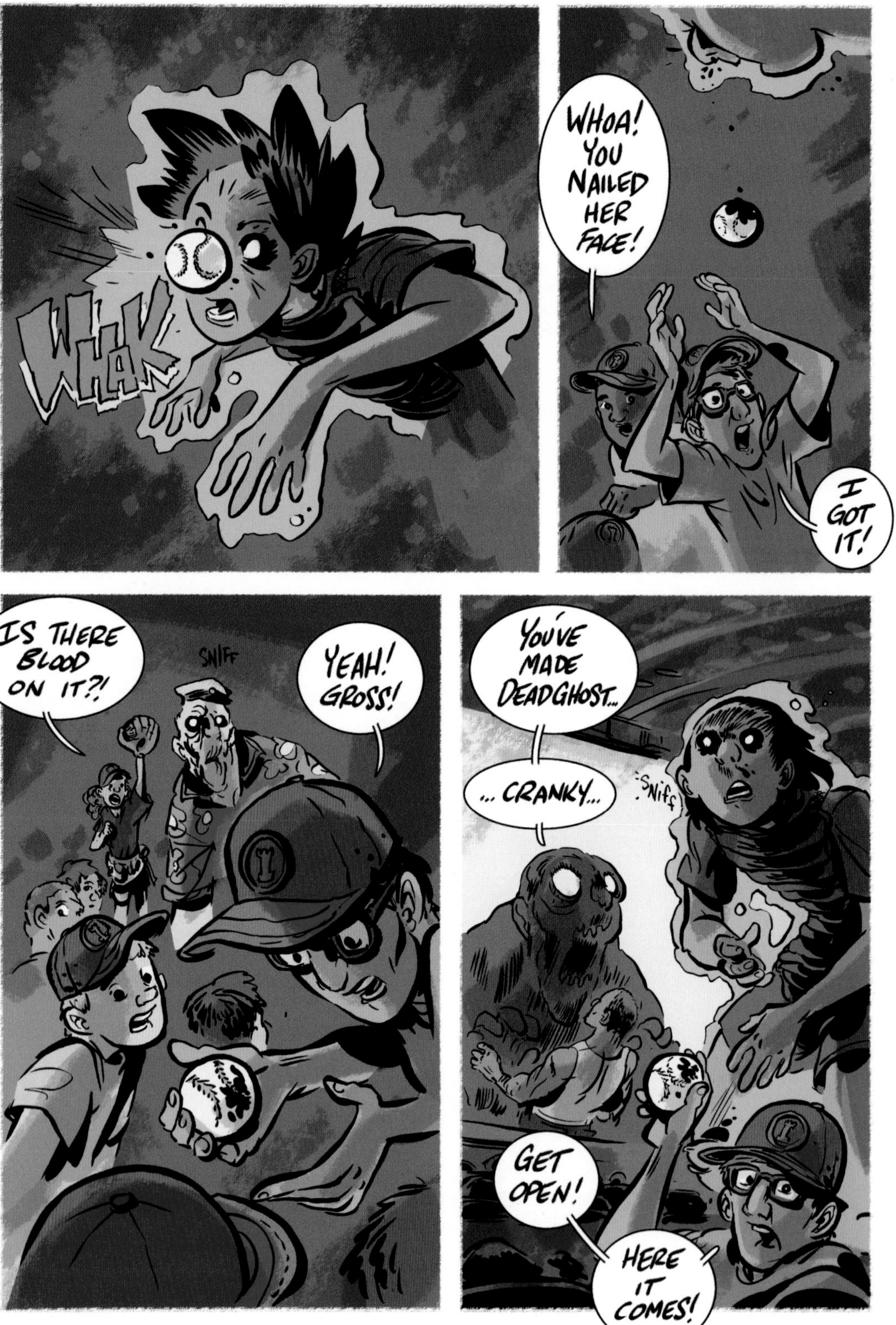
WHAK
WHOA! YOU NAILED HER FACE!
I GOT IT!
IS THERE BLOOD ON IT?!
SNIFF
YEAH! GROSS!
YOU'VE MADE DEADGHOST...
... CRANKY...
SNIFF
GET OPEN!
HERE IT COMES!

224

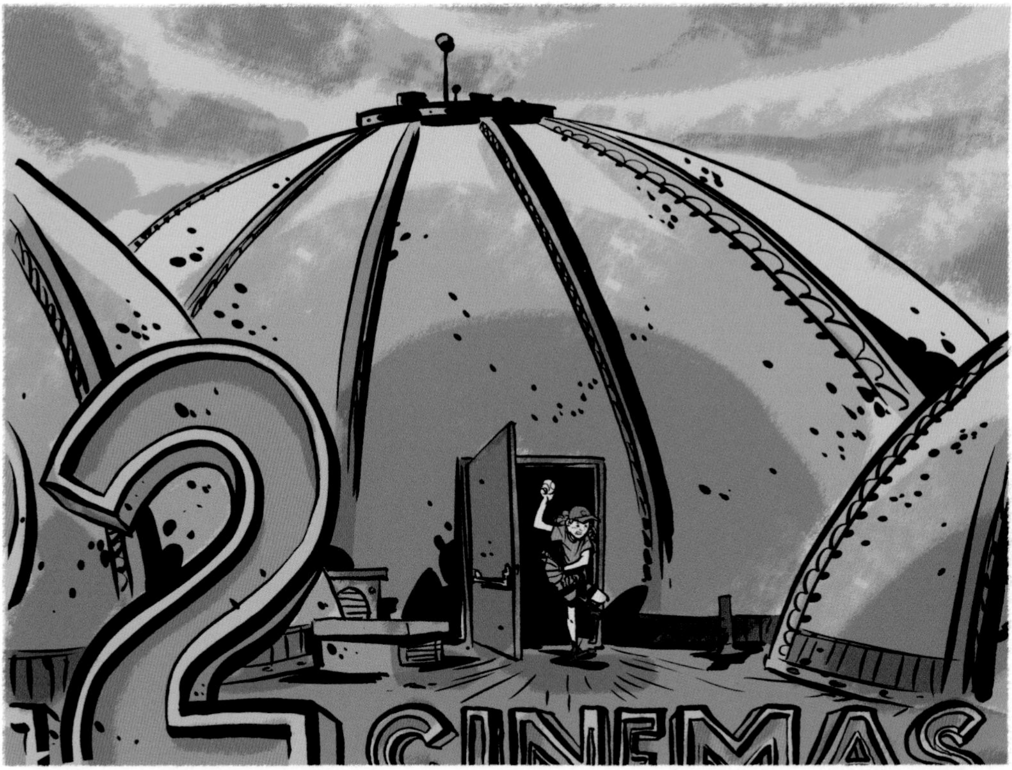
2
CINEMAS

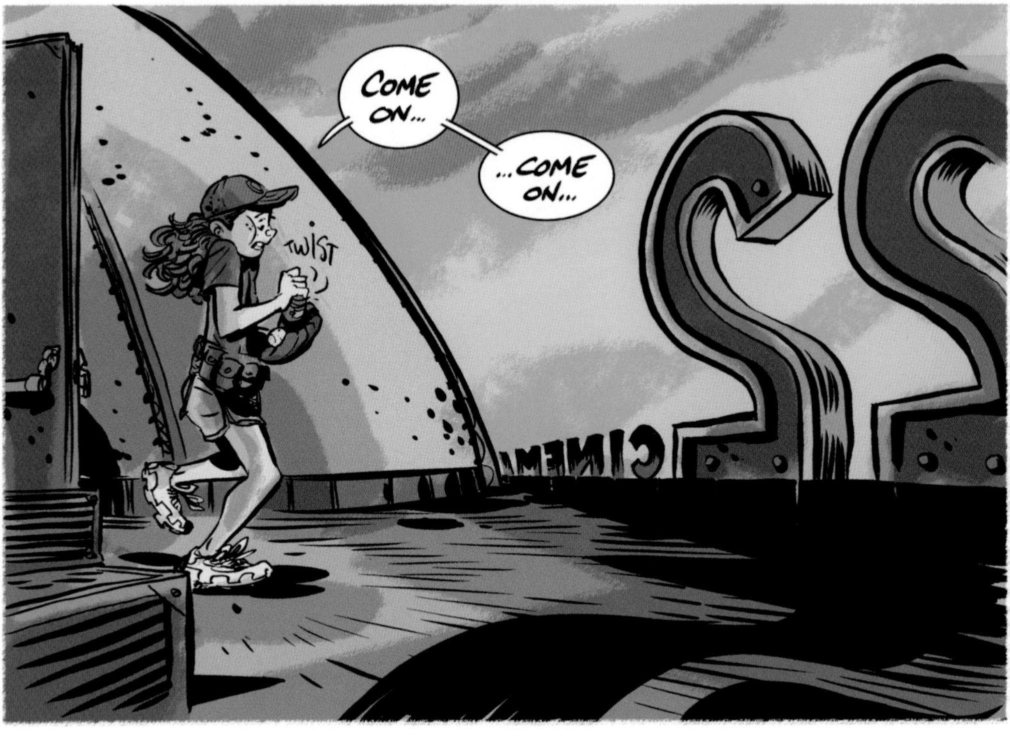
COME ON...
...COME ON...
TWIST

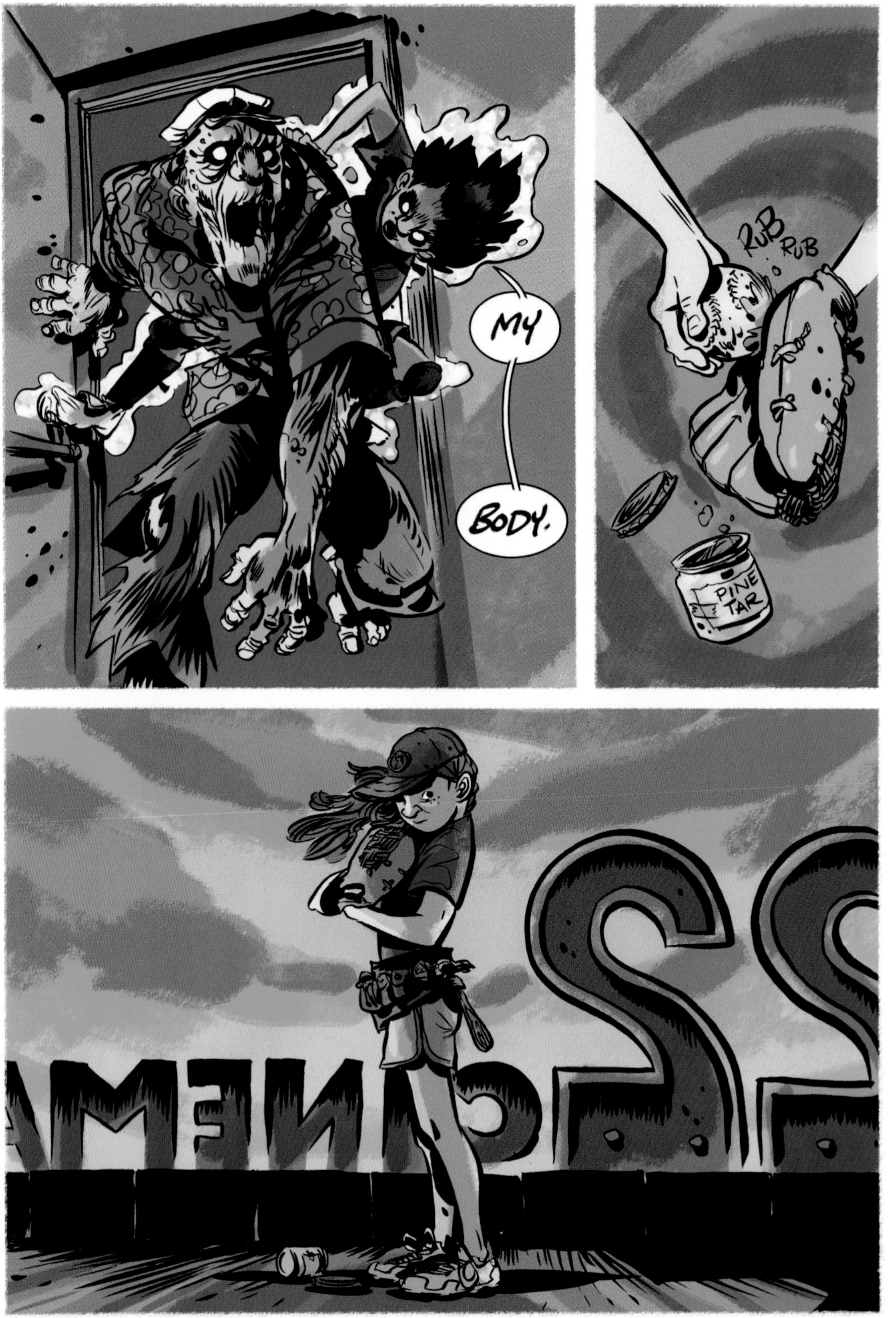
MY
BODY.
RUB RUB
PINE TAR

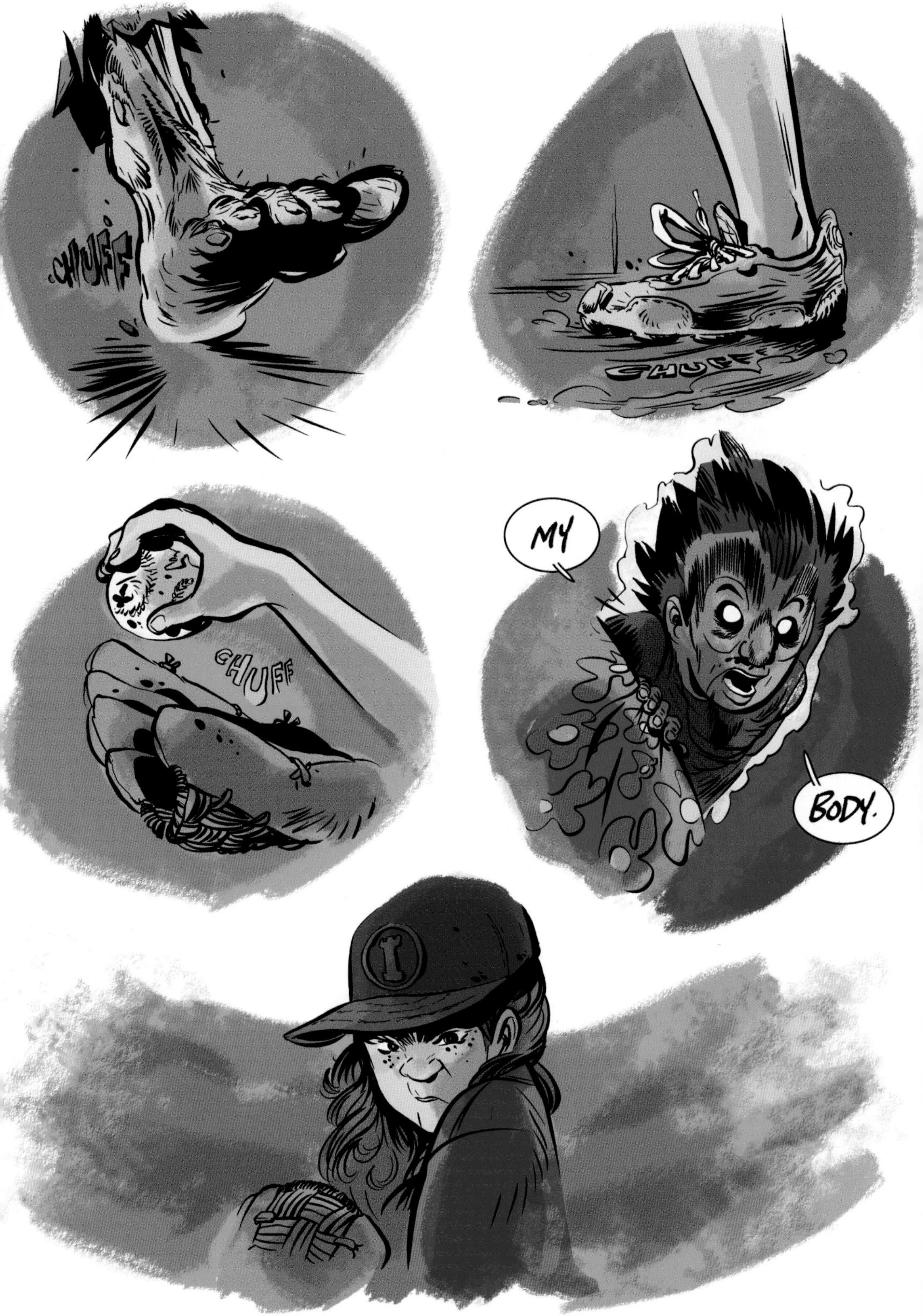
CHUFF
CHUFF
CHUFF
MY
BODY.

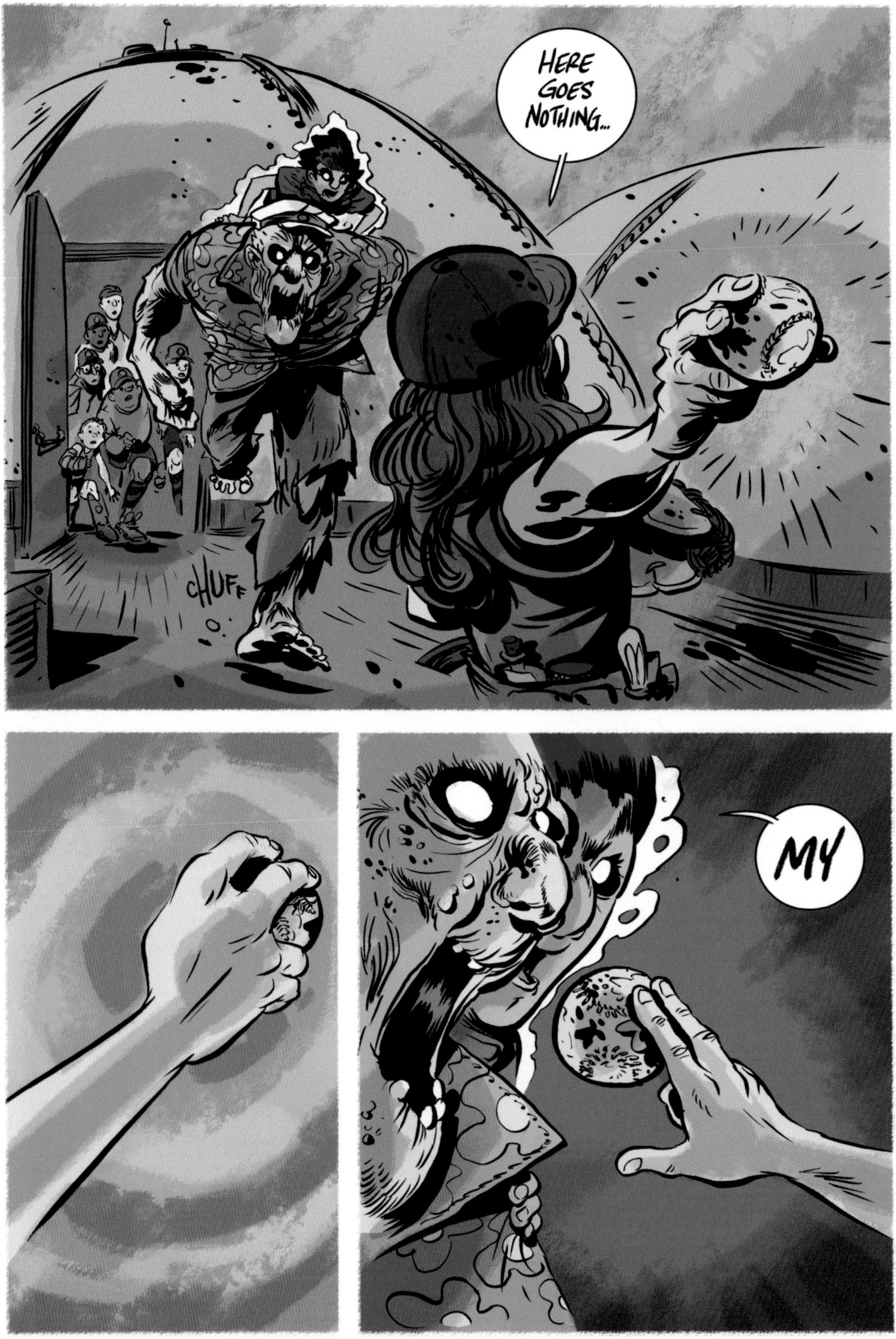
HERE GOES NOTHING...
CHUFF
MY

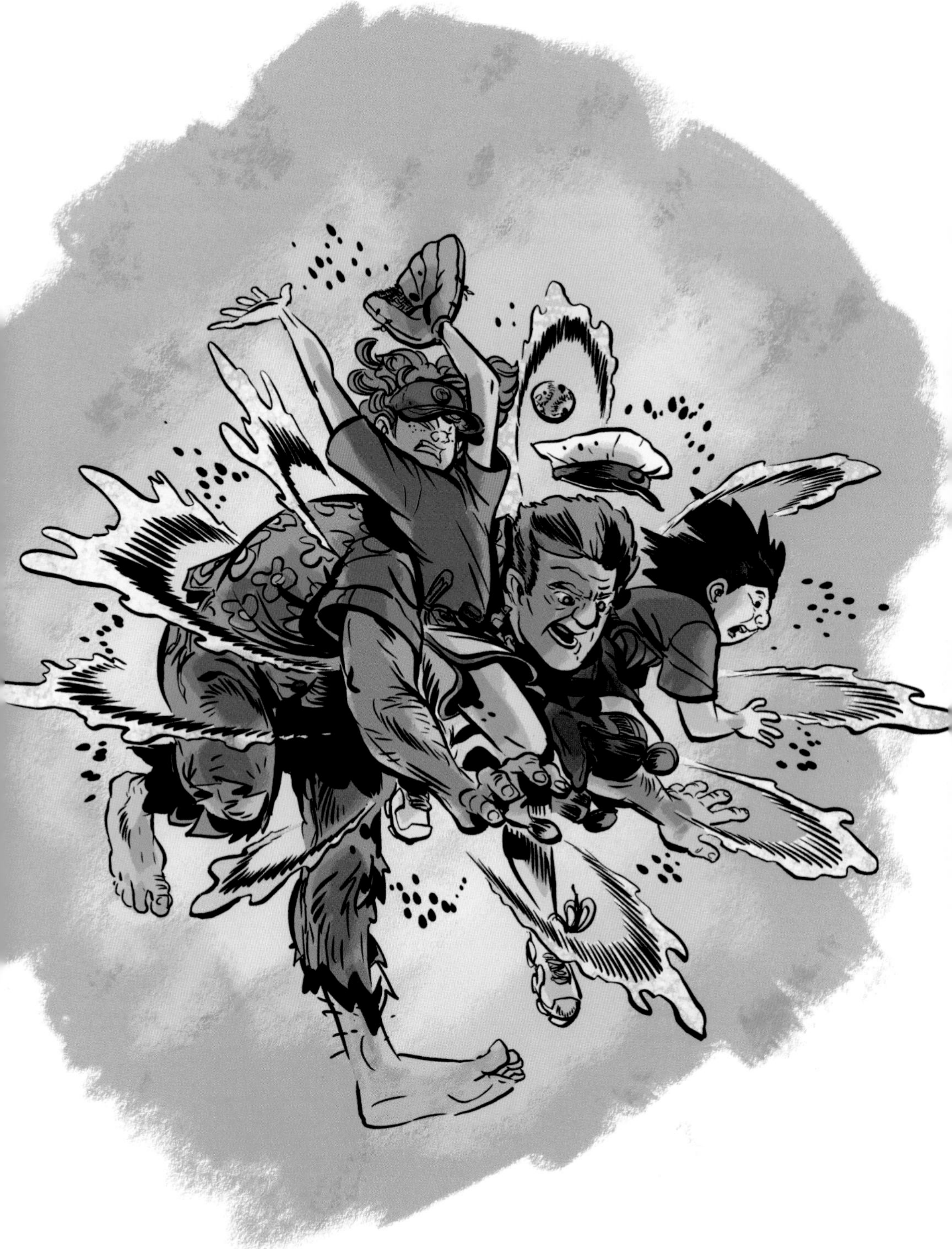

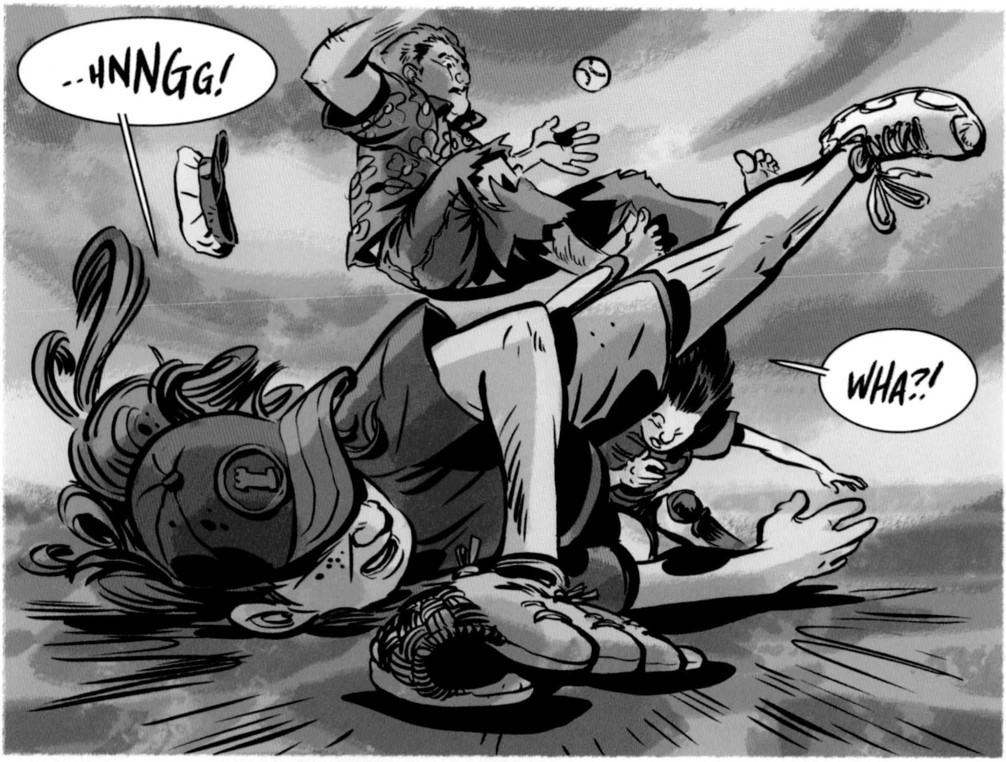
--HNNGG!
WHA?!

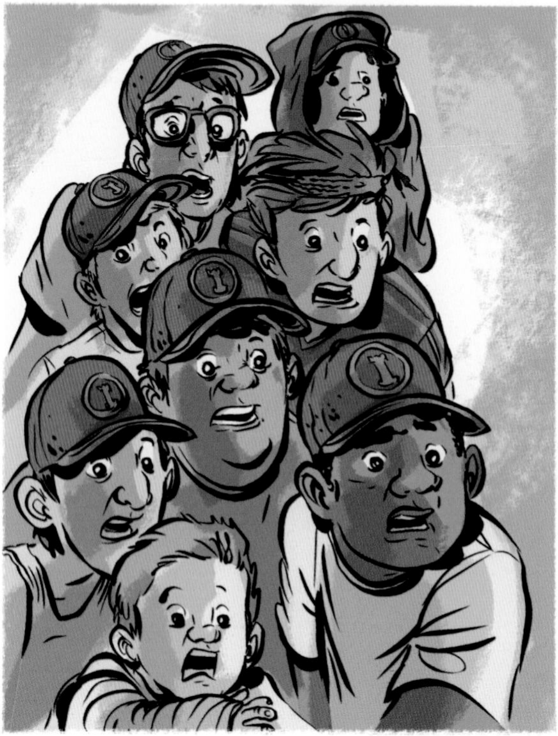

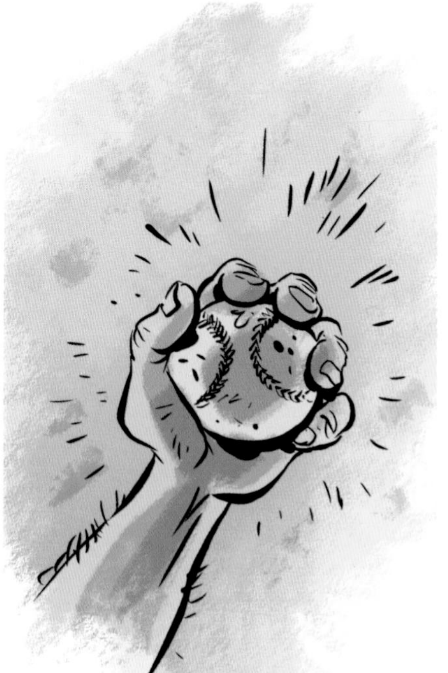

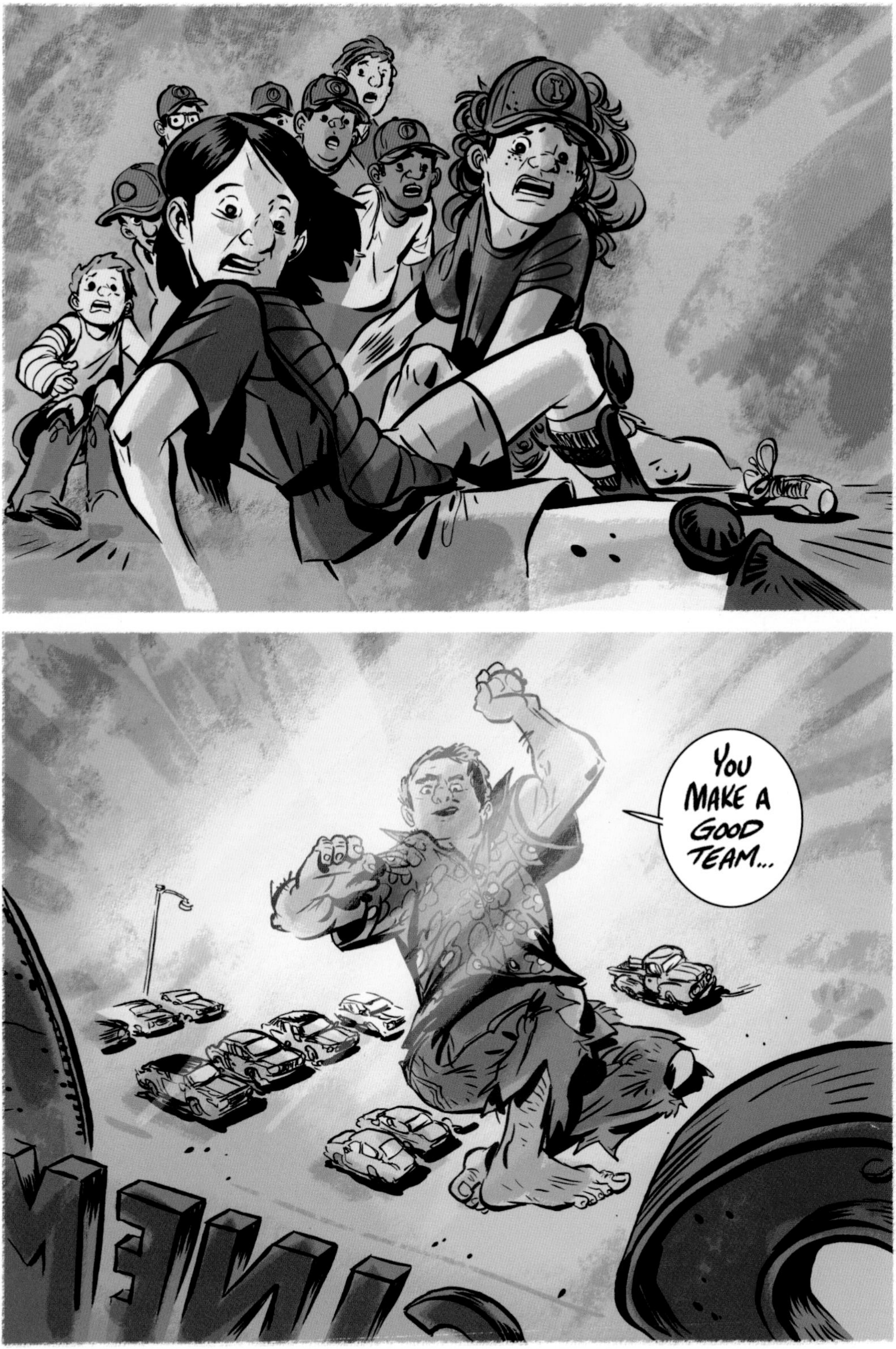
YOU MAKE A GOOD TEAM...

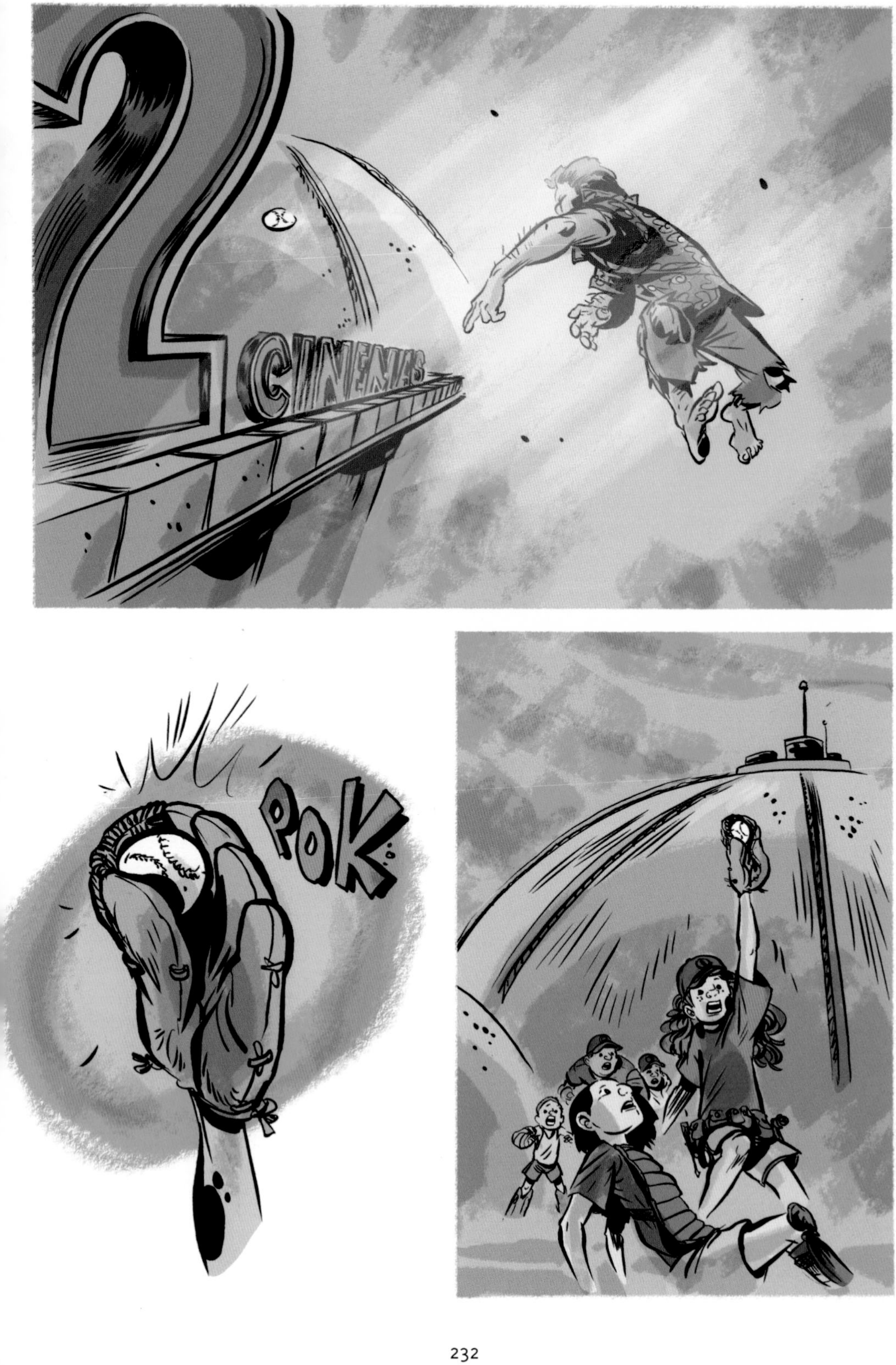
CINEMAS
POK

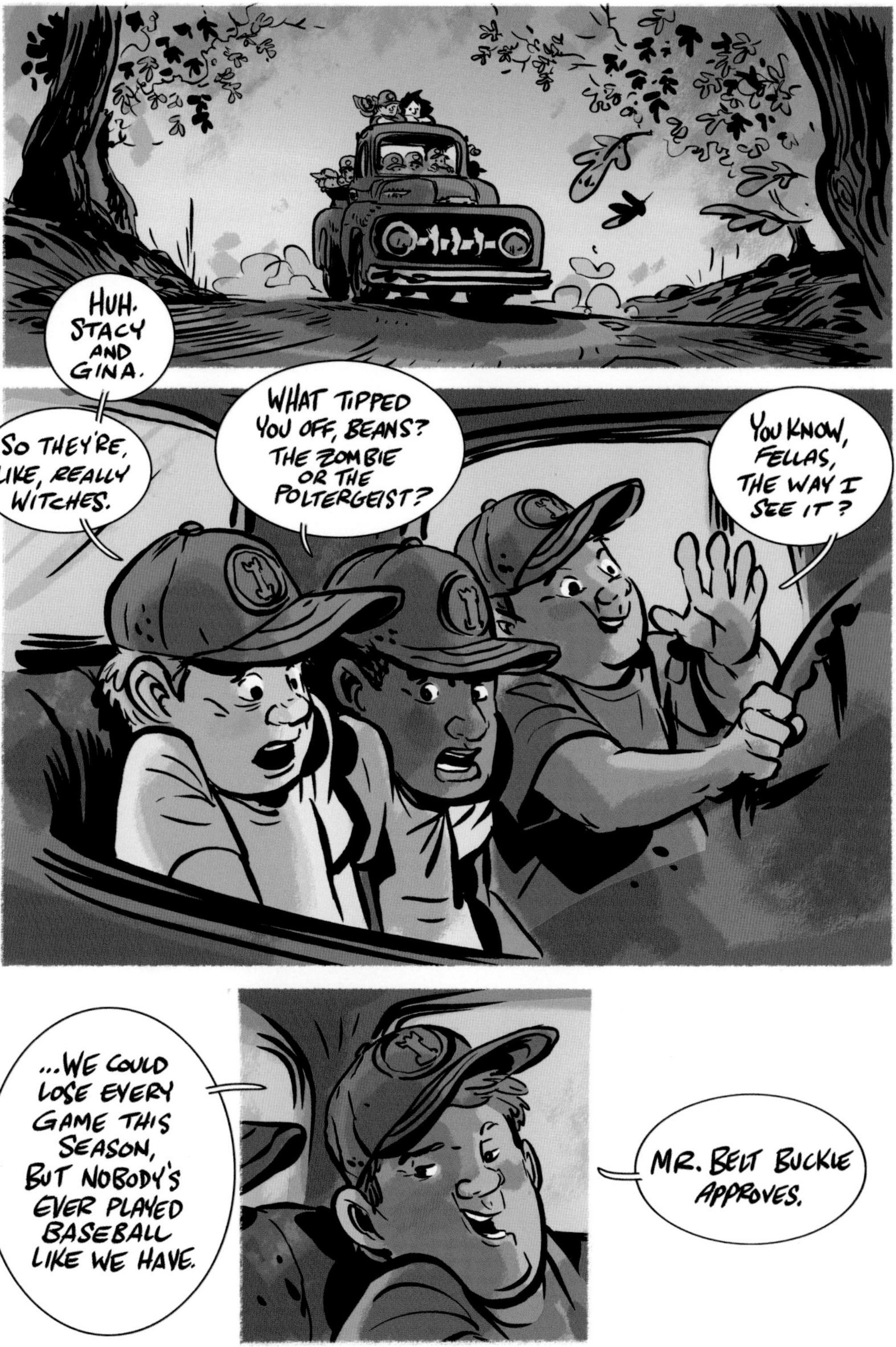
HUH. STACY AND GINA.
SO THEY'RE, LIKE, REALLY WITCHES.
WHAT TIPPED YOU OFF, BEANS? THE ZOMBIE OR THE POLTERGEIST?
YOU KNOW, FELLAS, THE WAY I SEE IT?
...WE COULD LOSE EVERY GAME THIS SEASON, BUT NOBODY'S EVER PLAYED BASEBALL LIKE WE HAVE.
MR. BELT BUCKLE APPROVES.

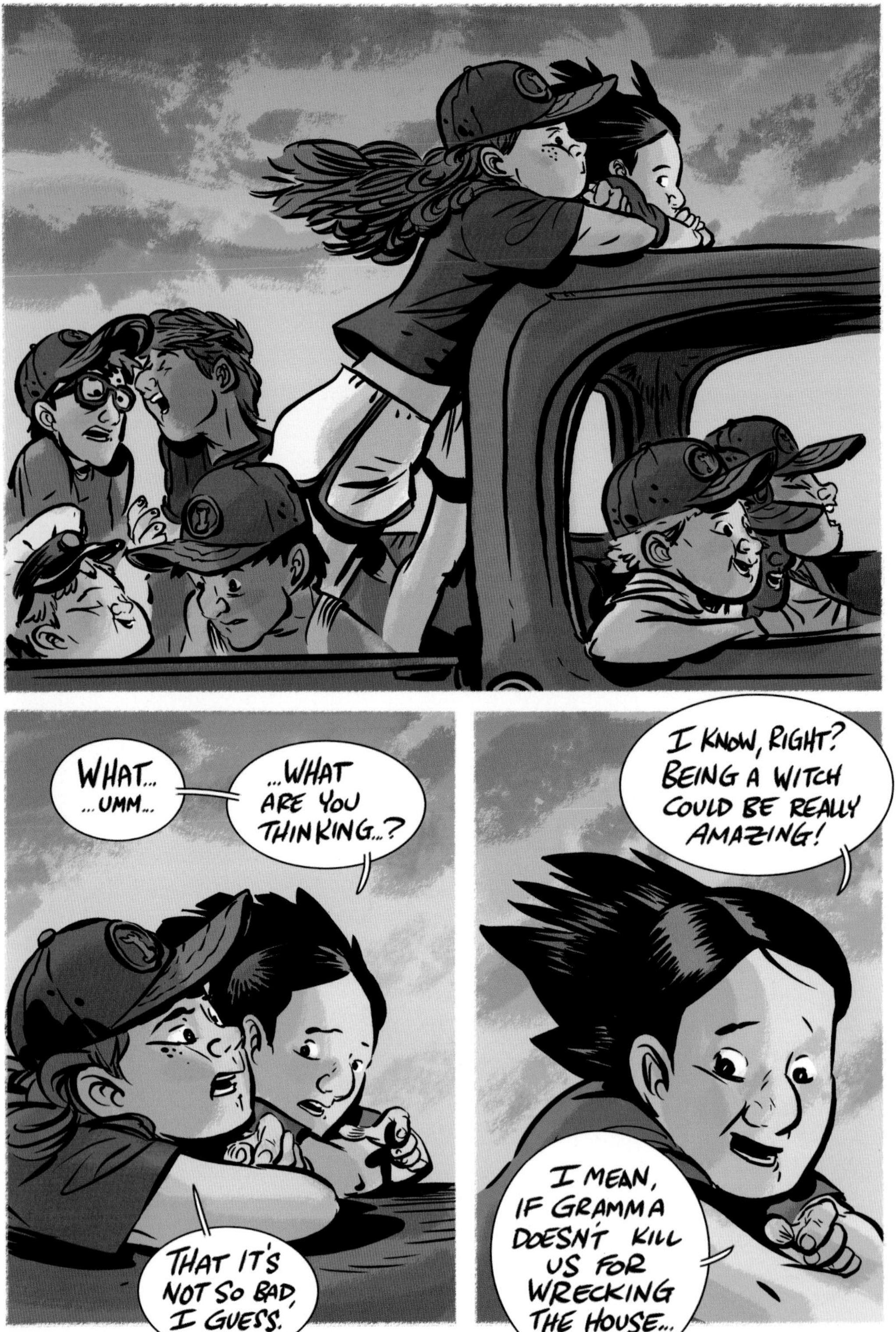
WHAT... ...UMM...
...WHAT ARE YOU THINKING...?
THAT IT'S NOT SO BAD, I GUESS.
I KNOW, RIGHT? BEING A WITCH COULD BE REALLY AMAZING!
I MEAN, IF GRAMMA DOESN'T KILL US FOR WRECKING THE HOUSE...

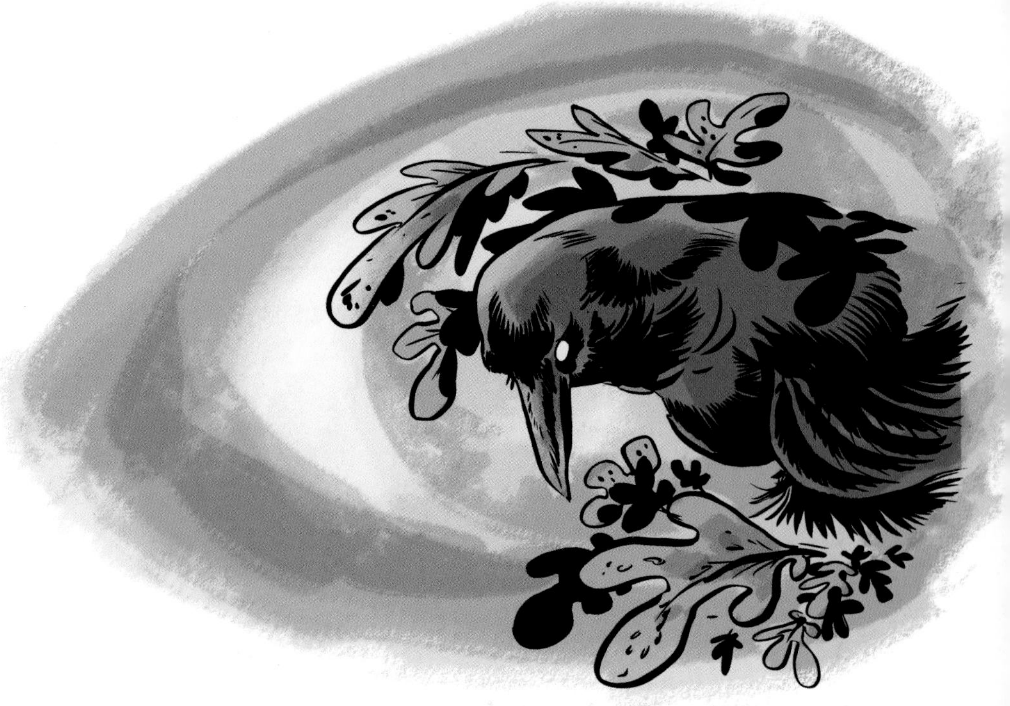

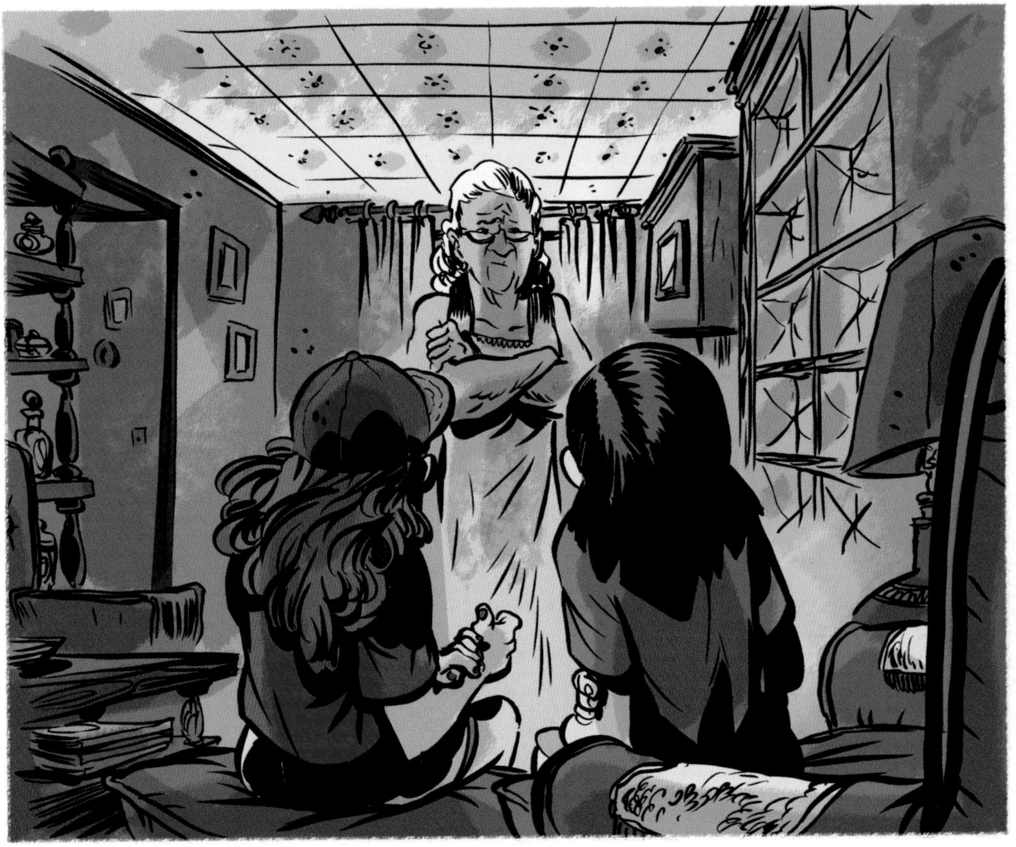

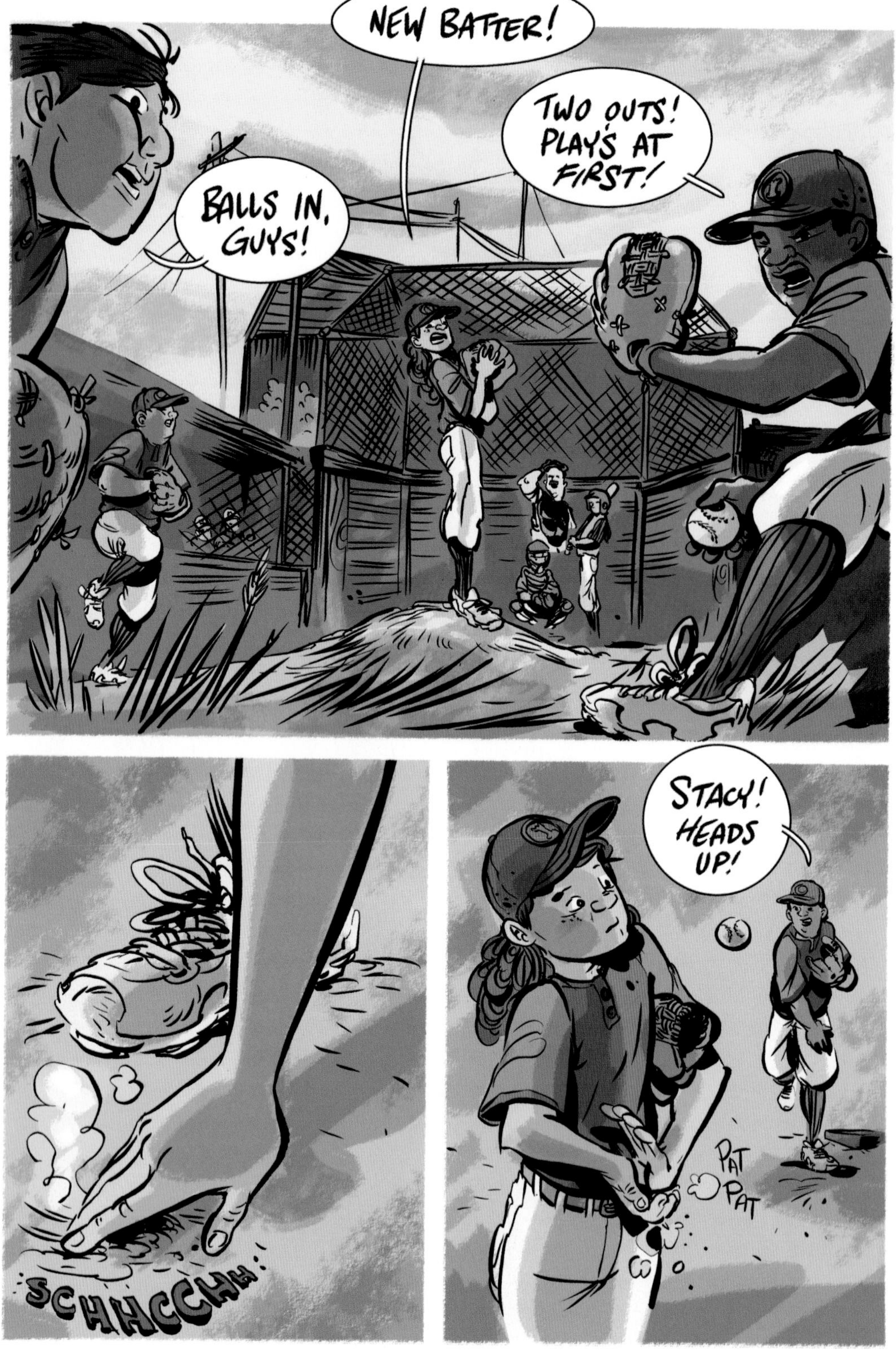
NEW BATTER!
BALLS IN, GUYS!
TWO OUTS! PLAY'S AT FIRST!
SCHHCCHH
STACY! HEADS UP!
PAT PAT

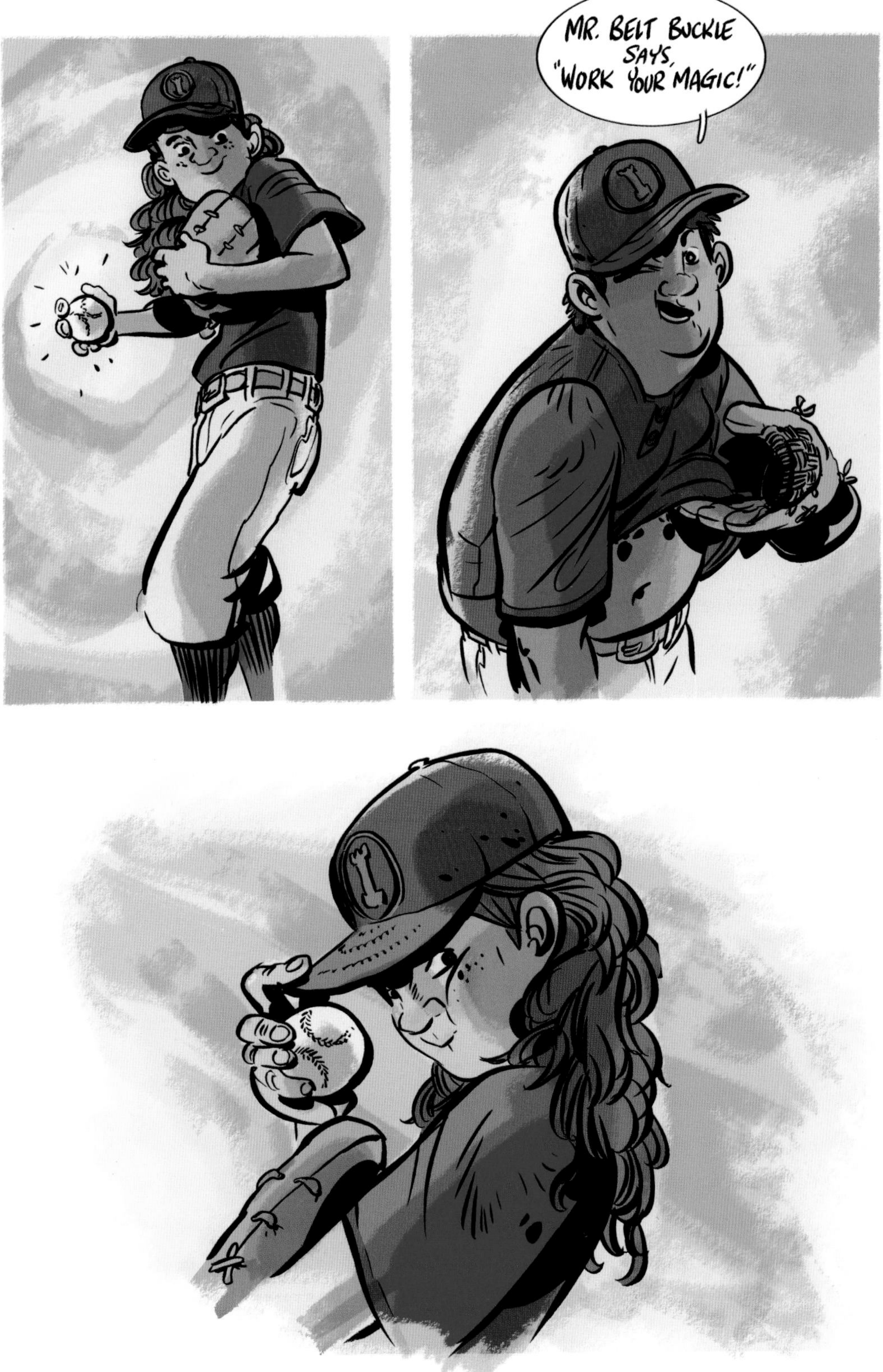
MR. BELT BUCKLE SAYS, "WORK YOUR MAGIC!"

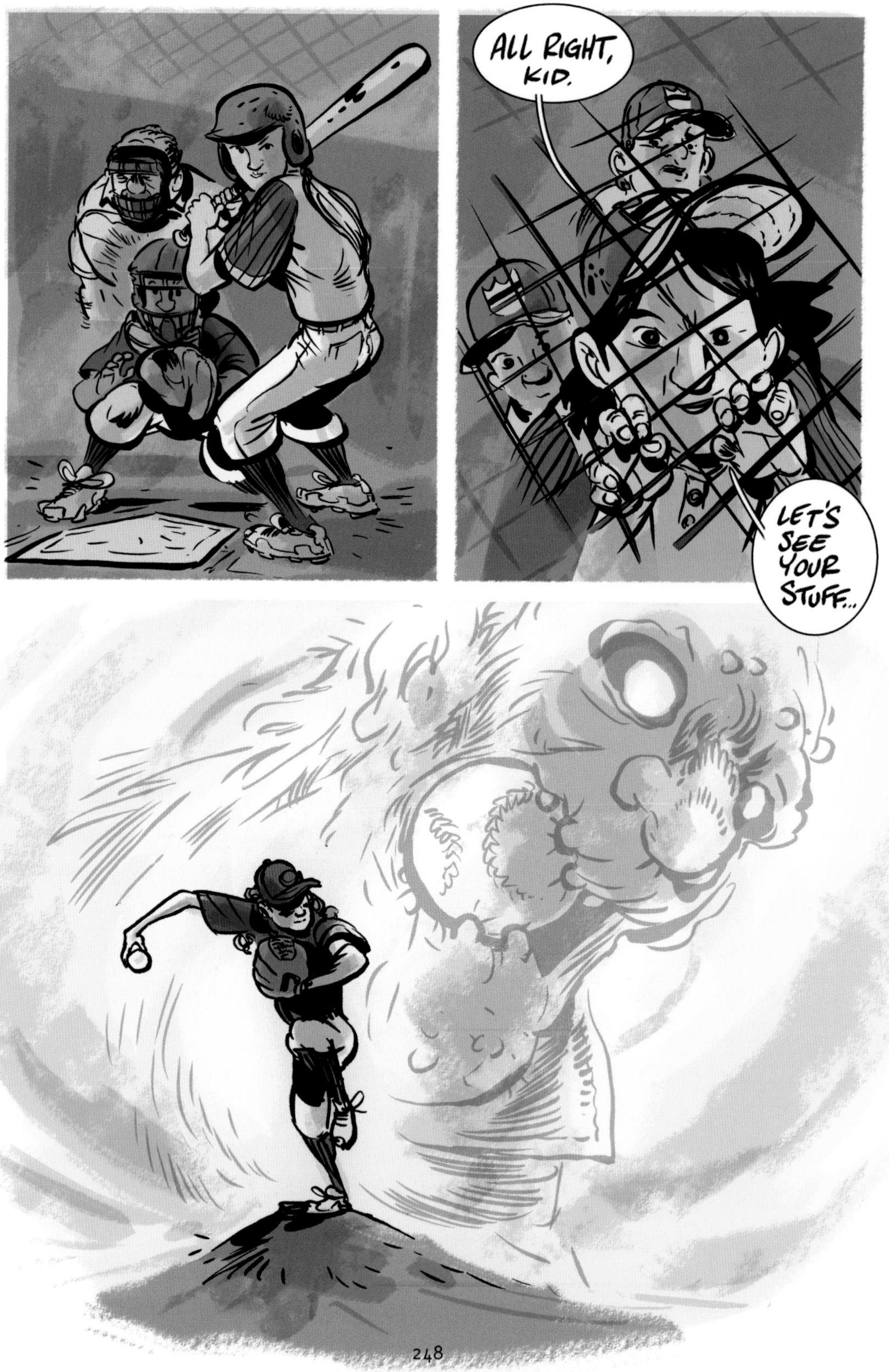
ALL RIGHT, KID.
LET'S SEE YOUR STUFF...

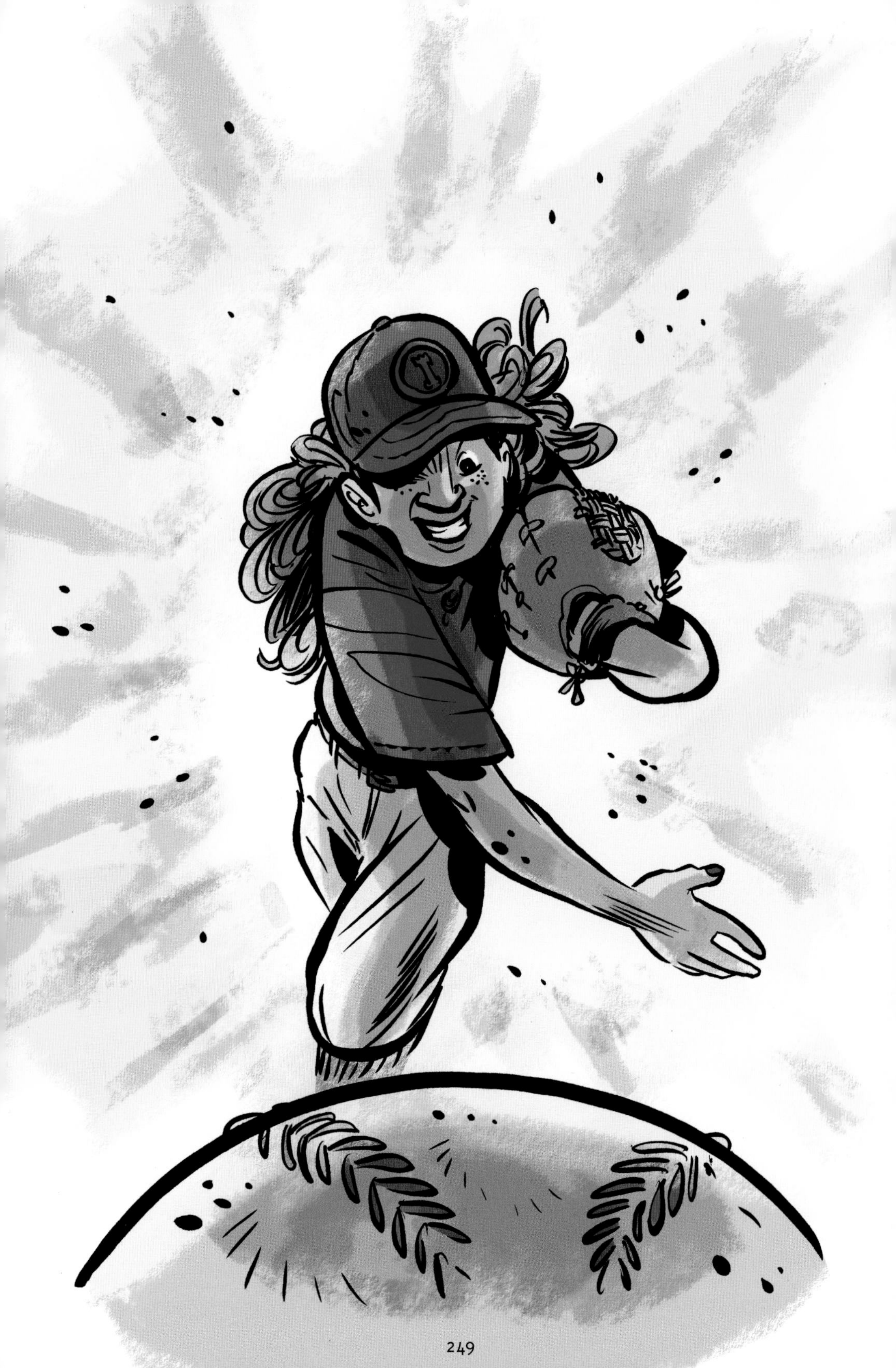

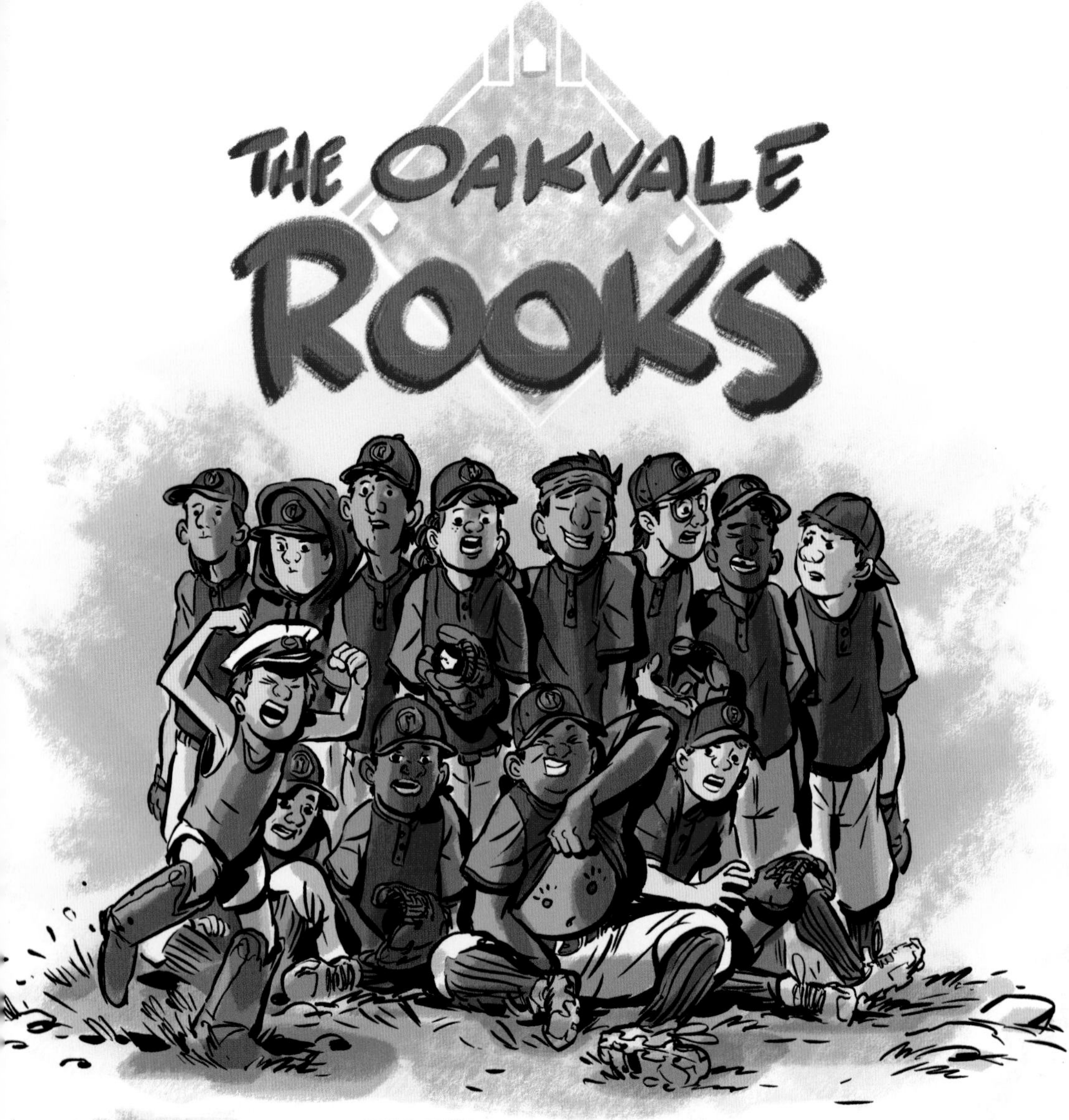
THE OAKVALE ROOKS

BACK ROW: JOAQUIN MARTINEZ, TEDDY GRASSO, TYLER SANCHEZ, STACY CAVALLARO, CASEY GOMEZ, BILLY TAKEUCHI, SOLOMON HAMPTON, MARKO LARSONOVAN

FRONT ROW: LEVI ISACCS, CHRIS GORDO, LOUIE "KILLROY" NUNES, PETEY "BEANS" DWYER

PHOTO BOMBER: HENRY "BOOTS" SANCHEZ

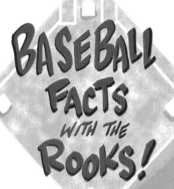

SCOTT MORSE is the award-winning author of many graphic novels for children and adults, including the *Magic Pickle* graphic novel and the Magic Pickle series for Scholastic/Graphix. In film and animation, he's worked with Cartoon Network, Nickelodeon, Disney, and Pixar. He's built old cars with his Dad (including the 1951 Ford truck featured in DUGOUT!) and has coached ten Little League teams. He lives with his family in Northern California and rarely draws faces on his belly.